# ONE
# TRUE
# SENTENCE

# Also by Craig McDonald

*Print the Legend*
*Toros and Torsos*
*Head Games*
*Art in the Blood*
*Rogue Males*

# ONE
# TRUE
# SENTENCE

## Craig McDonald

MINOTAUR BOOKS

A Thomas Dunne Book

New York

This is a work of fiction. All of the characters, organizations, and events portrayed in this novel are either products of the author's imagination or are used fictitiously.

A THOMAS DUNNE BOOK FOR MINOTAUR BOOKS.
An imprint of St. Martin's Publishing Group.

ONE TRUE SENTENCE. Copyright © 2011 by Craig McDonald. All rights reserved. Printed in the United States of America. For information, address St. Martin's Press, 175 Fifth Avenue, New York, N.Y. 10010.

www.thomasdunnebooks.com
www.minotaurbooks.com

Library of Congress Cataloging-in-Publication Data

McDonald, Craig, 1962–
    One true sentence / Craig McDonald. — 1st ed.
        p. cm.
    ISBN 978-0-312-55438-5 (alk. paper)
    1. Novelists—Fiction.   2. Murder—Investigation—Fiction.   3. France—
History—1914–1940—Fiction.   4. Hemingway, Ernest, 1899–1961—Fiction.
5. Stein, Gertrude, 1874–1946—Fiction.   I. Title.
    PS3613.C38698O54  2011
    813'.6—dc22

                                                            2010039078

First Edition: February 2011

10  9  8  7  6  5  4  3  2  1

This novel is dedicated to Madeleine and Yeats McDonald:

*"Be careful in choosing your path; nor walk in a dangerous way. For all of tomorrow hinges on how you've handled today."*

# ACKNOWLEDGMENTS

As always, first and foremost, I again thank my wife, Debbie, daughters Madeleine and Yeats, and James and Betty McDonald for making this novel, like all the others, possible.

Also, a nod, and a pat, to Duff.

A very special salute to my St. Martin's Press/Thomas Dunne/Minotaur editor, Kat Brzozowski, for the deft, eleventh-hour course correction; for getting us back on plan and making *this* novel the next published in the Hector Lassiter series. Also thanks to Sarah Melnyk, Monica Katz, Peter Wolverton, Andrew Martin, Kenneth J. Silver, and Fred Chase.

Much gratitude again to Svetlana Pironko and Michael O'Brien.

A very special thank-you to Alison Janssen.

I also salute Madeira James and team Xuni for all the great work on www.craigmcdonaldbooks.com and to Recorded Books' Tom Stechschulte, the one true voice of Hector Lassiter and all those who people his world.

Thanks to Melissa McClelland for providing *this* novel's soundtrack in the form of her sublime album *Thumbelina's One Night Stand*.

I'm indebted to all the independent bookshops and mystery specialty stores and booksellers who have taken the Hector Lassiter series to their hearts and urged the novels on their customers, as well as librarians who've recommended the books to their patrons. Particular thanks to Patrick Millikin and Barbara Peters of Poisoned Pen; the sorely missed David Thompson of Murder by the Book; Scott Montgomery of Book People; Sharon Kelly Roth of Books & Co.; Robin and Jamie Agnew of Aunt Agatha's; Helen Simpson of Big Sleep Books; and Toni and John Cross at Foul Play. Also to Denise Birkhoff, Pamela Coyle, Cathy Lantz, and Steven Lee.

*Muchas gracias*, also, to Corey Wilde, Naomi Johnson, Jen Forbus, John Kenyon, Keith Rawson, Jedidiah Ayres, Doug Moe, Rod Wiethop, Vince Keenan, Peter Dragovich and to "Day" in Texas . . . also to Ruth and Jon Jordan. Thanks also to Leslie Hutchings and Stephen Miller.

A salute also to artist Kevin D. Singles who, at this writing, is hard at work on the *Head Games* graphic novel (an illustrated spin on the Edgar- and Anthony Awards–nominated first Hector Lassiter novel), forthcoming from First Second.

Lastly, and too-belatedly, my sincere and deep acknowledgment to Ernest Miller Hemingway, who inspired me to "go far out beyond where a writer should go."

This novel concludes what is, in a sense, the Hemingway trilogy within the eight-book Hector Lassiter cycle.

*Vaya con dios*, Papa.

It is the fate of every myth to creep by degrees into the narrow limits of some historical reality, and to be treated by some later generations as a unique fact with historical claims.

— NIETZSCHE

# PARIS
# FEBRUARY 1924

*Snow falling on the* Seine.

It was half-past-two and it was quiet as it gets with the heavy falling snow and Hector was just starting to cross the Pont Neuf, heading home after a long night of writing. He was alone and cold and slightly drunk.

Icy fog crawled across the river. The lights of the bridge glowed strangely in the fog, not illuminating anything, but instead casting hazy, solitary cones of weak light that receded off into the cold mist.

From the other end of the bridge, much farther than Hector could see, he heard a scream, then the sound of the rubbery, thin ice breaking below . . . water splashing.

Hector called, "Hey there!" and began running, his leather soles slipping and sliding on the slick bricks. Hector thought he heard other feet hitting the pavers.

He crossed the bridge, knowing he'd passed the halfway point when the grade changed. Hector ran to the spot where he thought he'd heard the splash and leaned out over the stone rail, peering into the fog. Squinting, Hector could see a black patch below— standing out against the thin veil of snow covering the iced-over surface of the river. Wisps of steam from the warmer water trapped beneath the ice drifted from the black spot, curling into the mists of the fog. Hector watched a few moments, waiting to see if there was any sign of motion from the hole, but he saw nothing like that.

A suicide, probably . . . there was never any shortage of those.

He looked at the steps leading down to the river's edge. The bridge's lights glowed meanly across the slick steps. And if he got down there without falling, Hector knew he'd still be faced with just that hole in the ice. The current would likely have already swept whatever—*whoever*—had gone through dozens of yards from the steaming hole.

Reluctantly, Hector backed away from the railing. He decided going to the authorities would do little good. And doing that might just make Hector a fleeting suspect if they fished a body from the river later, after the thaw.

There were fresh footprints in the thin crust of snow . . . spaced far apart, like the person who left them was running. The weight of the impact on the hard snow made the size and the shape of the footprints indistinct . . . impossible to tell if they were those of a man or a woman.

He looked around again; saw nothing; heard nothing. He thought about trying to follow the footprints in the snow, then decided against it.

Hector shook loose a cigarette and struck a match with his thumbnail. He pulled his collar up higher and tighter around his face and jammed his hands deeper into the pockets of his overcoat, continuing his solitary way home.

By morning he'd nearly forgotten about all of it.

# COVEN

*They were gathered in* a private room off the back of a café called the Grand Néant.

The speaker wearing the black mask surveyed them sitting there, sipping their wine or anise: gaunt, intent-eyed men whom the self-dubbed "Nobodaddy"—a moniker borrowed from the poet William Blake—had personally selected as likely converts.

Dark men with darker sensibilities. Cynical vets, jaded rich boys, and bitter men who viewed life after the trenches and horrors of the World War as a gauntlet—a thing to tear pleasure from at any cost and with no eye toward consequences.

Fellow travelers.

A lost generation. Prospects. Worthy candidates for Nobodaddy's dark campaign.

Nobodaddy said, "As a movement—as an organized entity—we can impose our artistic and philosophical vision on the world. Here, in the City of Lights, we stand at the center of the beating heart of the arts. Every writer, painter, and poet of consequence is *right here.* If we seize control here in Paris, our vision, our artistic aesthetic, can be carried forth to the world."

The German—the tall dark one with the hawk nose and the terrible scar down the side of his face—shook his head. Werner Höttl said, "*Your* aesthetic. *Your* artistic vision. For surely, it is not mine. You embrace nihilism . . . wallow in your concept of nothingness and the futility of life. Insofar as you dismiss religion, I applaud you. Particularly because the artistic community of this city is too in thrall to the Jew. But my medium is film, and film is a communal experience. It can elevate an audience. A master filmmaker can make an auditorium of strangers feel the same things . . . react the same way. All you offer is sterile, black loneliness. This does not appeal to me."

Höttl studied the speaker in the black mask again. He was still trying to decide it if was a man or a woman. The voice was odd . . . rather androgynous.

The other dark-haired, hawk-faced one—Donovan Creedy— cleared his throat and nodded. "Herr Höttl is right about the Jews and the way they're poisoning and warping the artistic scene in this city. They run all the little magazines. Their salons are hives of indoctrination to their vision of the arts. I'm all for grounding out their influence. But I don't see how your campaign in any way enhances the prospects for our artistic success. Your vision of Nada renders life meaningless. If you have your way, everyone will be throwing themselves out windows or under trains. They'll be drinking poison and shooting themselves in the head to escape the barren world you've handed them. I want no part of this."

Creedy rose, putting on his hat and scooping up his overcoat from the back of his chair. The German, Höttl, also stood, said, "I'll follow you out, *Herr* Creedy."

Dejected, Nobodaddy looked to the young critic—handsome, tow-headed . . . a trust fund baby. "And you, Quentin?"

The art critic blew twin streams of smoke out his nostrils and shrugged. "What can I say? Either you aren't a good ambassador for your cause, or your aims are simply unfathomable to anyone who is remotely sane. All I've heard is an argument for the meaninglessness of all human effort . . . all artistic endeavor."

Quentin ground out the stub of his cigarette; lit another. He said, "I'll confess, I have artistic ambitions myself. Until I get a better handle on how I mean to realize them, I'm furthering my own education under the cloak of art criticism. From where I sit, you and your group—if it extends beyond yourself—are at odds with my interests. Hell, if everyone starts believing as you do, *nobody* will be painting, writing novels or poetry...writing plays. Hell, as those two odd birds who just cleared out said, all the artists who fall for your pitch will be too busy killing themselves to create."

Quentin Windly stood up, stretched, and said, "Afraid I'm going to take the air, too. Thanks for the drinks. I was you, I'd try drinking more myself. Maybe it'll change your black state of mind. Oh, and lose the mask—it doesn't engender trust. Hell, it makes you seem, you know, *insane*."

Nobodaddy had used the name "Elrond Huppert"—a fanciful alias he'd partly borrowed from a Leeds professor named Tolkien—when he'd solicited their participation; he hadn't told them to expect a masked host. "When you'd joined us I meant to reveal my face," Nobodaddy snarled, close to losing self-control.

Quentin grinned. "For someone who believes in nothing, you ask for big leaps of faith."

Nobodaddy watched the art critic go. Nobodaddy stood alone in the room, staring at empty chairs.

Well, soul winning wasn't an easy task, particularly when you were trying to win converts to a faith as black and pitiless as this one.

But there had been successes. The "church," for lack of a better word, was growing—those who'd just left would probably use another word...maybe "festering."

But a dark course had been charted.

It was just a matter of staying true to that plan and vision. If Nobodaddy couldn't win them over—all the artists, all the opinion shapers in the artistic community of the City of Lights—well, then, Nobodaddy and his minions would just continue pitching them into that black void, one at a time.

Maybe one couldn't kill them all, but one could surely try.

After all, God was dead; actions no longer carried consequences.

# PART I

vendredi, samedi, & dimanche

# One

*Hector took the mail* handed him by his *femme de ménage* and sorted it. He opened two envelopes from magazine publishers in the States and found two checks—each made out for several stories. It was enough to carry Hector well through the fall . . . not that he was as hard-pressed for money as so many other writers in the Quarter.

Germaine LeBrun handed him a café au lait and he sipped it gratefully. She said, "It is good news?"

"It is very good news," Hector said, sipping again and winking. He took out his fountain pen and signed one of the checks over to his landlady and kissed her cheek. "So you won't have to set me out."

"You're not even late," she said, touching her cheek where he had kissed it. She was an older woman and stocky and she had appointed herself his surrogate mother, Hector thought, though she was closer in age to his grandmother, if he still had one.

"This will ensure we stay on our good footing," he said.

He climbed back up to his room, carrying the breakfast tray she had prepared for him: eggs over easy, toast and bacon, and a cup of yogurt. She'd also added a flask filled with more of the strong coffee Hector favored. He smothered his eggs in salt and pepper and dug in, reading a couple of newspapers while he ate.

Hector was startled to see that an acquaintance had been murdered...found stabbed and left propped in a doorway of a vacant shop on the Rue de Moussy. Death had come from a single puncture to the heart, probably administered with a long stiletto, according to the report.

Hector sipped his coffee, added a little more cream and sipped it again. There would be no shortage of suspects for the murder, Hector figured.

Hell, most of the young writers on the Left Bank—Hector excepted—had good reason to want Murray Panzer dead.

Murray had come to Paris from Greenwich Village in '21, a trust fund intellectual with heady notions of starting a literary magazine. He kept his overhead down by paying his hungry contributors in extra copies of his magazine...in itself not an unusual practice. Paris was lousy with little magazines that did the same—"little reviews" and chapbook periodicals filled with drivel Hector couldn't read.

But Panzer, it had recently been learned, had been reselling his unpaid contributors' stories to other, *paying* publications in Spain and Germany...passing the material off as the work of writers whom Panzer invented pen names for, and then pocketed the money. Panzer's subterfuge had been found out by Constance Wright... a poet who'd been traveling with her lover in Berlin and who had found her own poem featured in *Der Querschnitt*—but now allegedly the work of a poet named "Gwendolyn Roquelaure."

Several of the literary writers and poets of the Left Bank were bitterly calling for Panzer's head.

Ernest Hemingway had not been among those burned, but he could vividly imagine himself having been one of those taken in. Hem had insisted that Hector should join him in a "visit" across the river to Panzer's apartment on the Rue Coquillière: "We'll knock him back on his ass, Lasso. Get a little money back for ours."

"No way," Hector had replied. "And I only write for paying markets, where they find *other* ways to screw you." Hector was forever taking shots for writing for the crime pulps back home, for "whoring" as some other young writers put it.

Hector had decided to use it to his advantage for once. "But at least I get paid in *currency* for my stuff," he'd told Hem.

"Well, someone should sure do something about that thieving son of a bitch," Hem had said, frowning.

Hector finished with the newspapers. He saw nothing about a body having been pulled from the Seine. He dressed to go out— pulling a cable-knit sweater on over his undershirt, shirt, and the sweatshirt he'd already put on. He shrugged on his big leather jacket with the fleece lining. He pulled on his leather gloves and scooped up his chocolate brown fedora.

It was cold on the street and exhaust from the cabs roiled in the chilly wind. The snow had hardened and it crunched under Hector's work boots.

"Lasso, wait up!"

Hector turned and saw Hem running toward him . . . running with that limping, shambling run of his caused by a weak, reconstructed knee. Hem was dressed in layers, like Hector—sweaters over sweatshirts, a scarf and black fisherman's cap and gloves with the fingertips cut out. Hem was four or five days unshaven and his clothes smelled of peat fire. "Where are you headed, Lasso?"

"Sylvia's . . . figured to browse awhile."

"Me too. Walk together?"

"Always," Hector said. "But just a minute." He rested his gloved hand on Hem's shoulder to steady himself, then raised his right leg and fished around under the cuff of his pants. Hector pulled the silver flask from his boot and smiled. "For the cold walk."

Hem beamed and accepted the flask and took a swig as they crossed the Rue d'Assas. "Gotta get myself one of these," he said, handing the flask back. "And Pernod . . . that's sure the right stuff for a morning like this."

Hector took a swig and slipped the flask in the pocket of his leather jacket. He took his off his glove and fished loose a cigarette and a match and got his smoke going. They were headed north on the Rue Guynemer, skirting the gardens. Hector slipped back on his glove and said, "See where somebody punched old Murray's ticket?"

Hem was surprised by that. Hector then told him about what he had read. When he finished, Hem said, "That's two, then. Hear word they found Lloyd Blake dead in his bed yesterday. His throat had been cut." To stay warm, Hem was trading punches with his shadow on the passing walls; with his reflection in the storefront windows.

Lloyd was another of the little magazine publishers. He'd taken on several investors recently to try and keep his little magazine going—much of it money taken from aspiring or struggling writers who couldn't afford to be underwriting little magazines. When he'd apparently garnered all the "contributions" he was apt to obtain, Lloyd had announced he was shutting down the publication after all.

Rather than refunding the money taken from his contributors, Lloyd had instead upgraded his living quarters and began hanging out with a smarter set on the other side of the Seine. Or so the gossips claimed.

Hector said, "Seems the literary life is suddenly becoming bloody."

Stopping his shadowboxing, Hem smiled and said, "Couldn't have happened to two better prospects, though. You can't disagree with that." He reached into Hector's jacket and took out the flask. Hem took a drink and raised the flask and said, "Farewell to that son of a whore."

Hector accepted his flask back and took a swallow. "To both the dead sons of bitches," he said.

# Two

*Because of the raw* weather, foot traffic was light on the Rue de l'Odéon. Heavy wet snow was drifting down again, but it didn't seem to want to stick to the cobblestones.

The writers stamped the slush from their feet and ducked into the bookshop . . . into the dry warmth from the shop's fireplace with its low-set mantel. Sylvia Beach, the owner of Shakespeare and Company, clapped her hands and ran around her desk to embrace them. Hector brushed her dark brown hair back from her forehead where it had been pushed by the brim of his hat when she hugged him, then placed his fedora on her head. Sylvia adjusted it to a rakish angle and winked one brown eye as she checked her reflection in the glass panel of a barrister bookcase. "You may have trouble getting this back from me, Hector," Sylvia said. "I look dashing in a chap's hat, don't I?"

"Very fetching," he agreed.

Hem squeezed her arm. "Mail for me?"

She smiled and walked back around her desk, still wearing Hector's hat. She reached in a drawer and handed Hem a thin sheaf of envelopes bound in a green rubber band.

Hem said, "Think I'm gonna browse." Then he drifted off somewhere to read his mail in private. Hector figured that was in case any of the letters were from the slick magazines back home. Given Hem's raw subject matter, they would probably be more rejection letters.

Hector slipped off his gloves and wadded them into the pockets of his leather jacket and then shrugged off his jacket and slipped it over the back of a chair by the fireplace. From behind Sylvia, a pantheon of writers' photographs stared down on Hector—Joyce, D. H. Lawrence, and Joseph Conrad, among others. Scattered throughout the bookstore were the photographic portraits of more writers, living and dead. Hector and Hem had a friendly bet about which of them would be the first to be honored with a glossy posted on Sylvia's walls.

With his steady stream of short stories appearing back home, Hector figured he should have some kind of edge, but he also figured Sylvia was waiting until one or both of them had a published novel under their belts.

Hector said, "How's Ade?" Adrienne Monnier was another bookseller on the Left Bank, and Sylvia's lover.

"Oh, she's just fine." Hector checked the spine of the book Sylvia had been reading when they came in: Havelock Ellis's *Erotic Symbolism*. Sexually charged books, a lesbian love affair, publishing Joyce's *Ulysses* ... Hector thought Sylvia had come a long way from her American roots and puritanical childhood as the daughter of a Maryland minister.

But Paris seemed to do that to young Americans.

Sylvia was also an avid gossip: "I haven't seen the newspapers yet, but I heard that someone murdered Murray Panzer," she said, warm brown eyes inquiring. "Is that true, Hec?"

"And how." Hector gave her a lurid account of the murder ... embroidered a bit by his own imagination and the way he saw the crime scene in his head.

He finished and Sylvia said, "And now I hear that awful Lloyd Baker was killed, too."

"Hem was just telling me about that one. Seems to be hard times for underhanded literary lights, eh?" Hector smiled and accepted the cup and saucer she handed him. The coffee tasted of vanilla but he was glad for the warmth of it, and for the effects of the caffeine. She handed him a brioche.

"Well, that makes three of them," Sylvia said, sipping her own coffee. She pushed Hector's hat back a little on her head so she could see him better.

Hector scowled. "Three? Christ, who else is dead?"

"Natalie Champlin—you know, who runs the quarterly poetry magazine *Janus*. They pulled her out of the river this morning."

Hector could hear the scream and the breaking ice and the splash again in his head from the night before. Maybe it had been Natalie he had heard going off the bridge. He said, "Suicide? Creditors at the door?"

"Might have been taken for that but for the wound. Natalie was stabbed through the heart."

"Just like Murray," Hector said, shrugging off a little chill.

He finished up his coffee and rose. "Going to wander the stacks," he said. "And see if I can find Hem. Soothe whatever his mail might have done to him."

Hector pushed his hat down lower on her head and kissed the back of Sylvia's neck, taking delight in her husky giggle. He thought again what a shame it was she was only attracted to other women.

# Three

*It was half-past-four* and Hector and Hem were still making the circuit together . . . still catching up.

"Christ, but it's good to be home," Hem said. The Hemingways had been back in Paris for just a few days. Ernest and wife, Hadley, had spent several ill-fated months in Toronto awaiting the birth of their first child. There, Hem had briefly returned to newspaper work under the direction of a sadistic editor—"A son of a bitch of the first water," as Hem put it.

The Hemingways had broken their lease and snuck out in the night, fleeing back to Europe on storm-swept seas with their newborn son, Jack. With Hector's help, they had found a new apartment above a sawmill at 113 rue de Notre-Dame-des-Champs, behind Montparnasse.

Hem said, "Any good plans for tonight, Lasso?"

"Just the usual. Starting out at the joint under your old place tonight I think."

"When?"

"I'll be there by six."

Hem glanced at a clock in a shop front. He said, "You checked out the Café du Dôme since it reopened?"

"Nah," Hector said. "Why don't we do that now?"


Hem had gone to fetch Hadley.

Hector sat at the back of the raucous *bal musette*, a tiny place on the Rue du Cardinal Lemoine. An old man was playing accordion and stamping time on a tambourine he'd tossed on the floor.

"Hello there, Hector."

He smiled and pulled out a chair and then scooted it in for her. "Hey, sweetheart. What'll it be, Molly?"

"White wine."

Margaret Wilder was two years in Paris from Elgin, Illinois. Margaret—Molly—was an aspiring poet. Soft-spoken and virginal (at least Hector figured so), she was blond and pretty in a fresh-faced way. Her eyes were violet and her thick, wavy hair was bobbed to the angle of her jaw. She wore little makeup. She slipped off her coat and let it fall carelessly across the back of her chair and held her hands up to the candle on the table between them. Hector said, "Where's Philippe?"

That was her boyfriend, though Hector wasn't sure how serious that relationship was from Molly's perspective. As nearly as Hector could tell, Philippe Martin worshipped Molly... very protective... obviously adoring her. Philippe was an aspiring French painter of meager talent, in Hector's estimation. And her boyfriend spent much of his free time in the Rotonde, that sorry catch basin at the corner of the Boulevard Montparnasse and the Boulevard Raspail where it was always amateur hour—a kind of Mecca for bohemian poseurs. The kind that talked more than worked. All of that only furthered Hector's assumptions about the young painter's low talent. In Hector's experience, the Rotonders were a sorry-ass lot.

"Still plugging away at the day job," Molly said. "But he should be along soon." The waiter leaned in and Molly said, *"Un petit vin blanc."*

Hector said, "Whisky for me, neat."

"I was by your place earlier today to see if you wanted to get lunch, Hec," she said.

He smiled. "Sorry I missed you. It's the first day since Hem has been back that he and I have gotten to spend any time together," he said. "So we've been making the bar and book circuit. Sylvia's and La Maison des Amis des Livres to see Adrienne Monnier. Spent a little time in the Place Saint-Sulpice trying to sober up. But the lions are all covered in ice and it's just too damn cold for sitting outdoors, even for a couple of lit writers. So we went back to the bars... and coffee drinks. You know—get sober and tight all at once."

She smiled. "Are you tight now?" Candlelight played in her violet eyes that seemed almost too exotic for her face. The man with the accordion was playing "Parlez-Moi D'Amour."

"No," Hector said, smiling. "Not between the cold and all the walking." He accepted his whisky and hefting it said, "But I am working on it."

Molly sipped her wine and said, "Me too."

He winced a little at the burn, then licked his lips as the whisky began to warm his belly. He said, "You had something in last month's issue of Panzer's magazine, didn't you, Molly? Did you hear about Murray Panzer?"

She wrinkled her nose. "I did hear about that," she said. "Everyone is talking about that. A horrible end for a horrible man. But not so horrible as to deserve that." She shook her head. "Nobody deserves that. And I suppose now there's one fewer market to publish in."

Hector almost balked at the term "market" being applied to a little magazine that paid in copies. But he held his tongue on that front. Instead, he said, "And then Lloyd Blake, too." Hector toyed with his glass. "Christ, I hope you weren't one of Blake's investors. You weren't, were you?"

Molly shrugged, looking away. "Just a few francs. Nothing I'll miss, really."

Molly's Parisian lifestyle was grudgingly underwritten by her mother back in Illinois.

The old woman, Molly had confided to Hector, hoped her daughter would soon come to her senses and return to the States and be a poet back there. She had written Molly again about that wish in the most recent of her letters to her daughter. Molly occasionally read her letters from home to Hector. She was nearly always left badly shaken by her notes from home . . . by their cold tone and their harsh words regarding her poetic ambitions.

A letter from home almost always resulted in days of sulking.

In one of the last letters Molly had shared with Hector, her father had threatened to disown Molly for the "deplorable example" she was setting for her younger sisters.

When she had spoken of the last batch of correspondence to Hector, Molly had said, "And of course my mother's notion of poetry is of something that's lightly lyrical and that rhymes. Like the stuff back home—you know, in all the slick magazines."

Hector didn't have much interest in modern poetry, or really any sense of it at all, so he couldn't render a judgment as to whether Molly was hopeless, a mediocre talent, or a real prospect. Hector did think that Molly was out of her depth in bohemian, Left Bank Paris. It was good she had found Philippe, Hector thought. He hated to think what might have happened to Molly if she hadn't had the good fortune to find what seemed to be a decent enough young man in her middling painter.

Molly seemed to Hector a little like the girl-next-door slumming in Sodom and Gomorrah. The town hadn't yet worked its dubious wonders on Molly. At least not so far as Hector could see. Hector thought he was mostly unchanged, too. He found that his own solitary childhood in coastal Texas was a stubborn thing to grind out.

Yet, in Paris, Sylvia Beach had turned from a prim minister's daughter into a lesbian bookseller and sometimes purveyor or even publisher of smutty, erotic, or banned books. Sylvia was the template for Parisian self-reinvention.

But Molly?

In most respects, she was still like a pretty, young wide-eyed thing from Illinois.

"I'm sorry I missed you for lunch," Hector said again.

"Me too." A sad smile.

Hadley Hemingway had confided to Hector her suspicion that Molly was infatuated with him. But Hector had met Philippe before he had met Molly and so he had a hard time thinking of Molly in that way.

And Molly seemed to cling to Philippe—to demand too damn much of his time.

Hector savored his solitude. He valued the options engendered in his lone-wolf lifestyle that assured him the time to write whenever he wanted. For Hector, it was *solo lobo*, all the way . . . or so he was always telling himself.

None of that stopped Hector from pushing the line, though.

Flirting a bit, Hector closed a hand over Molly's and said, "Where would we have eaten, Molly?"

She smiled, her head on side, and stroked the back of Hector's hand. "A new little *brasserie* I found just off the Rue Mouffetard. Thought we'd sit by the fire and watch the workers shiver in the streetcars."

"That would have been . . . nice."

Hector took his hand away and she frowned a little. He got out a cigarette. He offered one to Molly, who shook her head. He remembered then that she rarely smoked. He struck a match with his thumbnail. He waved the match out and tossed it in the ashtray on the table between them. She said, "I've been reading some of your stories."

Hector bit his lip, frowning. He blew smoke through his nose. "Yeah? How?" Hector took no small measure of solace from the fact that his "crime stories"—the proof of his "whoring" to other would-be and unpublished writers in the Quartier Latin—were unavailable in Europe. "Where in hell did you see any of my stuff?"

"Sylvia's. She's been quietly subscribing to *Black Mask*, to some other pulps from back home. She shared some of them with me. They really are quite wonderful stories, Hector. With a little tweaking they'd be—"

Hector shot her a look. "What? More literary? No thanks, honey. And I reckon I'll have to have myself a little chat with Miss Beach."

Molly took his hand again. "Don't be cross, and please don't be angry with her, Hector. Please. Sylvia is quite proud of you. She only shows them to a few close friends. I loved the stories. I love the way you write. I was grateful to get a chance to see them. I mean, since you won't ever show me or anyone other than Hem anything that you're working on."

Hector stared off across the room . . . out at the street where the snow seemed to have abruptly shifted to a cold hard rain. Across the street, a *boucher* stood under the canopy of his shop in his bloodied apron, staring up at the gray sky with his still bloodied arms hanging loosely at his sides.

People passed by the front window of the *bal musette* with hunched shoulders, their heads tucked down. Some clutched sodden copies of newspapers spread open over their heads.

Molly said, "Be nice to be someplace warm and sunny, wouldn't it?"

Hector smiled back at Molly and took her hand again. She squeezed his hand harder. "Sure, I guess," he said. "But I like the rain, too." He checked his pocket watch: a bit before five.

Molly said, "You're meeting someone?"

"Hem and Hadley. But not for an hour or so."

"We could go somewhere quieter until then, couldn't we? Someplace where you can hear yourself think?"

"Sure, let's do that."

## NOBODADDY

The little magazine editor was crawling across the floor of his flat, trailing blood as he dragged himself on elbows and blood-slicked knees on the parquet floor.

He was wimpering and pleading for his life.

Nobodday was on the verge of being sick. This wasn't what he was, not *really*.

The masked killer raised a statuette—a bronze copy of Michelangelo's *Duke of Nemours*—and brought it crashing down on the man's skull.

"For my one true love," the little magazine editor's killer whispered over and over.

It was all and always for *her*. Well, it *started* that way. She was still the driving force. But Nobodaddy was also looking after other interests, too. The masked killer collapsed back against the wall, staring at bloody hands. The hands of a self-styled poet.

Poetry was a recent preoccupation—an attempt to pierce the veil of Parisian literary society. They'd mocked him for his efforts in fiction writing . . . penniless, unpublished "literary writers" who tore into him when they learned he had a reasonably lucrative writing career underway writing short stories for the fantastic pulps back home.

At some point it occurred to Nobodaddy to expand his quest to further her work by taking the dark, pitiless vision of his own fictional pulp-lit creations and fashioning them into a cosmology for the dark, empty times—a siren's song of the void that would speak to this so-called lost generation of war vets and women made wanton and wild by the horror of the last decade's war.

If he couldn't win them to his side as readers or artistic allies, he would force his vision upon the world as a kind of dark messiah.

The body on the floor twitched once...twice. Some spark of life not yet ground out of it.

Sighing, Nobodday hefted the statue and set to work again.

# Four

*The bar to which* Molly led Hector was relatively quiet for perhaps the first twenty minutes that they were there. She had found them a booth close by a stone fireplace.

Rather than sitting across from him, shivering, Molly had squeezed into the booth alongside Hector. She sat pressed close against him. Her leg was warm against his and he could smell her perfume. She smelled like lilacs.

"I'd take that cigarette now, Hector," she said, raising her voice over the din from the growing crowd of drinkers. Surprised, Hector lit her cigarette and was shaking out the match when there was more commotion...some loud crowd coming their way.

A group of giggling young men shouldered their way through the drinkers, clearing the way for the woman with them.

Hector watched the woman: tall...proud shoulders and ivory skin. Her blue-black hair was cut in a severe and short bob and worn in bangs...looking a little like a gleaming black helmet. She was wearing a gray skirt, black sweater, and carrying a long coat. Her dark eyes briefly considered Hector, then looked around the room a bit more.

Molly, sounding a bit perturbed, said, "You don't know her, do you? I'm frankly surprised."

"No, I don't," Hector said. "And why surprised?"

"She's rather famous around the Quarter and elsewhere. Or infamous, rather. Her name is Brinke Devlin. She's a kind of professional muse."

"What's that mean?"

Molly's violet eyes were hard. "She moves from painter to writer to poet. Brinke takes them on as lovers and delights in claiming she pushes them to greater works. Then she moves on to her next find. She's really just an expensive whore. But a very attractive one...no denying that. That coat—it's a Poiret. Very pricey."

"Whore" got Hector's attention—Molly never used that kind of language. Thinking about that, and feeling her leg still tight against his own, Hector thought perhaps he should take Hadley's assessment of Molly's interest in him a bit more seriously.

"This 'muse,' she's French?"

Molly shook her head. "No, Brinke's like us...another American."

Brinke Devlin and her "escorts"—most, if not all of them, homosexuals, Hector figured—were looking for a place to sit. He checked his pocket watch again and said, "By now we're probably leaving your boyfriend, or Hem and Hadley, waiting. We should go." He sensed Molly bridling at his choice of words to describe Philippe.

Molly slid out of the booth and Hector helped her on with her coat. He shrugged on his leather jacket and picked up his hat, aware now that Brinke Devlin was watching him again.

He winked at her and waved a hand at their vacated booth. "All yours," he said to the "professional muse."

Walking back through the mix of snow and rain, Molly clinging to his arm, Hector paused to watch a young girl singing on the street corner for coins. She couldn't be more than ten, Hector figured. The little girl was unusually petite and her hair seemed quite thin ... as if she might be sick in some way. She was singing "La Petite Tonkinoise," singing it a bit off-key:

> *Je suis vive, je suis charmante,*
> *Comme un petit oiseau qui chante ...*

There were just a few coins in the hat she'd put down at her feet. Hector said, "How much do you make on a good night, darlin'?"

The girl, her eyes tightly closed, continued singing.

A merchant standing in the recessed door of his shop for a smoke said, "She's quite deaf."

Hector nodded. He pulled out a five-franc note and crouched and lightly shook the girl's shoulder. Her eyes flew open, searching Hector's face. Smiling, he handed her the bill and then picked up her hat full of coins and handed her that, too. Still crouched down so she could see his face, perhaps read his lips, he said carefully, "Go along home now, little sparrow. Go along home and get warm."

Molly squeezed Hector's arm and said, "She'll just be back here again tomorrow night. I've seen her before."

"And I might be by this way again tomorrow night, too," Hector said. "You know, to send her on her way again."

"You're a soft touch," Molly said, walking on tiptoes to kiss Hector's cheek.

The *bal musette* they had vacated earlier still wasn't filled to capacity. Hector looked around and saw their former table was still available. He led Molly there and helped her off with her coat.

Hector smiled and waved as he saw Hem and Hadley threading their way through the tangle of dancers and diners and prostitutes. He threw his coat over Molly's and pulled an extra chair over to their table.

He hugged Hadley and she gave Hector a kiss on the cheek and then shook Molly's hand.

Hem gave Molly a bear hug and slapped Hector's back. He said, "Bumby's with Marie, our *femme de ménage*, so we have the night, if needed."

"Swell," Hector said. "What'll it be?"

"Burgundy," Hadley said, smiling. She brushed snow from her short thick, raggedly cut red hair. She was pale-skinned and her cheeks were red from being outside. Hadley's blue eyes were also watery with the cold. She wore a worn coat that buttoned tightly across her chest—she was still carrying a good deal of extra weight from the baby. Shivering, Hadley kept her coat on. She was eight years older than Hem, who was just a little older than Hector, and she treated Hector like Hem's flirtatious kid brother.

"Same for me, for now," Hem said.

Hector went to fetch their wine.

A hand on his shoulder. Hector turned to face a good-looking blond man with violet eyes. It was Philippe, Molly's boyfriend the French painter. Philippe smiled and said, "You're not dancing with Molly, Hector? I wouldn't have minded. I, you know . . . I trust you with her."

Hector smiled and said, "That's your job, Phil—dancing with her. I'm not much of a dancer. And Molly? Well, it'd be like kissing your sister."

Philippe frowned, and Hector said, "Sorry, it's an Americanism. What I mean is, I think of your lady as a kind of kid sister. Back home, we don't often dance with our own sisters."

Philippe nodded uncertainly, said, "Where are they?"

"Back and to the left," Hector said. "Get you something to drink?"

"No, I just came from the Rotonde. I'll wait a while." The young painter drifted toward the back to find their table.

Hector returned to the table with Hadley's and Hem's wine and then realized his own glass was empty. Hector went back to the bar.

There was some commotion. Hector was suddenly flanked by two young men with unnaturally yellow hair and matching camel's-hair overcoats. They looked familiar. Hector checked the room reflected in the mirror behind the bar and saw several more young men . . . surrounding Brinke Devlin.

An older, overweight man with a monocle, sitting at a table near the bar, raised his glass. He said, "Brinke! Why are you here? All the other chic children are at Boeuf sur le Toit."

"Good a reason as any *not* to be there," Brinke called back.

Hector thought Brinke and her gang should all actually be at a *bal musette* off the Rue de la Montagne Sainte-Geneviève—that joint catered to homosexuals.

Brinke moved to the bar and one of the men next to Hector stepped aside to make room for her.

"I know you," Brinke said to Hector, smiling. She frowned then, thinking. "*How* exactly do I know you?"

"We met next door. I witnessed your entrance with your entourage there. Quite an entrance. You took our booth."

"Oh yes. You were with the blonde. Your wife? Your lover?"

"My friend."

She smiled. "Oh."

Hector smiled and held out a hand. "Hector Lassiter. And I know your name, Miss Devlin."

"That could be good or bad," Brinke said, shaking Hector's hand. "Your name is known to me, too, Hector." He couldn't figure out how that might be.

He smiled and said, "So as the Count, or whatever he is over there asked, why aren't you at Boeuf sur le Toit? It is a Mecca for the smart set, isn't it? A *monument poétique*?" The Boeuf, located on the Rue Boissy d'Anglas, was a kind of voguish hive for would-be writers.

"Hell, I'm no poet," Brinke said. "And you're not there, either. You're probably not there for the same reason that I'm not there—it's on all the tourist maps now. All the out-of-towners flock to the

Boeuf and to the Rotonde to see what passes for bohemians in those places. Three years ago, there were six thousand Americans living in Paris. Now they say there are thirty thousand of us. It's amateur night in Paris, nearly everywhere, all the time. Gertrude—you know, Stein—calls it the curse of a great exchange rate."

Brinke picked up Hector's fresh drink as it was set before him and sampled it. The light over the bar gleamed in her blue-black hair. She looked at his glass, then sipped some more. "It'll do," she said. "Better order another for yourself, Hector."

Hector held up a finger and pointed at his stolen drink. The bartender winked and nodded.

"So why are you here?" Hector took his new drink and sipped a little. He said, "This place isn't on anyone's map."

Brinke smiled and sipped some more of Hector's liberated drink. "Last time I was at the Boeuf, I spilled some claret on Maurice Ravel. His companion gave me a terrible tongue-lashing for it."

"Probably marking territory," Hector said, watching one of Brinke's "escorts." He smiled at Brinke and said, "I mean, Proust is freshly dead . . . Maurice is available again."

"You've heard those stories, too," Brinke said. "Well, anyway, I'm still living it down. And this place? This place seems to me to be . . . very real."

"Working-class, you mean?"

"Authentic, I mean," she said. "And the people are interesting. Take you, for instance. You write crime stories published back home. They're quite good."

Hector was taken aback. "How do you know that? How have you read them?"

"Sylvia Beach showed me a few of your stories a couple of days ago."

Hector sipped his whisky, seething. "Why the hell would she do that?"

"Because I write similar stuff. Well, not so similar, maybe. Mine are more mysteries, I'd guess you'd call them."

"You write mystery stories?"

"I write mystery novels. I write them under a nom de guerre. 'Connor Templeton.'"

Incredulous, Hector said, "You're Connor Templeton?" He had read a few of Templeton's books. Not really Hector's cup of tea, and very much mysteries. But they were sly and sardonic and easy, fun reads. Smart . . . often sexy.

"That's right," she said, sipping more of the drink she'd taken from Hector. "But please keep it quiet. Only you and Sylvia know what I really do. I have a reputation as a dipsomaniacal dilettante to live down to."

"Sylvia's better at keeping secrets than I give her credit for," Hector said. Then he added, "Unless they're my secrets, I guess."

"You have nothing to be ashamed of, Hector. You have no reason to hide your work from all them." Brinke gestured vaguely behind her. "What you write is gritty and real and gripping. I write comedies of manners with bloodless murder stirred in."

"You could adopt another pen name . . . write different sorts of things under that name."

"It's not that simple. It's not quite the way I work . . . or draw inspiration."

"Someone told me you're a professional muse."

"I hear that a lot, too," she said, smiling. "I don't discourage it. Saves a girl paying for her own drinks and dinners. Mystery writing doesn't pay what you might think."

"Nobody seems to know you have any inclination for writing anything yourself."

"Better that way. And with my looks, they'd never take me seriously, anyway." Brinke shrugged. "And if they knew I wrote mystery books for sweet little old ladies back home? I'd never get a free drink again."

Hector looked her over again and winked. "That's just self-delusional."

"I don't carry off self-deprecation convincingly, huh?"

"It's a longer reach for some than for others," Hector said. "I still can't match you to this place."

"Jean-Paul over there likes it."

"In a looking-down-his-nose way, you mean?"

"Sneering, sure. He thinks it's 'rustic.' He says the working men who come here are like those 'fellows with dirty fingernails' in D. H. Lawrence books. The ones the haughty ladies have lusty affairs with. Now, me on the other hand?" Brinke waved a hand in the vicinity of her long neck: "I'm up to here with bloody accordion music." She looked in the mirror. "Looks like your friend is spoken for." With her other hand, Brinke gestured with her drink at the dance floor. Philippe, the blond painter, was spinning Molly, who was giggling.

"That's her boyfriend," Hector said. "He paints."

"So, she is just your friend," Brinke said. "But she doesn't look at you that way. I could see it in her eyes at that place next door. You're missing an opportunity there."

Hector said, "You want to go somewhere with no accordion music?" He hesitated, then said, "And without your prissy, praetorian guard?"

"That could be . . . nice."

"Give me a minute." Hector drained his drink and weaved his way back through the dancers to the table where Hem now sat alone. Hadley was dancing with one of Brinke's escorts. Hem seemed amused by that for the moment, but Hector figured that sentiment could turn on a dime. It was good he was leaving, he thought . . . it would save Hector the risk of being Hem's coat holder in case Hem decided to thrash Hadley's dance partner.

Hem winked and said, "I saw. You're off someplace with her?"

"For a while, okay?"

"Hell, I'd do it. She's a dish."

"You know of her?"

"Of her, yes. But not so much about her. But I can see all I need to know to understand why you're leaving now, Lasso. Do that right now, before Molly sees. I'll come up with some story for her and for Hadley." Hem raised his glass and winked. "Bang her once for me, buddy."

Hector shrugged on his leather jacket and was about to slip on his hat when Brinke took his fedora from him and put it on her own head, tipping the brim low.

"It suits you," he said. He led her out onto the wet street and looked around for a taxi. "Horse, or horsepower, Brinke?"

A light snow was falling and the wind had dimmed.

She shrugged. "Where do you propose to take me?"

"Deux Magots . . . sit on the terrace maybe and watch the snow fall?"

"Deux Magots would be quite fine, but inside, where we can eat and talk, too. So, I think we go by horse."

Hector waved down a taxi and said to the *cocher, "Aux Deux Magots."*

They were jostled back as the coach jerked into motion. It had been a while since Hector had ridden in one and he savored the hollow clop of the hooves on the slushed-over cobblestones. There was a heavy fur blanket rolled up on a shelf facing them. He spread that over them and Brinke snuggled closer and Hector wrapped an arm around her shoulders. "This is very nice," she said.

She watched a young man with a missing leg limping along outside in the snow, balanced on a crude crutch. "So many of them ruined," she said. "You served?"

"Sure. I was injured and ended up in Italy, driving ambulances."

"How badly injured?" He felt her hands on his legs under the blanket, squeezing to see that they were real.

"I'm fine now."

Her hand strayed . . . he was surprised. She fumbled with the buttons, then her hand was there, warm and firm, moving slowly back and forth, stroking. "Just making sure everything is as it should be," she said, smiling.

He leaned into a long kiss. Her tongue parted his lips. She pulled away just long enough to say, "You know, you have a free hand, too, Hector."

Hector slid his hand under the blanket, letting it roam down Brinke's flat belly and under her skirt as he leaned into another kiss.

# Five

*Hector freshened their glasses* of wine and helped himself to another oyster. He said, "So how, precisely, did you become Connor Templeton?"

Brinke picked up an oyster and said, "I read a few dozen too many mediocre mystery novels and decided I could do better. So I wrote one. I put it away for a month, then read it again fresh and didn't hate it. I sent it off to New York. They loved it, but thought it might a little too 'bold' to be written by a woman. It was strongly suggested to me such a book written by a woman expatriate might not fly in Boston, or anywhere else back home. My editor said it would likely move better—meet with much less resistance and scandal—if readers thought it was the work of some man of the world or kind of debauched gentleman rogue. So Connor Templeton was born."

"I've enjoyed reading them," Hector said. "That's no kind lie—they're really quite swell."

Brinke took the last of the oysters from its bed of crushed ice ... a few shallots tumbling from the shell as she raised it to her mouth. She tipped it back, then deposited the empty shell on the tray of ice. "God, but these are wonderful," she said. Reaching for her wine, she said, "Let's have some more."

"Let's do that."

Hector ordered another dozen oysters and a second bottle of Pouilly-Fuissé.

She said, "And you, Hector—are you working on a novel yet?"

"Fitfully."

"Your stories are truly wonderful," Brinke said. "I wish they'd let me write books that have the atmosphere and grit and gravitas of your stories."

"The stories are to live on," Hector said. He drained the dregs from his glass, hesitating. He finally said, "The novel will be ... well ..."

"More literary?" Brinke sipped her wine and said, "That's what you were going to say, isn't it? The world doesn't need any more of those sorts of books, Hector."

He shrugged.

"How much have you written, Hector?"

"The same eighty or ninety pages ... several times."

"Because you're not following your passion." Brinke reached across the table and took his hand. "Like I said, the world doesn't need more books like Anderson's or Ford's or Fitzgerald's. You need to write books that read like your stories. Do that, and I'll bet you'll have a manuscript in hand before false spring ... and a sale before summer."

"You could be right. And it's not as though I'm trying to give those men you mention a run for their money in the short fiction department." Hector got a cigarette and plucked a matchbox from the ashtray between them. "And you can't eat copies of little magazines, which is what they seem to pay you with here in Paris."

"That's right, and even if you could eat them, you'd find the fare getting spare given recent events around here."

"What? You mean the killings?" Hector bit his lip and said, "What do you make of those? I mean, as a fellow crime writer?"

"You're the crime writer ... I'm a mystery writer." She smiled and shrugged her shoulders and ran a hand back through her thick black bangs, ruffling them. "It's pretty hard to say, isn't it? Perhaps some disgruntled, hungry author whose story got rejected one too many times? Some perturbed poet? Or maybe it's just some other little magazine editor, hell-bent on thinning the competition."

Their second plate of oysters and bottle of wine arrived. Hector went through the usual nonsense about the cork, Brinke smirking all the while at his obvious irritation to have to go through the motions with the sommelier.

Hector downed another oyster, chasing its coppery passage with more of the dry white wine. He said, "As we're paid writers, and not in those rarefied literary stakes, the only thing I'm reasonably sure of is of our mutual innocence. In this matter, I mean."

Brinke smiled and said, "Yes. But one was murdered in his bed. He was naked, too. Apparently murdered in his sleep, based on his expression. Or his lack of one. Or so a friend of a friend of a friend of an inspector tells me."

"Hadn't heard that nuance," Hector said. "Does tend to cast things in a certain light regarding that particular murder, doesn't it?"

"Exactly."

They were making short work of the *portugaises*. As she again helped herself to the last of the oysters, Brinke said, "What time do you have, Hector?"

He fished his jacket's pocket for his watch. "Seven. You have someplace else you need to be?" He tried to hide his disappointment.

Brinke said, "Gertrude's, around eight. Can't really beg off. You'll escort me, of course." She smiled. "Won't you?"

It had been a while since Hector had ventured into Stein's salon. "Of course." He poured some more wine in Brinke's glass. He said, "Five francs says Alice still has a mustache."

Brinke said, "That's hardly a wager."

# Six

*They took another horse-drawn* taxi to Gertrude's salon off the courtyard at 27 rue de Fleurus.

During their second taxi ride of the night, they mostly kept their hands to themselves.

Hector said, "Does Gertrude know that you write? And what you write?"

Brinke turned to face him. "Okay, it goes like this: Gertrude is a fan. So Gertrude knows. Sylvia and Adrienne know. And now you know. You won't tell anyone, will you, Hector?"

"Only if you promise not to tell anyone that Sylvia is squirreling away copies of *Black Mask*."

Brinke extended a gloved hand to shake and said, "Secret sharers."

Normally, Hadley would have been consigned to the far corner—the wives' portion of the salon. There, Alice entertained the wives between hurling sharp, fast, and intrusive questions their way and eavesdropping on Gertrude's conversations with various painters, writers, poets, and playwrights who'd come to pay tribute to Miss Stein.

But because Hadley was an excellent pianist, Miss Stein had

evidently decided to allow Hadley to provide background music for the evening. Hadley was playing Beethoven's *Moonlight Sonata* ... one of Hector's favorites. Hem, looking surly, stood alongside the piano, a wineglass clutched in his hand. He smiled broadly as he saw Hector and said, "Tonight all roads lead to the House of Pretension, eh?"

Hector cast his leather jacket on a chair piled high with coats and helped Brinke off with her fur coat. She was still wearing his hat. He briefly introduced Brinke to Hadley and Hem. Leaning in close to Hem's ear, Hector said, "Molly didn't come along, did she?"

"Off dancing with her painter," Hem said quietly back. "She seemed sorry you'd left. Philippe seemed bothered by her reaction." Hem fetched a couple glasses of Gertrude's homemade black currant liqueur and handed them to Brinke and Hector. Gesturing at the floral arrangement atop the piano, with a crooked smile Hem said, "Lasso, what's better than a dozen roses on your piano?"

Before Hector could respond, Brinke chuckled and said, "Tulips on your organ."

Hem roared and squeezed her arm and said, "God, I like this one. Please don't fuck it up, Lasso."

Hadley, frowning, still playing the piano, said, "I don't get it: 'Tulips on your organ'?"

Hector leaned down and kissed her cheek. He said softly, "Hash, think T-W-O. Now, new word, 'lips.'"

Hadley thought about that, silently mouthed it, and then blushed.

Smiling, Hector sensed this presence—looked over, then down. Small, skinny Alice, who stood just four-eleven, nodded up at him. "It's been some time, Mr. Lassiter."

"It has, Miss Toklas."

"Who invited you?"

"I'm escorting Miss Devlin."

"Ah." Alice smoothed her freshly dark hair. Hector checked her top lip. No effort to dye the thin hairs there. Alice wore her hair in a style similar to Brinke's, but as much as the cut looked dashing and sexy on Brinke, the hairdo looked frumpy and severe on skinny, birdlike Alice.

Helping herself to one of the *visitandines* heaped on a plate positioned on the piano, Alice said, "I suppose it was inevitable you two would become . . . associated."

Hem, sensing Hector might say something precipitous said, "Think of the good-looking kids these two might produce, eh?"

Alice despised children. Just days before, she had gritted her way through the request that she, along with Miss Stein, consent to be Hem's son's godmothers. She'd agreed, Hem figured, only because Gertrude had been so delighted by the prospect.

Hector sipped the belly-warming, vodka-strong liqueur. He would have settled for the vodka, neat. He said, "That's one lovely frock, Alice."

Alice smiled uncertainly and nodded and said, "I think Miss Stein is summoning you." She smiled thinly at Brinke. "I mean, both of you."

Hem handed Hector a second glass. "What's this?"

"Single malt. Figure you'll need it, Lasso."

Hector deposited his mostly full glass of sweet liqueur on the piano and Brinke took his arm. Hadley segued from Beethoven to Erik Satie's *Ìère Gymnopédie*.

Hector said softly to Brinke, "You never know how this is going to go."

Gertrude's long, graying hair was pinned up. Her face looked a bit leaner, but the rest of Gertrude's body was as large and as ponderous as ever. She sat hulking in her chair under a portrait of herself painted by Picasso. She wore a long, striped scarf bound loosely around her neck and a tight-fitting floral print jacket. She seemed to be posed in the manner of the portrait hanging behind her.

"*There* is my cinema star," Gertrude said, remaining seated but beaming up at Hector. She was always commenting on his dark looks. He kissed her hand. Gertrude gestured at Brinke with her other hand. "And my other star is here, too. And like stars, your mutual gravities have drawn you together, is that not so?"

Hector looked around at the numerous paintings adorning the stained walls: Cézanne, Manet, Picabia, Gris, Gauguin. It looked as though Gertrude might have parted with a few other paintings that Hector remembered hanging during his last visit. But the walls were nevertheless heavy with paintings, in some places arrayed four or five rows high. The sitting room looked like a museum, and the antique chairs and couches were arranged backs-to-walls so that no matter where a visitor sat, they were confronted with rows and rows of paintings.

Gertrude gestured to an occupied chair: a poet fled to make room for Brinke.

Gertrude said, "Hector, are you mourning for Woodrow?"

Hector scowled and said, "Woodrow?" He thought a minute, and then said, "You mean Woodrow Wilson?"

The American ex-president had died a few days before.

Hector said, "No. Particularly not after old Woodrow got me sent to Mexico to chase Pancho Villa. Good to know the pinch-faced, patrician politician is safely on the other side of the dirt. He said he so-hated war, then dragged us into the war to end all wars."

"No serious man should place his fate in the hands of a man who wears pince-nez," Gertrude said. Then, "He died on my birthday, you know."

"I surely hope that didn't cast a pall over your happy day," Hector said.

Gertrude smiled. "Not at all. We have no politics."

"At least 'Double W' lingered a month longer than Lenin," Brinke said.

Gertrude shrugged her heavy shoulders. "If you call that living ... after the stroke, I mean. They say Wilson's wife was secretly president for the longest time."

Behind them, Hector overheard a couple of painters arguing: "*Non*, it is Breton's creation. He calls it 'Surrealism.' He calls it pure 'psychic automatism.' It's truer than true. Beauty will be *convulsive*, or not at all. It's far beyond. Far beyond the beyond of Dada. Miro is doing some interesting things with all that, even now."

It made Hector's head hurt to hear such talk.

Gertrude said, "I spent a wonderful morning at Shakespeare and Company reading Connor Templeton's *Blood Oranges*. Then, I read this remarkable little story called 'A Life in the Week,' by my wondrous, handsome Hector."

Hector slipped out his pack of cigarettes, smiling thinly. *Goddamn Sylvia, again*. He was proud enough of the story. It might even have been publishable in a little magazine. That is, if Hector had wanted to *give it away*.

But having Gertrude, the queen of all gossips, knowing about his stories and reading them?

And to have Gertrude talking about his work here in her salon?

Feeling a little sick inside, Hector struck a match. Watching him, Brinke opened her purse, pulled out a long, thin cigarette case, and selected a thin brown cigarillo. She bent into Hector's still lit match.

He shook out the match and then leaned over Gertrude to deposit the match in an ashtray. Hector realized Alice was close by again. Alice was always on the watch—assessing the motivations of all those around Gertrude. Alice moved quickly to undermine or destroy those who might threaten her position of primacy with the Great Woman.

Brinke edged a little closer to the fireplace. "I'm very ready for summer," she said, her back to the crackling fire and her arms and fingers spread to savor the heat.

Hector wondered if Brinke was deliberately moving the conversation away from their work.

Gertrude shook her head. She said, "The summer will be no better. Better there be no summer. Certainly not with the Olympic games. And the spring will bring only that which the summer will be. '*Citius, Altius, Fortius,*' That's the motto they've chosen for the

Paris games. The games will ruin the summer and the summer will ruin the spring."

Hector shrugged. "Latin, or whatever that is, is Greek to me."

Brinke said, "It means 'Swifter, Higher, Stronger.'"

Gertrude pursed her thick lips and said, "More like 'Crowded, common, and unremarkable.'" Gertrude looked across the room to the "wives' corner" where Alice was again seated. She said, "We shall go to Spain in the summer."

Maybe Hector would, too. He could spend July following the *feria*. Maybe he could persuade Brinke to be his traveling companion. He was a bit unsettled at how attached he'd already become to her. He thought of Hem's remarks about children. Brinke didn't strike Hector as the marrying kind.

Gertrude returned to her line of inquiry: "It was really a wonderful story, Hector, despite its sordid milieu and *that* woman. Really quite fine in its raw, pungent way."

Mystery and crime fiction were guilty pleasures for Gertrude. She had given Hector copies of Marie Belloc-Lowndes's thrillers to read when he had first arrived at her salon. She'd later urged the same books on Hem, who had also loved them. Gertrude maintained that one should read only the very great works of literature, or that which was "frankly bad." She seemed to lump Brinke's and Hector's efforts into the latter category. Gertrude called her favorite mystery writers "mystifiers."

Leaning forward, her big forearms resting on her massive thighs, Gertrude said, "I'm surprised but quite delighted that you are here tonight, Hector. This is serendipity of the best kind—you and Brinke both being here." She waved across the room to the wives' table and Alice leaned over and said something to the young woman sitting across from her there. Sotto voce, Gertrude said, "That young woman is Estelle Quartermain." Brinke looked up sharply. Oblivious, Gertrude said, "Estelle writes mysteries, though more of the puzzle variety. Do you know her work?"

Hector frowned and shrugged. "I don't read many mysteries. Connor Templeton's excepted, of course."

Brinke said thinly, "I've read a few . . . have to know the competition." To Hector, Brinke said, "Estelle writes a lot of things involving exotic poisons . . . murder-in-the-vicarage kind of stuff. Locked room mysteries. Her books all feature the same detective—an Albanian-accountant-cum-amateur-sleuth."

Hector blew some smoke through his nose and said, "Gee. Those sound . . . swell."

He rose and shook the woman's hand. Estelle wore her mouse-brown hair in an English approximation of a French bob. Her dress covered more of her than most women in Paris seemed to care to cover, despite the cold. Her eyes were dark and quick and her mouth full. She was moderately attractive, but she carried herself stiffly . . . too prim. Hector offered her his seat, then moved behind Brinke's chair, resting his hands on the back of her chair.

Looking back and forth between them and clapping her hands, Gertrude said, "My mystery pantheon is complete!" Hector bridled at being lumped in as a "mystery" writer, but smiled as politely as he could manage. Gertrude said, "Brinke tells me she has read your novels, Estelle. And have you read Brinke's books?"

Brinke's charcoal eyes turned on Gertrude. Gertrude waved a big hand. "Don't look at me in that way. We're among friends here. Brinke is secretly Connor Templeton."

Standing behind her, knowing her only a few hours, Hector could already sense that Brinke was seething. He placed a hand on her shoulder and squeezed. She reached up to hold his hand there.

The young British mystery writer smiled, closely examining Brinke now, and said, "I know them. They're quite clever and funny. Good after-work books."

Hector winced a little as Brinke's nails dug into the back of his hand.

Estelle said, "I've read some of Hector's stories, too." Looking quickly around, as if she might be misunderstood, she said, "My husband reads those dime magazines. He picks up pulp magazines as we travel. On a liner, earlier this year, he found some *Black Mask* magazines. He's held on to those copies to read and reread Hector's stories."

Hector nodded, realizing he was squeezing Brinke's shoulder a little too tightly. He said, "What do you think of them, Mrs. Quartermain?"

Estelle licked her lips. She said, "You're a real writer...your dialogue is very convincing and real. And there is an urgency and fear that comes through very strongly. With your abilities, you could..."

Estelle seemed to hesitate, not sure she should go ahead with that thought.

Brinke said, "With his abilities, Hector will eventually eclipse us both, I suspect. When he writes a crime novel, I wager he'll raise the bar and change the terrain for all of us mere mystery writers. Locked room mysteries can get a little deadening after a while. The same with drunken bon vivant detectives like those in my books."

Gertrude said, "I didn't bring you three together to talk shop or to posture."

Hector said, "Then why did you bring us together?"

Gertrude's eyes shone. "We need you to help us catch a killer."

# Seven

*Hector finally resorted to* the scotch Hem had handed him. He drained it at a pull. Alice was soon beside him with a decanter. She refilled his glass and said, "Poor, poor Natalie."

"So this is about the little magazine murders," Hector said.

"They were all dear friends," Gertrude said. So far as Hector knew, Gertrude didn't maintain many "dear friends" and long-term associations were unheard of. Gertrude turned or was turned on all of them by Alice.

Or so Hector had heard.

When Gertrude called the murdered magazine publishers "dear friends," Hector assumed she meant that they had published various of her pieces. Though Gertrude enjoyed a considerable reputation, surprisingly few of Gertrude's works were actually in print.

"The police are quite stupid and uninspired," Gertrude said, glowering. "I have no sense from the papers that the police have any inkling the murders have a literary connection. The police seem to be looking at these killings as random, isolated acts. But the police are always stupid, are they not?"

Hector figured Gertrude's low opinion of the authorities to have been shaped by reading too many "frankly bad" mystery novels.

He said to Gertrude, "And you truly think that we can solve these crimes?"

"You three, yes, with all of your experience and knowledge, and with my counsel as a student of the genre. Yes, I know that we can do this. Do it we shall."

Hector was struggling to maintain composure. He said, "It doesn't work the way it does in our various books and stories. We give ourselves—give our detectives—certain advantages." He looked at Estelle Quartermain. "Some of us give ourselves more advantages than some others. But we all do it—bend things toward the possibility of a solution. When you read a mystery novel, things glide along in their brisk and mandated way. Then you suddenly get an extra paragraph on some butler or chauffeur. The author is making you notice that servant or driver. Setting him up as the killer or as a red herring. It's a so-called fair-play convention . . . a sorry, tired device. Unfortunately, there are no such fair-play conventions that apply to real-life crimes."

Brinke said, "Hector is right. People kill for the reasons they do in his stories, not like in the novels that Estelle and I write. In life, arguments escalate and a too hard blow falls. A man comes home from work early because he's feeling ill and finds his wife in bed with his brother, or with the fellow down the hall. Sex fiends murder strangers as opportunity arises. Robberies go bad and somebody innocent dies. Killers simply don't kill for the complex or arcane reasons that they do in mystery novels."

Gertrude, clearly exasperated with Hector and Brinke, looked to Estelle Quartermain.

In her lightly accented British alto, Estelle said, "I'm reluctantly forced to agree with Miss Devlin and with Hector. Sadly, no crimes really get solved from armchairs, Miss Stein. In a perfect world, we might..."

Hector lost the thread then... tuning Estelle out. He was suddenly seized by this nasty image of himself with the British mystery writer. In his mind's eye, he saw himself bending Estelle over some couch... pushing her skirt up over her waist and making her snarl.

Gertrude held up a hand, silencing Estelle.

Slack-jawed, Gertrude pointed across the room at one of her guests who seemed to be having some kind of episode or profound seizure.

The man was bald and fat and he was clutching at his head and neck. His arms began to tremble and then his legs began to shake. He fell to his knees and his back arched suddenly. Gertrude said, "Hemingway, see to Charles!"

Hector was making his way around the back of Brinke's chair as the man clutched his belly a last time and then collapsed into Hem's arms.

Hem, who was a doctor's son, checked the man's airway, then rolled him onto his side.

Hector grabbed the man's fat hairy wrist and felt for a pulse.

Hem frowned and tore off the man's false shirt collar. He thrust three fingers up under the folds of fat, pressing up under the man's chin. Hem shook his head and said, *"Nada.* Luckless son of a bitch is dead enough."

"Roses . . . tulips . . . and now lilies," Hector said.


"He was a big boy. What do you think—a heart attack?"

Hem watched a doctor who lived across the courtyard working over the man. He sipped some wine and said, "My instincts are against it, Lasso. And he was clutching his head and neck first." Hem drained his wine. "Then, he grabbed at his belly and back, best he could with his arms shaking like that. Just before he died, everything was convulsing and twitching. I've never seen anything like it."

"Nor have I," the doctor said.

The man, Charles Turner, lay on the floor with his dead eyes widely staring up in the direction of the high ceiling. The doctor pulled at the dead man's arm and said, "Look at that. He's dead, what, perhaps ten minutes? Yet already the rigor has set in. Very very unusual."

Estelle Quartermain, standing alongside still seated Gertrude, said, "Some poisons produce that result."

Hector tipped his head on side. "You actually think he was poisoned?"

Estelle pointed at the plate atop the piano and said, "I saw him eating several of the *visitandines* a bit ago."

Hem said, "Alice was eating them, too, and Alice still looks . . . well, vertical."

Hector covered his mouth to hide his smile at that.

Estelle, indomitable, said, "You should smell the cakes. If it is strychnine, they should smell very bitter."

Hector leaned down and sniffed at the plate: "Smells sweet," he said. "So much for the poison theory. And where does this strychnine business come from?"

"The convulsions Mr. Hemingway described, and the order in

which they occurred, are common results of strychnine poisoning," Estelle said, looking from Hector to Brinke. "So is immediate rigor."

"That last I've heard of," the doctor said. "And his eyes . . . wide open . . . the blood vessels all burst. It could well be poisoning."

Gertrude shuddered and said to Estelle, "Would it have to be in something he ate, or drank?"

"It could even be inhaled in powder form," the mystery writer said.

Estelle seemed to be enjoying the limelight, Hector thought. He said: "How long after exposure until he'd turn tits up?" Hector ignored the cross looks his crass phrasing drew from Gertrude and Alice.

Her voice taut, Estelle said, "Maybe twenty minutes. Probably no more than thirty minutes."

Hector nodded. "And you know all this from your own books?"

Estelle tipped up her chin. "I was also a nurse during the war."

That shut Hector down. Brinke leaned over the doctor's shoulder. She said, "What's that in his hand?"

Hector knelt down and pried the man's right hand open. Everyone in the room shuddered at the crack from a couple of the corpse's fingers broken by Hector's exertions. He held up a small silver case. "Snuff," Hector said. Then he narrowed his eyes. To Estelle, he said, "You said it could be inhaled?" He opened the case. "Bitter you said?"

Brinke said, "For God's sake, Hector, don't smell it! If she's right, you'll be the next to hit the floor."

Hector sprinkled a little of the snuff on the piano top and then picked up a paper napkin and spread it over the light dusting of snuff. He leaned down and took a short sharp smell through the layers of napkin. He recoiled. "Christ, it's bitter as hell."

Hadley, standing on the other side of the piano where she wouldn't have to see the body, said, "Someone should call the police now, don't you think?"

# Eight

*"It's been a hell* of a first date, Mr. Lassiter."

Hector pulled Brinke closer under the blanket. The horse's hooves rung on the slick pavement. They had just dropped the Hemingways at their new apartment above the sawmill.

He said, "Is that what tonight has been? A date? Seven hours ago, I'd never even heard of a Brinke Devlin."

"What else to call it?"

"A 'date' it is." He kissed her. "We calling it a night?"

"Calling it a night on the town, sure." Brinke stroked his cheek. "But calling it a night? Lord, no. But my landlady is a nun . . . or she was. Or she acts like one. Like a vengeful, dangerous bitter nun. I'm not sure we can get by her."

"What about a hotel?"

"You're a struggling crime writer and you've spent enough tonight on oysters and wine and taxis. Thank you so much for all that, by the way. It's been a wonderful night. One of the best."

"Despite the murder?"

She smiled. "Maybe partly because of it. It's a night I surely won't forget."

Hector accepted another slow soft kiss and then said, "That leaves us with two prospects: the night *is* over, or we sneak past my surrogate mother of a *femme de ménage*."

Brinke adjusted the brim of his hat she was still wearing. "So, loan me your coat when we get there. I'll try and walk like a man. And I promise to be quiet when we get to your rooms. But do you have some wine at your place?"

"Red or white?"

"Red."

Hector said, "We'll need to make one more stop." He called up to the *cocher*, "We need to make a stop at the Rue Auguste Comte."

Brinke said, "Where do you live, by the way?"

"The Rue Vavin. Four floors up."

She smiled. "We're practically neighbors."

Hector slid from under the covers to place another log on the fire. He looked out the dormer window: the snow was falling again. He freshened their glasses of wine and said, "I hope you don't have to be up early."

"Only to write," she said, watching him. "But I think I might give myself the morning off."

"Me too."

"Good boy."

He slid back under the covers with her. They tapped glasses and Brinke said, "I thought you might thrash Estelle."

"That, among other things," Hector said. "Suppose the afternoon papers should tell the story as to whether she called it right with the poison."

"Suppose so," Brinke said. "Did you know this Charles?"

"Didn't know him from Adam. Did you know the fella?"

"Only in passing."

"What did he do for a living?"

"You really have to ask? He ran *Meridian*. You know—another little magazine."

An hour later, Hector rolled off her onto his back. Brinke scooted closer, holding him close, her thigh sliding across his belly. The muscles high up in her leg were still trembling.

From below and next door, Hector could hear a singer...

"Winter Winds Blow." In the song, a lonely man losing his grip addressed memories of former lovers.

Brinke's black bangs tickled Hector's cheek. He stroked her hair back across her forehead and said, "What do you think of the long-term prospects for a couple of fiction writers?"

Sleepily, Brinke said, "You mean, in terms of a life together?"

"Yeah."

"Depends on the writers, I expect," Brinke said. "And, of course, the respective size of the advances."

# Nine

*Hector requested an extra-large* breakfast from Germaine and tucked his mail between the tray and plate.

Brinke was sitting at his typewriter, pecking away.

He said, "Thought you gave yourself the day off?"

"Just making a few quick notes about last night. In case I ever decide to use it in a book."

Hector placed the tray on the table with the newspapers and his mail and read over Brinke's shoulder. He said, "Estelle Quartermain may beat you to that novel. In fact, I think she's already written it a half-dozen times."

Brinke turned, a dark eyebrow arched. She had her clothes back on from the night before. "You have read Estelle's stuff, haven't you? Despite what you told Gertrude."

"Two or three books," Hector said. "But I wouldn't want Gertrude knowing that. She'd construe it as peer interest or envy, and I don't want to be that British mystery writer's peer."

Brinke nodded slowly. "Right." She stood and stretched and kissed Hector. "What's for our breakfast?"

"That." He gestured at the table.

"What'll you be having?"

He smiled and shook his head. Brinke seemed to have an inexhaustible appetite. She also seemed to have an insane metabolism—otherwise, Hector thought Brinke might more resemble Gertrude Stein. "Honestly? I'm not really hungry. Maybe save me a croissant," he said. "But I do need some coffee. Lots of that." As Brinke poured his coffee from its metal flask, Hector sorted his mail.

"Something here from Gertrude," he said. Brinke, munching on a piece of bacon, squinting, tried to read over his shoulder.

"So, an audience at four," he said. "I suppose you have your own version of such a letter back at your place."

"Better be a safe enough bet," Brinke said. "Otherwise, my ego will be in a knot."

Hector said, "Daffy old bitch really wants to play amateur detective. She could better invest her time in rewriting her own prose. Maybe then it would sell."

Brinke paused, a forkful of scrambled eggs at her mouth. Without lipstick and makeup, she looked very young . . . almost fresh-faced. She said, "Gertrude sees all these magazine publishers going 'tits up' to borrow a phrase of yours, and she's probably in a blind panic that she'll have no outlets."

"Hem's trying to force Ford to serialize her *Making of Americans*," Hector said. "I've seen a bit of that, thanks to Hem. All I can say is, *Christ*."

Brinke rose and found her purse and slipped out a pair of reading glasses. Blushing, she put them on and opened one of the newspapers. "Please don't tell anyone about these. I'm nearly blind without them."

She continued eating and reading the paper while Hector sorted more mail. Another check . . . and an inquiry from an editor asking if Hector might not have some crime novel the magazine's allied publishing house might take a look at.

Hector had been thinking more about what Brinke had said. He'd never contemplated writing something crime-directed in long form. But God knew he kept hitting walls when he tried to write "straight." In the morning, he'd take a swing at that other sort of novel, he told himself. Then he looked at his table where Brinke sat eating and reading, fetching in her black sweater and tweed skirt and careless black hair. Well, maybe he'd start the big project the day after . . . or the day after that. There was always the next weekend.

"Not much here about last night," Brinke said. "Nothing about cause of death, though poison is mentioned as a possibility. Gertrude will love that . . . could leave readers with the sense she or Alice spiked the snuff."

"Yeah, about that," Hector said. "If it was poison in that snuff box, then it probably happened off-site—the tampering, I mean. Nobody was going to be taking sniffs from that slob's snuff box. Charles seemed to me, insofar as I even noticed him, to be off to himself for the most part last night."

"He was fairly antisocial," Brinke said. "He hung on the margins. He eavesdropped. Stood off a little bit from the groups, but close enough he might be confused for participating. If he didn't have his little magazine, I doubt he'd have had any friends." Brinke smiled. "Even 'dear friends,' like Gertrude." Brinke looked down at her clothes. "Would be very bad form for me to be seen wearing last night's clothes."

Hector said, "My landlady is going out around noon—she already warned me I'd have to fend for myself for lunch. We'll sneak you out then. It's getting you back in here that has me concerned."

Brinke smiled. "Oh. I'm coming back, am I?"

Hector sat down next to her. "Christ, I hope so."

"We look a little alike. You could say I'm your sister, visiting from the States."

"At the hours we're apt to come and go? With the things she might overhear? I wouldn't seem like much of a brother."

"We're creative types. We'll think of something."


Hector had dropped Brinke at her apartment to bathe and change. He walked from her building to Shakespeare and Company.

Before Sylvia could come around the desk to hug him, Hector said, "I'm feeling cross toward you, Syl."

Sylvia winced a bit and said, "Why is that?"

"You've been a loyal and supportive friend, ordering those magazines. I just wish you hadn't shared them."

"Oh," Sylvia said. "Who tipped you?"

"It wasn't her fault, but Brinke Devlin and before that, Molly."

"I didn't know that you and Brinke are acquainted, Hector. But you should be."

"This time yesterday, we weren't. Now I know her rather well." Let Sylvia make of that what she would.

"You two should get on well," Sylvia said. "And Brinke will be discreet. About your writing, I mean."

"Sure. But Gertrude? Molly?"

Sylvia winced again. "Gertrude too?"

"And how. Last night at her salon ... loudly."

"I'll stop."

"Thank you."

"Hem's somewhere in back," she said. "He told me about last night. What in God's name is going on? Who is doing this?"

Hector said, "Search me, but stay away from snuff."

"That I can promise."

His anger spent, Hector plopped his hat on Sylvia's head. She adjusted it to the angle she wanted and said, "Somewhere back there is also François Laurencin."

Hector said, "And what is a 'François Laurencin'?"

"A literary review publisher ... *Benchmarks*. In light of recent events, he's drawn some conclusions and he's in a bit of a panic. I think he and Hem are talking. François is terrified."

"Not without reason," Hector said. "And you've told me just enough to send me on my way." He held out his hand and Sylvia handed him back his hat. Hector gestured with it at the front window. It was raining again and the rain slid down the glass, blurring the view of the street. He said, "Have you sold any more copies of *Three Stories & Ten Poems*?" It was Hem's little book. Hector had incrementally bought five copies since its publication. He'd already reserved several copies of Hem's other little book, *In Our Time*.

Sylvia shook her head. "Not since last month's."

"Hem ask about sales?"

"He counts copies."

Hector nodded. He counted out fifteen francs. "Once again, we never made this transaction."

"You'll take it with you?"

Hector checked the passage to the back of the bookstore. "Nah. Just send it here." He scribbled down Brinke's address at Rue Madame.

Sylvia said, "Message, or inscription?"

"Sure. 'From Hector Lassiter, with love, to Connor Templeton.'"

Smirking, Sylvia said, "Fifty years from now, an inscription like that one could start a wild rumor."

Hector put on his hat and slipped on his gloves. He said, "You know what they say about any publicity."


Hector's next stop was at his barber's for a trim and a shave. As they were finishing up, Brinke slipped through the door, pushing it tightly closed against the pressure of the harder wind. She stomped the slush off her boots and shivered. She was dressed in trousers and a long masculine overcoat. She was wearing a man's felt hat, not dissimilar from Hector's own.

"I've been following your itinerary," Brinke said. "You spent much less time at Sylvia's than I expected."

"I was ducking scared little magazine publishers," Hector said.

Brinke nodded. She held up her hands to model her outfit. "What do you think? Think it's enough to fool your landlady?"

"Maybe. And then she'll just think I've switched sides."

Brinke was eyeing Hector's haircut. She nodded at his barber. "He does very good work." She took off the man's hat she was wearing. Brinke ruffled her dark hair with her hand and said to the barber, "Will you give me the same cut, but a little fuller on top and longer in the front?"

Hector said, "You sure about that?"

Brinke said, "After seeing Alice last night, I've been . . . troubled. So, God yes, I'm sure. I need a change."


Brinke took his hand and moved it to the back of her head. "Here, feel." He stroked her hair across the nape of her neck, feeling the shorter thick hair there ruffle under his fingers. "I like it very much," Brinke said.

"Me too." He was surprised to find that was true. Her black hair was close-cropped but a little longer in the front, and parted left to right. "It's a good thing you've got great ears," he said. *And good bone structure, too,* he thought. He traced the line of her jaw with his thumb.

"Just my ears?"

"Everything. Perfect." They were seated by the café's window and the rain was steadier now, washing away the last of the slush.

Brinke freshened their wine and raised her glass for a toast. She had selected the café. She said, "To amateur sleuths." That reminded Hector and he checked his watch: an hour until they were due at Gertrude's. Plenty of time to finish their wine and then walk the short distance to 37 rue de Fleurus.

"The poison is official now," she said. "I heard a newspaper vendor say so."

"Any suspects? Arrests?"

"Of course not."

"Of course." Hector realized he couldn't keep his hands off Brinke's hair. She seemed to like that. He said, "Ten francs says in a week half the women in Paris will be wearing their hair like yours."

"They don't know my barber. And what is it with you and wagers? Must everything be reduced to odds?"

Hector shrugged. He heard a scream and then saw cars veering to avoid collision. There were more screams and pedestrians jamming into the street, waving their hands to stop or redirect traffic. Hector said, "I think that's Hem over there." More screams.

Brinke picked up her hat and coat and said, "We should see what's happened."

Hector put on his jacket and hat and took her hand. "Yeah... pronto."

They crossed the street, weaving between stopped cars. Hector turned around sharply to get himself between Brinke and the possibility of her seeing the body in the street. The man was sprawled face down and at least two cars had passed over his body. The wheels of one had crushed his head and blood and brain matter was spreading out in the spaces between the slick cobbles.

Hem was suddenly on the other side of Brinke and he guided Brinke and Hector to the curb and away from the crowd of onlookers. "Nothing we can do for him," Hem said.

"Who the hell was that?"

"Laurencin. The guy who runs—*ran*—*Benchmarks*."

Brinke shot Hector a look. It said, *Christ, another?*

Hector said to Hem, "You were with François? What the hell happened?"

"Jostled, maybe," Hem said, looking flustered. "I looked away, then heard this cry . . . then the first car hit him. It was crowded. Hell, he might have been pushed."

"Given his vocation I think we can make that leap," Brinke said. "We should get to Gertrude's," she said to Hector.

Hem blinked back the rain. "Stein's?"

"We've been invited," Hector said.

"I'll come, too," Hem said.

"You're going to need to make a statement to the police," Hector said.

"What, and say I saw nothing?" Hem shook his head. "I can't do him any good now, Lasso."

Hector said, "If someone recognized you . . . ? Well, fleeing the scene of a crime can look bad."

"Only in one of your stories," Hem said. "Nobody saw me, let alone knows me. Let's go to Gertrude's now."

Hem suddenly narrowed his brown eyes at Brinke. Unthinkingly, he reached out and stroked the hair at the back of her neck. She hadn't put on her hat yet. She leaned a bit into his touch, turning her head, like a cat, to lengthen her neck.

Hem said, "*Love* the hair."

# Ten

*Alice ushered them in* past the stairs leading to the second floor where nobody, to Hector's knowledge, had ever been invited. Hector had often tried to imagine what the private area of Gertrude's living quarters must look like. Did the museum quality of the ground floor extend upstairs? Hem often joked about it . . . postulating some kind of Victorian lesbian-bordello motif with flocked wallpaper and swings . . . awash in brocade.

Alice looked quizzically at Hem. Hector said, "Hem and I are a team. You know, like Holmes and Watson."

Simultaneously, Hem and Hector pointed at one another and said, "He's Watson."

Hem grimaced and said, "Well, I do have the bum leg."

Frowning, Alice said, "Miss Stein's other, *invited* guests are already here." The little woman scowled at Brinke. "You've cut your hair."

Brinke ran her hand across the back of her neck. "Hector's taking me to the Riviera when the weather breaks," she said. "I thought something to get my hair off my neck and shoulders would put me in spirit of warmer places."

Hem said softly to Hector, "The Riviera? What, some rich aunt died?"

"It's news to me," Hector said.

Gertrude was just making her way back to her chair, leaning hard on her cane. Her heavy black skirt reached her feet. Hector had never seen Gertrude standing. He was always struck by her ponderous weight and that had given him a false impression of her overall size. Now he saw Gertrude wasn't tall—hardly an inch or more than five feet. She wore a cardigan sweater over a high-collared, ruffled white blouse, secured with a silver brooch. Gertrude saw Hem and said, "Hemingway, we've been thinking about the christening. We think we should look to an Episcopalian church."

Hem nodded. "Yeah?" He reached for a plate of sweet cakes. Hector noticed the other guests weren't eating or drinking: probably fearing poisoning.

"Yes," Gertrude said, smiling as Hem helped himself to the food. She settled into her chair and leaned her cane against the arm of her chair. "The Episcopalians seem . . . less dogmatic."

"That's a thought," Hem said. "We're having dinner tonight at

Nègre de Toulouse. You and Alice could come along and we could discuss it further."

Hector looked around the room. Estelle Quartermain, seated next to Gertrude, nodded back. Next to her sat a patrician-looking, slightly older man Hector took to be the mystery writer's husband. He wore pince-nez.

A mannish woman sat at Gertrude's right hand. The woman was dressed in a tailored suit that looked to Hector to have been borrowed from a brother. The woman's hair was cropped much closer than Brinke's—even closer than Hector's. She was smoking a pungent cigar. Hem introduced her to Hector as Joan Pyle, co-editor of *Intimations*. Joan wore a man's white oxford shirt with a necktie. Hector suddenly felt underdressed. "Joan's a brick," Hem said. And another of the literary *grandes dames de Paris*, Hector figured.

Hector gambled and shook the editor's hand like a man's. Joan, who seemed to approve, said, "Nicole will try to get here, but she's dealing with a printing problem."

"Nicole Voivin is the other editor of *Intimations*," Hem explained. Hector thought he was lucky Hem invited himself along, as Gertrude was often lacking in certain social graces. There was a presumption on her part that if Gertrude knew a person, that person automatically knew everyone else in Gertrude's orbit. And Alice wasn't about to do anything to undermine her lover's self-centered presumptions.

Brinke said, "I hope Miss Voivin is not alone."

"She's being watched," Joan said. "Georgette is close by . . . as is a friend of Georgette's who boxes."

Seated next to Joan was a fiftyish, portly man with a thick, walruslike mustache. The man's blond hair was graying and his eyes watery. His breath came in heavy wheezes—the result of surviving a long-ago mustard gas attack. Hector leaned down and clapped the Englishman's arm. "Ford—it's been a spell."

Ford Madox Ford nodded solemnly.

Hector said, "Is Ezra coming, too?" The poet Ezra Pound, Ford, and some others had recently launched their own literary magazine dubbed the *Transatlantic Review*.

In a soft, almost sibilant voice, punctuated by stops for deep intakes of breath, Ford said, "Ezra is wintering . . . in Rapallo. Presumably far enough away . . . to keep him safe . . . from all of this."

Ford always left Hector a little baffled. The utter image of a stodgy Brit, Ford nevertheless wrote some very fine tough books and stories . . . and maintained a string of beautiful young mistresses.

Hem despised Ford, and did little to conceal it.

Alice handed Hector and Brinke glasses of red wine and they took seats opposite Ford. Watching to see if they would at least trust her hospitality, Gertrude raised a hand to her mouth as if to say, "DRINK."

Alice pointedly didn't arrange for a seat for Hem; she also didn't offer Hem any wine.

Hem picked up the piano bench and plunked it down directly opposite Gertrude. Hector handed Hem his untouched glass of wine. Hem sipped some of the wine, prompting a smile from Gertrude. Alice grudgingly went to prepare Hector another glass. Alice handed Hector the wine and he tapped glasses with Brinke and they both sipped—Brinke a bit warily. Hector drank deeply, as if it were water. Gertrude beamed again. Evidently encouraged by Gertrude's approval, Hem said, "I'm helping myself to another of those little cakes." Hem tossed one to Joan and another to Ford, both of whom caught the little cakes as if they were pitched vipers. "Eat up, Ford . . . Joan," Hem said. "They're quite tasty. Come on now—hell, they won't bite you."

Frowning, they both carefully nibbled at the cakes, chewing with forced smiles.

Gertrude nodded approvingly at Hem and said to the room, "You see now, our refreshments are quite safe. Now, I'm interested in our progress."

Hector sipped more of his wine. He said, "Progress?"

"Yes," Gertrude said. "What have my mystifiers learned since last night?"

As if suddenly reminded about the body that had been sprawled there, Alice, carrying more glasses of wine for Ford and Joan Pyle, awkwardly stepped wide around that part of the floor.

Looking rather annoyed by tiny Alice's stutter-step, Gertrude said, "What have you gathered or learned since Estelle's theory about poisoning has been borne out?"

Hector served it up cold: "François Laurencin is dead, too. Just minutes ago, in fact. Someone shoved him into traffic."

Hem nodded solemnly. "It happened right next to me. Didn't see who did the deed, but he's dead for sure. Brains all over the pavement."

Her forearms resting on her knees, Gertrude bowed her head.

Alice said to Hem, "And you did nothing?"

"There was nothing to do, Alice," Hector said. "François's brains were pulp before Hem, or anyone, could have reacted."

Slouched down in his chair, holding his half-eaten cake, Ford said so softly Hector had to strain to hear it, "This is inconceivable." The English novelist struggled up to stand and paced a bit, feet at right angles to one another and hands thrust deep into his coat pockets. At six feet, Ford stood just a shade taller than Hem ... but a few inches short of Hector. "We're all ... going to have to take measures ... to protect ourselves," Ford said in his wheezing voice. "All us editors, I mean."

Hem, perhaps sensing an opportunity, said to Ford—who preferred that younger writers actually call him *Master,* "With Ezra in Italy, you could probably use some help at the magazine. You should name me as a subeditor. It'll keep me in position to watch your back ... *Master.*"

Gertrude said, "It's a very fine idea."

Ford nodded and sat back down. He pulled at his mustache and finally said, "Yes. Yes ... let's do that. We'll bring you aboard ... Ernest."

Estelle Quartermain suddenly blurted out, "*Thieves* kill with daggers. Common thugs, like those in Hector's stories, push people under cars. But the poison that killed that man in this room?" She waved a hand at the spot on the floor that Alice had stepped around. She said, "That murder took planning. Knowledge. Cunning and sophistication."

Hector, reaching for his cigarettes, said, "My guys would never throw someone under a car. That's simply amateurish, or killing on a whim. And the only cunning or sophistication last night's escapade required was a library card and a zeal for reading your flavor of mystery books, Estelle. You've taught all the old biddies about cyanide and boiling flypaper for its arsenic content and the like."

Brinke pulled out her own cigarette case and shared Hector's match. As he held the match for his companion, Hector watched Estelle watching Brinke. The British mystery writer's gloved hand strayed to her own hair. Brinke said, "To my mind, the key murder here—insofar as we might quickly learn something—is the killing of Lloyd Blake. He was murdered in his own bed. He was naked. I've heard a few things about that killing . . . things trickling back through authorities. The fact is, the murderer was probably taken to Lloyd's bed. So we're looking for a woman."

"Or a queer," Hem said.

Gertrude nodded slowly. Her dark-eyed gaze settled on Hector. In her deep, smoky voice she said, "And you, my star? I can guess whose side you'll take in this, but what are your thoughts?"

Hector expelled a thin stream of smoke, looking at Estelle. "I think there are too many change-ups."

Joan Pyle leaned forward, feet apart and elbows on knees. "What does that mean?"

"Sorry, it's a baseball term," Hector said. He sipped more wine and leaned forward, unconsciously echoing Joan's posture. He said, "Some kill only once . . . a robbery at gun- or knife-point that escalates. Some domestic mess. But professionals—assassins—they specialize. Even sex maniacs nearly always kill the same way."

Estelle Quartermain said, "And your point, Mr. Lassiter?"

"The only consistent thing about these crimes," Hector said, "is the vocation of the victims. The murders themselves, and their means, are all over the damn place. There's simply too much variation."

Gertrude said, "Elaborate."

Nodding, Hector said, "All the murders—except for the one that Estelle has fixated on—required close-in work. They display a willingness to get messy and to see the effects up close. Daggers driven into hearts. And, most telling of all, Blake's murder. Brinke is right: his killer likely crawled into bed with Lloyd. The murderer got Blake to lower his guard. That one would have been the bloodiest death of all. In the other cases, there would have been the single thrust of the blade, then the swift retreat from a sheltered doorway, or a hand pressed to a chin to tip a body over a bridge rail and into the river before the real bleeding began.

"But that killing in bed? Even prone, even sleeping, there would have been a terrible mess," Hector said. He took another hit from his cigarette. Through a curtain of smoke he said, "The arterial spray would have been profound. The blood would have come like a geyser until the heart stopped."

"So uncivilized," Estelle said, looking queasy. "Thuggish."

"Welcome to real-world murder, sweetie," Brinke said, watching the other mystery writer. "Poisoning, from afar, is the work of an aloof coward. Or a terrible kind of woman."

Gertrude said, "And now a man has been thrown under a car. Yes, all these variations, as Hector calls them, have been vexing us." She looked again to Hector. "And so, my star, what is your conclusion?"

"I conclude that we're not looking for a killer," Hector said, "not for some devious mastermind of the kind I get the inkling Estelle envisions. I think we're facing killers. Some kind of . . . well, team, or cooperative."

Gertrude sipped some wine and nodded again, slowly. In her deep voice she said, "We think that we concur."

# Eleven

*Brinke walked briskly alongside* Hector, long legs keeping pace, her arm hooked securely through his. In her man's overcoat and hat—and with her short hair—they garnered occasional curious looks until other passersby drew closer and saw that Brinke was a woman.

She said, "We're skipping dinner with Hem?"

"God, I want to. Especially as Ford will be along now. Probably with one of his mistresses. You know—so Hem can 'watch his back.' I'm not sure who I feel sorrier for in the days ahead—Ford or Hem."

Hector was also hoping to avoid any awkwardness with Molly, who knew all of Hem's and Hector's haunts. After Molly had dismissed Brinke as a "whore," Hector couldn't see bringing the two of them together. Particularly since the "whore" was now sharing Hector's bed.

"Alone together is better," Brinke said. "But I am starving."

That made him smile. "You always seem to be starving."

They crossed the Rue Madame, headed toward the gardens. "It'll be Connor Templeton's treat," she said. "But where should we eat?"

"There's a good place on the Rue Auguste Comte, close by where we stopped for wine last night."

"Sounds perfect. And we can pick up more wine, for later." She squeezed his arm tighter, shivering.

"We could get a cab," he said.

"No, the winter's walk will do us good. Clears the head." She squeezed his arm tighter and said, "What do you think of Gertrude's plan?"

Miss Stein had laid out a loose strategy for investigation:

Estelle and her husband were to pursue the poisoning angle (Estelle had insisted).

Brinke and Hector would nose around the murder of Lloyd Blake.

"We'll do our little piece, I suppose," Hector said. "Of course, I also mean to go outside the lines if we really do this. Charles Turner had a wife. We should talk to her. Estelle and her husband will never do that—too intrusive . . . too . . . un-English."

"We'll do that if the widow will see us. But not tonight," Brinke said, smiling.

"No, not tonight," he agreed. "Tonight is for good things."

They dined on *sole grillées* and salad. Still hungry, Brinke had just ordered *crabe rémoulade.*

Brinke said, "Estelle really gets under your skin."

Hector poked around at his salad. At Gertrude's, as Estelle had disparaged the criminals in Hector's stories as "thugs," he'd been seized by another vision of himself with the British mystery writer—naked together on some Oriental rug . . . bathed in sweat . . . writhing . . . Estelle's nails at his back. He said to Brinke, "She doesn't rub you the wrong way?"

"Utterly." Brinke smiled. "But probably for different reasons."

"Such as?"

Brinke shook her head. "Doesn't matter now. You really think these killings are the result of some team effort?"

"I do."

"Me too, since you said it. But it's crazy. And who is doing it? And why?"

"All fine questions for tomorrow," Hector said.

They turned the corner onto the Rue Vavin. There were light snow flurries underway and enough wind to create small squalls in the rare spaces between the buildings.

"This is odd," Hector said.

A woman was sitting on the steps outside Hector's building. The woman's head was in her hands and her shoulders were shaking. Flakes of snow lay heavy in her thick auburn hair. She was wearing a threadbare wool coat.

When he recognized her, Hector ran the last thirty yards to her. He called, "Hash! What in God's name is wrong?"

Hadley rose and ran to Hector's arms. Between sobs, she said, "It's Ernest! He's been arrested."

Brinke said, *"Good Christ,"* and waved for a taxi.

"Arrested?" Hector squeezed Hadley tightly to him. "What on earth for?"

"Suspicion of murder."

# Twelve

*Hector directed the driver* to transport them to the station house in the 14 ème arrondissement where he presumed Hem would be taken.

As they bumped along, Hector said to Hadley, "And Ford, what did he do? He was to eat with you two, wasn't he? He didn't lift a finger to help?"

Hadley dabbed at her eyes with Hector's handkerchief. "We never made it to the restaurant. The police came to our apartment, before we left. I can't believe this is happening."

Brinke said, "And whom do they think Hem killed?"

"Some man who was crushed by a car," Hadley said. "And that's just crazy. They asked about the poisoning at Gertrude's, too. And about this man Murray Panzer... seems Hem was making threats because of all of the writers Murray swindled. But you know that's all bluster on Hem's part, right, Hector?"

Hector patted her hand. "Absolutely."


A uniformed underling pointed toward a broad-shouldered older man wearing a too large heavy black overcoat with a velvet collar and a black bowler hat. The man shook his head and said to the room, "Can't we get some goddamn heat in here?"

The man in the bowler and black overcoat turned to face Hector and took a pipe from his mouth.

Hector stuck out a hand and said, "Commissaire Simon?"

Aristide Simon nodded. "You're not that fool from *Gazette de Liège*, are you?"

"What? A reporter? No." Hector kept his hand out and said, "Your men brought a friend of mine in for questioning earlier this evening."

The commissaire took Hector's hand then and shook it—a firm dry grip. "Ah," the policeman said, "a friend of this Hemingway person, are you?"

"Yes, he's my good and quite *innocent* friend. I'm Hector Lassiter."

"Oh, yes. You're another to whom I wish to speak."

That surprised Hector. "I am?"

"Yes. You were present at the party last night at Gertrude Stein's salon. I'm told you tried to render assistance to the victim."

"For all the good that did. My friend whom you're holding also tried to 'render assistance.' Hem did a good bit more than me."

"I'm told that, as well," Simon said. "But Monsieur Hemingway was also standing alongside a man killed earlier today. Perhaps murdered . . . *par une voiture*. Monsieur Hemingway fled the scene before he could be questioned."

"Mr. Hemingway had no answers to provide you," Hector said. "He saw nothing."

"And so he claims." Simon took a draw on his pipe and said,

"You were close by that murder scene, as well, Monsieur Lassiter."

"Across the street, in a restaurant, with a friend. I saw the aftermath."

"And so you can't say definitively that your friend Hemingway *didn't* kill François Laurencin, as I pointed out to Monsieur Hemingway when he tried to use you and a Mademoiselle Brinke Devlin as alibis ... or at least as friendly witnesses."

Hector opted for a "change-up." He said, "How did Hem and I first come to your attention?"

"Monsieur Laurencin, poor fellow, had a parcel still clutched in his hand—in his undamaged hand. The left hand was quite mauled. Anyway, the parcel was a book. A rare book, printed in English and just purchased. Where else would he have purchased such a book but at Shakespeare and Company?"

"Where else," Hector said, frowning.

Commissaire Simon smiled. "And there was a store bill of sale in the book, with an address of the store ... date and time purchased."

"And Sylvia Beach, somewhat grudgingly, I hope, told you that François left her store with Hem."

"That's right, Monsieur Lassiter. And Mademoiselle Beach indeed did so *quite* grudgingly." The cop waved a hand. "Come over here to the table by the stove. It's the only warm place in this goddamn drafty building."

They walked to a scarred wooden table by the stove and Simon shrugged off his big overcoat. Underneath, he wore a black serge suit. "Sit, please, Monsieur Lassiter."

Hector did that and accepted a cup of coffee. He said, "Hem knows less than me, and I know next to nothing." He tasted the coffee ... too sweet.

"*Pas si vite!* Tell me what you do know, Monsieur Lassiter."

"Several around the Left Bank believe someone is murdering

the publishers of small literary magazines," Hector said. "From where I sit, they're right."

"Yes, five now, with Monsieur Laurencin's passing," Simon said. He pointed at Hector with his pipe's stem. "Why would anyone do such things?"

"I have no idea," Hector said. "Probably I have just the same unsatisfactory notions you have, if you believe there is a link between these deaths. Maybe it's just some frustrated writer who got one too many rejections and snapped. As I said, I have no good idea."

"But you have other, worthier ideas it seems," Simon said. "You think there is more than one killer at work."

"Hem told you that?"

"*Non*, he's belligerent and tight-lipped. Monsieur Hemingway is a stubborn one. I had a visitor...this preposterous English mystery writer. She said that she, and you, and some others, including this friend of yours, Mademoiselle Devlin, are all working for Gertrude Stein. She said that you're all trying, like some silly mystery book characters, to solve the mystery of these murders, just like the amateur sleuths in her own silly books...like that amateur detective, that goddamn foreign accountant of Mrs. Quartermain's."

"Agreed," Hector said. "It's daft as hell. Like so many, I just smile and nod at Miss Stein when she talks and it's often confused as approval or agreement. This notion of Gertrude's, it is quite daft."

"And so is Mrs. Quartermain," Simon said. "She has the most extraordinary and fanciful lines of inquiry for me to pursue. She tried to assign me tasks. The insouciant temerity of it all would be quite amusing...if people weren't really dying and in such numbers. Silly English."

"I'd love to hear some of her tasks for you," Hector said, smiling. He was truly curious.

"Another time perhaps," the policeman said with a crooked smile. "Some evening over drinks perhaps, when we could talk about your works, too. Miss Beach shared with me a few copies of *Black Mask* magazine. I asked her to read a couple of your stories to me. I like your stories very much. Despite Miss Beach's rather spotty abilities at translation, your stories are quite authentic, from my perspective. And you give the authorities a fair shake in your stories . . . not like Conan Doyle or this flighty Estelle Quartermain."

"We should have those drinks sometime."

"And we will, Monsieur Lassiter. But for now, I want you and your writer friends to stand clear of all this. We're working the case, enthusiastically. We've made the connections between the crimes. This is to be left to the authorities now."

"Reasonable request," Hector said. "And you'll be releasing my friend to me now?"

"Will you honor my reasonable request?"

"I will."

*"Merci."*

*"De rien."*

"See that your friends do, as well, Monsieur Lassiter, *oui*? We don't need to be tripping over sleuthing young fiction writers, do we?"

"You certainly don't," Hector said. "I couldn't agree more."

The commissaire smiled. "Good. Good. That said, if you, as an individual, have any further thoughts—insights or observations—I might entertain your input."

Hector scowled. *"Pardon . . . Je ne comprends pas.* You said, quite clearly, I was to butt the hell out."

Simon shook his head. *"Non.* Not in so many words, Monsieur Lassiter. I just asked that you stop this silliness with Miss Stein. That's what I ask of you, in particular. But you might be of real assistance to me. You enjoy entrée to the literary community that I do not. It's a strange world to me . . . almost a foreign world with all you Americans packed into your little Quarter. *Bohemians. Expatri-*

*ates*. It's all very recherché, *n'est-ce pas?* Also, from your stories, I can see you have an astute eye for human weakness and motivation . . . of the low strong drives that can unbalance people. And some of your conclusions are also my own. You see, I strongly concur with your theory that more than one person is killing these people. So, if you hear anything, or think of anything that might help me, I will always accept *your* calls regarding this matter."

Simon extended his hand first. "We have a compact?"

Hector smiled. *"D'accord."*

Their housekeeper, Marie, who had been watching baby John, had left the Hemingways' new apartment a short while ago.

Hadley was nursing Bumby. Brinke sat in the dining area with Hadley, watching, but in line of sight of Hector and Hem. It was the first time that Hector had been in the Hemingway apartment after dark and he was surprised how quiet it was with the sawmill shut down for the night.

"You shouldn't have agreed to back off," Hem said to Hector.

"Wasn't much room for objection," Hector said. "And it doesn't mean I'll honor that pledge. And you've got your own full plate, Hem. You've got your subeditor's post at the *Review* now. And you've got to watch over Ford."

"If it was Ezra I was protecting, it might mean something to me."

"If you have anyone else you feel affectionate toward—I mean, who also happen to run literary magazines—you ought to urge them to go to Italy, too," Brinke said to Hem.

Hem nodded and rose and picked up Bumby, tossing him a few times in the air until he belched and giggled.

Brinke watched Hadley wipe at her large, milk-heavy breast and then button her dress closed. Shivering a little, Brinke said to Hector, "We should be going now." She picked up Hector's hat and tossed it to him. "It's getting late," she said. "Time for all good children to be in bed."

Hector hugged Hadley and slapped Hem's back. He said, "Lie low for a time, Hem. We'll regroup *demain*."

As they climbed down the stairs, Hector said to Brinke, "You sure were in a hurry to leave."

Her own felt hat in hand, Brinke said, "Dear God, all that domesticity . . . it was cloying. Wasn't it?"

"Not your ambition?"

Watching her feet on the narrow stairs, Brinke said, "Why do I think I should know your answer to that question before I supply my own?"

"Take it easy," Hector said. "I didn't ask it with intent."

They hit the ground floor landing and Brinke turned Hector around, pulling him close. Her dark eyes searched his face. She said, *"Really?"*

"Really." Hector put his hat on and said, "I'm from coastal Texas. Where are you from? I don't know. I'm twenty-four. I don't know how old you are. My folks are dead. I know nothing about your family or origins. Knowing so little about you, how could I presumably be thinking about so much with you?"

Brinke put on her own fedora and slipped her arm through Hector's. "And so, am I to infer we have to know one another's biographies, womb-to-tomb, or thereabouts, before we settle this issue?"

"There's really nothing to settle," Hector said. "I'm not looking to lay down roots, Brinke. I'm still happily *solo lobo*. Except of course for my nights with you."

They stepped out into the dusting snow.

They walked in silence for a while. Brinke broke it: "Hem's the perfect red herring. I mean, if life's events were playing out in one of my mysteries . . . or one of Estelle's. Hem's a good likely distraction—in terms of a false suspect."

"Christ, don't class yourself with that sorry bitch Quartermain," Hector said.

"Harsh," Brinke said. "You said 'bitch' like you intended an even cruder word."

"Maybe. Besides, I go Hem one better in terms of the possible-perpetrator-by-propinquity stakes."

"You're going to have to explain that one to me," Brinke said. "You're talking like Gertrude Stein."

Hector said, "Christ forbid. Okay. I mean, the night or early morning that Natalie Champlin was murdered, I was crossing the bridge from the Right Bank—crossing the Pont Neuf—and I heard a scream."

"A scream?"

"Yes, a terrible scream. Then I heard the ice over the river cracking . . . a splash."

"You think you heard Natalie being murdered?"

"With all my heart." Hector wrapped his arm around Brinke's shoulders, pulling her closer. "There were footprints in the snow from the scene of the fall. They were spaced far apart, like the one who left them was running."

"Could have been anyone's footprints, Hector."

"No, it was early morning, and I heard feet running away, and they were the only footprints in the snow. I thought about following them. The thing was, the footprints were going my way. They led right back to our neighborhood. But it was late, and I was very tired, and the snow began falling harder as I neared home. Eventually, the prints disappeared entirely before I could see where they led."

"Male or female footprints?"

"There was no telling."

"But definitely retreating back to our neighborhood?"

"No question."

Brinke said, "Despite what you told that policeman Simon, I don't want to let this go. The next one killed could be a friend. Or someone who matters even more to us."

Hector pressed his gloved fingers to her lips. "That's unlucky talk."

"You're right." Brinke shook off his arm and squared her

shoulders. "Hands off, now. We're almost to your place. Time for me to walk like a man."

"Right," Hector said, smiling and shaking his head.

"What were you doing on the Right Bank that night, Hector?"

"Writing. I'm mostly a morning writer, but you know how sometimes you get on a roll? I did that evening. But you can't write in cafés in the Left Bank anymore, you know that. Too many interruptions. Too many drink cadgers and food moochers. And you look like a poseur, even if you're really writing. Across the river, that's not the case. I found a little place on the Rue de Bourdonnais . . . reasonably priced wine and oysters. Quiet. A good place to write."

"You should take me there soon," Brinke said. "We could get adjoining tables. Might be the only way I'll get any writing done so long as you remain a bewitching novelty."

Brinke bit the side of her own hand, her ankles trembling against Hector's.

A few minutes later she said, "Sorry . . . I have a terrible tendency to be loud."

"Someday soon we'll have to find a place where you can indulge that urge," he said. "Maybe the Riviera." He rubbed at the imprints of her teeth left in the heel of her hand. They were just starting to fade.

"That Riviera remark was for Alice's sake," Brinke said. "I don't really want to go there. I have no interest in another tourist destination."

Hector stroked her breasts. "Any place that does interest you?"

"South Florida," Brinke said. "Key West, particularly. It's said to be authentically bohemian, like Paris was in the good old days, but sparsely populated. Remote. Can only be reached by boat. They ignore Prohibition there and live like they're in a kind of hedonist's nation-state. They swim naked on the beaches and have great seafood in abundance. A live-and-let-live kind of place. My kind of place."

"I can't square that remote Gulf island with Connor Templeton," Hector said.

"It's very 'square-able' with Brinke Devlin, writer," Brinke said.

"You're really getting tired of Paris?"

*"Très."* She stretched a little and sighed as his hand strayed down her body. "It's very warm in Key West, all the time. Remember summers back home, Hector? I mean, when you spent the summer with a tan?"

"I'm from Galveston," Hector said. "I remember sunburns."

Brinke raised her head a little and pulled at the hair on his chest with her teeth that were a little gray from all the red wine they'd been drinking. She hesitated, then said, "Okay. Here it is, Hector. My full name is Alison Boyton Devlin. Brinke, as in 'On the brink,' is a nickname, but I like it much better than 'Alison.' I'm twenty-nine years old. My parents are Yvonne and Stewart Devlin of upstate New York. I came to Paris to study literature at La Sorbonne and because Daddy thought Europe would do me all manner of good. I dropped out of school quite a few years ago, but never left the city."

Hector took all that in. He said, "You're an only child?"

Brinke smiled. "You really have to ask? I haven't seen my parents since 1922. Father and I are reduced to quarterly letters. Mother writes more often. She knows I'm Connor Templeton. Father doesn't."

Hector kissed her, stroking her back. He said, "You didn't have to tell me any of that, Brinke. But thank you for doing it."

Her fingers traced his lips: "Doesn't mean we have to pick out rings, right?"

"Right."

# Thirteen

*Hector woke up alone.* Brinke's side of the bed was still warm, but her clothes, once slung over a chair by his bed, were gone. Hector pushed up onto his elbows and saw a sheet of typing paper on her pillow. He unfolded it and read Brinke's note, written in a bold, clean hand:

> Dear Hector:
>
> I really simply *had* to get some writing done, so I'm sneaking out before your "mother" can raise a fuss or you can stop me.
>
> You should write, too.
>
> Here's my vision: We'll meet at six across the river at Harry's ... make ourselves homesick for America at its bar, perhaps.
>
> Later, but not *too* much later, I'll be wanting French cuisine: *des moules marinières, du homard* ... or perhaps *des cuisses de grenouilles*. Or something entirely else. It's early yet, and I'm not sure of my own tastes at this hour. But you'll find us the other restaurant ... (someplace with *une tarte tatin* would put you in *excellent* standing).
>
> That's your task.
>
> I'm leaving *right now*, before I let myself change my mind.
>
> > Kisses,
> > Brinke

Hector smiled and sighed and rolled out of bed. He dressed just to get warm, got a fire going, then checked his pocket watch. Not yet five A.M.

Using an old iron skillet and the fireplace, Hector prepared himself some black coffee outlaw-style, as he used to along the trail when part of the Pershing Expedition, chasing Pancho Villa.

He sipped his strong, bitter coffee and sat down at his typewriter and scrolled in a sheet of paper.

Hector didn't know why he felt he wanted a title—particularly when he had no real idea or a plot for a potential crime novel. But he felt he needed something to give himself a foothold or emotional stake to drive on.

Brinke had left a newspaper folded by his typewriter...some short account of the poisoning of Charles Turner. Below it was a small advertisement for the Bal Nègre in the Rue Blomet.

Hector looked at the ad for a time, then, on some kind of instinct, he typed:

RHAPSODY IN BLACK
by
Hector Lassiter

Hector looked at it for a moment, trying to think of some first line that might justify that title. One true sentence. That was always the goal. He and Hem had talked about the quest for one true sentence during countless late night, *deep talk* sessions.

He sipped some more of his *café noir*. Then, remembering some scurrilous rumors about current U.S. president Warren Harding, Hector recalled something that happened in Texas when he was a boy—something that had been the eventual undoing of a badass local lawman. Hector typed:

They killed Hale Jones for looking at a white girl. His killers hanged Hale from a light post with a piece of cut-down clothesline.

The man who tied the knot was Sheriff Billy Davis. The sheriff stood six-three and weighed two hundred and fifty pounds. He was a defrocked Texas Ranger with notches carved into the butt of his Colt.

The girl Hale's gaze had lingered too long on was Sheriff Billy's stepdaughter, Twila ... milk-skinned, blond, and busty.

Talk around town was Twila was barren from a third and badly botched abortion.

Hale hadn't yet turned ten.

Hector read it over. He wasn't bowled over by it. It read like journalese, he thought. But maybe something was lurking in there. He wrote until half-past-ten, when his landlady lightly kicked his door with her toe. Her hands were full with a breakfast tray. "I heard your machine and didn't want to interrupt," she said. "But a man has to eat and it *is* getting very late."

He thanked Germaine and took the tray and settled down to breakfast ... hungry and tired. Hector shook out the newspaper and began skimming it, looking to see if anyone else had been murdered overnight.

The café was getting noisy and Hector was thinking of leaving.

Hands over his eyes. "Guess who?"

He recognized her scent—lilacs. He was aware of a sudden knot in his stomach. Hector said, "How are you, Molly?"

"You've been scarce, Hector. I was beginning to worry you'd gone the way of some little magazine editor."

"It's been bloody, for sure," Hector said. Change-up time: "How's Philippe?"

She took her hands from his eyes and plopped down across from him. "Fine."

Molly looked drawn and a little thinner. There were dark rings under her violet eyes and her blond hair was tangled—as it if hadn't seen a comb or a brush for at least a day and a night and another day. Hector figured maybe Philippe was somewhere recuperating below the belt if Molly's appearance was any indication. Molly just didn't look so virginal to Hector anymore. That made him a little sad.

Hector said, "Buy you a drink?"

She nodded and caught a waiter by the arm: *"Du vin rouge."*

Hector watched her . . . wondered how she had found him. Hector had brought his morning's output with him in typescript in order to go over it and perhaps to write a bit more, longhand. Then he had picked the most out-of-the-way, underutilized café within easy walking distance of his apartment . . . someplace he figured he could write and revise, unmolested.

"Where have you been keeping yourself, Hector?"

He didn't want to lie outright to her. He'd get found out, eventually. He always did. And crowded as it was, their little corner of Paris was too small a place to hide a love affair. Hector said, "I started a novel. I helped Hem out of a jam. And I did get caught up in some aspects of these killings. Gertrude Stein was trying to recruit me and some other similarly disposed writers to poke around. Several of the victims were close friends of Gertrude's."

Molly nodded distractedly and pulled out a cigarette case. "That last sounds crazy," she said. Hector had never seen Molly carry cigarettes of her own. Frowning, he pulled out his box of matches and struck one with his thumbnail and held it out for her. Watching him shake out the match, she said, "You're not smoking, Hector?"

"Not right now."

Molly said, "I didn't know Gertrude had 'close friends' beyond Alice."

"Well, yeah, I get your drift. And you're right. I should have said, they were *publishers* of Gertrude's stuff." He looked Molly over again. A phrase from back home came to mind: *Rode hard and put away wet*. He said, "What have you been doing with yourself, M?"

Molly hesitated, then said, "My God, over there—I think that's Léon-Paul Fargue!"

"Fargue?" Hector shrugged. "Who's that?"

Molly scowled. "The poet, Hector . . . *Fargue*."

"He's famous?"

"He's wonderful."

Hector turned a little in his seat to look at the poet. Fargue was stocky and his dark thin hair was combed in long strands plastered across his white scalp. He had a dark beard and mustache and wore glasses. The stub of a burned-out cigarette dangled from Fargue's lips as he dug through a briefcase resting on his table.

"He's not writing," Hector said. "Go and introduce yourself before he starts."

"I couldn't."

"Then I'll introduce you."

"You don't even know who he is," she said.

"He's really big?"

"They call him the 'Poet of Paris.' He has so many honors, I can't list them."

Hector thought about it, then pulled out the small notebook he carried and tore out a fresh sheet of paper from the back. He handed it to Molly along with his fountain pen. "Here, write a note to him. We'll send him some wine as an overture."

She started to speak and Hector said, "My treat."

Molly agonized for several silent minutes over her note. Hector was grateful for her distraction. She finally capped Hector's pen and folded the note. Hector summoned the waiter and ordered the wine and asked the note be included. He slipped his fountain pen back in his shirt pocket.

Hector checked his watch. It was only one. He said, "I have to be somewhere in a bit."

Molly looked panic-stricken. "You start this, and then abandon me?"

"That's a little strong—'abandon.' He'll come over and thank you. Or, if he's truly some Grand Man, this Fargue fella will summon you to bask in his presence. Either way, you'll get to interact a bit. Maybe strike up some rapport that will help you professionally."

"It's not about that," Molly said, eyes flashing.

It was *always* about that, for *all* of them—any writer on the Left Bank expected it of another writer. It was the game. But Hector said, "I know *you're* not like that, Molly, so don't look at me that way. I'll stay fifteen minutes ... it's truly all I can afford."

"Where do you have to be?"

"Need to check in on Hem," Hector said. "Like I said—he had a scare."

"What happened?"

"Ever hear of François Laurencin?"

She nodded. "Certainly ... the editor of *Benchmarks*. I read he was hit by a car yesterday."

"That's right. Or maybe he was pushed under one. Hem was with François when it happened."

"Lord, that's awful." She licked her lips, watching Fargue again. "Hem saw it happen?"

Watching her watching the poet, Hector said, "In the sense of the car hitting Laurencin? Yes, Hem saw that. But Hem didn't see how it happened ... or if it was made by someone to happen."

"Oh God, he's waving."

"What?" Hector turned and looked over his shoulder. "Oh, you mean Fargue." He stood up and folded up his manuscript and stuck it in his coat's interior pocket and then put on his leather jacket. Offering her a hand, Hector said, "Come on, Molly, I'll walk you over to him. But then I have to go. Can't stay for chitchat or for more than introductions."

Molly seemed genuinely starstruck, so Hector introduced her—as a "fine young poet"—and then briefly introduced himself. Molly said to the elder poet, "You must get very tired of people like me bothering you all the time like this in cafés and restaurants and . . ."

Fargue rose and kissed Molly's hand and then sat down and said, "Valéry once said to me, and he has often repeated it, 'You are the victim of notoriety, Fargue, but then you are just the man for it.'"

Hector rolled his eyes and excused himself.

Once he was out in the cold rain, Hector trotted along the street and around the corner to the Boulevard du Montparnasse to lose himself in the crowd in the event Fargue gave Molly a brisk dismissal.

The rain was shifting to sleet and it stung as it struck his face. Hector ducked into a church and took a seat in a back pew. He watched a few candles being lit, then pulled out the beginnings of his novel and uncapped his pen and went back to work.

He reread the opening of his novel. It simply wasn't working. Maybe he could adapt it for a short story someday. But it wasn't the opening of a novel—not of a crime novel or any other kind.

But for some reason he couldn't let go of the title.

Staring up at the cross, Hector thought of his life in Paris and the events of recent days.

He thought about Brinke . . . her dark hair and eyes.

Physically, Brinke Devlin was the embodiment of a femme fatale. In his notebook, Hector wrote:

RHAPSODY IN BLACK

by

Hector Lassiter

Then he wrote:

> Nick Holt first met Alison Wilder in a café at six o'clock on a Friday night. By six-thirty, Nick had agreed to kill a man for her.

Hector read the sentences over a few times. He wrote another couple of sentences behind them.

A priest passed by Hector, nodding. Hector smiled and nodded back, then wrote the next sentence of his first novel:

> Alison was a busty, beautiful brunette—a leggy looker to put a bump in a bishop's robes.

That last might be too much. It bounced too high off the page, maybe, Hector thought, smiling as he read it.

Then again . . .

He'd worry about revision later, he told himself . . . after he had his first full draft in hand.

# Fourteen

*"How's life as an* editor?" They were walking along the Boulevard du Montparnasse and it was drizzling—a soft freezing rain.

*"Subeditor,"* Hem said. Hector had slowed his pace a bit to accommodate Hem's limp.

"Right. So how is all that?"

"Frustrating," Hem said. "Here they all sit in the City of Lights, the very seat of culture where the 'Twentieth Century lives,' as Gertrude says. They're up to their asses in young modern Turks—painters, poets, and fiction writers—yet they seem hell-bent on making the *Transatlantic* just another staid, safe review. Given the milieu, the potential talent pool, and the funding, hell, they should go for broke."

"Sure, it's what we would do," Hector agreed. "Who's watching Ford right now?"

Hem made a face, then smoothed his dark mustache. "I didn't agree to move in with the old bastard, Lasso. And I have my limits. He's with one of his young mistresses. And how do you figure that? How does that old, used-up, foul-breathed limey cocksucker succeed in banging all these pretty young things?"

"Spoils of literary lionship, maybe," Hector said. "Something for us to aspire to."

Hem snorted. "Christ . . . But, beats all hollow the alternative, I guess."

Hector said, "I finally ran into Molly earlier this afternoon."

Hem rubbed at his unshaven cheek. "No scene, was there? No confrontations about your new bedmate?"

"So far, so good," Hector said.

They reached Le Dôme. Hector held the door for Hem. Weaving between tables, Hector said, "Molly seemed distracted, though." He hesitated, then added, "And Molly looked pretty bad, too . . . wrung out. Maybe days in her clothes."

Hem selected their table—one by a window where they could watch the street. Hem said, "I've heard some things. I saw a little that night you met and left with Brinke."

"Go on." Hector threw his coat and hat on an empty chair.

"Just a crew Molly and Philippe fell in with just after you left. Some group they maybe know too well. Molly didn't quite seem to fit in. At least not like her beau did."

They both ordered rum St. James. Hector said, "This 'crew,' what, it consists of more poets?"

Hem rubbed his hands together, warming them. "Some of them are poets, I think. Some of them I didn't know. There was at least one other painter with them."

"And . . . ?"

"They're very much a clique," Hem said. "Supposedly affiliated with Aleister Crowley."

Hector said, "What? Crowley? The diabolist?"

Hem pointed at his own nose.

Hector frowned and toyed with his glass. "What do you mean, like some occult thing? That Temple of the Golden Dawn–style shit?" Hector knew that several major poets and writers in Paris and elsewhere in Europe had been drawn into the Kabbalah-derived Hermetic Order . . . not the least of which being the Irish poet W. B. Yeats.

"Not quite like that," Hem said. "It's linked to a former disciple of Crowley's. There was some kind of split or philosophical rupture, I hear."

"Who is this Crowley disciple?"

"A poet named Victor Leek," Hem said. "Heard of him?"

Hector shook his head. "Nah. But he's some kind of goddamn satanist?" He smiled crookedly. "No pun intended."

Hem smiled back. "Maybe he was back then. A satanist, or whatever stuff Crowley and his ilk are really all about," Hem said. "But Leek and Crowley had some big break, like I said."

Hector drank some of his rum. "So what then? Like some left-hand version of Martin Luther, this Leek has since gone off in a huff and formed his own church?"

"A little like that, I guess," Hem said. "Leek is a nihilist. He's still a poet, but a nihilistic one. And he is the head of a movement of sorts. Something like dark Dada, maybe."

"And he's attracting acolytes?"

"Appears so. Poets and painters, mostly. No fiction writers yet, as I can see."

Hector squeezed the bridge of his nose. "A nihilist novelist? Can you imagine enduring the writing of such a book? And would anybody ever read it?"

"Way I see it, writing it, or reading it, would be at odds with the underpinning philosophy that spawned it," Hem said. "Paradox."

"Jesus wept," Hector said. "Dada, Surrealism . . . Leek put a name to his tent show yet?"

"Nada," Hem said.

Hector nodded. "Probably just still casting around for that perfect moniker to put it over the top," Hector said.

"No," Hem said. " 'Nada' *is* what Leek calls it."

Running his fingers back through his dark brown hair, Hector said, "Dada, Nada . . ." He rubbed his temples with his fingertips. "We are truly living in the end times, Hem. Where are you getting all of this, anyway?"

"Jeremy Hunt." Hector recognized the name—a tubercular poet . . . and yet another little magazine editor. "They made a run at Hunt," Hem said. "Unsuccessfully."

"A 'run'?" Hector signaled the waiter for refills. "You mean they tried to recruit him?"

"And his magazine. They're hungry for an organ of their own," Hem said. "Seems nihilism, and liquidity, are an elusive mix."

Hector laughed. "I can see how that could be. But Hunt balked?"

"Yeah," Hem said. "He's a little too old to fall for Leek's nihilistic patter, I think. Victor seems to do better with what Gertrude imperiously calls 'the Lost Generation.'" Hem paused. "You know—*our* generation."

"And Molly's been drawn in?"

"Her boyfriend certainly has."

"I should talk to Molly," Hector said. He couldn't muster much enthusiasm for that.

Hem stared at his empty glass. "Sure. But you'll need to get her away from her painter, too, I think, for any of it to take or to matter. And I suspect the only way that will happen is if you can offer her some incentive, Lasso."

Hector didn't like where Hem was headed. He said, "You can stop there."

"Hadley says it's much much worse than you know, Lasso." Hem shook his head, grimacing. "Fuck. You're right. Forget it. This is pointless."

Seething, Hector said, "You've come this far, pal. Might as well finish it now."

The waiter brought them their fresh drinks. When he left, Hem said, "Okay. In the short time we were in the *bal musette* with Molly and Philippe—after you left with Brinke and before we crossed paths again at Gertrude's—Molly confided some things to Hadley." Hem hesitated again. "Lasso, buddy, I'm telling you, if I go on, it's only at your insistence. And with all my heart, I'm telling you, you don't want to know this bullshit."

Hector rubbed his jaw. "You push me back with one hand and beckon me with the other, Hem. Fuck this: *spill*. I can take it. My conscience is a pretty elusive target, anyway. So serve it up cold."

Hem nodded. "Between last Thanksgiving and Christmas, you were unattached. Or so Molly told Hadley."

"More or less."

"Right." Hem's fingertips traced the grain patterns in the table-top. "Molly thought she saw her chance. Christmas season . . . the romance of Paris. You get it. Molly had big visions. Then she saw you with someone else."

Hector rested his head on his fist. "Someone else" was likely Justine Joly, a dancer in the Folies-Bergère. The relationship had been all about the sex and it had been over before New Year's Eve.

"Molly took some pills," Hem said, his voice raw. "They filled her full of charcoal at the hospital. Brought her back."

Hector took several deep breaths, his head bowed. Hem said softly, "Lasso, you hanging in there?"

"*Yeah.* And Philippe? Where was he when all this was happening, Hem? What was Philippe's reaction?"

"Philippe never knew," Hem said. "They split—Molly ended it—when she anticipated being with you. They reconciled on Christmas Eve."

"How romantic," Hector said, and immediately regretted it.

Hem licked his bottom lip. "You know, Hector, sometimes no comment at all is the better way to go."

"You're right."

"So now what?" Hem still seemed fascinated by their tabletop's grain patterns.

"Damned if I know," Hector said. "I can't fake what I don't feel. Can't live some lie to get Molly grounded again. Particularly not now. Not with . . ."

"Brinke in your bed," Hem finished for him. "I agree with all that. And to try and talk to Molly to address any of this means confronting her unreciprocated feelings for you. And God only knows what effect all that might have on her. Poor kid."

"Offer me some advice?"

"Any advice you'd maybe best seek from Hadley," Hem said. "If it was me, I'd maybe leave everything as it is. Sometimes a holding action is the best strategy, Lasso."

Hector shook his head. "When a suicidal young woman, a *poet*, is sliding toward nihilism?" Hector drained his drink and picked up his hat. "Doing nothing doesn't seem an option to me."

"It wouldn't. Where are you going?"

Hector threw some francs on the table. "Sylvia's bookshop. Seems Molly's been getting peeks at my work there. I should maybe finally return the favor. Sample some of her poetry."

Hem scowled. "All this time knowing her, and you've never read any of her writing?"

"That's right," Hector said.

"Christ, this really has been a one-sided affair."

Hector's pale blue eyes flared. *"Laisse tomber."*

Hem held up his hands. He stood and said, "Like I said, sometimes no remark is the only remark to make. Tolerate my sorry company to Sylvia's? I need to check my mail."

"Sure," Hector said. "It's probably better you're with me, anyway. So I can watch your back, I mean."

They stepped out onto the street. "Yeah," Hem said, "and why is that? Why in hell would my back need watching?"

Hector said, "Because even with the prefix of 'sub' you're a little magazine editor now, Hem, and therefore a potential target."

# Fifteen

*Sylvia handed Hector an* accordion file folder. "I generally drop what's new in toward the back."

"That's good," Hector said. "I'd prefer to read them in publication sequence . . . figure it might mirror composition sequence."

"Given that it's poetry, and most of it very short, it might at that," Sylvia said.

Hector pulled out the folder's contents—a stack of small chapbooks, little magazines, a couple of folded broadsheets, and one small, leather-bound anthology. "More here than I figured," he said.

"She's really fairly accomplished for one so young," Sylvia said. Then she added, "You didn't know that?"

He could feel his own blush. "I didn't. Poetry isn't really my thing." He pulled an ashtray closer and offered a cigarette to Sylvia.

"No thanks, Hec. I prefer my own. Why, after all this time, are you suddenly interested in Molly's poetry?"

"I'll answer that, but . . . well, you read all these poems of hers as they appeared?"

"Yes . . . just like your stories, Hec."

Hector said, "Have you noticed any changes in Molly's work recently?"

"In her work, and in Molly, herself," Sylvia said. "What's going on?"

Hector held up in hand. "We'll get to that in a second. Indulge me, please, Syl."

Her brow furrowed. "All right, Hector." Sylvia bit her lip. "How to put it? Molly's poems seem to me to have become . . . darker. Darker, and a good bit less coherent."

"Well, goddamn."

"She hasn't looked so good the past couple of days, either."

"I know."

"Hec, what's going on with her?"

"I don't know. Or maybe I *do*. Have you heard of Victor Leek?"

This sour look. "Him I know. He's been in once or twice. I don't like him, not at all." Strong words from Sylvia.

"Tell me about Leek. Hem gave me a little, but not much."

Sylvia rose and walked behind her desk. She poured two cups of coffee and then splashed a little whisky in each cup. "I probably don't know much more than Hem," she said. "Leek, it seems to me, is more about reputation than accomplishment. He's also a former acolyte of Aleister Crowley's."

"So Hem said." Hector sipped his spiked coffee. It hit some spot he hadn't known needed hitting. "You've met him, Syl. What's your personal impression of Leek?"

"Intense," Sylvia said, furrowing her brow. She closed her eyes to help her memory. "Leek is charismatic enough in his way . . . darkly present. Black hair and mustache. He's trying to inaugurate a literary movement, I gather."

"Nada."

"That's right." Sylvia sipped from her own cup. "Daft, isn't it?"

"That's a polite term for it," Hector said. "Yet it's finding followers, crazed as it may seem to us."

"Hec, what's this all got to do with Molly?"

"I'm afraid Molly may have been drawn into Leek's orbit."

Sylvia sighed. *"Merde, merde, et merde."*

Hector nodded and opened the first chapbook, flipping pages until he came to Molly's poem.

"I'll leave you to read," Sylvia said.

"Thanks, Syl." He looked back over his shoulder at her. "Hey, do you have any published pieces by Leek around? I want to start taking his measure."

"You looking for a guru, Hec?"

Hector held up his fist. "More like a speed bag."

She winked. "I'll see what I can find."

Hector sipped his coffee, lit another cigarette, and began reading Molly's poetry. He still couldn't gauge its quality. Hector's experience with poetry was largely shaped by grade school readings of Robert Service and Rudyard Kipling.

He read a few poems by others in the first of the chapbooks . . . a poem by Pound and one by Eliot . . . another by William Carlos Williams. Hector thought Molly's poem stood up rather well against Ezra's and Tom's. Hector flipped to the second periodical, then to a third. Hector began to discern a recurring motif— unrequited love.

Increasingly uncomfortable, Hector pushed on, reading against a massing sense of guilt.

Then, in the last publication carrying a poem of Molly's, there was an abrupt tonal shift. Hector checked the publication date: the first of February 1924. Molly's most recently published poem read like a blank verse suicide note or wish for death . . . a dark, empty howl of despair.

Hector closed the magazine, profoundly disturbed. He restacked the various publications and slipped them back into their file folder.

A firm hand on his shoulder. "That last is very unsettling, isn't it?"

He closed a hand over the bookseller's. "You have a gift for understatement, Syl." Hector patted her hand and then reached across the table and ground out his cigarette. "Any luck on the Leek front?"

"No," Sylvia said. "Even my standards are evidently too high. Sorry, Hec."

"You've already been a great help."

"I wish I could do more," Sylvia said. "I'm very worried about Molly. I know enough about writers to be careful to avoid confusing persona for personality, but that new poem, 'The Dark,' that's not poetry."

"More like a distress signal," Hector agreed. After a time he said, "I heard Crowley might currently be in Paris."

"It's true," Sylvia said. "He was recently run out of Italy on Mussolini's orders. I sold him a copy of Assier's *Le Diable en Champagne* last week. Something old I had buried in the back. That, and *Jean Wier et la Sorcellerie*. Glad to get them out of my shop. His stay here is being underwritten by Frank Harris. Or so Crowley claimed."

"Harris, that name resonates, but I don't know why," Hector said.

Sylvia said, "He's a journalist; newspaperman from back in the States. Though he isn't originally American. Harris is from Galway, Ireland. He fancies himself a memoirist now, though his 'Life' is only available in German. He gave me a peek last year, thinking I might actually publish it in French. It reads like *The Autobiography of a Flea* . . . if Henry James had written *Flea*."

Hector didn't know what to make of any of that. He said, "I take it you're not publishing him?"

Sylvia said, "Hardly. Oscar Wilde had a wonderful observation about Harris. Wilde said, 'Frank Harris has no feelings. It is the secret of his success. Just as the fact that he thinks that other people have none either is the secret of his failure that lies in wait for him somewhere on the way of life.'"

Hector smiled. "Bravo, Oscar. Do you know where Harris lives?"

Sylvia returned to her desk and flipped open a tin box. She sorted through cards, then handed one to Hector. "I don't know about this, Hec. You calling on Crowley . . . he really is quite mad. Perhaps even dangerous. You probably shouldn't go alone."

"He won't be alone." Hem was standing behind Sylvia.

She smiled. "I suppose then I should fear for Aleister."

Hem shook his head, a thick finger to his lips. "No sympathy for the devil."

Voices down the hall; two men arguing over various ailments and whose were the worse. One of the men had an Irish accent. The conversation broke off and a fat, bald middle-aged man in a dark suit made his way down a dimly lit corridor to the foyer. From a distance he said, "I'd invite you in, but it isn't my house."

"That's all right," Hector called back. "We shouldn't be here long."

Crowley was clutching an old leather-bound book under one arm. Hem gestured at the book. "Wharton?"

Crowley smiled. It wasn't much of a smile. He was thick-featured and his eyes looked foggy. Hector guessed he was drunk on something . . . opium, laudanum, or cocaine, but *something*. "Bossard," Crowley said. *"Gilles de Raiz, Maréchal de France, dit Barbe-Bleue."*

"The child murderer and rapist," Hector said.

Crowley waved a fat hand. "And a lieutenant of Jeanne D'Arc."

"Some would call that the blind leading the blind," Hem said. "Or the crazy leading the criminally insane."

"You're Hemingway," Crowley said, extending his hand to Hem. "I looked over your book at Shakespeare and Company. I recognize you from the woodcut on the jacket."

Hem shook Crowley's hand. As he shook Hem's hand, Crowley nodded at Hector. "And you're Hector Lassiter. I've heard some good things about you. Though I've never found anything of yours to read."

"Hector's oeuvre is currently restricted to American publication," Hem said. "We really don't want to keep you. We came seeking a little information. A friend of ours may be in some trouble. A kind of dangerous state precipitated by her association with a former disciple of yours."

"Oh?" Crowley suddenly appeared tired . . . even bored. Hector figured the "Wickedest Man Alive" must get his fair share of such visits from worried spouses, children, or siblings of Crowley adherents. Loved ones worried for the souls of their beloved ones led down the "left-hand" path by Crowley.

"I'm in a delicate state of preparation presently," Crowley said, waving his meaty hand again. He seemed unsteady on his feet. "Perhaps next month, we could meet over drinks and discuss all this, yes? Then you'll be going?"

"No, that won't do," Hector said, stepping up close to Crowley. Hem moved around behind the diabolist, effectively pinning him between them. "This really won't take long," Hector said. He pressed two fingers to Crowley's chest. "I need to know all you can tell me about Victor Leek. I need to know that now, Al."

Crowley sighed and gestured at a couple of armchairs. He took one; Hem sat in the other. Hector remained standing. He liked that . . . preferred towering over the so-called Great Beast of the Pit.

"Simply put, Leek—which isn't even his real name—was unworthy," Crowley said. He began picking at something under a thumbnail.

Hector held his tongue. "Aleister Crowley" wasn't a given name either . . . just one in a string of aliases deployed over the years by the man born "Edward Alexander."

"He's a lost soul," Crowley said. "Leek, or Oswald Rook, which is his real name, is an inveterate believer feverishly seeking *something* to believe in. When Leek lost God, he replaced him with Satan. Despite the rumors, that's not what *I* believe in. When I realized Leek's true motivations, I excised him. Back in London . . . he was Rook, then."

"Just tossed him like that, eh?" Hector lit a cigarette. "I don't quite swallow it."

"Well, he shamed himself, as well," Crowley said, crossing his hands behind his head.

"How?"

"Poorly executed ritual," Crowley said. "Comically so. Leek took to cutting himself. Bleeding himself. He embraced scarification rituals . . . and branding. While branding his testicles with the mark of the beast, Leek contracted a form of blood poisoning . . . his wound became gangrenous. Surgeons eventually castrated him."

Hem and Hector both winced. "Sounds to me like he gave his all," Hem said.

Crowley smiled. "Leek broke down after that. He descended further into drugs and an unseemly state of self-pity." Crowley slid down low in his chair and interlaced his thick fingers across his belly. "As I said, Leek tried to replace God with Satan. When he lost Satan, Leek embraced nihilism. It's really quite a fine joke, if you think about it. Leek *has* to believe in *something*, so in the absence of something in which to believe, Leek has embraced the void. He's replaced nothing, with *Nothing.* Leek fervently believes in *Nothing. Nada* is his new God."

*Some fine joke all right.* Hector said, "Where do we find Leek? Nobody seems to know where he's living."

Crowley sat up and then struggled out of his chair. "His life fell apart after the castration. As one might reasonably expect. For a time he was living above Suzy." A terrible smile. "Given his affliction, the noise from below must have been quite maddening, don't you think? The last I heard he was living in a squalid little hole . . . the Hotel des Lions on the Rue des Ursins." Crowley stretched and yawned and said, "Now I'm quite finished with you both. I have to get back to my meditations." He turned, then hesitated. "This friend you're worried about. A woman?"

"That's right."

Crowley struggled to his feet. "Well, at least you don't have to worry about Leek taking any liberties, with her, yes?"

"It's not her virtue I'm so concerned about at the moment," Hector said. "It's her spirit. And the fact this student of yours may be beating the will to live out of her. Out of my friend and out of all the others drawn to this sorry son of a bitch you helped create."

Hem stood, edging a little between Hector and Crowley.

The diabolist, weaving again now that he was standing, winked at Hector. "Don't you believe in free will, Mr. Lassiter? Don't you know my maxim? 'Do what thou wilt shall be all the law.'"

Hem slapped Hector's arm. "Come on, buddy. Let's push on, Lasso."

Crowley said, "For writers, you're really not particularly cultivated, are you? Either of you. And women? Women are quite expendable and easily replaceable. Women should be brought round to the back door, like the milk. That's another of my maxims."

Hector nodded. "You know, I just decided."

Crowley's forehead wrinkled. "Decided what?"

"That I *wilt*."

Hector swung directly between Crowley's eyes. Hector felt something crack in his hand. Crowley sprawled backward onto the floor, his head smacking the tile.

"Now we push on," Hector said, massaging his fist.

# Sixteen

*Hadley heard them coming* up the stairs and called through the door, "Tatie, don't be crude—we have company."

"I have a guest, too," Hem called back. "Lasso's with me."

Hem keyed them in. Even though it was Sunday, someone was running the buzzsaw at the sawmill below, filling the apartment with a low whine.

Brinke rose from her chair as Hem and Hector slipped off their coats. "I couldn't kill any more time waiting until six," she said to Hector. Brinke accepted Hem's bear hug and said over his shoulder, "So I decided to impose on Hadley. Try and learn a little more about my favorite Texan. Talk about our handsome younger men."

"Uh-oh," Hector said. She moved to hug him and Hector kissed her forehead. He was surprised to find Brinke was dressed a bit more as she had been the night they'd met—a longish, houndstooth skirt, black leather boots, and a black turtleneck sweater. He said, "God, you feel good. Smell good, too."

"You feel good, too," she said. "But that smell?" She wrinkled her nose, sniffing at his collar. "You smell like . . . incense."

"From our last stop," Hem said.

Hadley hugged Hector and kissed him on both cheeks. "Want to hold Bumby?"

Recalling Brinke's remark about "cloying" domesticity, Hector lied. "Nah, I kind of messed up my hand. In fact, I need to get some ice on it, soon."

"How about now?" Hem headed for the kitchen. As he did, he said to Brinke, "Lasso took a swing at the devil."

Hadley said to Brinke, "I thought I knew all Ernest's euphemisms, but that's a new one."

Hector looked at his hand. The knuckles were barked and beginning to swell. "I took a swing at Aleister Crowley," he said. "Unfortunately for both of us, I also connected. That's also where we picked up the scent of the incense. Christ only knows what unholy stench that was intended to mask."

Brinke scowled. "Crowley?" Brinke and Hadley exchanged a look. Hector caught it . . . wondered about it. Brinke said, "Well, as he is the self-proclaimed 'Great Beast 666 of Revelation,' Crowley just may put a hex on you, Hector."

Hem shook his head. "That twisted bastard will never report it. Never let it be known he got knocked on his ass. Crowley has a wicked reputation to protect. It wouldn't do for the devil worshippers to know their dark messiah got decked by a mere fiction writer."

Brinke picked up Hector's leather jacket and tossed it to him. "Hope you found us a good restaurant, Hector. And I hope it's a restaurant that won't let you in dressed that way."

"We'll take a cab to my place so I can change," Hector said. "The day kind of got away from me. Thought I'd have time to change before now."

"And unfortunately, we've had to move our schedule up a bit," Brinke said. "So you're going to have to be a bit of a quick-change artist."

Hector zipped his coat and tied off its leather belt. "Oh? What's going on?"

"The four of us are invited to Joan Pyle's, later this evening," Hadley said, rocking her fat-cheeked son to sleep. "Joan is feeling skittish. She told Brinke she would feel much better, at least for the couple of hours we visit, in the company of you two 'bruisers.'"

"'Bruisers'? More like bruised," Hector said, flexing his swollen hand. "But if that's the plan, we really best get moving on." Hector kissed Hadley goodbye and slapped Hem's arm. "Thanks for riding shotgun."

Hector followed Brinke down the narrow flight of stairs. "You really do look terrific," he said, watching her from above and behind. "But I guess we're giving up on fooling Germaine by dressing you like a man."

"Your landlady is a woman of the world," Brinke said. "She's more, well, *attuned* to your ways than you give her credit for. She trusts a healthy young man to be a man."

"And how did you divine that, Brinke?"

"I really have been shamelessly inserting myself into your life today, Hector. I paid your landlady a visit earlier today. Ostensibly I went to visit you, figuring you'd be gone after two. So I chatted up Germaine. I told her we're secretly engaged. She's delighted. And now there'll be no more need for sneaking around her like that. She's quite fine with it all. And the breakfast portions will finally be correct."

*"Hmm."*

"You disapprove? If things don't last much longer you can simply say I broke the engagement . . . cast me as the villain."

"One subterfuge to obscure another? How like a mystery writer." They hit the ground floor and he wrapped an arm around Brinke's waist and pulled her to him—pulled her into a slow, languorous kiss.

"That was very nice," she said.

"Why 'secret'? Our 'engagement,' I mean."

"I said you wanted to be financially secure as a fiction writer before we made it public. Germaine understands a proud young man's ego. And she's frankly quite relieved about 'us.' She was growing quite flustered at your 'womanizing' and—"

"Jesus, stop, Brinke. Please. Leave me some illusions so I can soldier on with some remnant sense of my sweet and 'private' life as it stood ten minutes ago. You really have been busy, haven't you?"

"You only know the half of it. And it's just to make the nights and mornings easier. Marriage? Not my cup of tea, Hector. Too much like buying a room with a view."

Hector's head was spinning. He finally wrapped his good hand around the back of her neck and kissed her hard. Then he wrapped both arms around Brinke and hugged her tightly for a long time. She felt like home. "It really has been a hell of a day," he said.

She pulled back a little and her fingers stroked his mouth, wiping off lipstick. "We'll see if we can end it better for you."

"A tall order," he said. "It's really been pretty dreadful in some ways."

This strange expression on Brinke's face...something he couldn't read. She said, "I know, Hector."

They stepped outside and Hector waved at a distant taxi. As they waited for the taxi to reach them, Hector saw a silhouette in the lowly lit alcove of an apartment building kitty-corner to the one in which the Hemingways lived.

As the headlights of the taxi washed the facade of the opposing building, the figure stepped further back into shadow. Hector saw only the lower portion of gray, pin-striped pants and black shoes affixed with white spats. He thought he also saw a walking stick.

But that was all he saw. Brinke was watching Hector—she squinted as she searched the alcove Hector had been staring at.

"Something?"

"Maybe not," Hector said.

He held her hand as she backed onto the taxi's rear seat and swung her long legs in after her. As she scooted over, Hector slid in next to Brinke and slammed the door behind him. He gave the driver his address and then reached across the seat with his un-damaged left hand. Brinke smiled and took his hand in hers and rested them together on her lap. She said, "Did you write some to-day?"

"I started a novel," Hector said. "I wrote about twenty pages early this morning on the typewriter. But I binned it. A few hours ago, sitting in a church to get out of the weather, I started over, longhand. That one, I think, is a keeper."

Brinke smiled. "A crime novel?"

"Yes, I'm taking your advice."

She leaned across the seat and kissed him. "I'm thrilled," she said. "I *know* this is what you should be doing. I'm over the moon."

Hector said, "And you?"

"I finished the next Connor Templeton. It's set in Paris . . . *Murder in Montmartre*. I'm giving myself a few days' rest, then I suppose I'll start volume eight."

Hector nodded. "You don't sound enthusiastic about that."

"I'm getting a little bored with Pierce Thorp, if you want to know the truth."

"Pierce," who had inexplicable and seemingly bottomless reserves of wealth, was Brinke's dashing, dapper, and dipsomaniacal bon vivant sleuth.

"How about taking *my* advice," Hector said. "Treat yourself for a few days and try to write your own crime novel."

"I told you, they'd never let Connor, let alone Brinke, publish such a book."

"You're in the City of Lights and they're in the Big Apple. Pick another pen name. Something suitably scrappy. Something like, oh, Bud Grant, or Jake James. Merchant Marine turned author."

"Those names alone make me want to try," she said.

"I'm serious."

"So am I . . . I think."

"So do it, Brinke . . . *Bud*."

"All right . . . I will."

"Now it's my turn," he said, leaning across to kiss her.

Germaine was behind her desk as they descended the stairs. She clapped her hands and demanded Hector turn around once . . . twice. To Brinke she said, "I've never seen him in a suit before. I didn't even know he owned an evening suit."

Brinke smiled. "He really does clean up quite nicely, doesn't he?"

Arm in arm, they stepped out into the light snow flurries. Hector waved down another taxi. "We need to stop at my place now," Brinke said. "You've outdressed me, and that just won't do."

"Come on, Brinke . . . you look stunning."

"People would talk," she said, shaking her head. "Remember: muse, whore, or ne'er-do-well—take your pick—I have an image to live down to. Where are you taking me, by the way?"

"A place on the Rue Bayard."

She whistled. "You're crazy! Did you rob someone today?"

Brinke looked into the long, tall mirror hanging on the wall of Chez Savy. She turned a little, pointing one toe . . . posing. "We look like an advert illustration for *Les Arcades des Champs-Elysées*," she said.

"The beautiful and the damned," Hector said.

"You've read Fitzgerald? You like his stuff?"

"Some of it, sure."

They were given a table by the street. In the low candlelight they could see out the slightly fogged window and onto the street. Heavy flurries flickered in the hazy orange cones cast by the gaslights.

"It's shaping up to be a very cold and blustery February," she said. Brinke shivered a little then. She was wearing a black dress with thin straps that bared her broad shoulders and most of her back. Hector slipped off his dinner jacket and rose and draped it over her shoulders and then sat back down.

"At least February is a short month," Hector said.

Brinke was staring at her untasted drink. Hector said, "What's wrong, darling?"

"Nothing. *Nothing* is wrong . . . and maybe that's exactly what *is* wrong."

"What, you're *too* happy?"

"I guess you could put it that way," she said. "There's something frightening about us together. We're like second nature to me. Do you know how much that terrifies me? It's all too comfortable . . . too perfectly easy."

"Sadly, that'll likely change," Hector said. "Believe me, we can't just coast along like this. This world will never let us."

"Maybe . . ."

"Try not to sound so hopeful." Hector sighed. He'd spent his day worrying about a woman who seemed in danger of slipping into some despair-driven void. Now he was confronted with another woman who was *too* satisfied with her life. He muttered, *"De mal en pis."*

Brinke pulled out her cigarette case. She leaned into his match. "What do you mean?"

"A friend of mine is in some trouble."

"The blonde . . . the one who is in love with you? Molly Wilder?"

"You know her name?" Hector started to light his own cigarette and said, "And she's not in love with me."

"Oh, she is." Brinke blew a thin stream of smoke at the ceiling. "Or she thinks she is." Her dark eyes darted to one side. "I really have been intruding into your life, just as I said. I didn't really go looking, but I learned things. Hadley told me about Molly . . . and about her recent suicide attempt."

Hector rubbed his cheeks and jaw. He shook his head. "She's come under a very bad influence."

"Someone tied to Crowley," Brinke said. "Hadley's heard some things about that, too. Victor Leek."

"You know him?"

"No. Never heard of him until today. But he sounds quite mad. Mad, bad, and dangerous to know, to coin a phrase. You're looking for Leek. That's why this thing with Crowley happened?"

"I have a possible address now. But that's for tomorrow. Hem's going with me."

"Rather than doing that, you should really spend some time with Molly tomorrow. Might be time better spent, Hector."

"Maybe. I'll try to chisel out some time for her. But first, I want to go to the source . . . attack the problem at its base. That means confronting Victor Leek."

"On face, very practical," Brinke said. "Very logical."

"I'm sensing a 'but.'"

Brinke arched a dark eyebrow. "*But* Leek might be a *symptom*. The roots of her real problems may reside in Molly herself. Perhaps partly in her feelings for you."

"Can we not talk about this tonight?"

"Sure, Hector. But I don't have much more to say on this subject, other than, my jokes and little games with Germaine aside, I'm really not a woman who does well with one man. Never have been."

"So this may be something new for you. For me, too. What's your point?"

"What I'm saying now is, I don't need, and perhaps don't even want, an exclusive on you."

"An assertion like that would probably endear you to a lot of men, Brinke. But where are you going with this?"

"I'm just saying, if you think an affair with Molly might pull her out of this, that a few nights in bed with her here or there might anchor her in some way, well, you should feel entitled to pursue that."

Hector tipped his head on side. "I don't even know where to begin responding to that."

Brinke sipped some water, avoiding his eyes. "Whatever comes to mind first."

"The fundamental problem as I see it," Hector said, "is my feelings for Molly don't run that way. I'm not going to bed her out of guilt. But let's pretend I did. In the end, when she either found me out for having no deep feelings for her, or when I tried to ease out of the restorative or therapeutic 'little affair,' Molly might be pushed right over into that abyss she's only toeing now."

Brinke nodded, looking out the window. "That's all quite possible, darling. It was just an option I'm affording you, that's all. If you're not inclined that way, that's fine. I just don't want to see you have to cope with something very bad if she comes to a dark decision." Brinke took Hector's hand. Her black eyes searched his face: "If you do nothing, and Molly does something, you have to know it's not your fault. You didn't ask her or encourage her to become infatuated with you. And you didn't create or help to foster the kind of damaged personality she must have to be drawn to this twisted nihilist poet."

Hector shook his head. "No more of this talk, please, not here. Not now. This isn't the evening with you that I envisioned. I saw Romance. Candlelight dinner. You, me and racing hearts, okay? *D'accord?*"

Brinke smiled. "I'm sorry. You're right. Tonight, let's just wallow in our too good and easy life together."

She sat up straighter and squared her shoulders and pulled his dinner jacket closer around her. She looked around, her brow furrowed. Brinke said, "Now, given the steep prices in this joint, where the hell is our goddamn waiter?"

# Seventeen

*Brinke had insisted on* "horses' power" for the ride back to the Quartier Latin and on to Joan Pyle's apartment. As they clomped along, Brinke said, "So, tough guy, how did it feel to whip the devil?"

Hector realized then that he'd been massaging his right hand. He said, "Not the heady thrill it sounds. Apart from the fact that I think I broke a knuckle, it was a little like shooting fish in a barrel. Crowley was doped to the gills. Cocaine, maybe opium."

"Or both," Brinke said. "Or peyote, laudanum. They say Crowley uses all that, and more."

"Either way, Crowley never saw it coming. I just let fly."

"So where does this poet, Victor Leek, live?"

"Leek—or Oswald Rook, which may or may not be his real name—is holed up in some hovel of a hotel not far from Notre Dame."

Brinke said, "If we cross via the Boulevard du Palais we could take a look at it."

"I don't think so," Hector said. He squeezed her knee. "Besides, when Hem and I do go there, I may well go armed."

"But we'd just be passing by the front. I just want to see it."

"It's a sewer, sleazy." Hector figured if Crowley said so, it must be truly dreadful.

Brinke kissed him. She smoothed the lapel of his overcoat. "Admittedly, we're not dressed for squalor, but we'll just roll slowly by and keep on going. It's research, perhaps for my crime novel. Grist for Bud, or Jake, or whatever nom de guerre I settle on."

"How about 'Russ Crocker'?"

Brinke wrinkled her nose. "That one I don't like at all. Doesn't sound like a man who'd know how to throw a punch or please a woman." She smiled. "So, we'll do this?"

"We'll roll on by," Hector said, rapping the roof of the coach with his good hand to get the attention of the *cocher*.

"My God, I just didn't know such places existed in Paris," Brinke said. "It looked like Whitechapel."

They turned onto the Rue d'Odessa. Brinke looked over her shoulder and out the small, fogged window behind and between them. She squinted against the headlights from a trailing taxi that had been lighting up the interior of the coach for several minutes. She said, "The bastard could go around."

Hector said, "He certainly could. If he wished to." Hector fiddled with the door of their coach. "Wait here a minute. If anything bad happens, tell our driver to beat hell out of here. Go to the police and ask for Simon."

Hector stepped down onto the street. The taxi—a new Ford—was sitting curbside about thirty yards behind their coach, its engine idling. Hector began walking toward the taxi. The engine gunned and headlights flared as the cab peeled away from the curbstone, gears grinding and tires squealing. The taxi whipped around their carriage and tore off down the Rue de la Gaîté. As it passed by him, Hector rushed the side of the taxi, trying to get a look into the back seat. He saw the silhouette of someone turning and ducking down to hide their face. He couldn't tell if it was a man or a woman; large or small.

"Nice monkey suit, Lasso," Hem said.

Hadley said to her husband, "Hush. You could really do with some of Hector's style, Tatie." Hem grunted, rubbing at his unshaven jaw.

Joan Pyle, dressed in a dark pin-striped suit and black silk necktie, said to Brinke and Hector, "You two look like an advert for Vionnet."

Hector smiled and shook her hand like a man's. "You think?"

A knock at the door. Joan said, "That'll be Gertrude and Alice, I think."

Brinke said, "What?"

Joan said, "Gertrude thought a change of venue was in order. You know, for our next consultation."

"Whoa, there," Hector said. "We've been warned off this affair by the police. I gave my word to a commissioner we'd butt out."

"Miss Stein hasn't given her word about any such thing," a voice behind him said. Hector turned, looked down: Alice, fuming up at him. He thought about ducking down to kiss her cheek, just to bug her. Then he took another look at her upper lip and decided against it. Alice said, "The last time we checked the newspapers, there was no indication that any arrests have been made in connection with these terrible murders."

Hector said, "Jesus, but I really need a drink." Then he said to his host, "Just please please please tell me you haven't invited Estelle Quartermain."

"Estelle is indisposed," Gertrude Stein said, stepping up to Hector. She was wearing her black steerage clothes that reached nearly to her toes, and a heavy black shawl over what Hector took to be a black opera cape.

"You're looking very dashing," Hector said.

"And you look like an advert for Arrow shirts," Gertrude said. "You may simply be too handsome to write, Hector. Now, as I was saying, Estelle is indisposed. Because *she* is following up on her obligations ... continuing *her* promised investigations."

Hector nodded and turned his head away from Gertrude to hide the nasty smile he could feel forming. He surveyed the liquor bottles arrayed on a sideboard behind the couch where the Hemingways sat. Hem said, "Pickings are slim, Lasso. We opted for the red wine."

Hector looked at the bottles with increasing distaste—schnapps, Tanqueray, some kind of cherry-flavored vodka, and ouzo.

Brinke, looking over the offerings said, "Make mine *du vin rouge*."

"Yeah," Hector said. "Mine, too." He pressed his hand to the small of her back and whispered in Brinke's ear, "Please promise me a very short night in this joint."

Brinke chucked his chin with a gloved hand. "Done. I want you out of that tux."

"And you out of that dress . . . what there is of it."

Her hand strayed between his legs. She said, "My, *tu bandes*."

This low voice, following him: "Lassiter! What do you have to show for the past couple of days?"

Gertrude stood close behind him, scowling.

Hector poured Brinke a glass of wine, then another for himself. He said, "Miss Stein, may I make you a Sloe Gin Fizz?"

"We shall have coffee," Gertrude said. Hector tried to judge whether she was employing the royal "we" or meant coffee for Alice, too. Then Alice pushed Hector aside to make the coffee.

Hector sipped his wine, a Bordeaux, and said, "I have no progress. I had to beg off this campaign of yours in order to see a friend released from custody by the police."

Half-distracted, Gertrude looked around the room, then eyed the room's largest chair—one arranged to command the sitting room. Joan's partner, Nicole Voivin—blond, rather plump . . . very feminine—immediately vacated the chair.

Gertrude sat down in it, settling in and resting her forearms on her knees. "A friend was arrested? In connection with these crimes? Who?"

"Irrelevant," Hector said. He sensed he was forever burning a bridge with Gertrude, but he didn't particularly care. He wasn't a fixture at Gertrude's salon. Hector figured Alice actively despised him. And the Great Woman was in no position to help Hector as a crime writer.

Most compelling of all, Hector wasn't about to confide Hem's detainment by the police to Gertrude or Alice.

"The reality is the police have a full sense of the case and have made the connections you feared they hadn't," Hector said. "The man in charge of the investigation, a man who seems smart and good, ordered me to tell you to desist."

Gertrude curled her lip. She said, "Joan, please give us a cigar." Then, to Hector, she said, "This police has not told me anything directly. Therefore, I will proceed along as I please until such time as this police does that."

"It doesn't work that way," Hector said. "If you—or goddamn Estelle—get in this man's way, or interfere with his investigation, this *police* could arrest *you*."

"Nonsense," Gertrude said. "I'll not be scared off. *I'm* not yellow."

The room grew quiet.

Hem said, "I was the one in jail. And if anyone ever breathes a word about that, man, or woman, or in-between, they won't ever have to worry again about who is or isn't yellow."

Gertrude blew out her lower lip. "You were arrested, Hemingway? On what grounds? What on earth for?"

"Suspicion of murder," Hem said.

"That's absurd," Gertrude said.

"Exactly, and that's why you don't fuck around the fringes of something like this murder investigation," Hector said.

"That crude language isn't necessary, Mr. Lassiter," Joan said.

Brinke shrugged. "Frankly, to my mind, the word 'fuck' pales next to 'yellow' or 'coward.'"

There was another silence, then a soft grunt. "We apologize," Gertrude finally said.

Hector couldn't let Gertrude have it that easily. "Are *we* apologizing, or are *you* apologizing, Miss Stein?"

Alice handed Gertrude her coffee. As she did that, the dark-haired little woman glared at Hector. Gertrude waved her fat hand. "*I* apologize."

Hector smiled at Alice.

Hem said, "I got pinched simply because I was too close to one too many dead men," Hem said. "That's all it took."

Gertrude said to Hector, "So you've done nothing? You haven't looked into Lloyd Blake's murder, as we agreed?"

"That's right," Hector said. "And something else came up. A dear friend is in some trouble. Something involving the nihilist poet, Victor Leek. He's trying to foster some kind of literary movement, literally built on *nothing*, and a friend is being drawn in, and at considerable peril. Members of this movement, they don't last long. They tend to suicide."

"We've not heard of this Leek," Gertrude said.

"*We* have," Nicole said. "He tried to buy our magazine."

Joan handed Gertrude a cigar. Hector stood ready with a match. Joan said, "Nic is being very liberal in her description of the offer. It wasn't a serious negotiation."

Brinke said, "Not enough money on the table?"

"No money at all. More akin to a transfer of title, if title existed." Nicole fitted a Gauloise to a long ebony cigarette holder. "*He* seemed to want us to *give* him *Intimations*."

"*Give?*" Hector sipped his wine. "Did he threaten you?"

"Not in so many words," Joan said.

Hem said, "So what words, exactly?"

Brinke ran her hands through her black hair. She said, "Hector, why do I get the sense that two of your dilemmas just crossed? That maybe they're tangled up with one another?"

Someone was pounding at the door.

Hector said, "Christ, don't let it be Estelle Quartermain."

Hem handed his glass to Hadley and rose. "I can get it."

Joan balanced her cigar on an ashtray. "That won't do—we're the hosts." She motioned Hem back to his chair and went to open the door.

Turning, Hem said to Brinke, "What did you mean, 'two dilemmas' have 'crossed'?"

Brinke said, "These murders, and Molly. I think that—"

At first, Hector thought it was some pet of some neighbor's that had been horribly injured. There was a high-pitched, inhuman-sounding squeal . . . like that of a dog rolling under the wheels of a car, perhaps.

Brinke said, "What in *hell*?"

Hem dropped his glass and ran to the front door. Hector realized then it was a human's squeals . . . Joan Pyle's screams.

Joan backed into the room, her hands reaching for her face. Wisps of smoke trailed from Joan's blistering face.

Racing past her, Hector said, "It's oil of vitriol—don't let her touch her face or she'll burn her hands, too."

As he cleared the door, Hector heard Hem: "Hash, a jug of water, right now . . . towels! And Brinke, start banging on doors . . . find us a damn doctor."

Hector heard feet pounding on stairs. He ran halfway down the first flight, then rolled over the banister, dropping down to the midpoint of the next flight of stairs. As he landed, Hector caught sight of gray pin-striped slacks and the hint of white spats, just rounding the corner to the second floor landing. Hector vaulted over the railing again. As he fell, his foot struck the leg of his quarry, sending the man sprawling across the ground floor landing.

The man twisted around and poked at Hector with his walking stick. Hector heard a click, then saw light on metal—realized the man had a sword cane. Hector threw himself to one side as the man hurled his cane like a spear, aiming at Hector's head.

The point of the sword cane shallowly embedded itself in the plaster wall, quivering there a moment before clattering to the floor. The man scrambled through the door onto the street, slamming the door shut behind himself.

Hector hit the door with his shoulder, knocking it free from its hinges. The man was running across the slick, cobbled streets. He lost his footing and went sprawling again, nearly sliding under the wheels of a passing Model T delivery truck.

Hector finally got a look at the man's face—swarthy . . . a thick black mustache and a gold front tooth . . . a long scar down one side of his face.

The man saw Hector approaching. He crossed himself. Hector heard the man say, "Hail *nada*, full of *nada* . . . *nada* is with thee."

Then the stranger threw himself head first into the path of a passing taxi.

# PART II

lundi

# Eighteen

*"Vitriol pitching ... that's a* shade Victorian, isn't it?" Commissaire Simon pulled out a pack of Gauloises and offered them around. He didn't find any takers.

Hadley and Alice were in the bedroom with Nicole, trying to comfort her. The doctor who initially treated Joan was with them, preparing sedatives for Nicole.

Joan had been taken away with severe burns to her face and neck and scalp. Hem was convinced Joan might also be left blind as a result of her burns.

Hector said, "You'd likely have to dig back to a Victorian novel to find a 'vitriol pitching' by name. Most back in the States call it sulfuric acid now."

"There's at least one acid pitching in Conan Doyle's Holmes stories," Hem said.

"Estelle Quartermain included one in *The Mitre Square Menace*," Brinke said.

Simon said, "Yes. And all of you are gathered here, despite my instructions to the contrary. But where is Mrs. Quartermain?"

Hector looked to Gertrude. She shrugged and said, "Otherwise engaged."

"Monsieur Lassiter seemingly wasn't able to impress upon all of you the illegality of inserting yourselves into an official police inquiry. Is that a proper inference on my part?"

"This was supposed to be a social gathering, Commissaire," Brinke said. "Hector and I came expecting only the Hemingways to be here."

Hector said, "This man who pitched the acid at Joan, who is he? Have you been able to identify him?"

Simon nodded. "A Spaniard named Paco Sánchez. He is a poet. Or rather, he was."

Looking flustered, Gertrude asked, "An *actual* poet?"

"I suppose that depends on what conforms to your notion of an 'actual poet,'" Simon said. He ground out his cigarette and began preparing his pipe. "Sánchez was published, and often, if that's what you mean. He won a few awards, as well."

"And then he tried to kill a woman, and committed suicide," Brinke said. "How does a poet come to that?"

Simon said, "A moment alone, Monsieur Lassiter?"

"Certainly."

Hector scooped up his overcoat and slipped it on, following the cop down the stairs. As he descended the stairs, Hector realized his left ankle hurt a little ... probably from a bad landing chasing the homicidal poet. Hector figured he was lucky he hadn't broken a leg leaping over all those banisters and dropping onto the uneven runs of steps.

They slipped out into the sheltered alcove of the apartment building, standing against the wall to be out of the chilly wind. Hector saw that the dead man's body had already been hauled away.

Simon squeezed his arm. "So what has really happened here, Hector?"

Wetting a cigarette with his tongue, Hector toyed with his box of matches before lighting one. He said, "Brinke was being honest. We came here tonight thinking it was a small dinner party, and that we would be providing some handholding. Joan—and her partner, her lover—run the little literary magazine called *Intimations*. Another one of *those* literary journals. They were afraid for themselves."

"For good reason, as it has proven out," Simon said.

"We didn't know that Gertrude and her stooge were invited tonight," Hector said. "You may need to lean on Miss Stein, Simon. I mean really throw a scare into her in order to get her out of your way. Same with Quartermain."

"As she is at hand, I'll do that with Miss Stein before I let her leave. And Quartermain? Next time she is foolish enough to pay me a visit, I'll deal with her."

Hector said, "What's the real story on Joan's prospects?"

"Dismal, I'm afraid. She's certainly going to be left blind. Blind, and quite disfigured. She's also in some kind of deep shock. That could indicate there's been some kind of mental rupture. They say the next day or two will be critical."

"Goddamn."

"The poet, Sánchez, was at a reading at the same time François Laurencin was shoved under a car."

Hector shrugged. "So we infer from that he didn't commit *that* murder. But we've already agreed this isn't the work of one person, haven't we?"

Simon nodded. "But this Sánchez, did he say anything as you pursued him?"

Hector took a hit from his cigarette, buying time to think. Hector was inclining along the same lines as Brinke—he believed that Victor Leek and his literary movement were tied not only to Molly Wilder's steep decline, but perhaps also to the little magazine murders. If he was right about that, Hector wasn't prepared to point the police directly at Leek. At least not until he knew how that might or might not affect Molly. So Hector opted for semantic legerdemain in case he might later have to amend his statement:

*"Nada."*

*"Merde."*

"You don't owe me a favor," Hector said. "But would you consider granting me one?"

"Ask, then I'll answer."

"A name has come up once or twice."

"Come up in connection with the murders, you mean?"

"Perhaps peripherally," Hector said. "Oswald Rook. Could your people make some inquiries?"

"*Oui.*" A long draw on his pipe, then Simon said, "This man . . . Sánchez, he willingly threw himself in front of this car. That is confirmed by others. I just can't conceive of a man doing that—particularly not a man of words—without saying *something.*"

"*Nada,*" Hector said again. Then he relented, just a bit. "Paco said a few lines from a prayer, but altered. 'Hail *nada*, full of *nada . . . nada* is with thee."

"How strange."

"Probably just depressed."

"Depressed like Mueller Hawkins?"

"Now you've lost me," Hector said.

"Mueller Hawkins is another poet, Hector. Another American. He hanged himself yesterday."

"Mueller get himself some bad news," Hector said, "or what?"

Simon shrugged. "Who can say? But he had a slip of paper he'd clipped to his shirt."

Hector blew smoke up into the alcove light. He said, "A suicide note?"

"No, there was just a single word scrawled on the slip of paper," Simon said. "*Nada.*"

# Nineteen

*Brinke and Hector shared* a taxi with the Hemingways on the drive home from the crime scene. As they did that, Hector recited for his companions Paco Sánchez's strange prayer. Hem asked Hector to repeat it twice, writing it down in a small notebook.

They said their goodbyes and Hector and Brinke slipped out of the coach. Hector paid the *cocher* to transport the Hemingways back to their more distant apartment.

Hector checked his watch under a gas light: two A.M.

He sensed motion across the street; thought he saw someone lurking in another recessed archway of a building on the other side. He considered walking across, perhaps forcing a confrontation. But his ankle hurt more than before. Then Hector looked at Brinke in her slinky black dress; at her glistening black hair lightly dusted with snow . . . her dark bedroom eyes. *To hell with more foot chases*, he decided. Let the bastard stand outside and freeze his balls off while Hector made love to Brinke. That was the ticket.

They made their way up the stairs as quietly as they could. Hector keyed them into his apartment, nearly tripping over something heavy just inside the door. His first thought was that he'd stumbled over a body.

Brinke said, "My fault. Sorry, Hector." She turned up the key on the light by the door and a soft glow gradually illuminated the room. Hector saw that he'd tripped over a large battered old suitcase.

"I decided it was better to have some of my things here," Brinke said. "With Germaine's permission, I had this sent around while we were having dinner."

Hector kissed her. He picked up and set down the suitcase, weighing it: *heavy*. "For a woman fleeing commitment, you don't travel light," he said.

"My spare typewriter is in there, too," Brinke said. "Figured we may need to learn how to write in the same room. For as long as *we* last, I mean."

He smiled, stroking her cheek. "We'll make that work."

He slipped off her coat and hung it in the closet with his own clothes. She wrapped her arms around her bare shoulders and shivered. "Maybe a fire first."

"What, you're not tired? Don't want to go straight to sleep?"

"Keep wasting time and I might."

Hector kissed her forehead and said, "I'll get that fire started."

"This is all starting to truly frighten me," Brinke said behind him as he worked at the fireplace. "Think about it. Poets driven so deeply to despair by this literary movement they've embraced that they hang themselves and jump into the paths of cars . . . commit murders. What if Joan had allowed Hem to answer that door tonight? What if she had asked you or me to answer that door?"

"It didn't happen that way. Can't run yourself crazy with hypotheticals, honey."

"Hector, you really need to find Molly first thing tomorrow. You, or I need to. Maybe Hadley. But someone needs to reach her and fast. Before she's handed a gun or a length of rope."

"Yes, but no more talk about that until we wake up."


Brinke's arms were trembling as she pulled him back up to her. "I've never been that comfortable with *brouter le cresson*," she said. "Being on the receiving end, I mean."

Hector wasn't sure how to interpret that. He said, "I thought the French had another term for that . . . something more Latin."

He kissed his way up her torso. She dragged her palm across his mouth and then kissed him. "Either way, you nearly killed me," she said.

"There are worse ways to go."

"And we've seen some of them recently."

"Can't let it go, can you?"

"You've had a pretty picaresque life for one who's only twenty-four, Hector," Brinke said. "The Punitive Expedition...the Great War. You've seen terrible things. I've spent the past few years writing mystery books in which people die ... but I'd never seen violence like that up close. I'm not sure I can ever write another Connor Templeton novel after the past few days. They seem trite and wrong after what we've been grappling with. Something almost sinful in doing that."

"You're just in shock."

"Maybe. But in the morning, let's do what we originally promised Gertrude."

"I promised Simon ..."

"Please, you clearly have made a separate peace with him," she said. "I suspect you have more leeway with Simon than you realize. Or let on."

"All right. We'll do that. Squeeze it in before Hem and I go looking for Leek."

"And Molly, you have to save some time for Molly," Brinke said.

"I still don't know how to help Molly. I just don't know how to pull her out of this spiral."

"Then *I'll* give that some more thought," Brinke said. She ran her fingers through his chest hair. "They say you can tell a lot about a man and how he'll regard women—how he'll treat them—by looking at his mother and his relationship with her."

"They say that?" Hector reached for his cigarettes; Brinke took them from him and tossed them back on the nightstand.

She kissed his neck. "So tell me about dear old Ma Lassiter."

"Not much to tell ... I didn't have her so long. She died when I was eight."

Brinke paused; he felt her breath on his belly. "She fell ill?"

"My father came home unexpectedly and found her with a ranch hand. He shot them both."

Hector was still aware of Brinke's breath, hot on his belly. She said, "Did you see . . . ?"

"No," Hector said. "But I heard the shots. Grabbed a hunting rifle. There were always plenty of guns around. I didn't understand what had happened." Hector rested his palm on Brinke's head. "I shot my father. Didn't kill him . . . the state did that. Four weeks from commission to execution. Texas doesn't fool around when it comes to meting out what passes for justice. Anyway, I was raised by my mother's father."

Brinke made her way back up the bed. She searched his eyes, not saying anything. She hugged him tightly for a time, then slid over onto his lap; settled atop him. Moving slowly, she said, "Someday you have to tell me about your grandpa, and what he taught you about women."


Hector managed to squeeze in a couple of hours of sleep. At four, he was up and in a terry cloth robe. He'd awakened before the fire was spent and he stoked it up again. He sat in a chair by the fire with a notebook, writing his novel longhand . . . smoking an occasional cigarette and looking up to watch Brinke asleep in his bed. She slept "pretty," unlike some other women he'd known. Her mouth was closed and her eyelids flickered with her dreams. The back of one hand was under her cheek and her knees were drawn up, the other hand between her thighs. She was shivering a little and he tipped his chair back down on two legs and pulled the covers up around her chin, leaning down to kiss her cheek. She smiled in her sleep and turned a little.

He went back to his story, writing for perhaps another hour. He came to a break and looked up. Brinke was sitting up in bed, her back to the headboard, staring at him. He said, "How long have you been awake?"

"About ten minutes, just watching you." She smiled. "You have harrowing focus . . . and speed."

"I know where it's going, just trying to keep up now. But I'm spent for the moment."

She pulled the covers aside and he slipped off his robe and slid between the sheets with her. She said, "Have to be quick about this, Hector—I want to do some writing, too."

Brinke had balanced her typewriter on a stack of books on the bed. She had pulled on a pair of his pajama bottoms and one of Hector's flannel shirts. She wrote directly on the typewriter. ("The only way I can keep up; writing longhand bogs me down.") After an hour, she raised her glasses, rubbed her eyes, and flexed her fingers. Hector rose from his own typewriter where he had been transcribing his handwritten draft. He tried to shake the stiffness out of his sore ankle. "I'm making some coffee." He prepared more of his outlaw-style coffee in his iron skillet over the fire. He poured Brinke a mugful and she tasted it and wrinkled her nose. "I'll drink it. It's drinkable. But it could raise the dead."

At seven, Hector dressed and went down to fetch breakfast— two trays and two trips. Germaine placed a rose on Brinke's tray. "Say it was your idea," she told Hector.

They ate breakfast together, both reading from various newspapers. Brinke said, "How do you feel about funerals?"

Hector shrugged. "Provided they're not my own?"

"We have three I think we should really consider attending," Brinke said. "One today and two tomorrow. Lloyd Blake today. François Laurencin and Mueller Hawkins tomorrow. It's a way of getting around Simon. We'd be paying our respects. If some questions got asked and answered . . ."

"It's inspired," Hector said. "Where are they planting Blake?"

"Père-Lachaise," Brinke said. "Laurencin goes to Cimetière St-Vincent and they're burying Hawkins at Cimetière du Montparnasse."

"Going to make for a grim circuit, but we'll do it."

Hector stood and limped around the table to pour himself some more coffee.

"What's wrong with your leg, Hector?"

"Seemed to have sprained it chasing Paco Sánchez. I landed badly jumping over a banister. May be worse than it first felt. I'll wear my work boots today. Get some ankle support there. Couple of days, I'll be fine."

Brinke said, "How's your hand?"

"Swelling is gone. Just a little stiff at the middle knuckle," Hector said. "My own fault. Should never have swung between Crowley's eyes. Too much bone there. Should have gone for his jaw. Something with give."

Hem came by at ten. Hector said, "Brinke and I had a plan, but it's shifted a bit. So we can go visit Leek now. We just need to be back here by one for a funeral."

"Oh," Hem said, "whose?"

"Lloyd Blake," Hector said. "They're burying him at Père-Lachaise. Brinke thought we'd poke around. Try to ask a few questions."

"I'll hang around the fringes," Hem said. "Stand off a bit. Maybe see who else shows. Make a kind of inventory of the mourners."

"Good," Hector said. He winced a little as he stood and put weight on his leg. Once he got moving again he was a little better.

"I'm thinking that leg should be looked at," Brinke said.

"Me too," Hem said. "Could be a fracture. You don't want to make it worse. Be immobile for six weeks or more then."

"That I wouldn't want," Hector agreed. "Think Williams would see me?"

"As it happens, he's supposed to be coming by to check on Bumby this evening," Hem said. "Drop by. We'll have him look at that ankle."

Hector nodded. "Now we need to pay our visit to the Hotel des Lions."

"We drove by it last night on the way to Joan Pyle's," Brinke said to Hem. "It's terrifying...desolate, dilapidated. Looks like London's East End."

Hem nodded. "I brought this." He held up a leather-covered cudgel.

Hector scowled. "Where'd you get that?"

"Stopped a purse snatching a while back," Hem said. "Took it off the little Belgian who tried to use it on an old woman he meant to rob."

"I don't want to get close enough to have a chance to use something like that," Hector said. He limped to a tall old armoire, opened it, lifted some shirts, and pulled out a linen-wrapped parcel. He undid the twine binding the wrapper and pulled out the long and gleaming Colt wrapped inside. The gun smelled strongly of oil. Brinke whistled. "Looks like something from an Old West show."

"It's an 1873 Cav model. A Peacemaker."

Hem said, "From Pancho Villa days?"

"Abouts," Hector said. "I've got another roscoe here." Hector unwrapped a second parcel. He handed that gun to Hem. "The Krauts were arming the Mexicans there for a time," Hector said. "The Germans were trying to open up a front on our southern border to keep us out of Europe. It's a Mauser. Took it off a dead Villista a lifetime ago."

Hem smiled, brandishing the gun. "Let's go find that goddamn poet. Test the depth of his infatuation with the void."

Brinke looked uneasily between them. She said, "I don't want to throw a wet blanket on you boys' fun with your guns, but what would Simon say?"

When they reached the ground level, Germaine waved at Hector and passed him an envelope. "For you." A letter from Gertrude. They went in search of a pay phone.

Gertrude Stein said, "We're interested in an update."

Again, Hector wondered if she was using the royal "we." He said, "We?"

"I'm here with Estelle, we're discussing further investigative strategies."

"I can't talk now, I'm sorry," Hector said. "Late for a funeral."

"Whose?"

"Lloyd Blake's. Figured to nose around for clues there."

# Twenty

*"Brinke didn't do this* place justice," Hem said. "Really think it's a going concern?"

Hector hadn't been able to see much of the hotel the previous night. In the light, it looked like a derelict building. The hotel's facade was stained with coal dust and the paint was peeling. The windows looked crooked in their casings and the ground floor walls were covered with layers of posters and faded notices. Hector had one leg crossed over the other and he was massaging his ankle. He said, "Not sure I'd grant it 'going concern' status, but I think it's still open for business. Some of those piss stains on the walls below the windows looked relatively fresh."

Hem slipped out of the taxi. "The street smells of urine and the river," he said.

Hector said to the taxi driver, "Please wait; we shouldn't be too long."

The driver said, "And you'll not find another taxi this way. But if there's any sign of trouble with any of the ones who live around here, I leave. This looks like a fine place to get robbed."

"You'll be safe enough," Hector said. He slid across the seat to Hem's open door, put down his injured foot, and promptly fell to the ground. Hem bent to help him up. "Jesus, Lasso, you sure you're up to this?"

Hector steadied himself, putting more weight on his good leg. "Ankle is just weak."

"You going to be able to make it inside?"

"Let me lean on you, Hem, and let's just get this done." Hector rested a hand on Hem's shoulder and limped alongside his limping friend. They reached the door and Hector said, "I'm wearing gloves so let me get that knob." The brass knob was tarnished blue-green and covered in something Hector couldn't identify . . . not rust, but close in color. Hector swung open the door and blinked a few times; there was hardly any light inside the lobby.

Hector limped to the front desk, still leaning on Hem, and then put both hands on the counter to support himself. He called, "Concierge?" There was a rusted metal bell on the counter and Hector tapped it once, twice. Then, tapping it a third time—striking it harder—he finally got a kind of ring from the thing.

They waited in silence for a few moments, then Hem said, "I don't think anyone is working the desk." Hector took off his gloves, pulled out a box of matches, and reached over the counter to the desk below and scooped up a candle in a brass holder. He lifted it to the counter and struck the match. Once the candle was going, Hector reached over the counter again and retrieved the registration book.

Hem pulled on his steel-rimmed reading glasses, squinting in the low light at the registration book. He ran his fingers down the page, then said, "Judging by these dates, either nobody checks out, or this place is all but empty."

Looking up the narrow, uneven steps disappearing into gloom,

Hector said, "Our poet couldn't have made it easy, I suppose. I mean, by registering as Leek or Rook?"

Hem said, "No, but there's an A. Crowley."

"That'd be our bitter boy," Hector said. "Give me your arm again, buddy."

"I don't think so," Hem said. He bit his lip, then shook his head. "That leg of yours is getting much worse. No way you can get up those steps. Too narrow to go up side by side, and too dark, too." Hem reached under his coat and pulled out the old Mauser. "I'll go up and take a look."

"Not alone. You've got a wife and baby."

"Better for me I go alone than having you hang on one of my arms and pounding up those old steps like bloody fucking Ahab stumping around," Hem said. "Besides, you can watch the front door, Lasso. Or stop him if he gets by me."

Hector tried to put weight on his leg without Hem's assistance and nearly fell down again. Grabbing the counter, Hector said, "Dammit, it's too much. You're right about that."

Hem took the candleholder in his left hand and hefted his gun in his right. "Okay then."

Hector clutched the tail of Hem's coat. "One thing—be sure to hold that candle out away from yourself—"

"To draw fire," Hem said. "I've read your stories and so know the tricks, remember?"

"Good luck." Hector watched Hem disappear up the creaking stairs. He put his back to the counter and held his Colt at the ready. Hector wasn't sure how much time passed as he waited for Hem, but the interlude worked his nerves.

More creaking on the stairs. Hem tromped down the steps, gray-faced, his gun arm hanging loosely by his side. "I found the missing desk clerk," Hem said. "I think that poor bastard, in turn, found what's in that room. And he got himself killed for his trouble."

Hem was breathing through his mouth, Hector noticed. "It's

bad, Lasso. They've probably been dead a couple of days and the cold hasn't kept them like you might think. We need to call your friend Simon."

"What's in that room?"

"A couple of streetwalkers, I think," Hem said. "Their throats are cut. The hotel manager is in the hallway. I'm guessing he walked in on Leek when he was killing the tarts. He saw what was happening and was shot by Leek. There's a bullet hole in the concierge's throat."

Hector put his hand on Hem's shoulder. "Our taxi driver better still be out there so he can drive us to a phone."

"Yeah," Hem said. "But switch shoulders, would you, Lasso? You're stressing *my* bad leg."

Hector smiled and shook his head. "Jesus. Ain't we the sturdy pair?"


Simon was exuding skepticism. Hector pushed on: "This gets back to that guy I asked you to check up on."

The commissioner narrowed his eyes. "Oswald Rook?"

"Alias Victor Leek," Hector said. "That's right. Rook, or Leek, was a student or adherent of Aleister Crowley's. As a result of some stupid ritual, Leek ended up unmanned."

"Leek I've actually heard of, but in another context," Simon said. "And 'unmanned'? What are you talking about?"

"Leek lost his balls," Hem said. "Castrated."

Simon pulled his overcoat closer. "So you think he taunted himself with these prostitutes. Then, in an unsated sense of rage or lethal frustration, he killed them?"

"Something like that," Hector said. "Then the clerk stumbled in." He took a deep breath, snarling in pain. "I've gotta sit down." Groaning, Hector limped to a bollard and sat down on that, the rounded metal top cold against his ass.

"You were limping last night," Simon said, "but not like that.

Until you see a doctor—which better be quite soon—I might have something that will help." He excused himself and trotted across the street to his own car. He reached into the back seat and returned swinging an ebony walking stick. He handed the cane to Hector. "Sánchez's sword cane. Obviously, the late poet no longer needs it, and it isn't strictly evidence. I'll just trust you to use it for support, not fencing."

"You can trust," Hector said. "And thank you."

"Show your gratitude by telling me where I might next look for Leek."

"Crowley said Leek was previously living above Suzy."

Simon grunted. "The brothel? Rue Grégoir-de-Tours?"

"That's the place," Hector said.

Smirking, Simon said, "A eunuch living above a house of pleasure? It's almost funny."

"It certainly had Crowley in stitches," Hem said.

"Well, I'll try to find Leek there, but I'm frankly pessimistic," Simon said. "But, going to the place, just perhaps, I'll at least learn where the women upstairs came from. Perhaps who they are. Rather, who they *were*."

Hector rose from the bollard, putting weight on the cane. He was pleasantly surprised how much it helped. He said to Simon, "We can go?"

"I don't see why not." They shook hands. Simon said, "Until the next calamity then."

"God forbid," Hector said.

Hem closed the door of the taxi after Hector, then walked around the cab and climbed in on the other side.

Hector checked his watch. He said, "Just time enough to pick up Brinke and reach the graveyard."

# Twenty-one

*They bumped along the* cobbled path and through the imposing, stone gates of Père-Lachaise into its sprawling grounds of spires and statuary. Hector thought it was good funeral weather—a slate-gray sky peeking through low, charcoal-colored clouds . . . another sleeting rain.

His leg was propped up on the opposing seat and Brinke had taken off his boot. She was sitting across from Hector to massage his ankle that had swollen to twice the size of its mate. "You're through walking until you see a doctor, I think," Brinke said, clearly worried by the appearance of his leg.

"I want to argue, but I know if I tried to get out there I'd just be taken for a drunk as I fell down, over and over," Hector said.

"Then stay here in the coach, Hector," Brinke said, handing Hem an umbrella. "We'll do the snooping around. You audit the crowd."

The graveside service was underway as they rolled alongside a string of parked coaches and taxis. Brinke and Hem shared the umbrella. Hem wrapped one of his burly arms familiarly around Brinke's trim waist as they stepped out into the cold drizzle. Hector shook his head, watching them and thinking, *Right, Hem . . . you horny bastard.* His friends picked their way amidst the ancient headstones and crypts to the open graveside.

Hector knew very little about Lloyd Blake, so he didn't know whether or not to be surprised by the relatively small number of mourners. Most were men, shabbily dressed, whom Hector took to be poets. There were two or three equally unkempt and modestly dressed young women ... thin, wan, bespectacled—writer-types, Hector decided.

A woman in mourning clothes held the hands of two teenage children. One of them, a girl, was sobbing, and the boy, presumably her brother, was rubbing her back, looking like he was also on the verge of a breakdown.

A few black carrion crows were perched in the naked limbs of a sheltering tree, cawing at the proceedings below.

At some distance—too far away for Hector to make out faces— seven men in gray suits and black armbands passed bottles of ivory-colored liquid back and forth, taking deep drinks and then shouting various Dadaesque strings of nonsense poetry Hector thought worthy of the worst of Gertrude Stein's "automatic writings." One of the revelers squeezed a concertina, playing a drunken rendition of the funeral march.

A smaller group stood off some ways from the Dada contingent. The second, silent group consisted of two men and two women dressed in dark clothes. One of the women, who wore a black veil, held her head up and seemed to be looking in the direction of Hector's coach. Hector looked at Brinke again; squinted. She was pointing behind herself with a gloved hand.

On a distant hill, far from the funeral attendees, there was the figure of a woman in white, shoulders hunched ... head bowed in grief. Hector first thought she was a statue or grave marker. Then he saw the shoulders of the figure were shaking. A hand reached to a white-veiled face.

Hector tapped the roof to get his driver's attention, then said, "Take us around the path to the east. I want to see something on that hill over there."

As the coach pulled away, Hector saw Brinke watching, nodding. Her arm was hooked through Hem's and they stood close together under the dripping black umbrella.

Hector watched the passing crypts and headstones and statues, making out an occasional name or date. His leg hurt a little as they began to climb the hill and more weight was placed on his ankle as he was tipped forward toward the opposing seat by the incline. Hector twisted around to better see out the window. When they crested the hill he saw the woman dressed in white, and he rapped the ceiling with his bruised hand. "Stop here, please."

Hector cleared his throat and did his best to feign an authentic French accent. Unlatching the door of the coach, Hector swung it open and said, *"Mademoiselle . . . s'il vous plait?"*

The woman in white half-turned. He said, gruffly, "I am Commissaire Simon, Mademoiselle, and I require a word with you. I require a word with you *right now.*"

The woman turned to face him; she was slender, rather tall. She moved like a young woman; her face was obscured behind her long white veil. Hector beckoned her into his coach. "Right now," he said again. "I promise that I'll try to make this brief."

The woman turned her head a little, looking back at the distant funeral, then her shoulders rose and fell with an audible sigh. She picked her way around some dirty puddles standing in the brown, winter-shocked grass and then planted her foot on the coach's step and wrapped a hand around the door frame. Hector extended a hand and helped her in as best he could with his bad leg splayed out in front of him. He apologized for his condition and said, *"Comment vous appellez-vous?"*

Hector narrowed his eyes. Through the fabric of her white veil, he could see she was young . . . perhaps twenty-four or twenty-five. She was blond and her eyes were hazel. She was also American. "Kitty," she said. "Kitty Pike."

Hector switched to English, leaving a little of a French accent there to further his ruse. "White is an unusual color to wear to a funeral, particularly in winter."

Kitty Pike shrugged. "I wasn't entitled to wear black. Or I didn't think so."

"You were trying to avoid provoking someone, is that it?"

"Something like that I suppose."

"Why so far from the proceedings?"

She shrugged again.

"You're not family of Mr. Blake's, are you?"

"No."

"A business associate . . . affiliated with his magazine as a partner, or investor?"

"Not quite that."

"You were lovers, then?"

She looked up sharply. Hector said, "I'm police, and you must answer."

"Yes," she said, looking away from him.

"And you stood back here, in white, to better blend into the surroundings? To avoid antagonizing Mrs. Blake? To evade some scene, or perhaps spare scandalizing his young son and daughter?"

"That's right."

"How long have you *known* Mr. Blake?"

"It would have been a year in March."

"You're a writer? A poet?"

"An illustrator."

"A painter?"

"No, a commercial artist. A designer. Lloyd hired me to illustrate some advertisements in his magazine. That's how we met."

"When was the last time you saw Mr. Blake?"

She stared at her hands . . . stroking the fabric of her ivory gloves tighter to her fingers. "Please, you must promise not to make a record of this. You must promise to keep my name out of this. When a few days passed, I was certain I'd be spared this kind of thing."

"I'll do as you ask, so far as I can, if you'll just answer my questions."

"Very well," Kitty said. "I'll do my best."

"When did you last see Mr. Blake?"

"The night before he was murdered. I . . . I spent the night with him, at his place. His wife and children were out of town for several days."

"Were you also planning to see him the night of his death?"

"No, he said he had a business dinner . . . a meeting with someone who wanted to buy the magazine from him. The magazine wasn't doing particularly well. I could tell that from the number of adverts—or lack of them—that I was asked to design. His magazine was hemorrhaging money and Lloyd was close to shutting his review down when an interested party approached him."

"Did he mention who this potential buyer might be, Mademoiselle Pike?"

"He did mention a name, but I can't recall it right now. I do remember him commenting that it was an American."

"But you don't remember this man's—this American's—name?"

"No, and it wasn't a man, it was a woman. I think she might even have been one of his investors."

Hector nodded, discouraged. He'd been expecting her to name Victor Leek or Oswald Rook. Hector said, "You said that Blake was thinking of closing the magazine. I had heard he had done that already. That he had solicited funds, then announced he was shutting down operations. The story goes that he took the money he'd collected and moved to the Right Bank and into a better apartment with his wife and children."

Kitty Pike shook her head. Hector could see through her veil that her cheeks had reddened. "No, Lloyd had plenty of money of his own," Kitty said. "Lloyd was quite well off. That's a lie about his absconding with his patrons' money. He'd simply skipped a publication date . . . you know, as many periodicals do in December-January."

Hector took out a cigarette, slowly lit it. He said, "This is awkward. I apologize in advance, but I have to ask. Mr. Blake, he was murdered in his bed, you know that don't you?"

"I read it."

Hector was riffing now. "Blake was murdered by someone

whom he'd taken to his bed. There is no doubt about that. As you noted, his wife was out of town—"

Real venom— "I told you, I last saw Blake the day before he died. I—"

"I'm not insinuating anything, Mademoiselle," Hector said. "You're not being accused of anything. You are not a suspect. But I have to ask. Were you aware of any other . . . well, *lovers* whom Mr. Blake might have had?"

*"No."* She looked out the window at the distant ceremony. "There was nobody else. He spoke of marrying me. He was going to break the news to—"

Hector lost the thread then. He could already finish the sentence for Kitty . . . and he figured he could probably go a good bit beyond. There would have been the inevitable promise of a quick, Paris divorce . . . a new apartment somewhere a few arrondissements away from his present home, which in Paris could be made to feel the equivalent of moving to another country. And Blake would have promised to marry Kitty, of course.

Hector almost felt sorry for Kitty. Then he saw that Blake's widow was on her knees in the wet, slushy grass, beating on her husband's coffin as her children clutched at her. Hector saw Hem step away from Brinke to wrap an arm around the widow and drag her to her feet.

Hector tossed his cigarette butt out the window of the coach and said, "It seems to be ending, Mademoiselle Pike. Do you have a car or a cab waiting for you down there?"

"Yes."

"We'll drop you there." Hector signaled the *cocher* and they started off down the hill. Hector said, "You can't remember the name of this potential buyer? This woman?"

"No . . . 'White' maybe. No, that's not right. But something with a 'W' . . . I remember that." Then Kitty said, "That's my taxi."

Hector called up to their driver to stop. Kitty said, "Oh, I *do* remember the first name now. I remember thinking at the time that the woman's name was the same as my mother's."

Hector nodded. "And what is your mother's name?"

Kitty stepped out of the coach and into the sleet. She closed the door and said, "My mother was named Margaret."

# Twenty-two

*Brinke said, "We came* up bust. The widow was too distraught for us to even attempt to approach or question her. Hell, Hem had to practically haul her off the coffin."

"I saw," Hector said, distracted . . . thinking of what Kitty had told him. "Terrible."

Brinke nodded, rubbing Hector's ankle. "Yes, what did you learn up there, Hector? Who was that woman in white you had in here?"

"Lloyd Blake's mistress. An American named Kitty Pike."

Hem said, "You think she's the one who stabbed him to death?"

"No, not at all," Hector said. "She's torn up, too. Not desolated enough to crawl into the grave after him like Mrs. Blake looked to be trying to do, but the mistress is mourning, as well."

Brinke said, "And did you learn anything from her?"

"Not really," Hector said. He could tell Hem believed him; Brinke looked skeptical. Hector almost smiled. Brinke fully had his number. In just a few days, she'd taken his measure and evidently learned to read him too well. Hector said, "Hem, I want to find a phone. Can you ring up Dr. Williams? Ask him to come by my place? I think if another hour or two passes, I'm going to be an invalid."

*   *   *

Dr. William Carlos Williams, poet and physician, said, "The tibia, fibula, and talus all seem to be intact. I was afraid at first it was a Pott's fracture. It does seem to be a slight dislocation, but the tendons and ligaments seem undamaged."

Williams, dark, slender, vaguely Spanish-looking—and whom Ernest insisted upon calling "WCW"—was talking mostly to Hem, who had already ventured his own layman's diagnosis regarding Hector's injured leg. Hem had essentially determined Hector was suffering from some kind of dislocation at the joint. Williams said, "Your assumption was correct, Ernest. You might have been a gifted physician yourself, I think."

Hector thought that assertion seemed to please Hem, perhaps too much.

Williams grabbed Hector's foot and gripped it. He said, "Ernest, if you can get hold of his leg, just below the knee, and hold it rock steady."

Hem did that. "Got it," he said, closely watching everything that Williams did.

Williams said to Hector, "You may want to lie back now, Hector, and prepare yourself. Perhaps bite on a wallet, or something."

Then the physician-poet abruptly twisted Hector's foot and there was a pop. Straining, Hector bit through his lip, tasted blood.

"There," Williams said. "Better to surprise you. And that's got it. I'll give you something for the swelling, but it should go down on its own now that the joint is properly aligned again. I'll give you a little something special for the pain, too."

Brinke said, "How long until he can get up and around, Doctor?"

"Give it at least a day," Williams said, running a hand back through his close-cropped dark hair. "I'll wrap it, and teach you both how to wrap it for him, for extra support." Williams nodded at Brinke and at Hem in turn. "See that he gives it the rest of the day, and tomorrow, to recover." Then, to Hector, Williams said, "Maybe tomorrow evening you can start putting some real weight on it. But go ahead and use that cane there, anyway. You'll probably need that for a week or so. And suffice it to say, no running for a while and particularly not any more of this jumping over banisters."

"Right," Hector said, grimacing. The pain in his ankle was already receding but now there was a pins-and-needles sensation of intense tingling.

He mentioned it to Williams. The doctor said, "Circulation is returning, that's all. Out-of-skew as your foot was, your circulation was disrupted. That could have created its own problems. Gangrene in time, or possibly the formation of a clot that might have migrated and caused a heart attack. Perhaps even a stroke, or brain seizure."

"Can't thank you enough for the house call," Hector said. "This was killing me."

"A dislocation can be more painful than a break in some ways," Williams said, rooting through his bag. "And as I said, given time, it might well have killed you."

Brinke said, "As you're here, would you mind checking his hand, as well, Doctor?"

Williams looked up from his bag at Brinke and said, "What's this? Another stairwell injury?"

"He cuffed Aleister Crowley," Hem said, grinning.

"For that alone I waive my fee," Williams said. He checked Hector's hand, making him extend his middle finger. Then Williams asked Hector to shake hands. As they gripped one another's hands, Williams said, "Squeeze my hand, Hector, hard as you can." Finally, Williams kneaded Hector's purple-blue knuckle. "Not broken, I think," Williams said. "There's not much to do for it but to give it some rest. Keep it limber, but don't strain it. And don't go around swinging on any more diabolists. At least not for a week or two. Anyway, the proper thing to do to diabolists is to shoot them. Preferably with silver bullets."

There was a knock at the door. Hem put a hand on the knob, then hesitated. He called through the door, "Who is it?"

A deep, husky female voice: "Hemingway? Is that you? Open the door. It's Gertrude Stein."

Williams, whom Gertrude often publicly and privately criticized, rolled his eyes. Hector smiled and winked at his poet-doctor. "Me too. But what can we do?"

"Leave," Williams said, "with all dispatch." He smiled and patted Hector's good leg. "Or at least, *I* can. You? Punishment perhaps for playing at the dime-novel hero, eh?"

"Then it's another sorry lesson learned the hardest way," Hector said, dropping his head back on the pillow as he heard Hem open the door for Gertrude. Hector braced for some biting remark from Alice. He smiled up at Brinke; she was sitting next to him on the bed, stroking his forehead. He said, "Darling Brinke, this day . . ." She smiled.

Gertrude said, "Dr. Williams, Miss Devlin." Gertrude stood at the foot of his bed, smiling frostily at Hector. "My poor poor star. Hadley dropped off some books at Sylvia's while Alice was there and thusly does word spread." Gertrude pointed at his leg. "This is from chasing that horrible Sánchez, is it? It's not broken is it?" Gertrude had also studied medicine. Hem had told Hector that Gertrude had been inches from obtaining her medical degree when she walked away from it all to write fiction.

Williams answered for Hector. "Badly dislocated, but I've fixed that."

Gertrude smiled and nodded. "*Doctor* Williams. It's so good to see you functioning in your true métier . . . *Doctor* Williams."

"He'll be fine." Williams handed Brinke a small paper envelope. "For his pain. Give him two pills, shortly. Then one more this afternoon, and perhaps another later, before he sleeps. After that, he can take them as he feels he needs them. But they're pretty powerful, so sparing is better."

Hector said, "Any reason I can't drink while I'm on these pills?"

Williams furrowed his brow: "The pills should make you quite numb, all by themselves, my friend. But a single glass of wine would be all right, I suppose. But no more. The wine will likely magnify the effects of the painkillers. As you're rangy and have what I sense to be a high tolerance for pain, I suppose the wine might even be advisable in some ways. At least it will keep you in one place. But I really think you'll find the pills enough in themselves."

Williams closed his bag, then turned to Hem. "I'll see you later this evening regarding Bumby. We should think about his circumcision, too. I could do it this evening."

Hem made a face. "*Yeah* . . . we'll talk about that. I'll walk you out, WCW."

Brinke thanked Williams. As Hem and Williams stepped out of the room, Hector saw that Estelle Quartermain was standing quietly in the doorway. She had previously been obscured behind the two men. Hector smiled meanly: the British mystery writer had cut her hair, and quite short. He guessed that Estelle had attempted to approximate Brinke's new haircut, but whatever stylist she had found had taken it to too mannish extremes. The resulting effect was closer to Joan Pyle's masculine crop than Brinke's sleek, boyish cut. Hector thought her new hairstyle made Estelle look like one of the many lesbians in the Quarter striving for archly male appearance. Estelle patted her head self-consciously with one hand as she noticed Hector focusing on her cropped hair. In her other hand, Estelle clutched a white cardboard box.

Gertrude gestured to Estelle and took the box from her and placed it on the bed by Hector's wrapped and elevated foot. "A special treat Alice baked for you," she said.

Hector was tempted to say, "Made with hemlock?" but said instead, "That was very kind of her. Please thank Alice for me." Hector was proud of himself for his graciousness. He said to Gertrude, "Despite the bum leg, we *did* poke around the Lloyd Blake murder a bit today."

Gertrude edged around and sat on the foot of the bed. Hector winced a little as the bed dipped and his ankle rolled a little toward Gertrude, who seemed oblivious to the effect that her settling bulk was having on Hector's posture in his own sickbed. She said, "So you said you intended to do. At his funeral, you said. And what have we learned?"

"We have learned that Lloyd Blake had a mistress . . . a mistress who said that Lloyd was approached by a woman who was trying to buy his magazine," Hector said. "Lloyd was supposed to be meeting with this woman the night that he was murdered."

Gertrude said, "And what is this woman's name?"

"Blake's mistress didn't know that," Hector said. "But this mystery woman *is* American. We know that."

"Nearly everyone in the Quartier Latin is American," Gertrude said, glumly. "The Quarter is teeming with you—you generation of lost, drunken, and promiscuous young Americans. The curse of devalued European currency."

"Nothing lasts forever," Hector said, accepting a glass of water from Brinke.

Estelle said, "You're *sure* she didn't say something that might tip us to this woman's identity?"

"I'm sure."

Hem closed the door behind himself. Hem took the envelope of pills from Brinke, shook loose two pills, then handed them to Hector.

Hector took his medication, drained the glass of water, and dropped back on his pillow. To Estelle he said, "And you? Anything new to report on the poisoning of Charles Turner?"

"The snuff arrived as a gift to Mr. Turner, a few hours before the gathering at Miss Stein's salon," Estelle said.

"A gift from . . . ?"

"It was an anonymous gift, according to Mrs. Turner. It arrived with an unsigned congratulatory note praising the quality of the latest issue of Charles's magazine. Mr. Turner often used snuff and most who knew him seemed aware of that, according to his wife."

"So the suspect pool is vast," Brinke said dryly. "That's convenient for *someone*. Anything else, Estelle?"

Estelle tugged at her shortened forelock, looking at Brinke's hair. "No," she said tersely. "I'm afraid not."

Gertrude said, "So now what, Hector? Hemingway?"

"I'm benched until tomorrow night," Hector said. "So I suppose for now we all best do what I'm ordered to do—hunker down. Bide our time. If we ever do identify a good target, we'll go to Simon if the evidence seems prosecutable."

Estelle moved closer to see Hector's eyes. For his part, Hector was suddenly seized by more violent, erotic images of himself with the mystery writer. He saw himself taking her from behind . . . roughly.

Hector could feel himself getting hard and he raised his good leg a bit before his erection could make a tent of the sheets.

Hector also felt deliciously warm and realized then that his pain pills were kicking in.

The British mystery writer said, "And if it isn't prosecutable, Hector?"

"Then we may have to take matters into our own hands," he said, smiling. Hector thought he might even be leering at the mystery writer.

Estelle wrinkled her nose and said, "Nietzsche said that it's wise counsel to 'distrust all in whom the impulse to punish is powerful.'"

Hector waved a suddenly heavy hand, realizing he was already feeling profoundly dopy from his pain medication. "Well, I'm not sure it's prudent to allow the ramblings of a man who died of syphilis to direct one's thinking, Quarts."

*Shut up*, Hector told himself. *Your tongue is loose from the drugs Williams gave you and you might say anything now. You're sounding like an idiot. Shut up.*

"You're slurring," Gertrude said to Hector. She lightly patted his bandaged ankle. "The doctor probably gave you morphine. Well, sleep now. We'll plan on talking tomorrow night." Gertrude looked to Brinke, said, "You'll arrange it?"

"We'll see how ambulatory he is," Brinke said. "You might have to come back here to Hector, otherwise. Or perhaps the night after next."

Hem said, "I'll make the decision on that. Hector's in my care now." Hem took Estelle's arm and steered her to the door.

Brinke said, "You're coming back, aren't you, Hem?"

"Sure," he said. Hem turned and took Gertrude's arm. "I'll walk you two down. Tell you about what Hector and I discovered about Victor Leek this morning."

Brinke said her goodbyes to Gertrude and Estelle. When Hem closed the door behind him, Brinke leaned down and kissed Hector's lips. She said, "You still with me, Tex?"

He groggily reached out, took Brinke's hand, and then placed it on the sheets between his legs. He could hear the drunkenness in his voice, but couldn't do anything about it. "This enough to prove I am? Take off those clothes and come to bed."

"I'd love to, darling, but Hem's coming back."

"He won't mind."

Hector felt very drunk now. He almost felt as though he needed to put his good foot on the floor to stop the room from spinning. Yet when Hector was truly that drunk from alcohol, there was always a sense of nausea—an awareness of an impending need to wretch.

But now Hector felt warm . . . infinite.

He wondered what the hell Williams had given him. And he badly wanted to be inside Brinke . . . wanted to come.

Brinke moved her hand from his lap and said, "Put that away for now. Save it for later. I'm going to ask Hem to sit with you for a time, Hector."

"You stay, too," he heard himself say, his voice thick.

"No, I can't, Hector. While you were with Hem, while you two were looking for Victor Leek, you had a visitor. Your friend, Molly Wilder. I was coming down the stairs as she was climbing them. It was . . . awkward. But we talked for a time and I invited her to a late breakfast. We talked a good deal more while doing that. Now, at least, Molly knows about us. We agreed to meet again for lunch—to talk about you and to talk about her poetry. I even confided to her that I'm Connor Templeton. Wanted to give her more of a sense of me than just some 'muse' or 'whore.' I like her well enough, Hector. I think Molly might even like me, despite some other feelings. But she seems very fragile, too. Very lonely. Yet, I think I can reach her."

"—S'good."

"God, you're flying, aren't you, Hector?"

"Sure."

"Sleep then," Brinke said. "I'll spend a few hours with Molly. Try to see what I can do to prop her up some more."

Hector found moving his lips had become more than he could manage. He wanted to caution Brinke about being alone with Molly. He wanted to warn Brinke against being alone with *Margaret W*ilder. He knew he needed to tell Brinke about what Kitty Pike had said about the alleged, interested potential buyer of Lloyd Blake's magazine—some American woman named "Margaret W."

But all Hector could manage was, "Molly . . . *no* . . ."

Her voice, fading. "She's truly reconciled to us, I think," Brinke said. "I can tell."

Hector tried to shake his head. But that, too, was now something far beyond his capability.

He heard Brinke and Hem briefly talking, but couldn't make out their words. The door closed. Hem leaned down so close to Hector that he could smell the peat smoke on Hem's clothes. Hem said, "I'm going to borrow your typewriter, if it won't keep you up, Lasso. Need to transcribe some manuscript pages. It's a new story about an Indian camp up in Michigan. About a pregnant squaw. I think it's damn fine. Maybe my best yet."


A woman's voice . . . Hector wanted to reach out to it, but he still couldn't move. The voice said, "It's Hadley, Hector. Tatie had to check in on Ford. Ernest said it's time for another pill. Here, now."

He felt her lifting his head, then felt her fingers at his lips. He tasted something hard and bitter in his mouth. "No, don't *bite* it," Hadley said. "Here." Then he felt the drinking glass at his lips . . . pushed up against his teeth. He drank from the glass, then drank some more.

Languor, mounting.


Voices . . . drunken giggles.

"The corkscrew is over there."

"Think four bottles will be enough?"

"Can always stretch it out with the Perrier."

"What are these?"

"Some kind of brownies or cakes that Alice B. Toklas baked. Gertrude left them. Help yourself. And maybe get one for Hector, too. See if you can't get him to eat a bit. It's been hours since he last had food and those pain pills are probably shredding his stomach."

Hector felt another pill being pushed into his mouth. Brinke's voice: "Here, wash it down with this, Hector."

He tasted wine.

Another voice—the voice of the second woman: "You sure that's a good idea? Wine to wash down medication?"

"Dr. Williams said it is fine if Hector had a glass."

That other voice, close by his face . . . the scent of lilacs: "Here, Hector—take a few nibbles of this."

Hector tasted of the small cake that had some scent about it he couldn't identify. He realized then he was hungry and allowed whoever was feeding him to give him all of the cake, and then a second piece. The voice: "He's starving, I think. I wish we had some-thing more substantial to give him."

Brinke, sounding quite drunk: "Later . . . when he comes out of this."

Then, a voice, he wasn't sure whose: "Then come over here now."

*   *   *

Voices again . . . more giggles.

"This is crazy . . . We *can't*."

Then sounds of kisses and low moans.

"Ordinary morals are for ordinary people."

It *sounded* like Brinke speaking, but it sounded more like something that Crowley, the diabolist, might say.

Again: "B, this *is* crazy, isn't it?" Then, *"Oh . . . oh."*

More whispers . . . the voices blending to a jumble. He picked out:

"But delicious fun, yes?"

The sound of more kisses.

Motion on the bed. Low moans and coos. Fabric, hitting the floor.

The bed was gently rocking, then Hector felt himself being undressed. He felt warm soft skin pressing against his skin. Breasts pressed against his naked body; breasts were touching him, brushing against him, seemingly everywhere, all at once.

Lips and tongues on his mouth, neck and chest . . .

A thigh sliding across his thigh . . . warm and wet. This thrusting against him, over and over.

Another thigh was moving above him—brushing against his cheek. He kissed the inside of the thigh, felt a flutter, then turned his head to kiss the other thigh.

His tongue was there then, nuzzling against that which was moving—*rocking*—gently against his mouth. The scent of musk and lilacs was strong in his nose.

Voices between kisses: "This is so . . ."

*". . . Delicious."*

"Delicious, yes . . . and wicked."

"Wicked, yes . . . and *wonderful*."

Another giggle: "I hope we don't kill him."

Hector felt himself coming, then later, coming again, and still later, perhaps even a third time.

Hands all over him . . . thighs . . . hair tickling his neck. The weight of heads settled on either of his arms. He felt lips brushing his chest, either side.

A voice, not Brinke's: "I'm destroyed."

Brinke: "You don't looked destroyed to me. You look ecstatic."

The other voice: "I may start loving Mondays."

Hector felt himself drifting away again.

Sweet oblivion.

# Twenty-three

*A long warm body* was spooned up against him. His hand was cupping a heavy, moist breast. Short hair tickled his nose. He was still inside her and he realized that he was hard again.

He began to move slowly; heard a low groan and felt hips pushing back against him. Hector kept moving, his eyes closed, savoring the sensation that almost hurt a little from all that had come before. He sensed he might even have some kind of friction burns down there.

He nuzzled the back of a long neck, brushing his nose in her close-cropped hair. Her moans deepened, and she rolled a little over onto her belly. Before he could slip out, he rolled with her, spreading her legs wider with his own legs so he could thrust more deeply inside her. He moved more quickly, sensing she was close to peaking, then he came again. He came with a hollow, piercing sensation because there was so little left in him.

Hector collapsed across her damp back, his lips grazing the back of her neck. He opened his eyes, saw blond hair. Startled, he raised himself up on his elbow and she half-turned under him . . . smiled at Hector.

Molly said, "That was passing wonderful."

"Yes," Hector said slowly. He gently eased out of her body. She shuddered a little as he slipped free. She rolled onto her back and pulled the sheets up over them.

Remembering the damage to his leg—still bewildered and unsettled—Hector rolled onto his back. Brinke was sitting on the window ledge, close by the fire. She was wearing a long silk robe that had fallen mostly open so he could see that she was naked underneath. Her eyes were sleepy behind her reading glasses. She was smoking a cigarillo, and some manuscript pages were clutched in her other hand. He could see that Brinke's exposed nipple was erect. She tossed the manuscript pages on his desk and said, "He has risen. How was that, Hector?"

Brinke ground out her cigarette, then stood and stretched. Her robe fell open. She shrugged it off and stretched out alongside Hector. She put her reading glasses on the stand by the bed.

"At least you can't run away," Brinke said, stroking his chest. "Not for another day anyway."

"Holy Jesus," Hector said. "What time is it?"

Molly, red-faced now, said, "A little after seven. Seven at night, I mean."

Hector looked back and forth between them. He had a tremendous headache and felt badly hungover. He said, "Everything that I'm now remembering and think happened, it *really* happened?"

"Probably much more than you're remembering," Brinke said. "You're weren't in much condition to resist. And you seemed strangely compliant."

"Morphine and wine are a killer combination," Hector said. "Sometimes literally."

"Doctor's orders," Brinke said. "But if it'll ease your bourgeois Texas conscience, there was another, unexpected potion in the mix, I think. Something else breaking down our self-control."

Hector rubbed his eyes. "What are you talking about?"

"Alice's baked goods," Brinke said, fingers tracing his lips. "Just a bit ago, having tasted another of Alice's cakes and soon enough feeling the effects from it, well, I figured it out. I've heard about Alice's recipe, but never sampled it before. Alice calls them 'Hashisch Fudge,' though they're actually made with cannabis. Cannabis, and some spices . . . fruits and nuts."

Hector was furious. "That little crone made us drugged desserts?"

Molly, sounding more than a little nervous now, sounding a good bit self-conscious, said, "Maybe she thought it would help with the pain of your ankle."

Hector looked at her again. Molly had pulled the sheet almost up to her neck. Her lips were swollen, from what Hector guessed to be hard kisses—his own, or Brinke's, or perhaps both. And Molly's thick blond hair was cut exactly like Brinke's now . . . some of the natural wave had even been straightened or cut out of her hair.

Molly's violet eyes were smoky and unfocused . . . dark-ringed. But she was still lovely. Hector smiled uncertainly at her and stroked the hair from over her right eye. Molly started to say something, then hesitated . . . averted her eyes. She pulled the sheet up a bit higher around her neck.

Brinke was stretched naked on top of the sheets. There was the dark red trace of a too hard kiss—an actual hickey—high up on Brinke's right thigh. Hector wondered which of them had given Brinke that.

Brinke looked at Hector, her eyebrows raised expectantly . . . waiting to see what he might say. He finally fell back on the pillow between them. He urged his arms under their heads and gathered them close against himself. He felt Molly's hand stray across his belly and close over Brinke's hand. He felt Molly squeezing Brinke's hand.

Molly said, "This is so awkward. I'm sorry, Hector. Sorry to presume . . . and with you drugged up like that . . . ?"

"Shut up, Molly," he said. He leaned his head her way, and then bumped foreheads with her. "I'm sorry for that. Jesus, how could I hate this?"

He sensed Brinke wasn't buying it. Brinke threw him one of his own Lassiter-style change-ups. "Isn't Molly's hair wonderful? My barber did the deed. I mean, your barber. Couldn't have her ending up butchered like Estelle, could we?"

"God forbid." Hector smiled at Molly. "You look beautiful, Molly. Very desirable."

"You proved that a few minutes ago, Hector," Brinke said. "As well as in several other ways earlier this afternoon." Another change-up. "How's that foot?"

"Okay. I think I could even walk a little."

Brinke shook her head. "Not yet. Don't push it. Besides, you've got your two nurses. Your two wet nurses."

Molly said, "Do you need another pain pill, Hector?"

"No, but wine would be wonderful. And soon we should eat. But not more of those damn cakes. Jesus ... *drugs* ..."

Molly started to pull the sheet with her, to wrap herself up in it, realized it was wrapped around Hector, too, then blushing, slipped naked from the bed. She padded to the sideboard to pour Hector some wine. Molly poured herself a glass, and said to the wall, not looking back at them, "And for you, Brinke?"

"We'll share," Brinke said.

Hector didn't know if Brinke meant she'd share his wine, Molly's wine, or both.

Walking back to bed, a wineglass in either hand, Molly finally met Hector's gaze again. Molly's body was rounder and a bit more womanly than Brinke's. Molly had wider hips but she was smaller-breasted than Brinke. The hair between Molly's legs was thick and chestnut-colored. Hector took the glass from Molly and said, "Jesus, but you're lovely."

Molly smiled uncertainly, then sat down on the bed. She crouched a bit to kiss Hector. It was a tentative kiss, then it became deep and slow. She used her tongue.

Hector felt Brinke stroking his lower back.

Brinke leaned in and kissed the back of Hector's neck. He felt her teeth. Seemingly apropos of nothing, Brinke said, "I was looking out the window a bit ago. The church across the street has a new sign posted. It reads, 'Don't Let Worries Kill You . . . Let the Church Help.' They meant to phrase that differently, don't you think?"

Hector said, "We can't all be writers."

It was eight o'clock and Molly had elected herself to be the one to go and bring them back some proper food. Brinke had insisted Molly dress in some of her clothes that she'd sent 'round in her bag on the off chance Germaine might be at the front desk. "Pull your fedora low and just wave if you pass by her," Brinke instructed Molly.

They were alone now, and Brinke was still naked in bed with Hector. She said, "Wipe the goofy smile off your face. How do you really feel about this?"

Hector raked his fingers through his dark hair. "My own selfish hedonism aside?"

Brinke winked. "Sure, if you can actually get around that. I know I can't get round my own most times."

"Disaster."

She nodded. "For whom?"

"Molly. Maybe us. Probably for me."

"Hector, you *can't* be *hating* this. And I told you, I'm not good with exclusivity. And I did find myself attracted to her . . . I can't deny that."

He shook his head, lit a cigarette. "You did?"

"She's not my first, Hector. Have no reason to think that she'll be my last. I've had several female lovers. Here and back home. And I'm not Molly's first, either. I read some of her poetry the other day. I knew Molly had been with other women as soon as I read her poems, 'Other' and 'Perfumed Sighs.' It was all right there. Her bisexuality, I mean."

Hector remembered those poems ... but he had not detected any Sapphic undertones. He promised himself another visit to Sylvia's to read them again.

Brinke said, "It *was* fun in the moment. Good, dirty, and harmless fun, Hector. And I have to admit that Molly seems engaged again. Overwhelmed, sure. Divided, I suppose. But alive. Molly is *feeling* again. Moored to life. And she's *had* you now. She's seen that while you're a wonderful enough guy, you're still just another man. She's seen you have feet of clay." Brinke's hand there. "And she sees you can be led around by this. All that may get you out of her system, so to speak. And you enjoyed yourself, lots ... even if you don't remember it. I could tell."

"And you?"

"Had myself a time, like I said." Brinke shrugged. "Helped a new friend, maybe. Certainly have some sexy memories for my dotage."

"And you changed the conditions of *you and me*. You did that unilaterally."

"I didn't exactly act alone."

"I was pumped full of morphine, wine, and cannabis, Brinke."

"You're fond of betting, Hector. A wager—I'll bet it could have been made to happen with you stone cold sober."

"But I wasn't. Jesus, Brinke, seduction via drugs?"

She shrugged. "I didn't know what was in those damn cakes of Alice's, Hector. Let alone how potent they are. Besides, are you changing your way of living? You drink, Hector. *A lot.*"

"Different," Hector said. "I can handle liquor. I can ration and control it. Drugs? I fucking hate what they do to me. I don't like losing control like that." He hesitated. He shook his finger at her. "You've used them before. Drugs. I mean ... haven't you?"

Brinke shrugged again. "Cocaine, now and again. Smoked some opium. Not much more than that." She smiled. "But I wouldn't say no to another of those brownies. I'm going to have to ask Alice for her recipe."

Hector leaned his head back against the wall. "What's going to happen to us?"

"*Us,* in the sense of you and I? Or *us,* as in Molly, too?"

"Any of us. All of us."

"We go along as we have, Molly in or out of the picture, as far as I'm concerned," Brinke said. "I'll say it again . . . I haven't had much success with long-term exclusivity."

"Brinke, I tried to tell you something this morning, before you left to meet Molly for lunch," Hector said. "But those pills of Williams's had knocked me flat."

Brinke propped her head up on her hand, her breasts close to his unshaven cheek. "What did you mean to tell me, Hector?"

"Blake's mistress—she told me things I didn't share with you and Hem."

Brinke leaned in close. "I *knew* it. I knew you were holding back today. What did Blake's lover say?"

Hector sipped his wine. He said, "According to Kitty Pike, the American who purportedly wanted Blake's little magazine was a woman whose last name begins with a 'W.'"

Brinke nodded. "That's all? A 'W'? No more than that?"

"No more of the surname," Hector said. "But the woman's first name was 'Margaret.'"

Brinke hung her head, sighing heavily. She looked up and at Molly's pillow. The pillow was still dented where Molly's head had rested. The room smelled of sex, but through all of the musky scent from their three bodies together, Hector could smell the faint odor of lilacs on the pillow where Molly had rested her head.

"Søren Kierkegaard said that life can only be understood backwards, but unfortunately it must be lived forwards," Brinke said. "Makes for a pretty treacherous split, doesn't it? Particularly in times like these. So what do we do, Hector?"

"We don't confront Molly, not now. Not after . . ." Hector gestured at the empty portion of his bed. "Or, at least not *yet.* We watch her, I suppose. See how all this crazy stuff with the three of us that's been set in motion plays out alongside the other, I guess."

Brinke searched his face. " 'Crazy stuff.' You hate the prospect of having us both, maybe for some time, that much, Hector? *Truly?*"

"No. I don't hate it at *all*, darling. But I guess I maybe fear that it's its own kind of problem. It's like running the risk of heightening, and eventually, jading the palate."

"That could be, Hector. But, playing devil's advocate, do you know how many successful ménages à trois there are both sides of the river? Dozens, maybe hundreds. Some happy trios contend it's the ideal male-female compact."

Hector remembered something then. He repeated, " 'Ordinary morals are for ordinary people.' Where did you get that, anyway, Brinke? That doesn't sound like any axiom you'd truly subscribe to. You're not that effete. Not the jaded libertine."

"It comes from Crowley," Brinke said. "I read a little of one of his books at Sylvia's today. Pretty selfish and self-centered stuff. But I thought it might help me reach Molly."

Sourly, Hector said, "Seems to have worked."

There was a small stack of books on the table by what Hector had already come to regard as Molly's side of the bed. He reached over and picked up the three, haphazardly stacked volumes. "Yours?"

"We picked them up at Sylvia's," Brinke said, looking at them. "Novels that Molly had reserved."

Hector sorted them: *The Assassination Bureau, Ltd*, by Jack London, *The Island of Dr. Moreau*, and Turgenev's *Fathers and Sons*. "Eclectic," he said.

"I was trying to figure out that mix myself," Brinke said. "Sylvia and I had a moment alone when Molly excused herself to the restroom. Sylvia said all three of those novels are regarded by those who incline that way as seminal nihilist texts."

Hector checked the loan cards in each of the books . . . saw Hem's name in the Turgenev. Hem had rented it some time ago—the first weeks he'd lived in Paris.

"Fucking wonderful," Hector said. "I hate to see Molly enveloped by this vile, misanthropic boondoggle that Leek is promulgating."

"Seems we're working on fixing that," Brinke said. "Seems to me that we've awakened her to sensation, to pleasure. If not to love, at least loving affection. *Passion*. I told you—I can already see a change in her. Thanks to you and this wonderful tool. What's it like, having one of these?" Hector felt Brinke's hand there again, stroking. He winced, twisting away a little. Her smile dimmed. "What, it hurts?"

She raised the sheet and looked at his penis. "Yikes...that looks like it *could* hurt. You're raw in several spots. We'll need to go easy on him for a while. Damn."

# Twenty-four

*Hector poured the wine.* He'd managed to hop over to the dinner table on his good leg, leaning on his sword cane.

Brinke had put some Satie on the phonograph. The two women had dressed for their dinner in.

*It's all so civilized,* Hector thought as the three of them sat down for their late meal.

As they ate, despite his earlier cautions to Brinke, Hector began to press Molly, just a bit at first: "Other night, Hem said he saw you with this group, Molly. These people tied to some offshoot of Aleister Crowley's . . . for lack of a better term, we'll call it *church*."

Molly's violet eyes turned on him. Hector said, "I've heard about this group. It scares me a little, honey, you being exposed to that."

"They're friends of Philippe's," Molly said. She searched Hector's face. He supposed to see how he would react . . . either to the simple fact of her assertion, or to Molly mentioning her boyfriend after Hector had made love to her more times and in more ways than he could claim to remember. Had Molly thought she could make Hector jealous? In a funny way, Hector had to admit to himself that he wasn't sure that she couldn't.

"So you're not *of* them then," Hector said. "Just *among* them?"

Molly stirred her food with her fork. "What about 'them,' exactly, scares you so much, Hector?"

Hector was aware of Brinke, sipping her wine and watching the dance with her quick dark eyes.

"I've had some crossings with this Nada bunch in the past few days," he said. "Partly how I hurt my leg." He raised his hand. "And how I got this."

For the first time, Molly seemed to see the bruises on Hector's knuckles.

She pointed. "What happened to your hand?"

"I punched Crowley where his mystical third eye is supposed to reside."

Molly's chestnut-colored eyebrows knitted. "Crowley? How'd you cross paths with *him*?"

"I was looking for a student of his. Or, a former student. I was looking in conjunction with the police. I told you the other day, just before we met Fargue, that I'm finding myself confronted with the police, often, lately."

"Why were you looking for this 'student'?"

"It may be tied up with all this business of the murders of all these magazine editors these past few days."

Molly put down her wineglass. "Are you accusing me of something?"

"*No.*"

Brinke said, "Mol, honey, a name has come up several times in connection with these murders. The name, or alias, is of this man tied to Crowley. Hector and Hem went to a hotel earlier this morning where this man was supposed to be staying according to Crowley."

Molly said, "And what did you find there, Hector?"

"Three corpses. Two murdered prostitutes whom this man had commissioned, and the murdered hotel manager. He slit the throats of the women and shot the man. But this poet, a fella named Victor Leek, had vanished."

Molly sat back in her chair. She sipped her wine and then crossed her hands across her belly. "Then you can rest easy. I've never heard of Victor Leek. Who is Leek?"

"He is the éminence grise of this movement he's dubbed Nada," Brinke said. "A movement pretty clearly tied to these murders."

"Oh, please," Molly, said. "It's a 'movement' I suppose, yes, but hardly some kind of murder cult or whatever you're both insinuating. It's like Dada . . . Cubism . . . this new thing they're calling Surrealism. It's a label to describe a collective of artists and writers with shared sensibilities."

Hector reached across the table and took Molly's hand. He stroked the back of her hand with this thumb. "Can embracing the void really be called 'a movement'? It seems to me more akin to self-annihilation. A kind of suicide pact."

"Believing in nothing doesn't literally mean to believe in nothing, Hector," Molly said. "Nothing isn't *nothing*. In Nada, *nothing* is treated as *something*."

Hector raised his eyebrows. "Then why not just go ahead and believe in something?"

"Because we believe in nothing," Molly said.

Hector's head was swimming. He sipped more wine. He said, "If you believe that life, all of this, is nothing, then what are you living for?"

Molly smiled. "For *nothing*, don't you see?"

Hector raised his hands, looking to Brinke for help.

Sighing, Molly looked between them, then said, "Hector, do you believe in God?"

"Not for some time."

"Yet you act like a moral man, so far as I can tell, "Molly said. "You're looking for this alleged killer-poet . . . working with the police. You're courteous, conscientious. You're a loyal friend. You give money to little deaf singers. Why do you do all this if you don't expect to be punished or rewarded when you die?"

"Because even if I choose to believe there is no God, I think it's critical to act as if I believe there is," Hector said. "It's what gives life order . . . separates us from the animals."

"So in the face of nothing, you knowingly choose to live as if you believe, even though you don't believe." Molly tipped her head on side. "So how are we different?"

"That's all semantics . . . metaphysical three-card monte," Hector said.

"No, it's a matter of perspective," Molly said, pulling her hand from under Hector's.

"There is a difference, Mol," Brinke said. "Hector's knowing self-deception is informed by a desire to create order. It's toward the collective good. But Nada is driving adherents to despair and some to suicide—a poet named Mueller Hawkins, for instance. He hanged himself, the word 'Nada' pinned to his chest. And it's driving people to murder."

Molly said, "You have proof of that?"

"My leg," Hector said, "I hurt it chasing another poet—a man named Paco Sánchez. He threw acid in the face of Joan Pyle when she answered the door of her apartment. I chased him. He tried to kill me with this." Hector raised his cane and twisted the handle. Both women flinched as the spring-loaded steel blade slid from the end of the sword cane. "I chased him into traffic. He saw he couldn't get away. He recited a bastardized form of a Catholic prayer, inserting the word 'nada' in a few strategic places. Then he threw himself in front of a car. The police have confirmed both of these poets were part of this Nada movement. They're actively investigating the movement now."

Molly looked at her hands. "I didn't know."

Hector said, "Who do you know in this Nada business beyond those ones Hem saw you with? You have to tell me. In circumstances like these, secrets can kill."

"Nobody, really," Molly said. "I should talk to Philippe, see what he knows."

"I don't think that's the best notion," Hector said. "At least not yet."

"What, you think Philippe knows about these killings . . . these suicides?"

"Maybe, yeah," Hector said. "You said you didn't know the name Victor Leek. Who do you—who does Philippe—think heads this movement?"

"I never really thought about it having a leader per se," Molly said. "Maybe Philippe is the same as me—blissfully ignorant of any structure."

"I want to talk to Philippe anyway," Hector said. "Soon as I'm on both feet."

Molly nodded slowly. "Think that's the best thing? Particularly after you and I and what we've shared? After today and all that has happened between us?"

Hector waved a hand. "One is apart from the other."

"I don't see how that can truly be," Molly said. "We've been one person."

Hector thought about questioning Molly regarding Lloyd Blake. Then he decided he'd already pressed her too hard for the present time.


There was a good deal of awkwardness after dinner.

Molly and Brinke cleaned up the table a bit. As they did that, Hector hopped back over to the bed to prop up his leg. He'd so far forgone any more pain medication and meant to continue to do that if he could manage it. As he had truly confessed to Brinke,

Hector couldn't abide the self-annihilation—or at least the *self-compromise*—exacted from him by drugs.

So instead Hector concentrated on the wine...making himself numb, but nowhere near drunk.

Hector wasn't sure what to expect next. He thought about making a joke about breaking out a deck of cards since he was housebound. His lack of mobility put him in mind of something Estelle Quartermain had said about a certain subgenre of mystery novels: "Nobody really solves mysteries from the confines of an armchair."

*More's the pity*, Hector thought, surveying his bandaged leg as he lay in his rumpled bed.

He realized then, with perhaps unconscious expectation, that he had positioned himself in the middle of his bed. He scooted back to the left side of the bed—Brinke's side, in Hector's mind—and shoved off, hopping on one foot to the window.

Molly said, "You're going to break your neck."

"I'm fine," Hector said. He sat on the windowsill and looked out the dormers. Across the street, a trio of men stood in the shelter of the church's entryway. They were all dressed in black and standing far enough away from the gaslights to keep themselves bathed in shadow. Hector might not even have seen them but for the glowing ends of their cigarettes. The angles of the cigarettes all shifted at once and Hector sensed they were looking up...perhaps watching him as he sat backlit in the window. He realized then what a fine target he might be presenting if there was something sinister about the three men and their presence on the street below his window. If they had a rifle or two hidden under their coats?

Hector said, "Molly, you see anyone as you were coming or going? Anybody give you any trouble?"

"No. Why?"

Hector shrugged. "Just being paranoid, probably. I mean, people answering the door and having acid pitched in their faces... being stabbed and pushed off bridges...thrown in front of cars, or throwing themselves in front of cars. Murdered prostitutes. It accumulates on a man's mind in a nasty way."

Hector stood up and hopped back to the couch. He noticed Brinke drifting to his vacated window and looking around. He saw her head drop a bit to the angle of the church's entrance. She said, "It's starting to snow again." Then she closed the curtain and moved to the next window to close that one. She said, "Anything else you're going to need right now, Hector? Because this jumping around is too risky. And it's got to be driving your downstairs neighbor to distraction."

"No, I'm all done for the moment," Hector said, settling back on his couch. He smiled and said, "Hem was likening me to Ahab this morning."

After Brinke left it, Molly drifted to Hector's window. She pulled back the drape and peeked through. Watching her, Brinke said to Hector, "So, who's your Moby-Dick?"

From the window, not looking back to give Hector any sense of whether or not she meant it as a joke, Molly said, "I sense that might be me."

Brinke looked at Hector and shook her head. She poured three glasses of wine, handing one to Hector. Brinke turned down the lights. She handed a glass to Molly, then said, "Dessert?" She held up the box of Alice's remaining brownies. "Six left. Just enough for two each," she said.

"You two can share mine," Hector said.

Hector was still sitting on the couch, watching them sleep. He'd been sitting there for perhaps two hours, still dressed . . . still nursing his wine, just watching them.

He'd watched them for some time before they fell asleep, too.

Brinke had sat next to Molly on the window ledge as they sipped their wine and ate their drug-laced brownies. After a while, Molly had taken Brinke's empty glass, then kissed her.

It went like that...the two of them eventually drifting to the bed to make love.

Occasionally one of them would look at Hector—Molly blushing; Brinke challenging him with her dark, bedroom eyes.

For his part, Hector had sat there, dressed, watching. He sat there with his bum leg, sword cane, and wineglass...like some decadent gimp libertine, or Aleister Crowley–manqué. *C'est de bon goût.*

Hector had tried to convince himself it was some kind of penitence to watch and not participate. Except that he very much enjoyed watching.

They were naked under the sheets now, tangled in one another's arms. Molly was softly snoring. There was room for Hector on Brinke's side of the bed. He checked his pocket watch: nearly midnight. He should take off his clothes and join them in his bed...for sleep. He was a little sorry they'd left no room for him in the middle.

A soft knock at the door. Frowning, Hector picked up his cane, decided, *Fuck it,* and put a little weight on his lame foot. It seemed fine...felt good, actually, to work it a bit. He limped to the door, carrying his cane in his hand. Mindful of the potential for an oil of vitriol pitching, he said, *"Qui va là?"*

"Lasso? Open up."

Hector opened the door and Hem squinted in the low light. He looked Hector up and down. Hem said softly, "You're having a late one. And you're not supposed to be on that foot yet. Frankly, I expected to find you laid low by WCW's goodies."

"They'd do the trick, too well. I know from earlier. So I'm weaning myself. And I can't sleep. *Nuit blanche.* Probably from all the 'sleep' earlier."

Hem was looking at the bed. He turned his head on side. "Is that what it looks like?"

Hector couldn't resist. "It was a few hours ago."

Hem smiled crookedly. "Jesus. Having a wife who won't lose

the baby weight, and a kid who cries twenty hours a day... You know, Lasso, sometimes it's a bloody fucking bitch being your friend. Jesus. Well, at least you've effected a rapprochement between the two women."

"That's one word for it. For the record, I didn't instigate it."

"But you didn't say no. You lucky son of a bitch."

Hector winced, leaning again on Hem's shoulder. Now his foot hurt a little. "Yeah, well, you got the last part right. And I await the savage balancing of the scales. What brings you around, Hem?"

"Bad news. Two items. Joan didn't make it."

Hector cursed, then said, "In some ways, based on things Simon told me about her injuries, that might actually be the kindest thing."

"My feeling on that score, too," Hem said. "Joan was wrecked by that acid. I saw. Wouldn't have been much of a life if she had pulled through. At least she's gotten it over with. The dying, I mean."

"What's the other bad news?"

"Jeremy Hunt."

Hector said, "Your friend, the tubercular poet?"

"Not anymore. They found him in his office, stabbed in the chest."

# PART III

mardi

# Twenty-five

*Hector reached out, his* eyes still closed. He found that he was alone in his bed. Another note from Brinke lay on her pillow:

Our dear Hector:

We decided it was best to slip out very early, before we'd risk any embarrassing entanglements with Germaine.

We're going to freshen up, then have breakfast together. Maybe visit Sylvia's for a time, too.

We want to meet about four at your little café on the Rue des Bourdonnais. A place, we figure, where we can have some part of Paris—and you, of course—to ourselves.

Right, then. See you at four.

Your girls,
M & B

Below that was a hastily scrawled postcript:

Hector:

Think I'm going to be meeting some of *them,* soon. I swear I'll be careful.

Love, Brinke

That last didn't please Hector.

As a precaution if Molly returned, Hector tore up the letter and threw the fragments in the wastepaper basket by the nightstand on Brinke's side of the bed. He stretched and felt himself there; he wasn't so raw or sore anymore. He flexed his foot a bit as best he could with all the traction bandages bound around his ankle. No pain there either. He sat up and swung his legs to the floor. Hector put a little weight on his injured ankle and found there was hardly any discomfort.

He figured with the ankle support of his boots he could be reasonably mobile.

Hector finished dressing after his breakfast and bath. He re-wrapped his ankle, forced his foot into his boot, and stood. He walked to the window without his cane, with just the slightest of limps. He pulled back the drape and looked for signs of anyone watching his building. Nothing suspicious. The downside of that, he decided, was that any sentinels might have followed Brinke and Molly.

He checked the time: not yet eight. There was time for some writing . . . it was early yet. Hector looked at his typewriter . . . saw a pile of manuscript there, but then realized it was not his own. He brushed a single black hair from atop the stack of papers, turned them over and read,

TRIANGLE
by
Bud Grant

Hector told himself that Brinke would likely sneak a look at his novel in progress—do it without a second thought—if she was afforded access to it. And Hector had been pretty liberal with his own manuscript . . . leaving it by his typewriter or the bed. Probably—or so he convinced himself—Brinke had already read what there was of *Rhapsody in Black.*

Hector gathered up Brinke's manuscript. He muttered, *"Quid pro quo,"* and began to read.

Hector took his time, walking slowly down the Rue Guynemer, cane in hand, its shaft resting on his shoulder. Hector was determined not to baby his leg, but rather to force recuperation through use.

As he walked, his thoughts kept returning to Brinke's manuscript. In a sense, he was intensely proud of her. The sometimes florid, always urbane, and frequently mocking third-person voice that Brinke employed in her Connor Templeton novels was nowhere to be found in the pages of her crime novel.

In its place, Brinke had adopted a blunt, first-person point of view. The story seemed to be inspired by the little magazine murders. Brinke's narrator was a young American hard case named Horace Lester, a dark-haired, blue-eyed expatriate caught between two beautiful young American women in a treacherous three-way love affair.

Hector, of course, recognized himself immediately in Horace Lester. Anyone who knew Hector and eventually read Brinke's book would recognize him, too, he figured. *Triangle* was shaping up to be a brazen roman à clef.

But in estimating Brinke's probable composition speed, and measuring that against her initiation of their ménage à trois with Molly, well, that was where things got a little unsettling—deeply perplexing Hector.

He found himself feeling a little like a chess piece: some pawn caught within a pitiless artist's ongoing project of creation.

Hector often felt he wasn't really living in his own life in the sense of being entirely *present* . . . never fully in the moment. He always found himself a little outside himself when life became intense. A part of himself was always standing back, reflecting on things as they unfolded . . . gauging his own reaction to a dangerous situation, to an argument, or to a particularly passionate moment in bed. The writer in him was always a little apart from Hector, watching. Sometimes, Hector thought that made him a monster. It hadn't occurred to him that anyone else could be like him in that sense. And it had also never occurred to Hector that someone with his own traits might endeavor to shape their own life and the lives of those around them toward a particular artistic end.

The more he reflected on all of it, the more Brinke's manuscript chilled him.

At the same time, Hector grudgingly admired Brinke's audacity. And more importantly—most importantly of all—Brinke was succeeding in her experiment to stretch herself as a *writer*. She was convincingly putting across a male voice and attitude . . . catching Hector's own cadences and much of his swagger.

But the shadow play of Brinke's crime novel and her love affair with Hector—and now, Molly, too—rattled him.

Hector kept trying to chicken-and-egg it all. He tried to settle in his own mind whether Brinke's life informed her fiction, or instead whether she was presently living her life—driving Molly's and his own life—as fodder for Brinke's new creation.

And he couldn't decide which was the more unsettling prospect.

Hector's mind wouldn't let it go . . . dropping it for a time, then circling back to gnaw at it again.

Then *life* intruded.

Three men were following him. Hector saw them reflected in the angled glass of a storefront's display window. The three men wore black suits. They had glum demeanors. Hector sized them up: *aesthetes.*

Hector veered into a café, hat pulled low so nobody could describe him well later. In profile, he ordered a whisky, neat, then watched in the mirror behind the bar as the three men picked a table nearby him. Hector slammed back his whisky, then asked for directions to the restroom.

He picked up his cane and walked along the bar to a narrow corridor leading to the restrooms. Across from the men's room, there was a door opening onto an alley. Hector tried the door, found it unlocked, and stepped out into the cold. He dropped his sword cane on the ground across the door's threshold, blocking the door from closing. Hector made his way down the alley and back around to the front of the café. Through the café's front window, he watched the men inside confer. One checked his pocket watch. He nodded at the other two. The man's two companions rose and walked back toward the restrooms. Hector saw them veer through the open door into the alley.

Hector slipped back into the café and walked briskly up behind the remaining black-clad man. The man seemed to Hector vaguely Asian. Hector was carrying his leather jacket over one arm. He walked up behind the man, leaned into his ear and said, "Stand up and walk out with me. I've got a gun pressed to your spine. Come *now.*"

Hector got a handful of the man's collar in his hand and walked him out of the café. They moved several doors down and turned a corner . . . walked a ways and then turned one more corner. Hector stopped at a café with some chairs and tables still set out front in spite of the weather. He said, "Sit."

Hector spun around a chair across from the stranger and plopped down, his left arm draped across the back of the cane chair, his right arm under the table. "Now sit still," Hector said, "or I'll shoot and leave you here with the same predicament as your guru, Victor Leek. You know—all yearning and no plumbing."

The man looked over Hector's shoulder. Hector could see behind himself in the reflection of the café's window. There was nobody behind him. Hector said, "Don't look so hopeful. Your friends don't look too sharp. They could be hours finding you. It's just us now, pal. What's your handle, Ace?"

Confusion: " 'Handle'?"

"Your name, what is it? *Comment vous appelez-vous?*"

"I don't want to tell you."

"You don't have that option. I have a gun pointed at your crotch. That means I get my way."

"You've outsmarted yourself, Monsieur Lassiter. You won't shoot me here in the streets. Not with so many passing by."

"Don't be so sure. And either way, you're my prisoner short of instigating a footrace, and then you'd just piss me off. I'd likely shoot you in the legs or ass to drop you. That would be the *first* shot. And let's be realistic. This is Paris. We're surrounded by Frenchmen who are going to blanch at the prospect of engaging a tall crazy American waving around a very big gun. Now, what's your name, Slick?"

"Ravel ..." Hesitation. "Jacques Ravel."

Hector sighed. *"Ravel?* Like Maurice Ravel? And *Jacques*, like the name of this joint here?" Hector inclined his head at the café's stenciled window. "Pretty lame lying, *Jacques*. But the phony moniker will do for now."

A waiter, bald, round, and annoyed, ducked his head out. "Come inside you two, yes? It's warm. Come inside and I'll take your order."

Hector smiled. *"Pardon, non.* My friend is claustrophobic. Now, what'll it be, J?" While he waited, to the waiter Hector said, *"Une bière, s'il vous plaît."* Hector smiled at his prisoner. "C'mon, for you, Jacques?"

Silence.

*"Jacques* ... drink with me. If I start thinking of us as mates, I'm less likely to do something you'll hate. You know ... like sending you off somewhere. You know—*aller simple.*"

The man said, *"Une bière."*

"Make it two each," Hector said to the perturbed waiter. "We're parched and it'll save you another trip out into this barbarous cold."

Hector smiled at his captive. "Now, no more sorry lies. You're what, a poet? A painter?"

Silence.

With his left hand, Hector pulled out his cigarettes, shook the pack, and pulled one out with this teeth. He struck a match on the underside of the table. "I'm beginning to think I kidnapped the wrong nihilist."

Hector tossed a cigarette and a match to the man. "Smoke it. Smoke it like it's your last. Because you keep foot-dragging like this and that's how things are apt to go. You need to modulate your attitude, pronto."

The stranger lit his cigarette. Hector said, "Look, pal—Jacques—*whatever*. I just want to know where to find Victor Leek . . . Oswald Rook. Just give me the name your goddamn guru is employing today and where he can be found. Simple, *n'est-ce pas*?"

The man blew smoke through both nostrils. "You're a fool. Do you know how many of us there are?" He blew a little smoke at Hector's face, but the wind blew it back in his own.

Hector smiled and said, "Keep stonewalling and your club is going to be smaller by at least one." Hector looked at the man sitting across from him . . . a small man smoking his cigarette and trying to look insolent.

Hector wondered what Horace Lester would do if confronted with the nihilist. Probably shoot the bastard in cold blood. Horace didn't seem to fuck around.

Then Hector was seized by another option. He dipped his left hand into his jacket's pocket, emptying the paper envelope of pain pills given him by Dr. Williams. Hector counted out four capsules, cupping them in his hand.

Their waiter returned. Hector lined the amber bottles up in a row, one behind the other from his prisoner's perspective. As he arrayed the bottles of beer, Hector dropped the pain tablets in the rearmost bottle. He gave them a second to dissolve, then scooted the rear two bottles around and pushed them across the table. "Drink up, J."

Fifty-fifty the man would drain the tainted bottle of beer first.

Hector suppressed a smile as the man picked up the drugged beer. Hector raised his own bottle, said, "Shall we drink to *nothing*?" They sipped. Hector said, "'Hail *nada*, full of *nada*...*nada* is with thee.' Who came up with that ditty?"

The stranger shrugged. With a shaking hand, he dragged his sleeve across his mouth, wiping off a drool trail. Hector figured he badly misjudged how long it would take the pills to affect the nihilist. The man was much smaller than Hector...and he'd been dosed with twice as many hits of morphine than Hem had administed to Hector.

Their waiter, still palpably annoyed, leaned out again. "All is all right?"

Hector winked. "Great. *Les toilettes?*"

The waiter pointed behind himself.

Counting out francs, Hector said, "You don't look so well, Jacques. C'mon." He hauled the stranger to his feet and half-carrying him walked the man to the restroom. "WC time," he said. Jacques could barely support himself now. One man was in the tiny restroom—standing at a urinal. Hector figured he didn't have much time before his captive fell into full swoon...maybe even lapsed into a coma. His arm around Jacques, one hand working at the nihilist's belt buckle, Hector, with what he hoped sounded like carnal urgency, said to the man at the urinal, *"Bonjour.* You won't be much longer will you?"

The stranger looked at Hector, looked at Jacques, then quickly buttoned his own pants and left the restroom.

Hector opened the stall door and wedged Jacques inside, pushing him back onto the toilet seat. Hector unbuttoned the man's pants and unstrapped his belt. Hector pulled the man's pants and underwear down around his ankles. Then Hector backed out and closed the stall door. He climbed atop the radiator. He leaned over the partition until he could reach the lock on the inside of Jacques's compartment. Hector threw the bolt, locking the nihilist within the stall.

Hector stepped down off the radiator, went to the sink, and

washed his hands. As Hector dried his hands, he called back to the man he'd locked in the stall: "Sweet dreams, J... until we meet again."

Hector hadn't forgotten Brinke's plan for visting funerals to gather information. François Laurencin was to be buried at noon at Cimetière St-Vincent. Mueller Hawkins was to be interred at two at Cimetière du Montparnasse. Hector returned to his apartment to change into something mourning-appropriate. He checked his dark suit in the mirror. He figured he looked like quite the nihilist, once he put on his black fedora.

Germaine, watching him plod down the steps said, "You look as though you're dressed for a funeral."

"*Deux.*"

She looked sad. "Not friends I hope? How are you bearing up?"

"*Comme ci, comme ça.*"

"You look very tired."

"It's been a trying few days." He kissed her hand. "I'll see you later."

"Have you and your fiancée set a date, yet?"

"*Non.* But you'll be the first invited."

"She is very smart... very beautiful."

Hector nodded. "Isn't she?"

As he stepped out into the cold, he ran into a blond, violet-eyed young man of about his own age. Hector said, *"Pardon,"* then, scowling, "Philippe?"

Molly's boyfriend, the painter, nodded, without saying hello. "I'm looking for Molly... have you seen her?" He sounded a little drunk.

"Not recently, no," Hector said. He figured if he wasn't asked to define "recently" his lie would stand well enough. Philippe looked a bit haggard. Hector had never really studied the young painter before, though he'd known Philippe for perhaps two or three months longer than he'd known Molly. There was a shiny small scar on Philippe's cheek, and another under his left ear, disappearing down into the collar of his shirt. His eyes were close in hue to Molly's unusual shade of violet. Hector figured it might be the only thing the two had in common.

Philippe said, "Where are you going, Hector? I could walk along . . . talk."

"Sure, Phil, for a few minutes."

"What's the rush?"

"I've got a friend to bury."

"Oh. I'm sorry." Phillip seemed to hesitate, then said, "About Molly . . . I'm not sure we're going to make it, Hector."

"What do you mean?"

"I think we're growing apart."

Hector nodded slowly. "Don't you love Molly anymore, Phil?"

"I love her very much, Hector. She's my life." Hector sensed he meant it. Philippe said, "But her mind is . . . elsewhere. Surely you must see it . . . must have sensed it these past few months. She's in love with you, Hector. I want her to be happy. No hard feelings, *n'est-ce pas*? If you can make her happy, then you two must be together."

Hector stopped walking, turned to face the painter.

"You must be mistaken, you must—"

"Please," Philippe said. "Don't do that. I know you know what I've said is true. You're too smart, too insightful to miss the looks she gives you. What, you're not attracted to her?"

"She's very attractive."

"But you still think of her as . . . a sister?"

Hector didn't think he could lie outright, and given the previous day's and night's events, he wasn't sure he should. "Less all the time."

"Good. Then I'm going to break it off with her, Hector. Clear the path for you."

"Slow down, Phil. And I'm not sure that's the best idea, Philippe, even if I maybe welcome that 'clear path' you're offering." Hector checked his watch. He was in danger of being late.

Philippe said, "You have someplace to be?"

"I told you, Phil, a funeral. Look, please don't do anything rash. Let's try and get a drink. I'll drop by the Rotonde later today or tomorrow. We'll talk more about this." Hector bustled off, not waiting for a reply, whistling for a cab, showing the painter his back.

Another gray day in another cemetery. Hector sat in a taxi, watching the mourners. He saw no woman in white on a hill this time.

The widow Laurencin was being comforted by another woman in black. The second woman looked familiar to Hector. Something about her black dress . . . something in her posture. Then he remembered the widow from the previous day's funeral . . . the woman whom had thrown herself across her husband's coffin. Hector nodded slowly—one newly widowed woman consoling another. As the wives of little magazine editors, it made sense they'd be acquainted.

A quartet of black-clad men stood off a ways from the other mourners. One of them was playing an accordion. Hector scanned more mourners' faces. He thought perhaps he'd spot Brinke or maybe even Molly, but apart from Lloyd Blake's widow, Hector saw nobody he could identify.

He felt under his coat and patted the butt of his Colt. He made up his mind. Hector said to his driver, "Wait here, please."

He set off toward the four black-clad men. As he approached them, the one playing accordion stopped, then pointed at Hector. The four men began walking away, turning and stalking off, hands thrust deep into the pockets of their black coats . . . the one swinging his accordion at his side.

Hector picked up the pace. As he drew closer, he said, "One of you boys wouldn't be Victor Leek, would you?"

The men were walking faster now.

Hector called, "No? How's about Oswald Rook?"

One of the men looked back over his shoulder, saw Hector was closing on them—that man began jogging. The three men with him also shifted to a trot. "What, you boys like to kill folks, then come and fuck up their funerals?" Hector looked back over his shoulder. They were out of sight of the mourners. His ankle was starting to hurt from fast-walking. Hector pulled out his Colt and called, "Next man takes a step gets shot in the back of the knees."

The four men stutter-stepped, exchanged looks, then bolted.

Hector knew he couldn't give chase. Cursing, he holstered his Colt. He limped back toward the funeral site. A woman in black was walking to meet him—Lloyd Blake's widow. "Thank you," she said. "Thank you for chasing them off, the cretins. I wish you had been around yesterday. They made a mockery of my husband's funeral."

He took her hand. "My name is Hector Lassiter, Mrs. Blake. All condolences. I was present yesterday, but in a coach. I injured my leg."

"Yes, you're still limping. Here, take my arm."

Hector slipped his arm through the widow's. "You knew my husband then, Monsieur Lassiter?"

"*Non*, but I know people who knew him. And there have been so many killed like Monsieur Laurencin, and your husband. All these magazine editors attacked. I've been working a bit with the police. These men I chased away, do you know who they are?"

Mrs. Blake shook her head. "No. *Agents provocateurs*? Dadaists, perhaps?"

"You're asking *me*, Madame?"

Mrs. Blake said, "I thought perhaps you would know—since you saw them yesterday, and chased them away today."

"Actually, I thought they might be people interested in buying your husband's magazine. I'm told the magazine is for sale."

"It's not. And I haven't decided what I'll do with it now. The magazine was his great passion. I hate to end it, if for that reason alone. And who told you it was for sale?"

"A woman I met yesterday at your husband's graveside service." Hector bit his lip and decided to risk it. "A young woman named Kitty Pike told me that. She said she was a kind of, well, employee of your husband's. An artist and ad designer."

"Oh." The widow scowled. "Granted, I was in a state, but I didn't see Kitty. I'm very surprised she made the effort. I wonder how I missed her?"

Hector was confused. There was no tone of anger or jealousy that he could detect in the widow Blake's voice. He said, "Well, she was hanging on the fringes, a good deal off from the other mourners. I saw her there, by herself, and I was intrigued enough to seek her out. To chat for a while."

"You sign, then?"

"I beg your pardon?"

"You sign? You communicate through sign language? You know, on account of Kitty's condition?"

"Her condition?"

The widow disengaged her arm from Hector's. "Who are you, really?"

"I really am Hector Lassiter. And I really am working with the police ... informally. You can confirm that with Commissaire Aristide Simon."

"If you met her, 'chatted' with her, then why don't you know that Kitty Pike is quite deaf?"

Hector frowned. He pulled his overcoat's collar up around his face. "Why indeed?" He stopped and took the woman's arm again. "You'd better describe Kitty Pike to me."

"Perhaps thirty. Heavyset. She has diabetes, as well. She wears glasses ... very thick lenses. Last summer, she lost her right leg below the knee as a result of bad circulation. She's housebound now. That's why I was surprised you said she had attended the service."

Hector said aloud, "So whom did I meet yesterday?"

"You're starting to frighten me," Blake's widow said. "What did this woman who passed herself off as Kitty Pike look like?"

Hector described her. Mrs. Blake wrapped her arm through his again and began walking. "I don't know anyone meeting that description," she said. "Not at all. This is quite unsettling."

"You're going to be offended, or angry at me again," Hector said. "But I must confess that she claimed to be your husband's mistress."

The widow's voice went flat: "My husband seems to have had at least one of *those*."

"Was there a name you ever heard for her? Something with a 'W,' maybe?"

"Do you have a specific name in mind, Monsieur Lassiter?"

"Margaret. Margaret W."

"*Non,*" the widow said. "*Non.* That name is not remotely familiar to me. But this woman that my husband . . ." She took a breath. "This woman of his, I think, is a brunette."

"You've caught a glimpse of her?"

"I found black hairs in our bed."

"I'm sorry." Hector said, "There *are* other names that I'd like to run by you."

"Go ahead."

"Victor Leek?"

She shrugged.

"Oswald Rook?"

"Not him, either. I'm sorry, Monsieur Lassiter."

"Hector."

They had almost reached the graveside, hard up against an ivy-covered stone wall. Mourners were taking turns throwing cold, snow-kissed dirt onto the coffin. A symbolic gesture at best, Hector figured, since the coffin was to be placed in a crypt.

"This woman, Margaret? Someone you suspect?"

"Someone I know," Hector said. "She's worrying me because of some new acquaintances. Ones like the ones I chased off, maybe."

"*Mal entourée?*"

"Quite." They fell into the line in order to sift dirt onto the coffin. He said, "Madame Blake, do you have any theory about who killed your husband?"

"My guess is the raven-haired woman . . . Lloyd's whore."

His taxi driver said, "Where now? A bar, I'll bet."

"*Non. Je voudrais descendre à Cimetière du Montparnasse.*"

The taxi driver screwed up his face. "What, not another funeral?"

"That's right."

"*Pardon*: You must have very bad luck, Monsieur."

"Perhaps next month will be luckier."

# Twenty-six

*Wet fluffy flakes twirled* down on the latest band of mourners. For the third time in the same prayer, Hector took off his black hat and shook off the snow from the crown and brim. He pulled his collar up closer around his face. He'd decided Brinke had abandoned all effort to follow her own plan of attending the day's funerals for clues.

Maybe she and Molly had found warmer, sweeter places to be.

For his part, Hector had arrived early; killed a little time visiting Guy de Maupassant's grave. He thought about spitting on that of Charles Baudelaire—perhaps the first of the "abyss lovers." Hector spent too much time staring at a statue of a woman in a hood, bent over, head in hands . . . the embodiment of grief. He'd found himself moved to place a hand on her shoulder, surprised for just an instant to find her shoulder was cold and hard like the stone that it was.

A hand patted Hector's shoulder. "You're a marvel, Monsieur Lassiter. Yesterday, you professed never to hear of Mueller Hawkins. Today, here you are, paying your respects."

Hector said, "Commissaire Simon. Didn't know you cared so much for Hawkins either."

"I had some time. Thought it might be worth my effort to see who showed up. Your thought as well?"

"It was a thought," Hector said.

Simon smiled, his hand still gripping Hector's shoulder. "Unless you think it's bad luck, or you're caught up in the moment, I propose we go find a warm fire and some good coffee."

"I concur."

They wended their through the cemetery, past sculptures of winged, long dead children and lost loves. Simon said, "All this care and money for the dead. How long until you think they find some rationale for digging these up, like the ones gone before? How long until they find some reason to discard the bones of these deeper underground in order to make room for the next round of corpses?"

Hector said, "It's not an issue back home in America. I don't think we're capable of running out of room to bury our dead."

The cop lit one of his Gauloises. "The blessing and curse of a young and vast country, I suppose. And here is my car."

Hector slid in and Simon slid in beside him. "You live on the Rue Vavin, yes? I'll keep your walk short for your leg." Simon instructed his driver to take them to a café on the Boulevard Raspail.

In the café, Hector settled into his chair by the crackling fire and checked his pocket watch—a few minutes after two. He sipped his red wine.

Simon asked, "You have somewhere you need to be?"

"Not for a couple of hours yet."

"I won't detain you . . . *I* have places to be. But I did want some coffee. And perhaps some advice. I have some photos, if you're up to it."

"Surely."

"Crime photographs."

"I'm going to need some wine then." Hector signaled their waiter and ordered himself a bottle of red wine. Hector said, "These photos—anyone I know?"

"A man named Jeremy Hunt. He was a friend of yours?"

"No," Hector said. "But I know him by name. He was another magazine publisher. I hear he was murdered. You should caution your coroner, because Hunt supposedly had tuberculosis."

"I'll do that, though the information comes treacherously tardily." Simon lit another cigarette, shook out the match. "These literary types, they fall around you like flies, my friend. Yet you endure."

Hector sipped his wine. He shrugged. "You said you have photos."

"I do." Simon lifted a leatherette case from the chair beside him and unfastened it. He pulled out three black-and-white photos and handed them to Hector. "Not terribly gruesome. Not like some other things you've seen recently. But a corpse is a corpse is a corpse and that is always unsettling."

"May it always remain so."

Hector placed the three photos side by side on the table, staring at them. They might as well be the same photo, really—just taken at slightly different angles. One was cropped to encompass everything from the waist up.

"It's the peculiar posture that you'll of course note," Simon said.

Hunt, a dangerously thin-looking man with sparse, sandy hair and a wormy mustache, lay on his back on an Oriental carpet. He was staring up at the camera with sightless eyes, his mouth slightly opened. He wore dark slacks, an open vest, and a white shirt stained with blood. The man's thin legs were stretched straight out.

It was Hunt's hands and arms that looked unnatural. The man's right arm was crooked at the elbow. His hand rested palm-down, three fingers extended toward his toes; the pinkie tucked under the thumb. The left arm was also crooked at the elbow, but the left hand rested palm-up. Three fingers of that hand were also extended above his head; the left hand's pinkie again folded under the thumb. Hector could see only one interpretation; one he wasn't prepared to share with Simon. Instead he said, pointing at the left hand, "Hunt was American. He was a bit older than me. But three fingers, that could be the Boy Scout's salute."

Simon scowled. "As he was dying, he took the trouble for that? And what of the right hand?"

"Unconscious symmetry, perhaps? He was dying, as you said . . . hardly a time for thinking . . . not thinking enough to send messages." Hector curled his lip, "Not outside of one of Estelle Quartermain's unreadable novels."

Simon smiled. "You've shamed me with that, as I'm sure you intended." He inhaled some smoke deeply into his lungs and let it out slowly. "Still, my instincts are against this being anything less than a message of some kind. Perhaps *three* and *three*. Or, together, *six*. But what does *that* mean?" The inspector picked up one of the photos, held it close to his face. "Or, perhaps not *numbers* . . ."

Hector swallowed hard. An inspiration: "Where in the room was the body found?"

"Essentially, in the middle of the sitting room, not far from a couch. Why?"

"Was his head pointed toward, or away from the front door?"

Simon ground out his cigarette, watching Hector. "His head was pointed toward the door."

Arching an eyebrow, smiling as if he was sharing some epiphany, Hector said, "Then perhaps he meant for you to see what he was trying to tell you this way, as you would approach his body upon entering. Upside down, I mean. From the perspective you have right now, sitting across from me and looking at this photo in front of me."

"Upside down, so to speak. Yes, that's quite astute of you. You'd really make a fine detective, with the proper training." Then Simon frowned. "But, *non*, look, it's the same either way . . ."

Hector sat back in his chair, lifted his glass. Well, he'd tried. He looked at the photo facing him. He looked from the dead man's right hand to his left. Hector couldn't imagine the fingers imparting any message other than initials: MW.

"You should take more care with yourself, Hector. Visiting these funerals, giving these men chase. You'll make yourself a target, if you haven't already, my brash friend."

Hector shrugged, posturing. "*They've* made it a matter of life and death. Provoked, I will respond. *A la guerre comme à la outrance.*" Hector held up a photo. "May I hold on to this for a time?"

"I'll allow it. But don't share it around."

"No. I just want to look at it some more. Brood over it. May spark some further epiphany. Any luck at Suzy?"

Simon said, "Ah yes, this Leek or Rook—your bête noire. And mine, too, I suppose. No, nothing turned up at that brothel."

Simon was barely out the door of the café when Hem wandered in. Hem whistled at the photographs of Hunt's body. "Jesus, like something from a mystery novel, isn't it?"

"Exactly. I figure it for posed," Hector said.

Hem pulled on his glasses and looked again at the photo. "Posed? You mean, like by some photographer, going for composition? *Mise-en-scène?*"

Hector sipped his wine. "More like someone who has read one too many facile mystery novels and is trying to frame someone. 'Posed' was a poor word choice. *Staged.*"

"Yeah? By whom?"

"Look at those fingers in tandem, Hem. Molly Wilder is my bet. I mean, as object of the frame."

"But you're concerned Molly's tied up with this Nada stuff, Lasso. What, you change your mind about all that when she crawled into your bed with Brinke?"

"I'm going to ignore that crack, Hem, and only confide that I suspect I've been made to be concerned about Molly's so-called ties to these killings."

"By whom?"

"You . . . maybe others. You in innocence, of course." Hector hastened to add that last as he saw Hem's neck and cheeks flush. "But you colored my thoughts on this, Hem. You locked me into a kind of tunnel vision that others may be exploiting now. There's more, too. But I've got to go."

"Where?"

"Men's room, a ways from here."

"Why not use the can here?"

"I left something in the other one."

"They're burying Joan tomorrow."

Hector said, "Think there's some record for the number of funerals attended in a single week?"

"Not any record I'd want to break." Hem pointed at Hector's half-finished bottle of wine. "You're not going to finish that?"

"Haven't the time. You do it for me."


The men's room was empty save for the stall—the one that Hector had locked the nihilist inside.

Hector climbed back atop the radiator, mounting with his good ankle.

"Jacques Ravel" was still there, head against the stall wall, a long drool trail sliding down his neck. But his eyelids were fluttering . . . he was close to coming to.

Hector lowered himself from the radiator, let himself out, and took up a seat close by the hallway leading back to the restrooms. He sat with his back to the hallway. He pulled out his notebook and pen. He checked his watch—three o'clock. Hector worked on his novel's newest chapter for about fifteen minutes before he heard heavy footfalls on the tile of the corridor leading back to the bathroom. A shadow crossed his table. He watched "Jacques Ravel," awkward and heavy on uncertain feet, stumble through the café and out into the gray afernoon light. Hector closed his notebook and followed.

Jacques walked past six or seven storefronts, leaning heavily on bollards and benches to keep from falling. He finally decided he needed a taxi. Hector signaled for one, as well.

Hector's taxi pulled curbside and he slid in. He said to the driver, "See that taxi there? Where it goes, we go."

The other taxi journeyed to the Rue Quincampoix. Hector knew the street by low reputation—a string of hotels housing prostitutes; a varied array of houses of pleasure.

"Jacques Ravel," a little steadier on his feet now, Hector thought, exited his taxi, spilling bills to the driver. One or two notes fluttered into the slush of the street. Some prostitutes approached Jacques and he waved them away with a shaking hand. Hector said to his taxi driver, "Don't leave. I'll be back, and quite soon, I think."

"Back soon from one of these?" His driver nodded at the pleasure houses, looking skeptical.

"I'm police," Hector said. "That man is a suspect. Now wait for me."

Hector followed the man to what looked like a private residence, but for the red light above the door. He gave the man ten minutes, smoking two cigarettes and turning down the overtures of perhaps a half-dozen street tarts in the interval. Then Hector rang the bell.

An enormous ex-whore-graduated-to-madam met him at the door. She shook a brass bell that she carried in her pudgy hand and several girls in various states of undress lined up near the door. Hector walked along the line, looking them over. One wore more clothes than the others. She looked new to the job. She held her shoulders straighter than the rest and met his gaze. Her eyes were blue—cobalt and darker and deeper than Hector's own. Her hair was as black as Brinke's, but long and straight and worn very much against fashion. Hector thought there was something French in her features and pale skin. But not French "proper"—more like Creole-French, from back home.

He said to the whore, *"Comment vous appelez-vous?"*

"Solange."

A strong American accent. Hector smiled at the fat, buxom madam. *"Solange* will do me fine."

"You pay *me*," the madam said. Hector bought fifteen minutes of "Solange's" time.

That prompted some giggles from the other whores that the madam tried to stifle with a quick stare.

Hector took Solange's hand and followed her down a corridor to an anonymous, relatively clean room.

"We haven't much time," she said. "What is your preference?"

"I'm American, like you," Hector said. "I don't know a single 'Solange' back home. What's your given name? Mine is Hector."

The black-haired woman said, "Are you here to talk? To try and save me? What are you? Some missionary? A romantic?"

"I'm police, investigating some murders," Hector said. "I won't threaten your position here, and I won't require more of you than some honest answers, which, frankly, may save your life. Your life, or the lives of others of these women in this house."

"Victoria, that's my name. I'm . . . I don't mean to stay here long. Doing this work, I mean."

Hector thought to himself that none of them ever did. And every day, a few more fallen women who never got off their backs or knees for one reason or another proved him right. "You're quite beautiful," Hector said. She was—despite some palpable self-hatred. But she wasn't hard-looking yet. Hector sensed she hadn't fully given up hope. If Victoria cut her hair and wore better clothes—squared her shoulders more—hell, she could be Brinke's younger, just as pretty sister, Hector figured.

As his mind drifted in different directions, Hector said, "A man came in before me. Do you know who he is?"

"Not a customer," she said. She hesitated. "More like a visitor. I could get in some serious trouble for telling you this. Discretion is everything here. We're supposed to be very discreet. And, occasionally, that woman you paid listens at the door. She looks through the keyhole to make certain that nothing, well, you know, *sinister* is going on."

Hector looked around. The bed was positioned on the wall opposite the door, in full view of the keyhole. He sat down on the bed and said, "All I want you to do is kneel in front of me, Victoria. Do that, and move your head a bit now and then. You know, as if . . ."

"I understand."

Hector tangled his hand in her long, black hair, occasionally gently moving her head as he would if she had really taken him into her mouth. He said, "This man who visits, whom does he visit?"

"Another man living upstairs."

"Does this man living up there ever ask women up?"

"Sometimes. A woman here I like, not a friend, but one who is friendly, she went up yesterday. I've not seen her again."

"I doubt you ever will. You should never go up there if called. Promise me that."

"I can't."

"Don't go up tonight at least. Find some excuse if you're asked. Say you have your curse. Run . . . take a cab. I'll leave you my address. If there is trouble, you come to me and I'll give you sanctuary."

"Who is this man?"

Hector saw a shadow in the crack under the door. He heard floorboards squeak. It occurred to him then that women of a certain size trying to be stealthy should never kneel.

He tangled his hand in Victoria's hair, a bit roughly, urging her head as though he was close to peaking. "That's it," he growled. "Faster. Use your tongue." He kept it up until he heard the floorboard squeak again . . . saw the shadow under the door drift away.

Hector tipped Victoria's face up, searched it. He said, "My

question to you, Victoria, is have you heard a name? Victor, or Oswald? Leek or Rook?"

"He's registered under the name Crowley."

*Perfect.*

"The man with him now, do you know his name?"

"No," she said.

Hector untangled his fingers from her hair, stroked it smooth. "Have you ever thought of cutting your hair?"

"No."

"That's good. It's quite beautiful. And so long, so dark." He ran his index finger down her cheek and lifted her chiseled chin. She was really quite lovely in her way. He said, "You live here?"

"No. Across the river."

"My side." He smiled. He counted out notes. "I'm going to guess this is equivalent to two days pay. Tonight, in a few minutes—after I've left—I want you to curse me for the worst degenerate known to existence and you quit your job here. Hole up at home for a couple of days. When I've taken care of this man, and settled some other things, I swear I'll come to you. When I do that, I'll either find you a better house in which to work, help you find your way home if that's your ambition, or help you find some other way in your life. Will you do this? You seem new to all this, and not without hope. That man upstairs is a murderer, but I'm not sure the courts can touch him yet. So you must quit *immediately.*"

"You're really police?"

"I'm here to bring this man to book for many killings. Including women in your present line of work. But I can't quite bring him to justice yet. At least, not tonight. Not until I know just a bit more."

"Solange"—*Victoria*—rested her head against his knee. She shook her head, trying to absorb it all.

He said, "You're wondering how you've come to all of this, aren't you?"

Her cobalt eyes searched his own much paler blue eyes. She said, "You're what, a psychiatrist, too?"

"No. I'm just a man. What brought you to Paris, Vick?"

"I wanted to be a singer . . . perhaps do some dancing, too. I did a little of that. But not enough to survive."

"Where is home?"

"St. Louis."

"Do you want to go back there?"

"No. My mother would take one look in my eyes and know. I know that. I write her letters. Letters about how good my life is here. Mother quit writing back last month. Guess I wasn't convincing in those letters about how gay my life is here in Paris."

"Two days, and I'll come for you, Victoria. You'll do this for me?"

"He really kills?"

"With a knife. He cuts women's throats. He's mutilated between his legs. He can't perform as a man. It's made him insane."

"But the other women here . . . ?"

Hector said, "I can't throw my arms around the world, pretty Vicky. But I can damn well get *you* out of here. Help you put your life back on track. I'll bet you're a lovely dancer. And I can tell from your voice that you would sing beautifully, as well."

Hector pulled out his notebook and fountain pen. "Now, it's time for an exchange of addresses."


Hector's taxi driver said, "Where to now? Headquarters?" Hector checked his watch: five minutes to four. He'd be fashionably late, but at least he was on the right side of the river. He said, *"Rue des Bourdonnais, vite!"*

# Twenty-seven

*Molly sat alone at* a table with three empty chairs. She saw Hector and waved. He shrugged off his overcoat and snow-dusted hat and threw them over an empty chair.

Hector wondered how Molly would play the greeting. Would it be the Mayfair kisses of the time before they'd slept together? A familiar hug? Something more passionate?

She hugged him tightly to her, looked up at him, then, closing her eyes, she leaned into a kiss. Hector kissed her back. He felt the tip of her tongue, went with it. He smoothed Molly's hair back across her forehead and sat down close to her, scooting his chair over to rest his hand on her thigh.

Molly said, "You really like my hair cut short like this? Like a boy's?"

"You look quite striking and you wear it well. I like you with longer hair, too."

She pulled at her short hair. "I'm going to let it grow out. It was exciting; a little scary to cut it. I still like it, but it leaves me few options. I miss feeling it on my shoulders."

"Then grow it back."

"Brinke is running late. Said it might be closer to five." Molly searched his face again—Hector guessed maybe for signs of disappointment. She leaned over and kissed him again. He felt his body responding.

He said, "It's good we have some time alone. To talk."

She smiled, looking a bit hesitant about what their talk might encompass. She ran her hand down the lapel of his black suit. "You look a bit like a Nadaist. Or as if you're dressed for a funeral."

"I've actually been to several funerals. And it sounds like I'll likely go to at least one more tomorrow."

"Some of our friends?"

"Little magazine editors and poets, yes. I thought I might see someone at their funerals. I thought that I might see something useful. It was really Brinke's idea."

"You really are poking into all this, aren't you?"

"I am. With police sanction. And someone seems to know that I'm a threat. I was followed this morning from my apartment. Three men in black suits. Have you and Brinke had any trouble today? Seen anything suspicious?"

"Not at all. These three men? What happened? Did you call the police?"

"No. I took care of it."

"How?"

"I handled it. Best to leave it at that."

Molly said, "You do seem to be getting around rather well, despite the leg."

"It's almost fully healed. I'm doing fine." He ordered a bottle of red wine and said, "Have you seen Philippe? He came by my place today, looking for you."

A little flash in her violet eyes. Molly looked at her lap, at his hand there, still familiarly resting high up on her thigh. "No. I've been pointedly avoiding that. Partly what you said, about Nada. About the crimes maybe tied to Nada. Partly because making love with you . . . with you and . . ."—nodding at an empty chair—"it's left me confused about what might be my future. Brinke is a fling. I can tell that. Or, I mean to say, I am. I'm Brinke's decadent fling, in tandem with you. I mean, the three of us, together. It's Brinke's sexy, wicked affair. What you and Brinke have, apart from me, I don't pretend to guess at. And Brinke has anointed herself as my

Pygmalion. Or at least I begin to think she thinks she is that."
Molly's fingers tugged again at her hair. "And you and I, Hector?
What do we really have at this point? We practically raped you
while you were doped up. You said as much yourself. I begin to
think Brinke is capable of anything. She's attractive, appealing.
But she begins to scare me, Hector. And this crazy thing between
the three of us? I think it's almost like research for Brinke. Between breakfast and lunch yesterday, Brinke insisted upon describing to me some of the manuscript of the novel she's writing.
Have you read it?"

"No," he lied.

"Then you're in for a terrible shock, Hector. It's *our* lives, Hector. Brinke's novel is about two women sharing a man, just like
we're sharing you. How can she do that? And my God, what she—
what *we*—did to you, *taking* you like that while you were half-
unconscious? I'm *so* sorry."

"I surely didn't hate it, Molly."

"If I find that I'm pregnant, you don't have to worry, Hector. I'll
pay for my own operation."

"Jesus, don't talk like that, Molly."

She shrugged. "I'm sorry. But I can't divide my feelings. Not
like Brinke evidently can. Not like you can."

"I'm not sure I can, either," Hector said. "I'm just as confused
and flummoxed by all of this as you are."

"Until I can sort this out better, I have to stay away from
Philippe, I know that."

"It's probably a good idea, anyway." Hector squeezed Molly's
thigh. Her hand closed over his, pulled his hand up a bit higher.
Hidden by the table, Molly pushed Hector's hand between her
legs.

She said, "I guess I don't really expect an answer. I won't be hurt
if you don't answer. But I have to ask: Do you think you might love
me, even just a little?"

Hector wrapped his other arm around Molly's shoulders. He pulled her into a slow, languorous kiss. "You matter very much to me. More all the time."

Molly kissed him again. "That wasn't quite an answer."

"It *was*. I don't want to lie, either way. Really, I'm still sorting through this, just like you." Another kiss, her tongue in his mouth.

Their waiter cleared his throat. Molly blushed. Hector paid their waiter, then checked his watch. He said to their waiter, "Bring us a third wineglass, won't you?"

Four-thirty. Hector said, "I need to ask you a little more about Lloyd Blake. Were you ever in his house? You said you were one of his magazine's contributors. How well did you really know him?"

Molly sipped her wine. Stared at her glass. "Hardly at all." She looked out the front window. "I don't even know where he lives."

"Ever hear of a Kitty Pike?"

She looked back at him. "No, Hector. Why?"

"Something strange happened yesterday. This must stay between us for now. You understand, Molly?"

"Okay."

"Promise me?"

"Yes, Hector. What's going on?"

"Yesterday, at Lloyd Blake's funeral, I met a woman who claimed to be Kitty Pike. She said she was Blake's employee and his mistress. Kitty said that the night Blake was murdered—stabbed to death in his bed—that Blake was to have a meeting with a woman named 'Margaret.' Kitty didn't know this woman's last name, but said it started with a 'W.' Kitty claimed this 'Margaret W' was trying to buy Blake's magazine."

"It's not me, Hector. There must be some other woman with my first name and last initial. They're not uncommon, after all. That's all I can think of to say."

Hector said, "Today I learned that the woman I met claiming to be Kitty Pike is *not*. She was an impostor. A fake who evidently meant to cast suspicion on you."

Molly shuddered, "Why *me*?"

"I don't know, yet. But it gets worse." Hector pulled out the folded-up photo from his jacket pocket. "This is a little grisly. It's a photograph of the body of another little review editor. He was stabbed to death. The policeman I'm working with is rather obsessed with the man's hands in this photo. He's obsessed with what message these hands may or may not be sending. I think the cop might have figured it out over drinks with me earlier today."

Molly swallowed hard. She took a deep drink of her wine and said. "I'm ready . . . show me."

Hector slid the photo across to her. "Oh my God," Molly said, "that's Jeremy Hunt! He just accepted one of my poems. He edits *Rain Shadows*."

"How well did you know Hunt?"

"Just in passing at a few parties. I met him once at Stein's salon."

Hector said, "Look at the hands. What do you see there?"

Molly looked up at Hector, her chin trembling. "My initials."

"Exactly."

"Oh my God! Who is doing this, Hector?" Molly looked close to panic.

Hector realized then, in a terrible moment of clarity, that he actually had a theory about that, a terrible, unthinkable theory. One he couldn't begin to share with Molly.

He sat back in his chair, feeling this void opening under him.

With a shaking hand, Hector slipped out his pack of cigarettes. He tried twice to strike a match with his thumbnail, then, licking his lips, he resorted to the strike bar on the side of the matchbox. He watched his hand trembling as he raised the match to his cigarette. Hector was looking at Molly, but he wasn't seeing her, wasn't thinking of her.

Hector was thinking of Brinke. He was thinking terrible things about her.

Hector wondered if his goddamn subconscious had been sending him signals for the past several days.

Hector asked himself if he had chosen to make the lovely villainess of his first crime novel Brinke's physical twin for some deeper reason than the fact that Brinke's physique and coloring embodied genre expectations. Had he also given his creation—this "Alison Wilder"—Brinke's given name and speech patterns for some reason apart from purely creative ones?

Hem had been arrested on the barest of circumstantial evidence that pointed toward the possibility he might be a murderer, or at least that hinted Hem might be culpable in several of the little magazine murders.

As he thought about it, Hector began to see how similar circumstantial suspicion could also be seen to swirl around Brinke.

Dark-eyed, dark-haired Brinke.

*Black*-haired Brinke.

Black-haired, just like the late Lloyd Blake's mysterious and perhaps murderous mistress.

Brinke, who spotted the phony Kitty Pike on the hill at Père-Lachaise. Brinke, who had literally pointed to the woman in white, directing Hector's attention to her.

And Brinke had given Hector suspicious looks when he was less than forthcoming about all that the phony Kitty Pike had told him.

Hell, it had been Brinke's suggestion that they go to the cemetery in the first place. Then, with Hector believed immobile with his injured ankle, Brinke had seemingly abandoned her own plans to visit the subsequent two funerals she had once insisted that they attend.

Then there was the matter of Victor Leek.

Hector had taken Brinke by the Hotel des Lions on the Rue des Ursins. He had told her of his plans to return to the hotel the next morning with Hem to confront Leek. He did that only to find the poet had fled . . .

Had Leek perhaps run as the result of some warning?

*Brinke.*

Brinke who quoted Aleister Crowley.

Brinke who spotted that killer snuffbox in Charles Turner's dead hand and then warned Hector against smelling from it.

Hell, it had been Brinke who invited Hector to escort her to Gertrude's in order to witness that murder by poison in the first place.

Hector thought again of Brinke's manuscript. It wasn't enough that it was tracking a three-way love affair just like the one that Brinke had inaugurated with Molly. No, *Triangle* was also spreading out to encompass a series of murders among the literary set of Left Bank Paris, just like the little magazine murders.

Again, Hector asked himself which truly followed which:

Was Brinke using the murders for grist for her novel?

Or was it possible Brinke was modeling her novel on the very crimes she had set in motion, or, at least, that she was complicit, too?

Was it conceivable that the murders and Brinke's novel were concomitant works in progress?

And was the ménage à trois something Brinke had inaugurated not just to fulfill her creative needs, but also as a means of distracting Hector as it became clear he was closing in on Victor Leek and his nihilist followers? Did their decadent affair spring from Brinke's recognition that Hector might in fact succeed in his role as amateur sleuth?

Brinke had picked their café across the street from the scene of François Laurencin's murder. Had that been more than grisly coincidence?

And Joan Pyle's party:

Hector had simply been told by Brinke and Hadley that they were expected to attend the cocktail party at which Joan was fatally attacked. But what initiated that invitation, exactly? *Who* initiated it? He thought about how Hadley had phrased it—something like, "Joan told Brinke..." Wasn't that how it had been?

And those three men camped outside Hector's apartment—they

hadn't followed Brinke and Molly. No, they had instead loitered with intent, then struck out after Hector.

Hector again began to feel like a kind of mark. Like some pawn being pushed around by a chess master.

Maybe Molly had called it all wrong out of the gate.

Maybe *Brinke* wasn't the muse, but Hector *was*.

Was it possible Brinke had cast Hector in the role of her own personal inspiration to drive her first real crime novel?

Hector remembered what he had told Hem about the possible posing of Jeremy Hunt's hands, "like someone who has read one too many facile mystery novels." Perhaps Hector should have instead said it smacked of the work of someone who had *written* one too many such books.

Someone like an Estelle Quartermain…or a "Connor Templeton."

*Quartermain.*

Brinke had been fascinated by Hector's instinctive animus toward her rival mystery writer. Hell, the poison that killed Charles Turner was right up Estelle's alley. And Brinke had pointed out to Simon that another of Estelle's novels featured a vitriol pitching. Was it conceivable that Brinke had first "cast" Estelle Quartermain in the role of murderer, before instead switching objectives to cast Molly as the killer?

Or perhaps Estelle had always been Brinke's red herring, her intended false suspect?

Hector was sweating; his heart was pounding. His palms were damp. Jesus, was it possible he was on to something with this crazy, dark epiphany?

He realized Molly was staring at him, her forehead wrinkled. "What in God's name are you thinking about, Hector? You look…haunted."

"I'm fine. And I mean to find out who is doing this to you, I swear, Molly. But until I do, you and I, we may need to stay close to one another."

She smiled. "I'm not arguing with that prospect. But I can't deny I dearly wish the reasons were different."

Hector's hand was there again. He squeezed gently, massaging between her legs. She sighed, spreading her legs a bit further apart; bedroom eyes. She leaned forward to kiss him again. Hector said, "In time they may become so."

"I'm really quite in love with you, Hector. Does that frighten you?"

He kissed her again; smelled lilacs. He tasted wine on her lips. Hector tried to decide if he wasn't falling in love with Molly. "I'm not afraid of that." Then he said, "You're going to need to stay at my place in the morning I think. I'm going to have to go out."

"I'll come with you."

"No . . . *no*. I found the poet—the one who heads Nada. I'm going to confront him tomorrow. Perhaps with the police, perhaps not. That part I haven't decided yet."

"Where? How did you find him?"

"The how isn't so important anymore," he said. "The where? He's living above a brothel on the Right Bank. I've confirmed that. With any luck, tomorrow morning, he will be neutralized. Arrested or otherwise. Hopefully, this Nada thing will collapse without him. It's the old and trusty strategy, you know? Cut off the head and the body dies."

At a quarter after five, Brinke finally appeared. Hector helped Brinke off with her coat. She was wearing her man's suit and overcoat again . . . her dark fedora. Brinke smiled thinly and sat down between them, taking Hector's chair. Brinke looked at the nearly empty wine bottle and poured the dregs into her own glass.

Molly excused herself to the restroom. Hector said to Brinke, "You're late. Where have you been?"

Brinke arched an eyebrow. "Actually, I was on time. Or very close to it. But as you had your hand up Molly's skirt and her tongue down your throat . . ." Brinke sipped her wine. "Thought I'd give you two lovebirds some time alone. I went for a walk in the snow. Brooded."

Hector started to raise his hand to speak . . . but he didn't quite know what to say.

Brinke said, "Don't even try. It's not really your fault. It's mine. That's what some cocaine over lunch, too much wine, and Alice B. Toklas's baked goods will buy a woman—an impossible situation . . . sharing her man with some arty, suicidal blonde."

Hector ground his teeth. "You regret this new thing we have going now?"

Brinke shrugged. "In the drunken, dissolute moment, it seemed fun enough. And I'm always for fun, you know that. Over breakfast, I'd said a few things to Molly similar to what I told you. About not being a woman who handles commitment well. I suppose, looking back on it, I thought it would make me—you and me—seem less the threat to her future. Earlier, I'd told Molly about the funeral you and I attended. Molly started talking about her Irish background on her mother's side. About how the Irish believe in making love after a funeral. In the cab back to your place, she kissed me. I liked that, quite a bit, I'll confess. The cocaine didn't hurt with any of that. I was taken aback, mind you, but I was tipsy, too. Flying on the drugs she shared with me. I responded. I told you yesterday, I find Molly attractive. I guess it all kind of started there in that coach. The three of us, I mean."

Going cold inside, assessing angles and weighing assertions, Hector thought about all that. He said, "Yesterday, after the three of us . . . Well, you still seemed rather enthusiastic about it all."

"I was still flying. Molly and I shared some more of her cocaine just before you awakened. She carries it in that snuffbox in her purse, and . . ." Brinke shrugged, weighing his expression. She said, "That's right. You wouldn't know any of that, because she reads you correctly. Molly's known enough not to show *you* that side of herself. She smokes opium, too. That's a recent development. Or so she claims. Me? Even I know enough not to chase the dragon. Nobody does that more than twice in a week and has it stay an indulgence."

Brinke drained her shallow glass of wine and helped herself to Hector's wineglass, which was still three-quarters full. "And I'm being such a bitch, telling you all this about your new honey. In some ways, you two are so young. Maybe you two *are* the couple."

Hector shook his head. "Oh, for God's sake. She's not my 'new honey.'"

Brinke sipped more wine. Over the top of her glass, from under long black lashes, her dark eyes drilled into him. "Really, Hector? See, my younger man, I read you as the sort of old-school-style swain who probably has a real problem separating love from sex. I see you as the old-fashioned kind who has to fall in love with the women he takes to his bed. A last-century man. Frankly, I at first figured that's what was happening between us. But I was just getting used to being your woman—your *fausse fiancée*—when the poetess crashed our pretty party." Brinke hung her head and ran her fingers through her short black hair. "Oh Christ, I've so wrecked everything, allowing that girl into our bed."

*Our bed.*

Hector suddenly felt sorry for Brinke. He put aside his suspicions long enough to reach across the table and take Brinke's hand. He said, "Jesus, if it weren't for those damned pills and my damned leg . . . Alice's fucking tainted cakes . . ."

Brinke smirked. "Sure, isn't it comforting to think so? Sorry, but I stand by my earlier wager. What I remember of it, anyway."

"What was that wager?"

"That stone-cold sober you wouldn't have walked away from the opportunity to make love to two attractive and willing women. No man would." Brinke looked up . . . over her shoulder. She looked very tired. "Maybe I should check on Molly. She's been gone a while."

"No," Hector said. "Here she comes."

"Goody."

"I'm afraid I have to go," Molly said, smiling. She picked up her coat and hat.

Hector said, "What? Why?"

"Message just arrived. I left word where I could be found . . . left word with my *femme de ménage*. Something has come up. Something maybe wonderful."

That seemed to interest Brinke. "What?"

"An opportunity. I have to have dinner with someone. She has a proposition for me."

Hector said, "She?"

"I can't say more. I promised."

Hector's gaze shifted to Brinke. He watched her, seeing if she would encourage or discourage Molly going.

"This doesn't make me too comfortable," Brinke said. "You know this person?"

"Well enough," Molly said. She looked to Hector. "I see. You think this might be some trick or trap, don't you?"

Hector said, "Don't you?"

"No. Not at all. Trust me, this is fine. It's good news . . . maybe the best ever."

Hector said, "We'll go with you. Or at least ride with you. We'll drop you and pick you up later."

"No, it's fine." Molly leaned down and kissed Hector on the mouth. She hesitated, then kissed Brinke on the cheek. Hector noticed Brinke didn't kiss Molly back.

"Wish me luck," Molly said.

*"Bonne chance,"* Hector said.

"Good luck, Molly," Brinke said, winking. "Break a leg, sweetie."

Molly said, "I'm not sure how long this will take. Perhaps we can just plan now on meeting for drinks tomorrow. Say, the Deux Magots? Perhaps around noon?"

"No, not there," Brinke said. "The Rotonde."

Molly smiled, waved and was gone.

Brinke said to Hector, "I just decided that girl is quite mad. And I couldn't bear meeting Molly at Deux Magots—not where you and I spent our first night together. Can we leave here, Hector? I feel like you two necking and groping one another in here have made this joint yours and Molly's place. I want to go somewhere I can think of as ours. Set about getting *us* back."

# Twenty-eight

*They sat a few* inches apart from one another on the seat of the enclosed coach under a shared blanket. Hector had his healing leg propped up on the opposite seat. For the moment, they were just aimlessly driving around the Right Bank, waiting for some place to strike Brinke's fancy Hector supposed.

Hector said, "That day in the graveyard—how'd you spot that woman behind you? That Kitty Pike?"

Brinke looked at him. "What brought *that* up? And why now?"

Hector looked around . . . looked for a lie. "Just being in a coach again, I guess."

Brinke shrugged. She pulled the blanket up closer around her. She said, "It was a girly thing, I suppose. First, there was the bad taste of wearing white to a funeral. Secondly, and maybe worse, there was the bad taste of wearing white in February. It was like that woman—that Kitty Pike—was deliberately trying to call attention to herself. I saw her as Hem and I were walking toward the grave. I couldn't help thinking there was something not remotely right about her. I thought you should check it out."

After some thought, Hector said, "Well, your suspicions were right. She wasn't what she appeared to be."

Brinke's black eyebrows knitted. "I don't understand."

"You abandoned your plan to attend funerals today."

"I was trying to keep up with Molly, to watch her. Thought I'd get an audience with her new friends. Molly hinted I might. But that didn't happen. It was all gossip and talk of you and Molly wanting to window-shop. *Ugh.* And I'm still regretting taking her to my—your—barber. Swear to God, I'm growing my hair back out, Hector. Quite long, I think."

"It would suit you," Hector said. "Hell, any look would. You have that kind of face. But I should warn you, Molly is talking about growing her hair, too."

"Having second thoughts, is she? Well, she's not the only one."

"She said she sensed you're trying to shape her."

"What? In my own image? Not my ambition."

"Really?"

"Why, did Miss Molly claim something to the contrary?"

"Not in so many words..."

"But enough to give you that impression. Isn't Molly the crafty one?" Brinke said, slowly and distracted, like something was dawning on her, "How'd you know I didn't go to any funerals today?"

"Because I went to them."

A bit cold: "See anything in the boneyards, Tex?"

"Not you. Saw Simon. I chased off some Nadaists, I think. And I spoke with Lloyd Blake's widow. Seems Kitty Pike is not Blake's mistress. The real mistress is some raven-haired, other unknown woman. And it seems the real Kitty Pike is an overweight, one-legged wretch who is housebound. The Kitty Pike I met was a ringer."

Brinke said, "A ringer who tried to frame your new honey."

"Funny you should say." Hector pulled out the photo of Jeremy Hunt's corpse. He struck a match and handed it to Brinke so she could see better. He said, "Anything about this picture strike you as, well, mystery novel–like?"

Brinke examined the photo. She looked at him in disgust.

"I think we're done talking, Hector. We're done period." Brinke banged on the roof of her coach and called, "Rue Madame."

Brinke tossed the match out the window and slid further across the seat away from Hector. She flung the picture back at him. "You're unbelivable. You might actually turn me off men."

Hector picked up the photo, folded it and stuck it in his pocket. "What the hell do you mean?"

Brinke slapped him. "You think *I'm* the one killing all these people? You think *I* tried to frame your little girlfriend with something as contrived as that woman in white on the hill and those silly hand signals for initials? You've read my stuff—including sneaking looks at my new novel, which I'm not pleased about by the way, not at all. Do you think if I wanted to plant seeds of doubt or to frame that little drugged-up tramp I couldn't do it with a good bit more finesse? Because, I could, Hector. Hell, I doubt that even Estelle Quartermain would stoop to the tactics you're ascribing to me."

"I haven't accused you of anything."

"Please. Suspect me if you will . . . hate me. But don't insult my intelligence. Not more than you already have. You goddamn Judas."

"I asked you some questions, that's all, Brinke. I'm at sea. Everything I thought I knew . . . everything I thought I could trust . . ."

"I don't care a damn about any of that. What matters to me is that your trust and faith in me wavered, Hector. That's what just happened. I'm just going to say this once: I'm not guilty of anything you're thinking, or that I think you might be thinking. That's it. That simple. I'm through with that little bitch poet. And I'm through with you. We'll end it with this: *I'm* no killer."

"I was followed by three men today."

Brinke's eyes blazed. She looked at him a long time. She said, "A lie? A diversion? That admission some tactic to knock me off stride? Maybe make me feel scared for you?"

"No."

"What happened?"

"Last night, three men were watching my building."

"I saw them," Brinke said. "I knew you had seen something looking out the window, so I looked for myself. Three men in black, smoking in the church's alcove, right?"

"Yes. They followed me this morning. But they didn't follow you and Molly, and you two left my place long before I did."

"Thus bolstering your suspicion of me," Brinke said. "You're not as smart as I thought you were, Hector. What, Molly spreads her legs and you lose your brains? Two things. First, based on the last thing I heard, you were supposed to keep your sleuthing self in bed and off that leg until late this afternoon. If those three had been my stooges, I wouldn't even have had them stationed outside your place because I believed, based on your own doctor's prognosis, that you were housebound—you know, like the 'real' Kitty Pike. Secondly, I wasn't the only one who left your place this morning. I had company, you know. And my company is known to run in *those* circles, Hector." Brinke smiled. "Here's something else. I was at that graveyard yesterday with you. I was far closer, physically, to Mrs. Blake than you were yesterday. Yet, with that long black veil she was wearing, I couldn't tell you now what the Widow Blake looks like. I never saw her features."

"Your point?"

"Have you met Mrs. Blake prior to today?"

"No," Hector said.

"Then how do you know that today you met the real Widow Blake, sleuth? Maybe today's widow was the 'real' *impostor.*" Brinke curled her lip. "Jesus, Hector, anyone can play these games, don't you see that? You're sliding into paranoia."

Brinke was right, of course. She had deftly poked holes in his circumstantial case against her . . . found all the flaws in his shared or implied scenarios.

His suspicions about her collapsed, just like that. Once again, Hector was all for Brinke. "I'm sorry, Brinke. You have every right to hate me."

"That much you've got right." She took out her cigarette case, said, "Light me."

Hector did that. She said, "You said three men followed you. What happened to them?"

"Two I shook. The third? I drugged him. When he came to, I followed him."

"Clever. I might use that in a book. Where'd the third man go?" Brinke blew her smoke in Hector's face.

He decided to risk it. If he could contrive to stay in Brinke's company until morning, and to perhaps go ahead and alert Simon to Leek's location before then, well, there should be no possibility for Brinke to warn the poet if they were in league in some way.

"The man I followed went to a whorehouse," Hector said. "I've confirmed Leek is inside that house of pleasure, hiding above it. He's registered under Crowley's name."

"A recurring motif in terms of the poet's chosen abodes," Brinke said, blowing more smoke at him. "And you must have tremendous stamina. I mean, you had to be subtle at that brothel, right? Couldn't just start a room-to-room search or blurt out a lot of questions for fear of spooking or warning the poet. You would have engaged a whore of course, and, no pun intended, pumped her for information. It's what I would have a character do in that situation."

"A character like Horace Lester?"

"You weren't supposed to see that yet. Not supposed to know about him."

Hector nodded. "Parenthetically, how'd you know I *had* seen it? How'd you know that I'd snuck a peek at your manuscript? Other than the fact you left it lying around?"

"I left it out because I thought I could trust you."

"So, how do you know I looked?"

She reached up to her head, took hold of a single black hair, and wincing, jerked it loose. She held it up between thumb and forefinger. "I put one of these on top of my manuscript before I left for the day with Molly."

Hector smiled. "You set a trap. So you really *didn't* trust me."

"Not without reason, as you're proven."

"How'd you know the hair had been moved?"

"I stopped back at your place before coming to the café this afternoon. Wanted some time alone to talk with you. Germaine let me in."

Hector said, "Well, on the topic of sharing, you kept your manuscript from me, but you talked about it to Molly."

"To my great regret," Brinke said. She inhaled some smoke ... held it for a while, looking at Hector. She blew the smoke over her shoulder. "And now what will you do about Leek, Hector? Will you kill Leek, or trust the cops to handle him?"

"Killing him had crossed my mind." Hector risked it—smiling he said, "It's what your man Horace would do."

Brinke wagged a finger at him. *"Stop.* I was just starting to spend some of my anger toward you." She shook her head. "Okay, here's the plan. You're going to let me read *your* manuscript, Hector."

Hector figured if he did that, then Brinke might be freshly angry at him. But he said, "It is only fair."

"That's right. It's only that." She looked at him for a time; he couldn't read her expression. "I'm going over things in my head," Brinke said. "Thinking of things about the past few days that might feed your suspicion of me. Thing is, if you mull it all, you could become just as suspicious of Molly. And we know for a fact that Molly, 'Margaret W,' is tied to Nada, and by extension, to Leek. And only a casual reader of mystery novels—you know, like maybe a poetess—would try to frame someone as hamhandedly as Molly has been set up."

Hector thought about that. Brinke seemed right, again. But Brinke was also very intelligent—a strategist and a master plotter ... her many novels proved that.

What if—Hector found himself wondering—what if this was some double bluff on Brinke's part?

What if Brinke was deliberately "hamhandedly" framing

Molly in order to deflect suspicion from herself as the mastermind behind Molly's fall? What if Brinke was counting on someone like Simon or Hector to expect a much more elegant conspiracy from the likes of Brinke?

That kind of thinking just made Hector's head hurt.

He thought more about what Brinke said about Molly.

Oftentimes, the obvious solution is the right one, he told himself.

*Except* in crime and mystery novels.

But this was life ... not some contrived world moving at the whims of an Estelle Quartermain or "Connor Templeton."

Hector could tell from the hollow sound of the horse's hooves and the smell of the air that they were crossing the Seine. He felt he was running out of time to patch things up with Brinke—that he would lose his opportunity to stay with her through morning on the off chance she *was* tied to Leek and determined to warn him of Hector's pending visit.

Impulsively, Hector leaned across and kissed Brinke. She pulled away as far as she could. Hector pressed harder against Brinke, pinning her to the seat with his weight. She bit his lip, drawing blood. She beat on his back with her fists. Then her tongue was in his mouth ... she slid to the floor, moved to all fours. He roughly pushed her coat up over her waist and unfastened her trousers and pulled them down around her knees. He tore Brinke's silk panties getting them off her. Hector took her from behind. They moved frenzedly and Brinke again bit her own hand to suppress her cries.

Afterward, still inside her, he kissed the back of her neck. He said, "Germaine believes we're secretly engaged. Why don't we really do that?"

He shuddered as she abruptly turned, his body slipping from hers. Brinke stared at him. "You mean that?"

"Yes. I love you, Brinke. Let's look for a ring tomorrow."

He saw her struggling with it. "I'm still dreadfully mad at you, you know."

"For good reason. Say yes, and I'll have a lifetime to repair the damage."

"I still get to read your book—what there is of it. *Tonight*. Yes?"

Hector said, "You might be madder at me, after."

"Like you said, you can spend years making up to me. Besides, I'm a writer, too. I understand the tension between the page and all this." Brinke gestured with her hand—indicating the world, Hector figured.

She said, "You truly certain about this proposal? What about Molly?"

"I want *you*. Only you." Hector had lingering suspicions about Brinke but he was following his own gut, bending to his own wild desire now.

"Hector, a few days ago, you said you're happily '*solo lobo*.'"

He kissed her again; tasted his own blood on her mouth. "Lone wolves are never truly happy."

Brinke wiped the blood from his lip. "And hawks don't share. But why do you do this now?"

How would the French put it? Hector said, *"Le coeur a ses raisons que la raison ne connaît point."* His hand caressed her cheek. "Will you marry me, Brinke?"

"I will. Yes. Yes, I will. But let's keep it secret a while longer, yes?"

They kissed, slow and hard. Brinke ended it. She hesitated, then said, "You have fresh sheets at your place? Because if you don't, I don't want to go back to your place."

"Yes, I have fresh sheets. In the armoire."

Brinke pulled up her slacks, buttoned them, and fastened her belt. She wadded her torn and discarded panties into the pocket of her overcoat. She rapped on the roof of the coach and gave the driver Hector's address. Brinke tried to smooth her hair. She said, "Just one promise from you, Hector. You ever have doubts about me again, you confront me directly."

# PART IV

mercredi

# Twenty-nine

*Placing his manuscript aside,* Brinke said, "No, I'm okay with it, really."

"I mean to change the names later," Hector said. "Just figured using names familiar to me would save me having to check constantly to remind myself who's who as the manuscript got longer."

"It's not a new trick, Hector. I do it, too."

"I'll change the 'Alison' to something else in the final draft."

Brinke shook her head. She took off her reading glasses and tossed them on the stand by the bed. "No, it's fine, really. 'Alison Wilder' sounds like a real dangerous 'twist.' Your 'Alison' was the femme fatale from the get-go?"

Hector squirmed. "Right."

"Life doesn't often imitate art. Learn that lesson now, Hector."

"So noted," Hector said. "Speaking of names, I've been thinking about yours."

"I'm keeping my maiden name, Hector. Partly for business reasons, partly for sentimental ones. But also because, well, frankly, 'Brinke Lassiter' doesn't ring for me in the same way that 'Brinke Devlin' does."

"I was going to suggest you keep it."

Brinke smiled. She was sitting nude at the foot of his bed, her head pressed against the footboard. Brinke was propped on one elbow and her left hand rested on her right thigh. Her legs were crossed at the ankles and she looked a little like a prettier take on Edouard Manet's *Olympia*. She said, "Maybe you're not so old-world after all."

"Not from the waist down."

Brinke smiled and crawled back up the bed. She straddled Hector. "So, when do you go back to that brothel?"

"In a bit."

"Armed?"

"Sure."

"I'm coming with you," she said. "Hem should probably come, too."

"I thought about asking him. When we get there, you should wait in the coach, be ready to run to the police for help. In case things should go badly, I mean."

"Sure."

He said, "We'll have breakfast, then go fetch Hem."

Her fingers traced his mouth. "Think you can do that at will? Hadley said that because of John's crying, Hem's taken to writing in cafés."

"There's only one good café for that—Hem's special café. We'll find him if we get there before ten. I'll dress and go down and get our breakfast."

He gently urged Brinke off his lap. Nude, Hector walked to the window, pulled back the drapes, and searched the street for black-clad men.

"Anyone?"

*"Nada.* I mean, that literally."

Brinke said. *"Un homme d'esprit.* God help me. Do you mean literally there is nothing there, or literally some of those Nada-types are lurking?"

Hector said over his shoulder, "There you go, editing me again. I mean the former. The proverbial coast is clear."

"Is that good news, or bad?"

Hector said, "I'll let you know when I decide." He turned, sat on the window ledge. He said, "You have any thoughts about what kind of ring you might want?"

Brinke rolled onto her belly, facing him, resting her chin on her hands and bending her legs at the knees, crossing them again at the ankles, her feet swaying in the air. "It's so funny. I saw one yesterday in the storefront of an antique shop on the Boulevard du Montparnasse. Very old, very French."

"Sounds lovely." Hector smiled. "If we hurry, maybe can we take a look at it on our way to find Hem."


"This place is new for me," Brinke said as Hector held the door for her at the Closerie des Lilas. "Thank God for a warm café," she said, rubbing her arms. She brushed snow from her shoulders and stomped her feet.

Hem was sitting at a table in the corner at the rear of the café. He sat with his back to the wall and facing the room. It was a gunfighter's table choice . . . or a writer's, Hector thought. It provided a man the panorama of the place. It was a prime spot from which to watch and absorb and perhaps eavesdrop on those close by. To listen for a snatch of dialogue or an interesting speech pattern to appropriate.

On the table before Hem there was a nearly depleted plate of oysters and a carafe of white wine. Hem's blue, student's notebook was closed and a pencil rested atop it alongside a pencil sharpener. The ashtray on Hem's table was full of peanut shells and pencil shavings. Hem saw them, rose, and said, "There's my girl." He gave Brinke a bear hug and squinted at her left hand. He took her hand and raised it to his face. He smiled at the ring there and said, "Happy Christ, is that what I think it is?"

Beaming, Brinke said, "It is."

Hem smiled and kissed her on the mouth. "I can already hear the hearts breaking all along both banks of the Seine."

Laughing, Brinke said, "Aren't you the silver-tongued devil, you writer you?" She smiled and hugged Hem again. "I'm being choosy about wearing this for now. Around whom, and where I wear it, I mean." Brinke said. "But it is what it appears to be. We want you to be best man, Hem. You will, won't you?"

"Just tell me where and when, Dev."

"We're still talking about that," Hector said. "But it is a closely held secret."

"Last month, I was a working journalist," Hem said. "I can keep a secret. But some advice for you, Lasso. Seal the deal quickly, before this beauty figures out how much better she can do than you." He clapped Hector's arm. "Congratulations, Lasso. You're definitely marrying up."

"I know." Hector looked around the café. Old men with beards were playing dominoes and arguing politics over cups of espresso or *tisane*. At the other corner of the café, his back to the rear wall, just like Hem, a one-armed man sat scribbling in a notebook. Hem saw Hector watching the maimed man. "That's Blaise Cendrars, the poet," Hem said. "He's one of the good ones."

Hector said, "At least there are no men in black suits. No obvious Nadaists."

"No," Hem said. "No danger of that here. Blaise is the only poet who ever comes here."

"Good news, that."

Hem pointed at Brinke's engagement ring. "Who else knows?"

She said, "Hector's *femme de ménage* and you. That's it."

Hem thought about that... looking at Hector. It was as if he could read Hem's mind: *What will Molly say? How will she react after what I saw at your place night before last?*

But Hem forced a smile and said, "I can tell Hadley, can't I? I mean, if I swear her to secrecy, too?"

Brinke nodded. "Of course. I want her to stand with me... Hadley, and Sylvia."

"I'll answer for both of them—of course they will," Hem said.

"We have a second reason for finding you here this morning," Hector said. "Interested in riding shotgun again?"

"Leek?"

"I've found him again."

"For certain?"

"As of last night, yes. A sporting house on the Rue Quin-campoix."

Hem said, "Just us? No police?"

"Just you and I, if you're game. Brinke will wait outside . . . to go and fetch help if it's needed."

"You bring that Mauser?"

"Sure."

Hem slapped Hector's arm again. "What are we waiting for?"


The street was crowded with gawkers and police . . . newspapermen and photographers.

The police presence seemed to be centered around the house that Hector had visited the previous afternoon . . . the one above which Victor Leek was hiding. Brinke picked up her purse. She said, "Uh-oh. There's Simon. And he's waving at us, Hector. Better put your guns in here." Brinke opened her purse and Hector and Hem thrust their guns inside.

Simon cast down a cigarette stub and leaned into the window of their coach.

"You're eagle-eyed," Hector said to Simon.

"I also instructed my men to look for you," he replied. "I expected you to turn up."

"Why?"

Simon wasn't his usual affable self. He said, "That will soon enough become apparent. Get out please, Hector. Your friends can stay here. In fact I insist they do that."

Hector swallowed hard. "Am I in some kind of trouble?"

"Time will tell. Get out now."

Hector obeyed. He closed the door of the coach and said to Brinke, "Back soon. I hope."

Simon took Hector by the arm, began walking him away from the commotion in front of the brothel. "It's very bad in there."

"What has happened?"

"What do you think? A slaughter, all of the women, killed. All of them. Nearly a dozen. *Le massacre . . .*" Simon shook his head. "It's insane in there, Hector. Bodies everywhere. And one man couldn't have done this. But then, we know that one man probably didn't do this, don't we?"

"Yes."

"Why are you here, Hector?"

"Why were you expecting me?"

Simon shook his head. He squeezed Hector's arm tightly enough to make the writer wince. He said, "You don't get to pose any questions this time, Hector. Not until my own queries are exhausted. Exhausted, and answered in full. Now begin."

Hector lit a cigarette. He said, "I was followed from my apartment yesterday. I managed to turn the tables on my shadow and followed him here yesterday afternoon. I engaged a woman, a prostitute new to the trade—an American—who told me the man I followed was upstairs with another man registered as 'Crowley,' just as Leek had been registered at the Hotel des Lions. Having been rendered a eunuch, I don't quite understand why Leek keeps coming back to prostitues like this. What do you think? *Nostalgie de la boue?*"

Simon wasn't to be distracted. "You knew all this yesterday afternoon?"

"Yes," Hector said. "Or, at least, I thought I knew it."

"But you didn't immediately alert me. It doesn't bear pointing it out to you, but I will, nevertheless. If you had called me yesterday, all of those unfortunate women back there might be alive now. Theirs were terrible deaths."

Simon was right. Hector didn't need to be told that. "I meant to call you this morning."

"Why the fatal delay?"

"To give my source—this American—time to get safely out last evening," Hector said. "To buffer my visit yesterday and Leek's apprehension today with some time so my source wouldn't be compromised . . . perhaps put at some further risk."

"Stupid. *Stupid*. But as you say, this harlot countrywoman of yours should be at no risk now. Not as everyone whom your 'source' knew in that place has since been slaughtered."

"I need to get into there," Hector said. "I need to see that my source did indeed leave last night."

"Impossible. It's a crime scene now." Simon relented, just a bit. "What does this woman, this American, look like?"

"Very attractive. Aristocratic-looking, in a Creole-French way. Pale skin . . . long, blue-black hair. Slender. She has very unusual, cobalt-blue eyes."

"There is nobody like that in there. The dead women are quite coarse-looking. Plump. There are none that look as though they would have been particularly attractive in life." Simon hesitated, then said, "Do you realize what you have done, keeping this from me? Leek is still out there and getting more destructive by turns. You're now in tremendous jeopardy because of what you've done."

Hector nodded, his mouth dry. He said, "For suppressing evidence. It's an offense, I know."

Simon frowned. *"C'est plus qu'un délit, c'est un crime.* I can't imagine there being a next time, but if there is, you come to me immediately. Understood?"

*"Bien entendu.* I swear."

"I don't envy you your conscience, Hector. Were you trying to protect someone, handling this yourself? Trying perhaps to protect someone other than this improbably attractive American prostitute, I mean?"

*"Non.* Next time I come straight to you, *Je le jure."*

Simon squeezed his arm. "The alternative will produce dire

consequences for you, perhaps on many levels. We understand one another, *n'est-ce pas?*"

"Entirely."

"Where do I find this American prostitute?"

"I don't know," he lied. "I didn't get her real name, or learn where she lives. Her working name was 'Solange.'" Hector didn't want to have the woman harassed by the police. If she'd gotten wind of what had happened, she might already have bolted.

"Useless."

"I'm sorry."

Simon turned Hector around, began walking him back toward the coach where Brinke and Hem sat waiting. "You may see some men in the days ahead," he said. "I will send photos of my men around to your apartment later, so you will know them by face. That way you may distinguish my men from others who might be watching you."

"I don't need any *garde du corps.*"

"It's not exactly like that, Hector. Not just that."

"You're having me watched because you don't trust me anymore?"

Simon nodded. "There is also that. But you've made yourself a critical target for Leek now. You asked how I knew to alert my men to look for you. There is a reason. We found this in the room where Leek was hiding." Simon handed Hector a slip of paper stained with a partial, bloody thumbprint.

Hector read:

> Dear Mr. Lassiter:
>   Now you become the quarry.
>   For you, it will be *une longue et terrible souffrance.*
>   *La reine le veut.*
>                                              —VL

Hector tried to brass it out. He shrugged and said, "*N'importe.* Let them hate, so long as they fear. That would make a fine motto, wouldn't it? What would it be in Latin? *'Oderint dum metuant.'*"

"I don't regard this as an idle threat, my brash young friend."

"You think he means it," Hector said.

*"Sans aucun doute."* Simon said, "That salutation, *'La reine le veut'*—'the queen wills it'—who is the queen?"

Hector handed the note back to Simon. "I don't know."

"You don't know, Hector? Or is it perhaps that you're not yet sure?"

"Perhaps both."

*"Peu à peu*, it comes. There is someone other than that prostitute you meant to protect. Another woman? That woman in the coach, perhaps? Mademoiselle Devlin? Is she the queen to whom Leek refers in this note?"

"Not her. I . . . I just can't."

"Then I'll arrest you now. Compel you under authority to tell me. Don't let others die for your misguided sense of loyalty, Hector. There's enough blood on your soul already."

"She can't know I'm the one who told you."

"It will remain between us. Who is this woman?"

"I think she's an innocent . . . a target of someone trying to implicate her in these crimes. This coda on this letter left in there for me is just more of the same. We already suspect Leek is calling the shots. Why should he suddenly allude to the fact that he's being directed by some mystery woman?"

"Who is this woman you're shielding? Tell me now or I'll arrest you . . . and I'll charge you as an accomplice, as well."

Hector sighed. "A young American poet. Her name is Margaret Wilder."

"Ah, the hands of Jeremy Turner and your rather odd theory yesterday about them are now explained." He patted Hector's cheek. "Well, what's left of your conscience can rest easy. That name is not new to me. I've been making inquires about Mademoiselle Wilder for some hours now, for reasons of my own. I, too, keep my own counsel at times, you see. There have been anonymous tips about a 'Margaret W.' So you've betrayed nothing. At most, you've merely mildly intensified my interest in this poet. Oh, on that note, our friend Victor also left this on the body of one of the women back there." Simon handed Hector another bloodied slip of paper:

### LINES FOR LASSITER

*The dark prince sounds his clarion*
*Sounds it from afar*
*Its song is carried on the night wind*
*Calling our numbers to arms*
*We descend, cunning wolves*
*Eyes on the too tender fold*
*Stalking, watching, waiting*
*Our minds cry for peace*
*Our heads ache with black pain*
*The voice in our heads crowds our thoughts*
*We say No.*
*Demanding, the man in our heads wrings his hands*
*We say No.*
*The dark man inside insists:*
*Exhorting. Accusing. Calling for his dues to be paid.*
*At last, unable to resist, we strike:*
*I strike.*
*Nameless, faceless, you cower*
*You surrender everything*
*Your blood is the claret that enlivens my tongue*
*I wash my hands with your heart*
*I make you small to make me larger*
*I see you grow small, taking the man with you*
*Until the next time*
*And the next time*
*And the next time.*
*Each time, the man calls again, stirring the beast inside*

*And I seek the wine of another*
*And another*
*And another.*
*Each one is just like you*
*Each time a tribute to you*
*Each time, I cut you down again*
*Each time, you make me grow.*

"What do you think, Hector? Of his poem, I mean?"

"Never much been one for poetry."

"*Oui.* Nor am I. And where are the rhymes?"

Hector tried to tamp down his anger. "What's next then?"

"You stay out of this now, Hector," Simon said. "You're no longer in my good graces. In time you might be again . . . if you behave. But no more secrets, *d'accord*?"

"No more. I understand."

"How despondent you look. Don't despair, Hector. Good may yet prevail. *Gardons la foi.*"


Hector settled back in the coach. Hem said, "What was all that?"

Hector said, *"Un mauvais quart d'heure."* Hector told them everything. He told them about the murdered prostitutes and the letter left by Leek. "I sense everyone—every American in the literary community—is a suspect in that man's mind now. He's digging deep into individual histories. Researching us all, I sense."

"I want us to leave Paris," Brinke said, a strange and unfamiliar edge of urgency in her voice. She looked genuinely terrified. "That was about as direct a threat as could be made . . . that letter and that crazy poem. We'll pack tonight, Hector. We'll leave in the afternoon. Nothing is worth the risk. Not squared off against someone who would do what Leek did to all those poor women. Perhaps we could marry in the morning and honeymoon tomorrow night somewhere far from here. Milan . . . Madrid . . . Switzerland.

Somewhere away from this bloody city. We'll go to London. Go home and make our way down to Key West. Start our life together there. Please, Hector, promise we'll leave this town before tomorrow night, as fast as we can."

Hector looked to Hem.

Hem reached across the seat and squeezed Hector's knee. "I'm with Brinke. And, hell, why not elope? You weren't going to do this with family, anyway, right? Marry this beauty in the morning and vamoose, Lasso. If you go to Italy, maybe Hadley and I will come, too. Ezra sent us an invitation. I'm sick of this goddamn weather. And you're right: I'm a target now, too, maybe, because of the fucking *Transatlantic*. The five of us will go to Italy. We'll be safe from them there until the police can wrap this up. It'll be far enough to discourage them following."

Hector said, "There may be no place that far."

Brinke squeezed his hand. Her ring glittered in the light. "I'm leaving Paris tomorrow, Hector. Come with me . . ." Her black eyes were besieging. "I don't beg, anyone, not ever, Hector. Not for anything. But I'm begging you. Please come. Don't gamble away this pretty life together you've talked me into."

Hector took a deep breath, let it out. He decided. "Fine. You choose the church, Brinke. See if it can be arranged for the morning. Us . . . Hem and Hadley and Sylvia. And Germaine, of course. Then we run. I suppose we'll consummate our marriage on some night train to somewhere."

It was against all Hector's instincts—beating a retreat. Then he looked at Brinke again, at her imploring, charcoal eyes. "Don't worry, darling," he said. "I've given you my word. Nothing will change my mind. Key West . . . you're certain of that?"

"It will be our place . . . our place alone together," Brinke said. "All ours."

Cupping her chin in his palm, smiling, Hector said, "Isn't it pretty to think so?"

# Thirty

"*Two nights ago you* had this embarrassment of riches," Hem said, toying with his *fine à l'eau.* "Now you're engaged to Brinke. How'd this come to be?"

Brinke was in a church a short distance away, seeing if she could find an amenable priest for a fast wedding. On the ride to the café, she'd vowed to lie she was "with child if it will speed the plow."

"Night before last—and earlier that afternoon—was just something bizarre," Hector said. "Brinke initiated it. Some crazy thing to try and give Molly some new preoccupation. Something to spark Molly's interest in life again. Molly talked Brinke into sampling some cocaine on top of wine. Brinke drank more wine at my place. Then we all ate those cakes of Alice's that Gertrude dropped off while you and Williams were at my place. Seems they were laced with cannabis. Inhibition, self-control . . . good sense . . . *any* sense, they all went out the window."

Hem slammed his hand down on the table. "That explains that night last April. I had some of those damned cakes of Alice's. Couldn't figure out what hit me so hard. I'd had a few glasses of wine, but never been affected by the vino the way I was that night. And hungry? I ate a bowl of Gertrude's pretzels that night." Hem shook his head, this crooked smile on his face at the memory. Then he said, "Molly may take this engagement very badly, of course."

"Hence the secret," Hector said. "We'll just beat out of town." Hector hated that last as he said it.

Hem said, "You three already agreed to no repeats of the other day's escapades?"

"Not in so many words. But both of them more or less told me individually they weren't interested in 'sharing' me anymore."

"I'm not liking the sound of any of this," Hem said. "And frankly it's cruel. Cruel to Molly. Running out on her tomorrow, I mean."

"It is craven," Hector said. "Well, we're granted a reprieve for a time, in terms of her finding out. Yesterday afternoon, Molly took off. Claimed she'd been invited to some important dinner with some mystery woman. Said it was something that might change her whole life."

"That doesn't sound comforting, either, Lasso."

"Molly claimed to know the mystery woman. She swore that there was no possibility of a trap or some other sort of subterfuge. Either way, it buys me a little time . . . time to maybe think of a way to break this to Molly."

Hector hesitated, then said, "You think I'm doing the right thing, Hem? Marrying Brinke, I mean?"

Hem smiled. "Brinke's a writer, but not competitive with you. Competition like that always sounds the death knell for love affairs between writers. Brinke understands the life. She's beautiful, obviously passionate. Handles her liquor well. And she's smart as a whip. I'm jealous as hell. I meant it earlier—bag Brinke before she wises up. You'll never find another like her."

"You'd really come to Italy with us?"

"Not tomorrow, but early next week, yes. Ezra really has been after us to do that. And we both are sick of this weather. There's a lot of flu going around the city. Doc Williams said we should get Bumby out of Paris until all that passes. So Hash and I were already talking about Rapallo."

"Sounds like we'll have us a time, then." Hector slowly shook his head. "Yeah . . . Certainly a better time than the last time we had together in Italy."

"A damn fine time," Hem agreed. "Be good to go this time as tourists. Bugs me though, and I bet you, too. Leaving so many friends here to the whims of those cocksuckers—to this Nada bunch, I mean. Goddamn that fucking Leek."

Hector rubbed his eyes. "We've both now narrowly averted being arrested. I don't think we can pull off a third dodge on that front. We've both pissed off Simon too many times."

"True." Hem smiled and nodded at Brinke. "God, look at her. She's sublime."

Brinke was returning, but frowning. Her black hair glistened with the melting snow. Her overcoat's tails were flapping behind her; her felt hat was clutched in her hand. She shrugged off her coat and slung it over the back of an empty chair and balanced her fedora atop it. "We were almost set. Tomorrow, nine in the morning at *Notre-Dame-des-Champs*."

She leaned in for a kiss. Hector kissed her and said, "I'm surprised they agreed to our crazy schedule."

Brinke smiled. "It wasn't that easy, I'm afraid. Connor Templeton was going to buy the church a replacement window. He was going to do that with his advance money from *Murder in Milan*."

Hem laughed. "A window in exchange for a jiffy marriage? Christ, is there nothing that isn't for sale anymore?"

Brinke said, "Well, they do call it 'stained' glass. But it seems you have to have a license, and there's some time involved in all that. And I can't believe I almost did this, and on a whim. Marriage has always been for other people. Never thought I'd take the plunge. One of you chaps buy me a drink and talk some sense into me before I almost sin again."

Hector knew Hem's money was tight. Hem never let anyone forget that. Hector raised a hand and ordered a bottle of Rioja Alta, a favorite of Hem's from the previous summer's holiday in Spain.

Brinke said, "Either way, we still leave tomorrow, Hector?"

"Agreed."

Their wine arrived and Hem filled their glasses. He toasted, "To the Lassiters! Whenever it happens."

They drank and Hector said, "Brinke's keeping her maiden name."

"Very modern," Hem said. "And a sign of returning good taste. Prettier sounding than Lassiter. Maybe *you* should take the name 'Devlin,' Lasso." Hem rolled that one around in his head, said, "Hector Devlin. Sounds like a good middleweight's name. He'd be a secret southpaw—only thing that compensates for his being a habitual rummy."

"I think we're witnessing the birth of Hem's next protagonist," Hector said dryly. He winced suddenly. "Oh God." He checked his pocket watch. "It's five past noon." Hector looked at Brinke. "Yesterday we told Molly we'd—"

"Meet her at the Rotonde," Brinke finished for him, looking a little sick. She sighed. "I'll call . . . tell her we're running late."

Brinke sighed again, sipped deeply of her wine, then stood and put back on her hat and coat. "I'll go see if I can find a phone."

Hem's brow was furrowed. He stroked his mustache. "The Rotonde? That was a risky choice, wasn't it, Lasso? That's Philippe's haunt."

Hector said, "Molly first suggested Magots. Brinke countered with the Rotonde."

Hem said, "Given what you said they both said about the cessation of the ménage à trois, I guess maybe Brinke figured to force matters to a crisis. I mean, by arranging to maybe run into Molly's beau there. Precipitate some break."

"Makes sense," Hector said, "but smacks of Machiavelli."

Hem smirked. "You may just have defined womankind."

Brinke plopped back down in her seat. She sipped her wine, poured in a little more. "Talked someone from the neighboring telegraph office into running next door and asking after Molly. Seems the dear little poetess stood *us* up. Molly left word she couldn't make it for our rendezvous, but instead said that we were to catch up with her at Joan Pyle's around eight." Brinke nodded at Hem. "She asked you be there, too, Hem, with Hadley. Asked if we could alert Gertrude and Alice … Sylvia. You know, all the usual faces."

Hector said, "To what possible end?"

"Molly said it is a surprise."

Hector realized he'd spilled a little wine on his hand. He dabbed at it with a napkin. "We going to go?"

"I don't want to," Brinke said. "But I think we better. We should leave town on the best note we can with her, don't you think?"

Hector nodded, feeling Hem's gaze on him. "Sure. Swell."

"Let's finish up," Brinke said, "then I'm going home to begin packing at least some of my stuff. For our getaway, I mean. When things cool down here we can return from Italy and do the deed and finish closing out our apartments."

"She who must be obeyed has spoken," Hector said to Hem.

He smiled at Hector, raised his glass. "Better learn to love it, Lasso," Hem said. "It's your brand-new beautiful life."


Hem said, "How's that stomach, Lasso? Dreading getting those women in the same room in a bit?"

Hector hoisted his glass. "It's the artist's curse, maybe. Sordid lifestyles, I mean. If I was an *homme d'affaires*, perhaps I wouldn't find myself in this predicament." Hector shrugged, said, *"Nous verrons ce que nous verrons."*

Hem snorted into his glass. "Right. Oh, Christ, look there. It's the fucking 'Master.' I knew this place was a mistake."

Hem and Hector had settled on a café close by Brinke's apartment. They had dropped her there for a couple hours of packing for the next day's hasty escape.

Ford Madox Ford saw the two young writers, waved and shuffled their way. Hector groaned and rose and shook the old British novelist's hand. Ford's mustache was stained with something Hector thought might be the detritus of onion soup. Ford's never pleasant breath also strongly attested to that possibility.

In his muttering, wheezing voice, Ford said, "Ah, the young . . . Yankee Turks." Ford helped himself to an empty chair, said, "This weather . . . hell on my lungs. Reminds me . . . of a winter's weekend . . . nearly snowed in at the offices . . . of the *English Review*. Henry—James—dropped in. Henry and I . . . we became . . . quite trapped. We—"

Hector began to lose the thread, almost immediately. Hector remembered something that Gertrude had once told him H. G. Wells purportedly said in describing Ford: "A copious carelessness of reminiscence."

As Ford droned on, Hector watched Hem. His friend had this indolent half-smile on his face. Hem's brown eyes looked attentive— Hem's eyes at least looked that way to Ford, Hector figured. But knowing Hem as he did, Hector could see the contempt in those quick brown eyes.

"—and so today . . . was like that day," Ford said. "And tomorrow? Commitment piles upon commitment . . . chore upon chore. Lads, the French . . . have a phrase. Do you know it?"

Hector shook his head, said, "Not until you say it. There are, after all, so many phrases."

"The French have a . . . phrase," Ford said again, as if Hector hadn't spoken. *"La semaine à deux jeudis.* It means the week . . . with two Thursdays in it. I sense this . . . is such a week. I remember . . . Conrad remarking that—"

Tuning him out again, Hector reached for his cigarette pack. A rotund, balding man with slicked-over strands of black hair and a black mustache and beard was standing a few feet away, looking over the busy café for someplace to sit. He seemed familiar to Hector. After a moment, Hector placed him—Molly's hero poet, Léon-Paul Fargue.

Hector said, "Pardon my interruption, Ford, but have you met the marvelous French poet Fargue?" Not waiting for an answer, Hector raced ahead: *"Non?* Let me introduce you." Hector waved and said, "Here you go, Monsieur Fargue . . . please, take my seat. We met the other day—Hector Lassiter. I was just leaving. But first, have you met Ford Madox Ford and Ernest Hemingway?" The French poet shook hands with Hem and then with the English novelist.

Hem picked up his own coat and hat. He said, "Yes, Hector and I have some things to attend to before first Thursday—let alone *second* Thursday—arrives."

Shaking hands, appraising one another, the two older writers seemed oblivious to Hector and Hem. Ford said to Fargue, "I've read much of your poetry."

"Stop there," Fargue said, urgently squeezing Ford's right forearm. "Opinions are for the mediocre, and you—the Leviathan of the Quartier Montparnasse—are not mediocre. Here," Fargue said to Ford, taking Hector's chair. "We'll sit before more see me. Look at them, the bourgeois rabble. Don't they have some lesser Fargue and Ford of their own class to stare at?"

"It is ... the thing we ... cope with," Ford wheezed in commiseration. "I remember ... Henry—James, that is—saying, 'Ford ...'"

Hem took Hector's arm and pulled him to the door. "Lasso, swear to me—if I get like that, you have to promise to put me down. The writing life—fuck all that. Jesus wept." Hem suddenly swung Hector around and ducked down behind the taller Hector.

"Holy Christ, Hem," Hector said, flustered. "Now what?"

Hem rose, spun Hector back and around and practically dragged him through the door. "That was Tristan Tzara coming in ... with Man Ray," Hem said. "Now this dump is the perfect train wreck, Lasso. We're getting out just in time."

"We still have to kill some time waiting for Brinke," Hector said.

Hem shrugged. "There is always another café."

# Thirty-one

*"What will your landlady,* the nun, say?"

Hector's head rested on Brinke's thighs. She raked her fingers through his hair with her left hand and fed him and herself bits of cheese with her right. They were sprawled across the wreck of her bed, nude . . . bathed in sweat from their lovemaking and from the fire crackling in her small, rustic fireplace.

It was the first time that Hector had been in Brinke's apartment. He had been surprised upon entering. He'd envisioned something a bit more . . . haughty. A *boudoir* or something more in the salon vein, perhaps. But Brinke's apartment was a rustic garret . . . exposed rafters and two unfinished, uninsulated walls. Frost had formed on the inside of the glass panes of the windows on those two walls. It was an impersonal space, too: no photos of her mother or father . . . no art or mementos.

Brinke had watched Hector wandering her room . . . looking around, checking the spines of the few books in an amateurishly built bookshelf, and had said, "It's a way station, Hector. An engine to live in. A cheap and good place to write because there are no distractions. I really only sleep here." Several racks on wheels held her clothes. The dresses and coats all looked expensive to Hector. Brinke seemed mostly to wear whatever money she was earning. A couple of large steamer trunks doubled as armoires.

Now she popped another cube of cheese in Hector's mouth and said, "My landlady is a moot point after tomorrow. And she's out of town for the next few days, anyway. Her sister is ill and lives in the country . . . a train's ride away. Farther than even her ears can hear."

Hector smiled, chewing his cheese. Brinke had been right—far from what she evidently considered other prying ears, Brinke was indeed loud in her lovemaking... uninhibited groans... lewd urgings in Hector's ear.

"Besides," Brinke continued, "it would be worth the risk, anyway. Your place isn't safe for so many reasons. Leek, for one. And Molly could show up at any time. Speaking of your place, did you get word to Germaine about going away tomorrow morning?"

"She's on the page."

"I adore her."

"Hem picked up our train tickets for us, too," Hector said, stroking her thigh. "While he did that, I packed, pretty hastily, but as it's Italy, and the country, I figure I won't need much. I'll arrange to have my bags delivered here later this evening." He turned his head and kissed her belly.

Brinke sighed and pressed his face against her belly, cooing and giggling as he thrust his tongue in her navel. "We should bathe and dress, soon," she said. "It's getting close to time for dinner with Hem and Hadley. Then on to Nicole's place. Where are we eating with Hem and Hash, by the way?"

"Place Hadley and Hem favor and nobody else much does," Hector said. "Vélodrome d'Hiver. Should keep us safe from uninvited dinner guests."

"We've not talked about children," Brinke said suddenly. "You'll want some someday, I suppose."

"Not necessarily." He figured that was the safest answer for the moment. "What about you?"

She shrugged. "Time will tell. Hell, a week ago, I would have sworn I'd never marry."


They finished dinner early and wandered next door to a *bal musette* for a couple of dances.

Hem and Brinke were cutting up the floor. Hector, nagged by

his ankle, sat with Hadley, sipping wine and watching their partners together. He said, "This might be the craziest thing I've ever done. Marrying that woman."

Hadley smiled, her freckled nose crinkling. "The 'craziest thing'? That covers a lot of ground. Hem's told me stories about you, Hec."

He nodded, said, "But this matter of Molly . . ."

"I heard of course, from Hem, about what happened between you three," Hadley said. "That was most unfortunate. But putting that aside—if it can be put aside in any way . . ." Hadley searched for words, settled on, "I mean, if it *hadn't* happened, I would say to you that you can't bend or live your own life in some way to save someone else's. You can't feel you have to do that just because this other person has gotten it into their head you're the only one for them. Frankly, I don't think you and Molly would last a week, Hec."

"And Brinke and I?"

"Should be quite an adventure for both of you," Hadley said, stroking his cheek with the back of her pale hand. "But you two are more alike than different. And more alike than I think either one of you realizes or is capable of seeing."

Hector pressed her hand to his cheek. "Sure there aren't any more like you at home, Hash?"

She shrugged and gave him a half smile. "Don't be daft. You and a woman like me together would be a disaster."


Hector spotted Molly across the room as they entered Joan Pyle's apartment. Molly merely smiled and waved . . . no reaction to the fact that Brinke was very much on Hector's arm—albeit sans engagement ring.

His gaze drifted to the ancient Oriental rug spread across the entryway. There were small holes burned in the rug here or there from the acid that had been thrown in Joan's face.

Nicole looked drawn and haggard . . . years older. Hector thought he even saw some gray suddenly crisping Nicole's blond hair. She thanked the four of them for coming. Hem gave Nicole a bear hug and she awkwardly patted his back. He said, "Anything at all, Nicky . . ."

"You being here is all that's needed, Hem," Nicole said. "Grab some wine and some seats. We'll be starting in just a moment. I have to get this finished. I *have* to."

They moved to the main room. Hector nodded and said hello to Sylvia and Adrienne Monnier; to Gertrude and Alice. Ford was there, still very much with Fargue. Ford was going on about something D. H. Lawrence had once remarked to him.

Hector shook William Carlos Williams's hand. The doctor-poet nodded at Hector's leg and said, "You seem quite better, Hector."

"Quite. Thanks to you."

Nicole held up her hands and Hector, Brinke, Hem, and Hadley hastened to sit.

"I want to thank you all for coming on such short notice," Nicole said. "I've made a decision about the fate of *Intimations*. I've created a trust to continue funding of the magazine for at least the next three years—ample time for its new editor to secure alternate, further funding."

Sylvia said aloud, "New editor?"

"That's right," Nicole said. "I'm relinquishing all editorial responsibilities, all affiliation with *Intimations*, effective immediately."

Some chatter ensued. Hector smoked a cigarette, watching reactions . . . listening to the others wonder aloud or make guesses as to who the new editor might be. To Hector's mind, being given control of a literary magazine in the present climate was no great favor.

Nicole said, "I could never have imagined doing this, not even a few days ago. Our magazine and its mission—finding new voices and showcasing promising writers, providing outlet to daring young poets—was a dear dream of ours." Nicole's chin began to tremble. She sipped some sherry, then pressed on. "Frankly, with Joan gone, I can't imagine continuing. So I'm not going to try. I've spent the past two days talking with some writers whose work Joan and I have both admired and published. I've been talking to the writers and poets I feel most share our sensibilities and vision for *Intimations*."

Hector continued watching the room . . . several strangers there. Obvious poets in bohemian or shabby dress; drunken literary writers Hector knew by face and reputation. Hem was looking around, too, Hector noticed. Little magazines were a good bit outside Brinke's realm, and so she struck Hector as looking a bit bored by it all, her gaze constantly returning to Molly.

For her part, Molly was attentive . . . kneading her fingers and licking her lips and closely watching Nicole. Hector focused his attention squarely on Molly.

Nicole said, "So, I have made some decisions, difficult decisions. Some that are yet to be made clear. But this one decision that I'm about to share with you came relatively easily to me. And so, the new editor of *Intimations* has been chosen. Please support the new editor as she settles into her role. She'll need much help. She'll eventually need contributors—financial contributors. And she'll need good friends. Friends such as those whom Joan and I so valued during our time with you. Please, join me now in congratulating *Intimations'* new editor, Margaret Wilder. Come up here, Molly."

Molly, beaming, put down her glass and rose, hugging Nicole. Gertrude and Alice, after scowling at one another, clapped politely with the more exuberant applause of Sylvia and Adrienne. Fargue, standing, put his hands together, shaming Ford to his feet. Fargue said out of the side of his mouth to Ford, "I've followed her career for some time now"—Hector rolled his eyes—"and early identified her as a comer."

Ford, nodding, said, "I've been after her . . . after Millie . . . for the *longest* time . . . to write a little something . . . for the *Transatlantic*."

Hem stood and helped Hadley up. Brinke and Hector were the last to stand. Hem and Brinke looked at Hector—looking at him as though they somehow expected him to have known what was coming and had kept it from them. Hector shrugged his shoulders, putting his hands together.

Hem cornered Hector at the bar. "You really didn't know?"

"Hadn't a clue." Hector handed Hem a whisky soda. "It's a little like hanging a target on Molly's back, though. I don't like it. Not under these circumstances. And can she edit? Can Molly balance books? I dunno."

"When it comes to literary magazines," Hem said, "I don't think accounting skills are paramount concerns, Lasso. Main thing there is just out-running the creditors."

"Suppose."

Hem clapped Hector's back. "Well, if she's anything like Ford, or Hunt, or any other of these little review editors of my experience, then I think we can safely say that you're back to one girl, marriage or no. Molly's days and nights are now spoken for. She'll practically live at that little magazine's goddamn office. Gets into their blood and pushes out everything else."

Hector poured himself another drink. "That been your experience with the *Transatlantic*? If it is, you've been hiding it well, 'cause you haven't seemed too scarce, Hem."

Hem sucked on an ice cube. "Well, if I had autonomy—any real say—I might, Lasso. But Ford directs his magazine as if he's still running the *English Review*. He's actually dug up some geezer who's writing his meandering memoirs. Ford's slated an excerpt in the next number. Honest to Christ, it opens, 'I first met Whistler . . .'"

Wincing, Hector said, "So quit. Leave Ford to the tender mercies of the nihilists." Hector's stomach kicked: Brinke had pulled Molly off into a corner. It seemed a very intent exchange . . . no smiles, but many nods from both women. Hector watched them, only half-hearing what Hem was saying.

"Yeah, well, I doubt even that murderous crowd has the patience to kill Ford," Hem said. "But it's the game, too—making the connections. We both know that. Making those connections, tending to the career. Kissing ass. And I think I've just about gotten the Master broken down to the point of publishing Gertrude's *Making of Americans*. And . . ."

Brinke opened her purse and handed something to Molly. Molly nodded a last time, smiled uncertainly, then embraced Brinke. They kissed one another—more like sisters. Then Molly smiled and put out a hand to Fargue as he stepped around Brinke and bowed before *Intimations'* new editor.

Brinke slipped over and confiscated Hector's drink. She took a slug, then whistled low through the burn. "Not smooth stuff," she said. Brinke feinted a punch at Ernest's jaw with her left hand and said, "Heard any good jokes lately, Hem?"

He shrugged. "Haven't talked to Ford in the past couple of hours," Hem said.

Looking puzzled, Brinke took Hector by the arm. She smiled at Hem and said, "I'm stealing your friend for a bit."

Hem nodded. "He's yours now to do with as you please." Hem drifted toward Sylvia.

Brinke said to Hector, "You as pole-armed as I am?"

"Every bit."

"I'm happy for Molly, make no mistake there."

"Me too. But frightened for her, too. The timing could be better."

Brinke pulled Hector down on a couch next to her. She said, "If the timing were different—circumstances different—Molly probably wouldn't have this opportunity. Have to take the rough with the smooth, Hector."

He was watching Molly work the literary crowd. Molly was vivacious, smiling. Molly was chatting with Sylvia and Adrienne and Hem . . . reaching out to touch their arms in confidence. She seemed much more like the old Molly.

Brinke, watching Hector watch Molly, said, "Even it we weren't leaving tomorrow, you'd likely have lost her for at least the coming few weeks. Suspect Molly'll submerge herself in this new role."

"You been talking to Hem, Brinke?"

"His prediction, too?"

"That's right."

"Hem reads people well. Molly intimated that was her intention to me when we spoke a few minutes ago."

"About that—what did you and Molly just talk about?"

Brinke said, "I apologized for the drugs and liquor and what followed. Didn't say I regretted what happened, but rather the way it happened. Said that I was sorry everything was made awkward and that your friendship with her has become warped and unclear."

"What did she say to that?"

"She agreed it's unclear. Then I told her we're leaving town for a few days. Going to Italy."

"How'd she take *that*?"

"Well enough. Said she'd look forward to catching up when we get back. Said her next few days were to be spent racing a deadline for *her* magazine's printer."

"You didn't tell her we're engaged?"

Brinke shook her head. "Incrementally, we'll bring her to that truth. We'll perhaps say things escalated between you and I in Italy, deepened into love. We'll come back having decided in Italy to marry, so far as she's concerned. I think it's best that way. If Molly knew what's happened between you and I now, well, it would be terrible for her, despite this other thing that has happened for her. This way, the blow will be softened a good bit."

"I hope that's the truth," Hector said, hating himself more than a little.

"You should steer clear of her the rest of the night," Brinke said. "When we leave, which we should do momentarily, I think, you should give Molly a big hug and hearty congratulations. Kiss her—on the *cheek*—and we'll bolt. Start acting like her big brother again, yes?"

"It's what we'll do," Hector said. "Though I can't help thinking Molly is going to need watching. You know, because of Leek."

Brinke squeezed Hector's hand. "Will she? Need watching, I mean? Really? Because it seems to me that perhaps the nihilists just assumed control of that little magazine they've been hankering to 'buy' or to 'steal.'"

"You don't really believe that, do you, Brinke?"

Brinke brushed a comma of hair back from Hector's forehead. "I'll answer your question with another, Hector."

"Okay . . ."

"Did you tell Molly about that brothel on the Rue Quincampoix, Hector?"

Brinke looked away from him. *"You did."*

Thinking about that, Hector said, "Not the *exact* location. You passed something to Molly. What was that?"

"Molly's having her period," Brinke said. "Just started. It was something to help with that. At least we dodged that bullet. You making her pregnant, I mean. What a calamity that would have been."

Hem was suddenly there next to them with Hadley. He said, "Lasso, we've agreed you should wish Molly well and we should go now. Go while things are calm with Molly and she's surrounded by well-wishers. Let's all go get properly smashed somewhere with real liquor."

"Yes," Hector said. "It was Brinke's thought, too. I'll—"

Hector took Hem's arm, pointed. Hadley and Brinke turned to see what Hector was pointing at.

Standing in the corner by the fireplace alone, Nicole Voivin took a last look around the room at all the literary lights now ignoring her—her circle of friends who were focusing instead on Molly. She was sobbing.

Nicole slowly raised her trembling left arm.

Instinctively, Hector and Hem began moving toward Nicole at a half-run.

When Brinke saw what Nicole had clutched in her left hand, she screamed to Nicole, "No—please don't do it!"

Other guests turned just as Nicole pressed the derringer to her temple and pulled the trigger.

The tiny gun sounded more like a champagne cork dislodging than anything like the gun shots of Hector's experience.

But the tiny gun was enough to do the job.

Nicole's eyes rolled up toward the ceiling. She wavered a moment on her feet, then tumbled into Hector's and Hem's arms.

Hector pressed his handkerchief to the powder-blackened hole in Nicole's left temple. The blood was pumping from the wound under his hand so he knew her heart was still beating. Then the pulsing pressure against Hector's fingers subsided and the red and purple stain on his handkerchief began to spread.

Hem said, "Dev, if Doc Williams is still here, fetch him. Hash, you call the police, *now*." Hem looked at Hector, said softly, "For all the good any of that will do."

Hector said, "It's too late, already, Hem … blood's gone to seep."

# Thirty-two

*Hem said, "Can you* imagine yourself getting that low? I mean despondent enough to do that? And in front of a crowd?"

Hector shook his head. "I've been through so much that might have pushed me that way. But each time, I've seen I can wait the despair out, wait for the wheel to turn. You hunker down and plow through. Regard it as a bad interlude to outlast. The void recedes, if you can wait the bastard out. What about you?"

"I can imagine it," Hem said. "I can conceive of giving into that kind of despair. But not with an audience. I would—"

"And so another calamity presents itself, and here are my two intrepid fiction writers. Blood on their sleeves and fully in the moment, talking of life and death. Such writers you two are."

Hector frowned at Aristide Simon. "This was a suicide," Hector said. "And not one driven by Nada. Not by the movement anyway. I think Nicole lost all hope all on her own."

"*Oui.* I was listening before making my presence known. She was a woman drawn to art and given to high emotion. A woman who had lost her life's one true love, or so my men are being told by your friends. So, for Mademoiselle Voivin, it was a succumbing to the *grand néant.*"

Hector said, "Why are we split off like this? Why were Hem and I brought to this bedroom, away from the others?"

"Privacy," Simon said. "Privacy from prying eyes and ears. I still have hopes for you helping me, Hector. And I deduce that Monsieur Hemingway here is your sounding board. I suspect he knows all that you know. So I save you the trouble of telling him.

And he's proven himself capable enough. Hemingway has demonstrated what my grandfather termed 'grace under pressure.' My men have taken the other guests to the backroom of a neighboring café in order to begin preparing the body for transport. I think, in this case, we can dispense with an autopsy. There being so many witnesses, after all."

"This is a suicide," Hector said. "No argument about that. So what brings you personally here?"

Simon waved a hand. He took a packet of Gauloises from his coat pocket. He held the pack out. Hem and Hector both shook their heads. Shrugging, Simon said, "Pretense. Camouflage. An excuse to catch you both up on some vital developments."

Hector said, "What's happened now?"

Simon said, "We have also bolstered our intelligence. We've learned some things." He smiled through a haze of smoke. "You Americans are a queer lot. Do you find it necessary to come here in order to reinvent yourselves? Can't you just move from one coast of America to another, or more simply, from one town to another, in order to recast yourselves in your own self-images? What is it about Paris that draws you all here to reimagine yourselves in some new persona?"

Hem shrugged. "I'm the man I always was, just more so. Hector's the same."

"Yes," Simon said, "admittedly some of you are steadfastly yourselves. And peculiarly, it's the ones with arguably the ugliest names. 'Hector Lassiter,' 'Ernest Hemingway' . . . 'Alice Toklas,' and most disagreeable sounding of all, 'Gertrude Stein.' Any of you four could be forgiven for adopting new names."

Hector got out one of his own cigarettes. He said, "You have a point?

Simon smiled. "I'll come to it. You have somewhere else to be? More sleuthing, or perhaps just another brush with death you're tardy for? Now, take Aleister Crowley . . . I find there is no such creature. He was instead born 'Edward Alexander.' Another reinvented man." Simon smiled and shook his head.

Hector said, "You've confirmed that Hem and I have clung to our given names . . . so you've been poking around into our pasts, too."

"As I said earlier. And I'm thorough. Hector Mason Lassiter, born in Galveston, Texas, on January 1, 1900." Simon looked at the glowing end of the cigarette gripped between his knuckles. "Tell me, Hector, I know this Texas of yours is a big state, but do you know another Texan named Vander Clyde?"

Hector looked around for a place to dispose of his match. "Nope."

"He performs every night at the Casino de Paris. Cocteau, among many others, is a great fan of this Vander's. Only many of those admirers of his believe that Vander is a woman. Your fellow Texan might be the most extreme case of 'reinvention' of which I'm aware. Vander is now an acclaimed trapeze performer most believe to be a woman named Barbette."

"Her—him—I've heard of," Hem said. "Can't wait to tell Ford. I think he has designs on this Barbette once his current mistress, Stella Bowen, comes to her senses."

Simon smiled, "Well, this fellow Texan of Hector's is an extreme example. Most of you Americans seem to lean more toward the kind of reinvention we see in Monsieur Crowley . . . in this Rook, who has rechristened himself 'Victor Leek.' Only there is no 'Oswald Rook,' either. We've run him to ground—his identity I mean. We've done that with the assistance of some rather tiresome, but dogged, genealogists in London. Oswald Rook is actually a man who was born 'Jackson Douglas Starr' in a state called Illinois. His parents were George and Irene Starr. He had one sibling, a younger sister named Lenore. In 1921, George and Irene Starr died in a fire that consumed the family home. The brother and sister, who both still lived with their aging parents—the siblings were both aspiring writers with no real other marketable skills, you see—were fortuitously away from home when the fire started. By the time home insurance investigators realized arson was to blame for the tragic conflagration, the Starr siblings had already liquidated their parents' assets and collected on two rather sizable life insurance policies, fleeing to London. Eventually they found their way here to Paris."

Hem said, "Leek—Rook—*Starr*, I mean, has a sister? Living here in Paris?"

"*Oui*. So it would seem." Simon reached over and took Hem's empty glass from his hand. He turned over his own palm and emptied into the glass the ashes from his cigarette he'd been allowing to collect there. Simon tapped the butt of his cigarette over the glass and then held it out for Hector to dispose of his spent match and to tap down his own cigarette's growing cone of ash. "We'll come to that momentarily," Simon said.

Hector said, "So Starr, and presumably this sister, murdered the mother and father for cash and a pretty new life in the Old World."

"Precisely," Simon said. "The sister, one presumes, is every bit as destructive as the brother. *La belle dame sans merci.*"

"You have passport photos? You know what this sister looks like?"

"No, we have genealogists. And a newspaper in America that is sending us a copy from its archives of the story that was run regarding the fire that killed the parents. Photos of the brother and sister ran with that article. The journalists were able to describe the brother and sister. Seems if the descriptions I've heard of Victor Leek are accurate, the brother, at least, has dyed his hair black. In the photos, he's quite fair, or so I'm told the journalists back in Illinois insist. The sister's hair? Harder to tell . . . she's wearing a hat."

Hem, the ex-newspaperman, said, "When will you have those materials in hand?"

"Friday at the latest, I would hope," the detective said. "We've been at this a while . . . we were looking for this Starr in connection with something else. A different crime. But it is a happy accident, *oui?*"

Hector said, "I'd like to see those pictures when you get them. Maybe I'll recognize the sister. Or maybe Hem will."

"I suspect *I* will recognize this sister when I see the pictures," Simon said. "You see, I have two candidates, two women I suspect of being this Lenore Starr. I'm fairly confident they can't both be wrong guesses on my part. It will be the one, or the other. I stake my career on that."

Hector braced for it: "Who are these women?"

"Indeed . . . who are they indeed?" Simon said. "This is going to be terribly distressing for you, Hector. You see, as I told you earlier, I've been investigating others around you beyond Hemingway here. And I've learned some things. Things that will be hard for you to hear. For instance, Hector, there is no such person as 'Brinke Devlin.'"

Hector said, "That's no revelation. 'Brinke' is a nickname. Her real name is Alison."

"Yes, Alison Boyton Devlin," Simon said. "Born in New York state. That's her story now. But there is no such person. Her last confirmed identity we traced to the Middle East. In 1922, she was living in Egypt under the name of 'Margaret Walker.' She was then writing her mystery novels under the pen name of Connor Templeton, of course. But she lived under this alternate identity. Prior to that, that 'Margaret' spent a year in Berlin. There she was 'Gretchen Pabst.' And, of course, the author Connor Templeton."

Hector felt a strange tightness in his chest. He could hear it in his own voice: "But you can't confirm that she's Starr's sister?"

Simon shook his head. "I'm sorry, Hector. I can't seem to grasp a thread that I can follow to a 'true personality' for this woman. By that, I mean I can't determine what name this woman who now calls herself Brinke Devlin was given at birth."

"She's not Starr's sister," Hector said. "I know she isn't."

"And you're perhaps right," Simon said. "She may be entirely apart from Starr, or Rook, and apart from all these crimes. But there is another issue, my friend. Perhaps other crimes, of which your 'Brinke' is not so innocent."

Hector swallowed hard. "What the hell are you talking about now?"

"In Berlin, in Madrid, and in some other places we know or suspect her to have been, there have been other crimes ... crimes strangely close to crimes described in various of Connor Templeton's novels. I have a young detective working for me who studied in America. He's quite fluent in English. He's been reading the Templeton books in their original English ... and making connections. A talented and diligent young man, you'll agree."

"Kudos to your boy," Hem said. "How do you know Brinke wasn't just drawing on crimes that happened in these places where she was living at the time? Lowndes modeled *The Lodger* after the Ripper murders, but nobody suspected her of committing the Whitechapel crimes."

"Well, that is the question," Simon said. "Which came first? The crimes, or the crime stories? I have no satisfactory answer for that as yet. Particularly because in at least two cases, the crimes, and the probable composition of the novels describing those crimes, seem to have unfolded almost simultaneously. Or so we're inclined to believe."

Hector said, "You're going to confront Brinke?"

"Not yet. Not until I have my photos. And these others crimes are outside my purview ... far outside my jurisdiction. Depending on what my young man finds in his researches, I may eventually turn the materials over to my counterparts in Spain and Germany. I suppose I should think about confiscating her passport. But that can wait another day or two ... for the newspapers from America to reach me. You'll of course want to keep all this from this woman, Hector. Particularly since she may be Leek's, or rather, *Starr's* sister, and thusly a murderer many times over. I'm sorry to put you in this quandary. I know you are lovers. But given today's earlier threatening letter, and that poem, I think it's only fair to arm you with information so you can protect yourself, Hector. You should perhaps find some excuse to stay away from her for the next couple of days."

"I'll see to myself," Hector said. "Don't worry about me."

Hem said, "You said there are two women you suspect could be Starr's sister. Who is the other?"

"A slightly more compelling candidate to my mind," Simon said. "And, in her current incarnation, she claims to have been born in the same small town where Starr was born."

"Illinois?" Hector said, "this small town . . . is it Elgin?"

Simon nodded, sighing. "I'm sorry, Hector, *oui*."

Hem said it: "Molly."

"*Oui*, Margaret Raeburn Wilder. For whom no authentic records exist, just like Brinke Devlin."

"Molly's shown me correspondence from Elgin," Hector said. "From her mother."

Simon nodded. "You saw the envelopes?"

"No," Hector said.

"The signatures?"

"No, she quoted the letters to me." Hector squeezed the bridge of his nose. *Jesus.*

"Could be forgeries . . . perhaps some adopted mother . . . or a woman who styles herself as this 'Molly's' mother," Simon said. "Or she made them up on the spot. She is the creative type. The fact remains, we have the Elgin connection. Fair hair. And she's of the right age to be Starr's younger sister."

Hector shook his head. "Name changes—at home they'd be sinister. At least eyebrow-raising. But here? *De rigueur.* As you said, many Americans do it. Man Ray is really 'Emmanuel Radnitzky' . . . I could go on and on."

Simons said, "Well, Friday we'll know all. Until then, stay away from these pretty, deceptive young women, Hector. That is my advice to you."

"I'll take it under advisement."

"My men continue to watch you," Simon said, "but that veil of protection only extends so far, Hector. It can't reach into the beds of apartments and garrets. I can only protect you *en plein air.*" Simon rose and said, "Now I go to speak to some other witnesses."

Hem said, "Molly? You'll confront her about this?"

"She was gone before my men arrived," Simon said gravely. "The only one of you to leave, it seems. So again, my suspicions are raised."

When Simon was gone, Hem slapped Hector's back. "You are bitched. I'm so sorry, Lasso."

"It's a goddamn mess," Hector agreed. "But I don't think Brinke is a murderer. And she's certainly not Leek's sister." Hector couldn't yet think of the killer poet as "Starr."

"So what do you do, Lasso?"

"First, find out if Brinke's ever been to Italy and written any books about Italy that might make her a suspect there. If not, she and I push on to Italy on the night train tomorrow. Do it before that cocksucker Simon can take her passport."

"Still going to marry her?"

"I love her, Hem."

# Thirty-three

*Hector was very aware* of Hem watching him. But he smiled at Brinke as she rose to embrace him. She kissed his cheek and whispered in his ear, "Hadley was terrified they were going to arrest Hem again, and you, too, this time."

"It wasn't like that."

"Then what was it about?"

He squeezed her arm. "Later, please." Hector looked around at the other party guests, then innocently asked, "Where's Molly?"

"The police want to know that, too," Brinke said. "She seems to have drifted off in the confusion after Nicole's shooting. Left before the police came. She's so unbalanced emotionally, hard to tell what seeing that did to her. I feel so sorry for her, in a way. There she was, given this great gift, having her big night thanks to Nicole, then Nicole does *that* and takes all the focus away from Molly and her new literary enterprise."

"Like you said," Hector said, watching Simon watching him with Brinke, "gotta take the rough with the smooth." Hector helped Brinke on with her overcoat.

"Most are staying on here to drink," she said.

"Exactly," Hector said. "Good reason for the four of us to find our own café. Speaking of the future—you ever actually been to Italy, Brinke?"

"Not until tomorrow." Brinke frowned. "We *are* still going, aren't we?"

"Of course." He stroked her hair back from where it had fallen over her right eyebrow. "Of course, darling."


"Another ghastly night," Hadley said, holding out her wineglass for Hector to refill it. Hadley sipped her wine and said, "Hardly feel up to the next stop."

Hem said, "Pardon, Hash? There's a *next* stop?"

Hadley said, "Invitation came while you were out with Hector. Adam Byron, who runs *Revelations*, is having a party in 'defiance of the recent murders' according to the announcement he sent. I wish I'd brought the actual invitation along. It's rather amazing. Covered with skulls and crossed bones. I'm sorry I forgot to mention it."

A husky voice over Hector's shoulder: "We are invited, as well. But I wonder about going after tonight's mess."

Gertrude and Alice had sidled up behind Hector and Brinke. Hector rose and pulled over a couple of extra chairs.

"Given the way these social gatherings are going," Gertrude said, "reticence seems the thing called for regarding tonight's next affair." Hector scooted in Alice's chair, then, with a good bit more exertion, Gertrude's.

"Excuse me, I want to make a quick trip to my place," Hector said.

Brinke's eyes on him: "What's up, Tex?"

"Just checking in with Germaine. Making sure there've been no visitors I might have missed." The name hung unspoken between them: *Molly.*

"Probably a good idea," Brinke said softly.

Hem: "A very good idea, Lasso."

Hector waved down a cab.

Germaine was behind her desk, working over some papers. Hector kissed her on the cheek and told her he might be away for the night. Then he said, "We're still thinking about a holiday away for a few days ... Italy," he said.

"Sounds lovely," Germaine said. Something in her voice. Hector felt his own pulse quickening. Might the poet or those bastards who followed Leek actually have threatened the dear old lady to get to Hector?

He said, "What's wrong? I hear it in your voice."

"Nothing, perhaps," Germaine said. "I just ... Some police came by. You're not in some trouble are you, Hector?"

"Not directly. I'm actually helping the police with something. Did they ask you questions?"

Germaine said, "No, they left an envelope for you."

Hector figured it would be the pictures of Simon's men that Hector had been promised—to aid in Hector's ability to distinguish the cops from other possible tails.

And that reminded Hector of another problem for Thursday: he'd have to lose his police shadows in order to flee France with Brinke.

But that was a problem for later.

"It's nothing, please believe me," Hector told Germaine. "Just some information to help me. Please keep them for me, won't you? I'll look them over later."

"Of course." Something still there in the old woman's voice.

"I really am fine," Hector said, smiling. He said, "I'm not in any trouble. Not with the police."

"I believe you, Hector." Germaine hesitated, then said, "I may have done something very stupid. Foolishly, I carelessly betrayed a confidence. You had a visitor a short while ago. A young woman, very attractive."

"Margaret Wilder?"

"That's her name, yes. She was asking after you. Hoping you'd come home from some event you were both present at earlier this evening. She seemed quite urgent about seeing you. I didn't think and, well, I said you were still out with your *fiancée*. Mademoiselle Wilder became quite upset then. She ran out, crying. I'm so sorry, Hector. I don't want to pry into your private life. But I sensed that you and this other woman . . . well . . . I've created a terrible problem for you. I know that."

"Molly's secretly been harboring an infatuation," Hector said. "I didn't know about it until quite recently. You did nothing wrong, Germaine. Don't worry about it, please. It's fine. I'll see you later."

Hector stepped back out to his waiting cab.

*Well, that tore it.* Hector massaged his temples with his fingertips. He wanted to be in Italy, *immediately* . . . before he might have to be confronted with some headline about Molly throwing herself off some bridge or under some train like the doomed heroine of some overheated Russian novel.

Hector paid the cabbie and slipped back into the warmth of the café. Brinke met him at the door: "What's wrong, Hector?"

Hector shook his head. "Germaine accidentally tipped Molly to our engagement. Molly was at my place just a bit ago."

Brinke slammed her palm into the wall next to the door. "Oh, Hector..."

He took Brinke's arm. "There's more...this party, let's go to it—token appearances—but take a coach there, alone. We need to talk. I need to know some things, Brinke. I need to know things about you, right now. I need to know them for my own piece of mind. Before Italy. Before I dismantle my life here to build that beautiful new life with you back home on that island."

Brinke's chin was trembling. "All right, Hector. Of course, darling. We'll go right now?"

"Right now."

"I need to make a stop first. Want to make certain that Molly hasn't paid a visit to my place."

# Thirty-four

*In the years to* follow, Hector would always remember the ride to the party: the sound of horses' hooves on cobblestones, the swirl of the falling snow through the coach's windows, and the smell of fires from the chimney pots.

There were also Brinke's sighs...his own mounting frustration at her many evasions. Her hand squeezing his so tightly—as if through her grip's mere pressure she could make Hector believe, or, at least, dissuade further questions.

Hector said, "I don't believe as Simon suspects, that you are tied to Leek, or as we now know him to be, Starr."

Brinke's eyes smoldered. "Well, thank God for that." Pure acid.

"But these other crimes I've been told about," Hector said, "I need to know more from you about what Simon is accusing you of in these other countries."

"Lies, Hector. Coincidences made to appear sinister by a man whose career is built upon suspicion. Innuendos built upon newspaper headlines I drew plot points from. Simon's theories are insane."

"And these other names? Gretchen Pabst? Margaret Walker?"

Names chosen for places I never meant to stay for long."

"What's you're real name, darling?"

"Brinke."

"Your *given* name? What's *that*? What's your *birth* name?"

"Brinke. Brinke Sinclair. I've come full circle." She squeezed his hand again. "It's true, darling. I've taken back my first name."

"Where were you born, *Brinke*?"

"Springfield, Ohio."

"Your parents' names?"

"Joe and Mildred Sinclair. I'm not from money."

"Any siblings?"

"No, I really am an only child, just as I told you."

"Your parents still living? Could I wire them and confirm all this?"

She hung her head. "I really don't know."

"Why not?"

"I haven't seen them since I was a child, Hector. I was raised by nuns."

"How'd that come to be?"

Their coach jerked to a stop. "We're here," she said unnecessarily.

"But we're not finished, Brinke."

"Everything, darling. I'll tell all of it to you, whatever the cost. I'll tell you what happened with my parents, tell you about my writing and what happened in Germany, in Spain, and in Egypt. I swear, my love, you, and only you, shall have all my secrets. But I have to think about how best to frame it for you. Because, and this is selfish, I don't want to lose you in giving you all my secrets. They aren't that bad, Hector. Not like that damned policeman seems to think they are. But the life I've sometimes lived isn't the life a Brinke Devlin would have lived. That's why I'm her now, I guess."

Hector stared into her eyes. "Tonight? Later? You swear to me?"

"Everything later, yes darling." She stroked his cheek. "Kiss me now, Hector. Before we go in there, kiss me."

She drew slowly away from their long, deep kiss, her lips swollen, her fingertips tracing his lips. "I love you, Hector. You're the only one I've ever said that to, the only one in the world. You're the man I love. The man I'll always love."

Hector lifted her chin, kissed her again. "I love you. So no secrets, Brinke...not on my side or yours."

She smiled sadly and he wiped away her tears with his thumbs. "Why are you crying, Brinke?"

"It's you...goddamn wonderful you."


Hector wished they had begged out on the party. He'd rather be alone with Brinke...drawing from her all her secrets between bouts of lovemaking.

But they rode the elevator in silence to the hotel's uppermost floor—the grand ballroom.

The party was a drunken who's-who of avant-garde Paris—painters, musicians, writers.

Brinke clung to Hector's arm, kissing his neck and telling him over and over how much she loved him.

Hector saw Estelle Quartermain and her husband chatting with Gertrude and Alice. Estelle had slicked back her mouse-brown hair from her forehead to disguise the damage of her disastrous hairstyle.

Hem and Hadley were wending their way through the crowd toward Brinke and Hector. Brinke kissed Hector again, passionately, her tongue parting his lips. Hector tried to say, "We have an audience."

"I don't care," she said. "But excuse me now, darling."

She nodded at the ladies' room door. Impulsively, Brinke leaned in for a last kiss. She pressed her palm to his cheek, her fingers fleetingly stroking down to his chin, then she was gone.

Hem, watching Brinke's back, said, "You told her didn't you, Lasso? Told her what Simon told us?"

"Of course."

"Get any answers?"

"A few honest ones I think." Hector squeezed Hadley's hand in welcome. "More are promised later tonight. So I want to make it an early evening. Meet the host and vamoose."

Hem said, "You're still going on to Italy with Brinke, aren't you?"

"Yes," Hector said. "I wish we were already on our way."

There was some commotion across the ballroom. A few screams . . . some laughs. Hector and Hem exchanged a look and then began shouldering their way through the revelers toward the source of the screams and guffaws.

Hector heard someone ahead of them say, "What is this, some kind of Dadaesque entertainment? How silly."

Hector and Hem broke through the lines and exchanged another look. Hem said, "Holy fuck!" Then, "Everyone *run!*"

A black-clad man stood with his back to a wall of windows, clutching two sticks of dynamite in either hand. The fuses were cut short and the flames descending down each fuse had nearly reached their terminus. A few partygoers were still laughing and pointing—mistaking it for some piece of theater.

The man was reciting a bastardized form of the Lord's Prayer: ". . . though I walk through the shadow of the valley of death, *nada* is with me . . ."

Years before, in a trench on Easter Sunday, a potato-masher grenade had plunked down in the mud near the feet of Hector and a circle of his spent friends as they were resting between salvos. For an instant, Hector had hesitated, then he had moved to throw his own torso over the grenade in a bid to save his buddies.

During Hector's fleeting instant of hesitation, Frankie Moore, a tow-headed, seventeen-year-old boy from La Plata, Missouri, had flung himself over the grenade.

Having seen the carnage of Frankie's body, and what the boy endured during the long hour before succumbing to his near total bisection, Hector had wondered if, faced with the same sort of life-or-death choice, he would again make the effort to take that self-sacrificial plunge.

Hector was running toward the man with the sticks of dynamite in either hand—Hector was running before he knew his brain had sent his legs the signal. He thought he heard Hem behind him, yelling, "Lasso, no!"

The crazed man looked from Hector to either of his hands—checking the progress of the fuses—then looked back to Hector, snarling. All the while, he continued reciting his crazed prayer, now dropping *nadas* into the prayer with such frequency it almost sounded like a chant.

Hector grabbed the black-clad man by both biceps, running hard and using his own size and weight to force the Nadaist backward on his heels, driving him toward a window.

Hector heard glass breaking, then he watched the man begin to scream, dropping the sticks of dynamite from his left hand in a vain attempt to clutch at Hector's sleeve.

*So much for the siren song of the void*, Hector thought. *Look at him, trying like hell to save himself now.*

Then Hector felt glass dig into his thigh and realized his own center of gravity was well beyond the window's ledge and that he was in fact beginning his own free fall to the pavement far below.

Behind him, Hector heard a guttural, "No!"

Hector felt a sharp jerk, his fall temporarily ceased. A hand was gripping at the collar of his coat, choking Hector, and another had gotten hold of his coat tails and belt.

Below him, perhaps seven floors closer to the pavement, the dynamite exploded. The falling, screaming man was enveloped in a red, orange, and black mushroom cloud, then the explosives in his other hand went off, shredding his body. The swelling fireball was rolling up the side of the hotel toward Hector.

His own free fall had ceased, but Hector was dangling above a rising ball of fire. Hector had seen burn victims in the war. He didn't want to become like the ones he remembered: some agonized, blind scab with no ears or nose. Better to dash one's brains out on the pavement far below. Hector struggled against the hands suspending him above the swift-approching plume of fire and smoke.

"Stop fighting, goddamn it, Lasso. Go limp!"

Hector did that and felt himself jerked back through the window. He felt a sliver of glass slide into his thigh, and another rake his belly, then a smaller ball of flame rolled in through the broken window, setting the curtains on fire. Hector was sprawled on his back atop Hem, who said, "We've got to get those curtains down before they set fire to the walls and ceiling!"

Ford and Fargue each grabbed hold of a flaming curtain and jerked the drapes down and to the floor, stomping out the flames. Grinning, forgetting himself, Hem said, "Atta boy, Master... Fargue!"

William Carlos Williams bent down over Hector, supporting him while Hem slid out from under Hector. Williams focused his attention on Hector's thigh. The doctor picked up a piece of broken glass, and inserting it into the hole in Hector's pants, slit the inseam of Hector's pants leg. Williams said, "Thank God, the femoral artery was missed—just. This will require stitches, however." Gertrude Stein forced herself into a kneeling position and ripped open Hector's shirt. She grasped a bloody piece of glass and pulled it out of Hector's belly. "Only an eighth-of-an-inch penetration, if that," she said. "Superficial, we're agreed, *Doctor* Williams?"

Williams checked Hector's belly and said, "It'll bleed plenty, but I concur... *Nurse* Stein."

Hector said, "I'm fine, really. Just bandage me up."

Ignoring him, Williams said, "It's that head wound that most worries me. The explosion must have blown some glass back up at Hector." Hector realized then he felt something warm and wet above his hairline. Then Williams's hand was at Hector's mouth, forcing in some pills. Hadley handed Williams a glass of water and he urged it down Hector's throat to wash down the pills.

Hector felt that familiar feeling of spreading warmth. More morphine, he figured.

The world receded.


In a haze, feeling himself lifted onto a stretcher, Hector heard Williams say to someone, maybe Gertrude based on the context, "A first, eh? A woman's emergency sewing kit to stitch a severe head laceration. If he keeps his hair in the years to come, the scar should never show."

Hector heard Hadley next—she sounded slightly manic—"I've looked everywhere, Tatie. There's no sign of Brinke."

Another voice (Estelle Quartermain?): "The bathroom is a shambles . . . it must have been a terrible struggle. There was some talcum powder knocked off the sink and a shoeprint left in the talc . . . size 12, maybe . . . and a woman's shoeprint, too. On the inside of the stall, written in lipstick, are two letters, an M and a W. It's clearly a kidnapping."

Hem: "Either way, the police are on their way up. Hash, you go to the hospital with Sylvia . . . stay with Hector there. I'll see what I can do to find Brinke."


The cold air and sleet against his face briefly brought Hector back around. A man in a white coat was strapping Hector to a bench in the back of an ambulance. Hector saw another man in a white coat was curled on the floor of the ambulance, huddled in a pool of blood. The man's throat had been slashed down so far that Hector could make out the spinal cord through all the severed soft tissue.

Across from Hector, sitting on a bench, was a man in a black suit. His black hair was slicked back and he had a pencil-thin black mustache. He smiled at Hector. Somehow Hector just *knew*. His voice thick from the drugs, Hector said, "Victor Leek?"

"That's right. We'll talk again shortly, Lassiter. Enjoy this last peaceful sleep."

# Thirty-five

*Hector was hanging by* his wrists from a chain dangling from a ceiling hidden in darkness. His shoulders hurt and he was cold. He realized then that he was also naked. He looked down and saw a good deal of dried blood trailing down from his thigh almost to his ankle. There was dried blood on his belly and matted in his pubic hair.

Hector blinked a few times, trying to squint into the blackness. In one corner there was a soft glow from a small fire. Hector said to the darkness, "Where's Brinke?"

A voice: "I don't know what you're talking about. And you have other immediate personal concerns you should focus on."

The man who had identified himself as Victor Leek—or *Jackson Starr*—emerged from the blackness, smiling...one arm behind his back. Hector found he could see a bit better now. The walls around him seemed to be covered with skulls and stacks of human bones. "Where in God's name are we?"

"In God's name, indeed," the poet said. "We're in the annex of the ancient graveyards of Paris. Les Catacombes. The City of the Dead hidden under the City of Lights."

"Your kind of place, Leek," Hector said. "Or are we going by 'Starr' today?"

The poet scowled.

"That's right, pal," Hector said, "the police have figured out who you really are. You, and your sister, Lenore. Or should I say Molly?"

Hector couldn't read the man's expression. The poet said, "You're confusing me, again. I'm Nobodaddy."

*"Sure,"* Hector said. He looked down at himself again. "I'm going to tell you right now, and tell you true, I have no information about anything that matters a damn. So there's no point in thinking about torturing me . . . I have nothing to give you."

The poet smiled. He pulled his arm from behind his back. Hector saw "Leek" was clutching a cat-o'-nine-tails in his hand. The poet said, "Torture, to use your term for it, isn't exclusively a means to an end, my friend. It can be an end in and of itself. I promise you pain." The poet raised his arm. Hector instinctively twisted around so the blows would fall on his back. The poet lashed out three, four times. After the second swing, Hector gave up trying to suppress his own screams.

The poet cast down his cat-o'-nine-tails. "Already it grows tiresome," he said. "And you've already lost a good bit of blood from your earlier wounds. Can't have you sliding into unconsciousness from blood loss. Not before the main course."

Between gasps, Hector said, "At least tell me Molly isn't tied by blood to you, you diseased son of a bitch." His back was burning and he could feel warm trickles of blood running down the small of his back and down his ass. If anything, the man more closely resembled Brinke.

"Dying in ignorance can be its own form of torture, Hector," the poet said. Leek turned, speaking into the blackness behind him. "Is it hot enough, yet?"

A voice from the corner where the small fire had been set said, "White hot."

"Bring it."

Another man stepped from the shadows. The second man was wearing thick leather gloves and clutching a pair of iron tongs. Gripped in the tongs was a branding iron, its tip glowing blue-orange.

The poet pulled on his own pair of leather gloves. He said to Hector, "You may have heard some stories about me. I'm told you confronted Crowley. Figure he told you all about my misfortune."

Hector said, "Did you enjoy killing prostitutes before your 'misfortune,' or does the resulting frustration drive you to that?"

The poet took hold of the leather-wrapped end of the glowing branding iron. "I'm going to help you answer your own question, Lassiter." The poet examined the end of the branding iron, then began walking toward Hector. "I say this with some authority: the pain you're about to experience will eclipse any you've known, or will ever know." He smiled. "Left, or right? Or perhaps split the difference?"

Squirming, screaming, Hector tried to back away from the glowing end of the branding iron, so close now Hector could feel the heat radiating from the end of the molten metal on his thighs and genitals.

Hector hit the end of his tethering chain as the iron moved closer between his legs.

One instant, the poet was in Hector's face, urging the iron toward Hector's testicles and murmuring, *"Similis simili gaudet."*

A second later, there was a shot, and the poet was clutching at a red hole in his shirt, halfway between his heart and belly.

The poet's cohort began to run, retreating further into Les Catacombes, but now the cavern was awash in torchlight and there was a second shot and the other man fell, blood spreading around the place where his face struck the floor.

"I'm deeply sorry, Hector," Aristide Simon said, his voice echoing off the macabre walls. "You shouldn't have had to suffer more than you already did back at the hotel. My men and I, we became lost in these damned tunnels." Simon began working at Hector's bonds. He said, "But it was, in the end, your screams that brought us here in time."

Hoarse, Hector said, "How'd you know to follow the ambulance?"

"One of my men I'd posted to watch you is the reason," Simon explained. "Just as I was arriving, he pointed out the ambulance was headed *away* from the nearest hospital."

Hector said, "Everything . . . blurred." He could still hear the drugs in his own voice . . . the slurring. He said, "Brinke, I thought I heard . . ."

His hands came free from the chains and Hector slumped into Simon's arms. Hector heard William Carlos Williams say, "He's in no condition for that, now. Give him more of these . . . make him dry-swallow them. I need to get to work on those whip wounds. We'll tell him the other sorry part later. Collect his clothes. I want to get him warm. Put on his pants and socks and we'll drape his overcoat over him when we carry him outside."

# PART V

jeudi
*(The First)*

# Thirty-six

*Hector was seething. Some* fool had left a newspaper in reach of his bed. Hem would know better. Hector figured it had to have been one of Simon's men—two men he figured to be stooges of Simon's stood sentry outside his door. After what had happened to Leek, Hector wondered a bit at that: there couldn't still be some threat, could there?

Whatever the case, Hector had seen the article in the paper about Brinke's abduction. An hour after Hector had unsuccessfully lobbied Williams for a discharge, and tried to press him for more information, Simon finally appeared. A sad smile.

Hector's heart kicked. "No . . ."

The French cop stood at the foot of Hector's bed. "There is little doubt, now, my friend. We're still looking for her body, but one of her shoes, her purse, and Madamoiselle Devlin's torn dress have been recovered at various points along the Seine. It's possible she might have become attached or tangled in some way to the underside of some barge and dragged out to sea, in which case we may never find more. There is also much debris down there on the bottom of the river in which a body might become snarled for some time. Perhaps forever."

"It doesn't make sense," Hector said. "If the intent was to kill

Brinke, why not do it right there in the ladies' room, with a knife or a gun? Why risk capture to drag her out of a busy hotel? And that's another thing—how'd they get her out of here past desk clerks and bellboys? Past elevator operators, hotel detectives, and doormen?"

"You talk like a mystery writer, my friend," Simon said, a bit patronizing, but his voice soft. "There are service and delivery doors all over the hotel. Nonpublic entrances and exits through kitchens and storage areas. Or, possibly, they had taken a room close by the ballroom. They might have held her there and waited until after hours to smuggle her out."

Hector said, "Now who's talking like a mystery writer? And again, why go to that trouble when they just might have killed her in the ladies' room?"

"They intended to kill you, too, Hector. But not right away. They took the trouble to kidnap you with the intent of torture and then death. I don't want to be morbid or give you more to pain you than you already have to cope with, but a similar intent might have directed their actions regarding Mademoiselle Devlin."

Hector couldn't bring himself to think along those lines. And he couldn't conceive of Brinke being dead. He said, "And Molly? Have you found her?"

"Missing, still."

"I notice I still have guards."

Simon nodded slowly. "How much are you up for, Hector? How much can you sustain hearing?"

"Everything. And I want out of here. I need to get out there, to look for Brinke."

That sad smile, again. "There's been a colossal complication, my young friend. Either we had bad information from the beginning—from that treacherous Crowley, whom, by the way, I've initiated steps to have deported—or else we have been fooled in another way. Frankly, I think the latter."

"What are you talking about?"

"Hector, the coroner provided some startling news regarding

the body of the man we believed to be Victor Leek. The man I shot down in those damned tunnels. The dead man's genitalia, they're quite intact."

Hector was raging: "So that man who tortured me was a stand-in."

"So it would appear," Simon said softly. "Particularly since my newspapers from the States have arrived and early." Simon opened up his leatherette case and passed a yellowing copy of a broadsheet newspaper to Hector. Hector scanned the headline about the fatal fire, then, under a heading slugged "Survivors," looked at the photos of the brother and sister Starr.

Hector's heart raced as he looked at the photo of Lenore Starr. It was a picture of a younger Molly Wilder, no question of that.

And her brother, Hamilton Starr, aka Victor Leek?

He was Molly's boyfriend, Philippe, her doting, mediocre painter.

Simon was watching Hector. He said, "I'm sorry, Hector. Truly sorry. We will get this 'Molly.'"

"Or I will."

"*Non*—we'll have no talk like that, Hector. The brother, do you recognize him?"

Hector folded the newspaper, handed it back to Simon. *"Non."*

# Thirty-seven

*Hem handed Hector the* note he had found tacked on the door of their flat when Hadley and he had returned home the night before:

Monsieur Hemingway:
    A flimsy door . . . a silly French woman . . . Only those

between your son and I. Stand down or face the consequences.

—VL

Hector cursed. He said, "Where are Hadley and Bumby now?"

Hem said, "In the waiting room out there. With a couple of
boxer friends. Safe enough for now. Jesus, to threaten a child . . ."

"That's the powerful thing about embracing the void, Hem—
anything goes when you believe your actions carry no consequences."

"Hadley wants me to take this letter to the police. To inform
Simon of the threat."

"Normally, I'd agree," Hector said. "But you do that, and Simon will put guards all over you. He'll make you his stalking
horse . . . you, and yours."

"Christ, I'm so sorry about Brinke, Lasso."

Hector raised a hand. "No. *No.* I haven't accepted Simon's theory on that one yet, Hem. It doesn't seem plausible to me. Makes no
sense to kidnap Brinke under those circumstances and with those
attendant risks, and then toss her into the Seine. These nihilists kill
with impunity, quickly and face-to-face . . . *except* for that poisoning. But whatever the means, they *don't* haul you off to do the
dirty deed."

"Except in your case, Lasso."

"You been talking to Simon? You sound like him about this."

"We talked a bit," Hem said. "Simon told me Molly is confirmed as the sister. Simon didn't have his newspapers handy, or I
might have been able to identify the brother."

*A lucky break.* "Or maybe not," Hector said. "Unlikely you
would have known him. I've been thinking. My wallet is here in the
drawer by the bed. Those train tickets are there. Take them and
you and Hadley get on that train tonight. *You* go on to Italy. Bumby
will likely be allowed to ride for free. If not, you can get a third

ticket for him at the station. As he's in-arms it's not as though he'll need a seat. Should be no problem."

"I don't want to run, Lasso," Hem said. "Or to leave you in the lurch."

"It's not like that, buddy. I'm going to end this thing tonight, Hem. Alone."

"Guess you haven't heard, Lasso. You're in here for at least the next three days. Doc Williams's orders. They're worried about your back infecting. Besides, with your back shredded like it is, and the stitches in your thigh and belly, you aren't going to be particularly agile."

"I'll cope. And I don't need agility. Just need to get back to my place and get my Colt."

"You need to get out of here first," Hem said. "You're under guard."

"That's how you pay me back for those train tickets and how you best help me, Hem."

"What do you mean?"

"Go out and quietly tell Hadley you're leaving for Italy tonight, Hem. Tell her that, but also tell her that you're going to be in here, in my room, for another hour or so."

Hem scowled. "To what end?"

"You're going to help me dress, Hem. Then you're going to loan me your hat and coat so I can walk out of here past Simon's guards. While I'm sneaking out, you're going to take my place here in bed . . . cover up to the chin and hide that mustache. Give me my hour to get home and get my gun. Then you and Hadley and John get the hell out of this city. I'll try and join you in Italy in a few days. Maybe I'll even bring company."

Hem said, "Hector, I don't want you carrying around a lot of false hope for finding Brinke . . . not alive. Simon is insistent she's gone."

"He's been wrong about other things, Hem. He may be wrong this time, too. You'll do this for me, buddy?"

Hem smiled uncertainly. He sighed, then reached out and shook Hector's foot. "Let me go tell Hash. Tell her not to react or call out when *I* walk out of this hospital in a few moments. And thanks so much for those tickets, Lasso. If I was a lone wolf I'd have your back all the way on this, I want you to know that—"

"Stop there, buddy. It's a given. Just make sure you don't have any black-clad, sullen-looking shadows when you get on that train tonight, Hem."

Germaine ran around her counter and embraced Hector through the door. She kissed him on both cheeks. He suppressed the urge to scream as she patted his back.

She said, "I thought you were in hospital . . . the stories in the papers are terrible. And poor Madamoiselle Devlin. I'm so, so sorry for you, Hector. I hardly know what to say."

He squeezed her arm. "That story may yet have a different ending. A happy ending, I hope. Have I had any visitors?"

"No. Some mail . . . that's all."

"I'll take it with me . . . read it as I can. That envelope the policeman left for me, do you have it?"

"Right here."

Hector looked over the photos of Simon's men. He committed their faces to memory. As least he'd be able to sort them from any of Philippe's or Molly's minions.

Hector bit his lip at the pain as he climbed the stairs to his apartment. He put on some fresh, warm clothes—work pants and boots, a flannel shirt and sweatshirt, and long leather coat. He thrust his Colt into an interior pocket of his leather greatcoat, then wrapped the Mauser up in paper and twine, wrapped that in Hem's coat and tucked it all into a bag. Hem would need his only winter coat in Italy, Hector figured. And the old German gun would provide Hem extra comfort.

Hector left the parcel with Germaine along with a few francs to have it delivered to Hem's *femme de ménage.* "If you can do it, it might be best you were away from here for a couple of days," Hector told Germaine. "At least through Saturday morning. Let the others upstairs fend for themselves for a day or two."

"I'm not sure I can do that."

"You *need* to do that, *please.* These people—the ones I'm helping the police to catch, the one's who took Brinke—they'll stop at nothing. Please go: I can't lose anyone else to this."

She nodded, squeezing both his hands. "Well, then. But you mind yourself, Hector."

"Nobody needs worry for me. Once I know you're safe, well, they'll have done all they can do to try and harm me."

Germaine shuddered. "What are you going to do, Hector?"

"I'm going to teach them there are some things worse than nothing."

Watching behind himself in the reflections of storefronts, occasionally ducking down side streets and circling back around or turning on heel, Hector looked for shadows but eventually determined he had in fact escaped any surveillance.

Assured of that fact, Hector began his search.

Hector didn't know where Philippe lived, but he did know where Molly resided. Hector started there; Molly's landlady insisted she hadn't seen Molly in at least two days.

Hector next limped to the Rue Delambre, where the offices of *Intimations* were located. A grim smile: one in a series of glass panels next to the door was missing. A piece of cardboard had been taped in place of the broken pane to keep out the cold. Hector pushed aside the cardboard and found that he could just reach the interior knob and he unlocked the magazine office's door.

He went in gun drawn, stepping in quickly and moving to one side to avoid being backlit by the graying sunlight through the door—a potential target in silhouette.

A mouse ran across the floor and scuttled under a barrister desk. The office smelled musty. Hector closed the door behind himself, resecured the piece of cardboard, and wandered around the small cramped office. A few new moustraps had been set up around the edges of the desk. Two had been tripped—dead mice lay with crushed heads in the bloodied traps. One was a very recent kill: its tail continued to twitch.

A cot rested in one corner. Atop it was a small valise. Hector opened it . . . recognized the dress Molly had worn the night of the day of the ménage à trois. He lifted the small pillow, held it to his face, and smelled lilacs. A Franklin stove provided heat to the office. Hector tentatively touched his palm to the stove's black iron surface. Still warm. There was a glow from the coals he could see through the grate. Molly, or Lenore, evidently hadn't been gone for long.

The place was otherwise empty . . . just various manuscripts from hopeful contributors stacked here and there . . . typed poems and short stories spread out on a battered white-pine worktable.

Hector picked up one of the submitted poems, flipped it over, and pulled his fountain pen from his pocket. He wrote a short note on the back of the sheet of paper:

> M.
>
> I know it all now. I know about you and your brother and his masquerade as your painter-boyfriend.
>
> I know what you two did to your parents in order to buy yourself these new lives in Europe. I know, because the police know and told me.
>
> What I don't know is whether your parents, the Starrs, were evil and abusive.
>
> What I don't know is how much of all that, and this bloody business of recent weeks, was your doing and how much of it was Philippe's.
>
> I want to know more about these things.

And I want to know what you, or what Philippe, has done with Brinke.

Depending on your answers—your honest answers—there may yet be some way out of all of this for you. Tonight at 9, and tomorrow at 9, I'll stand on the Left Bank end of the Pont Neuf, on the easternmost side. I'll stand there tonight and tomorrow until 9:15.

I want to meet you, and only you. We'll talk this out. I swear to give you a fair shake if your answers are the right ones.

If you find this note before the police (I figure they've been through here, and moved on), you should destroy this letter if you intend to accept my offer of a meeting. You wouldn't want it to be found and for there to be official company on that bridge.

No more than I want to see any other nihilists when we meet.

—H

Hector read his letter over again. The danger was that Simon had men watching the building who might follow Hector, or search the magazine's office to see what Hector had done during his time inside . . . underlings who might find his letter for Molly. Hector hadn't seen any police watching as he'd broken in; he'd be equally careful in his leaving.

Perhaps, owing to manpower considerations, Simon was having his men perform occasional sweeps of various likely locations at which to find Molly—her apartment, the magazine office . . . perhaps cafés Molly might be known to frequent.

But if the police came back and found the letter before Molly did . . .

Hector looked around again. Molly had left some toiletries on the table alongside all the submissions. Hector opened her lipstick. He rolled up the note and stuck it inside the lid. The lipstick seemed a place a male French cop—even a good one—wouldn't think to look.

Hector was startled by a sharp snap. He pivoted, gun out.

He saw another mouse twitching in a trap . . . the copper wires crushing its skull as its rear legs kicked a last time or two.

Hector looked out the window at the street . . . saw nothing out of the ordinary. He set the door to lock behind himself. As a last precaution, stealing a note from Brinke's bag of tricks, Hector pulled loose one of his own hairs, wet it, and spread it across the door near the ground—half of the hair clinging to the door, the other half to the jamb.

It was a wild notion, but it seemed to Hector one worth pursuing in the absence of alternatives. He stalked northeast to the Boulevard du Montparnasse. Hector pulled his hat low as he entered La Rotonde . . . checking faces.

At a corner in the back, at his habitual table, he sat. His back was to Hector, but his face was reflected in a mirror—Philippe Martin, aka Jackson Starr, aka Victor Leek, aka Oswald Rook.

Philippe sat with three black-clad men . . . young, saturnine, bleary-eyed . . . poets all.

Hector took up a position by the bar—a place from which he could watch Philippe from under the brim of his hat and through the bottom of a glass. A waiter was taking the nihilists' drink orders. The pass-through to behind the bar was just to Hector's left elbow—the waiter would have to navigate around Hector to reach the bartender to fill the orders.

The waiter moved to a second table to take more orders, then walked back toward Hector. As he approached, Hector fished out his wallet. He stopped the waiter and said:

"Those four men who just ordered. They're old mates of mine. I'd like to pay for their drinks, but make it a surprise before I go and sit with them. At least two of them have *appalling* tastes in brands. I'd like to upgrade their orders to some top-shelf stuff. What are they having this afternoon?"

The waiter shrugged. "Nothing that stands much improving for three of them . . . beer." He curled his lip, "In a pitcher." *Better and better*, Hector thought. "The other, the blond one, he ordered a wine . . . rather undistinguished," the waiter said.

That would be Philippe—he exlusively drank red wine . . . bad red wine.

"Appalling, as I said," Hector said. "Improve the wine . . . indulge yourself. I'll settle up as you come back through to deliver it." The waiter smiled and moved to consult with the bartender. As he did that, Hector took the last of his morphine tablets and ground them together into chalk. He cupped the dust in his hand. Hector reached over the counter and grabbed a swizzle stick . . . palmed it. The waiter approached with his tray burdened with the pitcher of beer and a glass of Châteauneuf du Pape. He placed the tray on the bar and told Hector the price. Hector nodded, counted out notes with one hand and passed the francs to the bartender—dropping them before the waiter could grasp them. "Clumsy of me," Hector said. The waiter stooped behind the bar to collect the bills that had fluttered to the floor. Hector dropped the ground morphine into the pitcher of beer and stirred it in quickly with the stolen swizzle stick. He smiled at the waiter as the man rose with the money he had retrieved. "Remember—a surprise," Hector said. "Let them think they're running a tab. It's been a long time and I want to surprise them when I appear."

"Of course." The waiter had his tip—that was all he cared about.

Hector ordered a scotch and soda from the bartender for himself, then drifted off to a table to wait.

Twenty minutes passed. The three beer-swilling nihilists were slumped back in their chairs . . . mouths agape. One actually looked dead. Hector had no real sense of what kind of dosage he'd delivered to the men through the tainted beer . . . eight or nine tablets' worth, Hector guessed. Maybe more.

Philippe was looking around furtively . . . trying to grasp what was happening. His back to Hector, the nihilist shrugged on his coat.

Hector slid out of his table and exited La Rotonde. He sidestepped to the right of the café door. He stood there with his cigarette pack and lighter cupped to his face, his hat pulled low—his features all but obscured.

Moving quickly, Philippe exited the café and veered left.

Hector followed.

They walked on awhile, then Philippe ducked down an alley. Hector followed as closely as he dared. The alley angled off and Hector edged around the corner. Philippe was standing in the middle of the alley, prying open a sewer lid. Hector guessed it must be some eventual access point to Les Catacombes.

Grunting, Philippe got his fingers under the edge of the heavy iron lid, beginning to raise the manhole cover. Philippe did the lifting with his legs, though Hector wasn't sure at what risk a castrated man would be for sustaining a hernia.

When the lid was about an inch off the ground, and all ten of Philippe's fingers were under its edge, Hector padded up behind Philippe.

Hector slid his good leg between Philippe's wide-apart legs. Hector slammed his foot down on the sewer lid, crushing all ten fingers and parts of Philippe's hands under the heavy iron lid. Hector heard bones crack, then Philippe was gasping for air, working up to a scream. Hector pistol-whipped Philippe into unconsciouness, then set about freeing the unconscious man's mutilated hands.

Philippe awakened upside down, dangling from a fire escape by his own belt, its end wrapped tight around his ankles and tied off to the rusted iron staircase zigzagging up the back of an abandoned building.

They were close by a printing shop and the clack of the Linotypes was deafening, even through closed doors.

Hector was reasonably certain any screams for help would go unheard. Philippe seemed to grasp that, too. He leapt straight to denials: "What the hell are you doing, Hector? Have you gone mad?"

Hector pulled up a discarded crate and sat down. "Drop the outrage, Philippe. And drop the phony French accent—though I'll allow, it's been a good one. But you're from Illinois. Your real name is Jackson Starr and Molly is your sister, Lenore. I've seen the newspaper pictures of you and Molly—'the survivors.'"

Silence.

Hector said, "And now you're quiet. I'll take your silence as confirmation. I met your would-be doppelgänger, of course—*Nobodaddy*. You come up with that one in your cups?"

"What are you going to do, Hector?"

"I want to kill you," Hector said. "And I should do that. Slowly and painfully. If it weren't so cold, you'd be hanging there naked now. You know, like your stand-in had me hanging down in those caverns I assume you were trying to escape to a few minutes ago. I know those hands of yours must hurt, but I owe you a good deal more pain than that. But, given what you've lost, and how, I suppose torture isn't much of a threat to you. Not like it'd be for another man. After all, you lack that which might most effectively be used to motivate a man under torture. But, fortunately for me, there's more than just yourself at risk. There's Molly."

Philippe said, "Leave her out of it, Lassiter. So far as our folks, Molly had nothing to do with that fire."

"And what of these recent murders?"

"I did it all for her, at least at the start. But she didn't know that . . . not until you and that whore Devlin told her. Molly couldn't break in here as a writer, just like me. I gave up trying to place my poetry long ago. My fiction? People *laughed* at it. You know how it is—mocking you for your pulp magazine writing, same as me. Yet we're the ones who could *sell* our stuff. I shifted to painting for a time because I could at least make a few francs doing that and be respected for the work, like it somehow mattered in the way my fiction didn't. But Molly held on to the dream. She spent *hours* writing her little poems, only to be paid in copies of the few magazines that accepted her work. I could hardly bear to see her suffer rejection after rejection. She was constantly giving money she couldn't spare to these damned 'publishers' in hopes they'd reciprocate by publishing her poems more frequently. Then, when she reminded them of her financial support, they'd blather on about how it was a 'meritocracy' . . . well, *fuck* them!"

Hector said, "So what then? Big brother punished the publishers by killing them?"

"*That.* And I tried to get Molly her own magazine. That was my solution. I thought about buying one for her. She and I discussed it. I figured those magazines couldn't be making any money, so the asking price for one should be nominal. I mean, really—how much could it cost to take one of those rags off one of these prissy, pretentious bastards' hands? But these artistic types had grandiose expectations in terms of sales prices. Each one saw it as their chance to cash in. *Idiots.*"

"You might just have started your own magazine," Hector said.

"That was the follow-up plan, at one point," Philippe said. He shook his head. "I'm getting dizzy—the blood is all going to my head. Will you cut me down?"

"Cope, cocksucker. So why didn't you just start that magazine and spare some of the little magazine editors' sorry lives?"

"Thinning the herd first, you could call it. Then, what do you know? That crazy lesbian bitch went and plucked Molly out of the ranks and all but gave her a magazine to run—an established magazine, one with what Molly called 'a fine track record.' Everything was great. Except for you . . . filling Molly's head with stories about this shadow poet who was heading Nada—Victor Leek, my alter ego and screen in the event the police ever decided to come after Nada."

"Molly didn't know you were Leek? Didn't know you were the ringleader?"

"Molly just thought I was a fellow believer. She never heard of Leek. I kept the name from her ... to keep her safe in case anything happened to me." He shook his head again. Hector figured the blood flow probably was a real problem—the man's face and ears were bright red. Philippe said, "You filled Molly's head with all these notions that Nada was behind the killings," he continued. "Molly was clueless about what was really happening. Until you started telling her all this stuff about Rook, or Leek. You and that goddamn whore—the two of you, seducing Molly ... *Lenore*. And after Molly nearly killed herself for you last Christmas? You can't imagine what it's been like for me, Lassiter, watching her hopes rise and fall again ... over you and her prospects for a life with you. Over that damned magazine she's been given. Jesus, that she nearly killed herself for you once ... and may yet do it again? She's truly the only thing in this empty black world that matters to me. What she sees in the likes of you ..."

Hector sighed. "Yeah, there's no accounting for tastes." A petty shot ... Hector already regretted it. He lit a cigarette, stood, and stamped his feet to shake off the chill. "So you swear that Molly has killed no one?"

"No. Never."

"What about this business the other night, with the dynamite?"

"A last shot at bringing all you fools down together—clearing the way for Molly and *Intimations*. Leave her as the only show in town."

"Where's Brinke? What have you done with her?"

"I don't know what you're talking about. I figured to blow her to hell with you."

Hector looked around the debris-strewn alley. He picked up a piece of wood, about the length of a baseball bat. Hector hefted it, then feinted a swing at Philippe's shins. Philippe said, "No, don't do that! I saw in the papers about her disappearance—about Devlin's things being found in the river. But *we* didn't do that. *I* didn't do that. I just hope you didn't drive Molly to it with your sick games. Devlin was no threat to us without you prodding her. That was my reading of the situation. I figured if you were dead, Devlin would ease off. So we did nothing to her. That's the fucking truth."

Hector raised the plank again. "Where do you want the first one?"

"We didn't do anything to her, I *swear*, Hector."

"Do you really think it's possible that Molly—?"

"Hell no. I mean, I don't *think* so. Jealous as she was of you two, Molly was kind of fond of that tramp. Molly said so, and I believed her. I didn't fucking do anything to Devlin. I swear it, Lassiter! If you're going to kill me, just do it now. But don't hit me with that thing. I didn't have her snatched."

"Then who the hell did?"

"I don't fucking know!"

Hector said, "On the door of the restroom stall where Brinke tried to hide from her attacker, Brinke wrote an 'M' and a 'W' in lipstick."

"I'm not following you, Lassiter."

"Your sister's initials. MW for Molly Wilder. The same clue you laid with that woman dressed in white on the hill at the cemetery during Lloyd Blake's funeral, doling out her hints about 'Margaret W.'"

"Are you insane? I'm not following *any* of this, Lassiter."

"*No?* What about Jeremy Hunt? That silly stuff with his dead fingers twisted into Ms and Ws? What was your rationale for pointing suspicion at your own sister time after time? What about that note you left with all those dead women's bodies, referring to the 'queen'?"

"I left no note. A poem, yes—I still dabble for my own amusement—but I left no note."

"A similar note was left on Hemingway's apartment door, threatening his child," Hector said.

He raised his broken hands, shook them at Hector. "I didn't do that, either. Nada has become more for me than the ruse it started out to be. It's of paramount importance to me—a thing that can give life purpose in a universe threatened by a dead God. Something to *focus* on and that speaks to our ruined, lost generation. I saw Hemingway as an important conquest, or recruit, if you must know. You, too, at one point. Around the Left Bank, you two are regarded as comers. Drawing you two into my movement would lend it legitimacy. I don't know what the hell you're talking about with all this stuff about initials and women in white . . . And Jeremy whatsis—who's *that*? We didn't kill anyone named Jeremy . . . let alone do anything to anyone's fingers." That seemed to remind Philippe of his own fingers. He held his hands up before his face, swallowed hard, and said, "Jesus Christ! What have you *done* to me?"

Hector raised the board again. He feinted a blow at the man's face, but didn't connect. He threw down the board. "For Christ's sake, Philippe, what have I done to make you think I'm this stupid?"

"I'm telling you the truth, Lassiter. I wouldn't frame my own sister, even as a bluff, which is the only thing I can figure you figure. That's harebrained . . . could backfire and leave Molly—*Lenore*—holding the bag for everything *I* did to help her. Jesus, I'm not a monster. I love my sister too much to put her at risk that way."

Hector was incredulous: "Oh, you're a monster to be sure—all those prostitutes you slaughtered . . ."

"I can't apologize for that . . . or explain it. If you lost your—"

"I'm not interested in that. Not beyond stopping you from ever doing it again."

"What, then? You're going to turn me over to the police, Lassiter? Going to risk letting me tell them about what you did to me in this alley? I don't think the French authorities are going to cotton to some unhinged Texan running around Paris playing vigilante.

Even against someone like me. I don't believe you're going to turn me over to the authorities. I—"

Hector heard something around the corner—it sounded like the report of a pistol . . . a bullet perhaps striking brick. Hector held his gloved fingers up to his lips to silence Philippe. Hector drew his Peacemaker and edged around the corner . . . walked a ways down the alley.

Then Hector heard something that sounded like a second shot. Between the traffic echoing down the alleyway, and the roaring Linotypes, it was hard to be certain. But Hector limped as quickly as he could back to Philippe.

The nihilist hung limply from the fire escape, a single bullet hole between his eyes.

His gun raised, Hector spun . . . looked around him. The rear access door to a building across from where Phillipe was hanging was now open. Hector thought about running into the building to search for the shooter. Instead, he ran back down the alley.

# PART VI

jeudi
*(The Second)*

# Thirty-eight

*Hector walked slowly down* the Rue Vavin, checking alcoves and recessed doorways—looking for any of the faces in the photos sent him by Aristide Simon . . . looking also for black-clad men . . . looking for Molly. Sometimes he found himself thinking he might catch a glimpse of Brinke.

Then Hector did see a familiar female face.

Estelle Quartermain was leaving Hector's building.

Hector trotted as best he could across the street with his still tender ankle and the stitches in his thigh.

The British mystery writer was just climbing into the back of a horse-drawn cab. Hector caught the door as she was closing it. She glanced up sharply. Hector smiled and said, "Hello, Estelle. Were you looking for me?"

It was one of the rare times Hector could remember seeing Estelle without a companion. They were in the cab together. He said, "What brings you to my place?"

"I tried to find you at the hospital," the British mystery writer said. "Opinions are split. I mean, split regarding whether you walked out, or were kidnapped. Either way, while I was there, that policeman, Simon, he was giving his men a frightful tongue-lashing."

Hector said, "Since you came to my place looking for me, I'm going to assume you were one of the ones who believed I walked out of there of my own accord."

"That's right," she said. A little smile. "You're a resourceful fellow . . . like one of those lads in your stories."

*Lads?* But Hector said, "Sure I am." He pulled out his pack of cigarettes. He said, "You don't mind?"

"Only if you share."

Hector handed Estelle a cigarette, struck a match, and got their smokes going. Hector couldn't remember having seen Estelle smoke before, but she seemed adept enough. He said, "So why are you looking for me, Mrs. Quartermain?"

"You can resume calling me Estelle . . . or just Elle, if you prefer." She looked at her gloved hands. "This that I have to tell you is awkward, on many levels." She inhaled from her cigarette . . . exhaled . . . bit her lip. Estelle had done something more to her hair. Hector realized it was several shades darker than he remembered it. Estelle still had it slicked back from her forehead and behind her ears. She blew some more smoke from the side of her mouth, away from Hector, and said, "This matter of Brinke's *abduction*—do you believe what's in the papers?"

He said, "About Brinke being dead?"

Estelle seemed a little taken aback at how bluntly Hector had put it. But she swallowed and nodded. "Yes."

"No, I don't believe it," he said.

"Why not?"

"It doesn't make sense, for one thing. Acid in the face . . . a knife to the heart? These nihilists kill on the spot, directly. Brinke's 'murder' doesn't fit the template." He held up a hand, anticipating Estelle's next remark—the one he'd already had thrown at him by Simon. "I was a special case. They wanted me to suffer before they shot or stabbed me." Hector narrowed his eyes, exhaled smoke through both nostrils. "I sense you don't buy her kidnapping either."

"Not the kidnapping, and certainly not the death," she said.

"Why not?"

"I've been doing some of my own sleuthing, Hector. You may not know that my husband is a kind of well, private detective."

Hector tried to suppress a guffaw. "You mean like . . . Sherlock Holmes? Arsène Lupin? Or your guy, the Armenian accountant?"

Estelle smiled like she thought he was silly, like she thought her smile was charming. "No, they're pretend, Hector. My husband works for a British detective agency. A kind of English equivalent of your Pinkertons."

That analogy didn't endear Mr. Quartermain to Hector. He said, "So that affords you what? Access to public record searches? To lab resources? To what, exactly?"

Estelle waved the question away. "That's not important now. What is important is that I began noticing some things a while back. I believed, as you did, that some—I qualify with *some*—of these murders in recent weeks were committed by the nihilists, just as you've asserted. But some others? Those, I think, had a different motive."

Hector thought about that. It wasn't the first time he'd weighed that possibility. But he suspected that his own candidate for at least one of those non-Nadaist-directed murders was going to be a very different one from Estelle's. He said, "Do go on."

"I think someone used the cover of the little magazine murders to settle some personal scores . . . old scores," she said.

Hector nodded. "Which murders in particular?"

"Jeremy Hunt, for one. Lloyd Blake, for another. And Charles Turner."

Her choices didn't surprise Hector. Lloyd Blake: the man with the faux mistress clad in white who had introduced the name "Margaret W" into the mix as a potential little magazine buyer and murder suspect. Jeremy Hunt: he of the arranged fingers . . . MW. And Turner . . . the poisoned man.

But Hector played along. He said: "Why those victims particularly?"

"Killed indoors," she said. "Not stabbed in some doorway or on a bridge. And the poison? That's never fit with the other murders, as you pointed out yourself."

"What else do you suspect?"

She shrugged her shoulders a little. "I'll confess I used some of my husband's connections to check into the backgrounds of some people around this whole affair. Not you, of course. And not Mr. Hemingway. You both seem good and sturdy men. Good American stock."

He smiled crookedly. "Thanks, Estelle, that's swell of you."

"It's only the truth." She smiled and shrugged again. "But I did take the liberty of investigating Brinke Devlin. I've been aware of her for some time—not as 'Brinke,' of course, I mean in terms of her nom de plume... Connor Templeton. I was driven to do so by whispers one hears within our sector of the writing community."

Hector lit another cigarette. Estelle eyed it. He slipped it from between his lips and held it out to her. She smiled a little uncertainly, then accepted. He lit another for himself. He said, "What kinds of whispers?"

They were heading westerly on the Boulevard du Montparnasse. Their driver asked for a direction or destination. Hector told him to turn right onto the Rue de Vaugirard and keep going until he hit the Boulevard Saint Michel. Hector figured they'd make the circuit around the Jardin du Luxembourg.

Estelle said, "The story I'd hear was that this Connor Templeton had a kind of penchant for writing what he lives and living what he writes. Apparently there was, from time to time, official interest resulting from odd parallels between actual crimes in various jurisdictions and plots and story points in Templeton's novels."

"We all draw inspiration from our lives," Hector said. "It's called writing. Experience a moment, then distill it down to one true sentence. You know—*writing*."

"But our writings don't *anticipate* events, Hector . . . particularly not criminal matters."

"And Templeton's do?"

"It's the story I've heard," Estelle said. "Time and again."

"*Whispers.* So you investigated."

"I tried a few times in the past . . . only to learn Connor Templeton was a pen name for some mysterious, unknown writer," Estelle said.

"Then Gertrude let the cat out of the bag at her salon," Hector said.

"Precisely!"

"And what have you learned as a result of that?"

"Brinke Devlin is another, well, kind of non de plume, if you will."

Hector tried to look surprised. "You mean . . . an alias?"

"I didn't want to be the one to say it. Alias implies criminality."

"Isn't that exactly what you're implying? What's her real name?"

"Margaret Walker."

"You're joking."

"No, it's quite true."

Hector nodded slowly. "Margaret Walker." He said portentously, "MW."

"Like the bathroom stall's door," she said. "Now you see."

"So what are you saying, Estelle? Whoever took Margaret—Brinke—knew about this other identity and wrote it there?"

"Or Brinke wrote it there herself. She knew I was closing in, perhaps. She sensed that Simon and I would confront her soon."

"So she faked her own kidnapping?"

"That's my theory," Estelle said.

"I'm confused. Why put her own initials up there like that?"

Estelle smiled, holding up a gloved finger. "I think it was a reckless bid to round off a larger gambit. That 'MW' came up in a couple of other contexts in the course of my investigations. Jeremy Hunt, for example. When the police found him, his fingers had been positioned in a very particular way. Three fingers on his right hand formed an 'M.' Three fingers of the other hand formed a 'W.'"

Hector said, "No! Are you serious?"

"Deadly serious."

"Of course." Hector was having some difficulty stifling the urge to laugh. "You think that this man, with his dying breath, tried to leave us some clue to the identity of his killer?"

"That's what the *police* here thought," Estelle said. "Silly Frenchmen."

"What do *you* think?"

"I think Brinke deliberately posed the fingers that way."

"To incriminate herself?"

"To exonerate herself . . . deflect suspicion from herself," Estelle said. "It's so obvious a frame, nobody would believe it . . . presumably not even these French police."

"Sounds a little too bizarre for me," Hector said. "Bluff and double bluff . . . brinkmanship. These are not games to play—not with your own life at stake."

"That's just it—the net was closing around her," Estelle said. "She knew that I was putting it all together. I'm convinced of it."

"Why are you convinced of it?"

"Her disappearance for one thing—and the fact that it was obviously faked. I forgot to tell you. Shortly before her disappearance at the hotel, a bellhop on duty that night told me he saw Brinke conversing with some man who handed her a bag in exchange for a few francs. The bellhop said Brinke opened the bag and pulled its contents out a little ways to examine them before letting the man take his leave."

"What was in the bag?" Hector was truly curious . . . this story he found himself believing for some reason.

"A man's shoe."

"Large, I guess we should suspect . . . to press into the spilled powder," Hector said, "to leave a man's footprint in the ladies' room."

"To bolster the deception," Estelle said. "Precisely. And then the package arrived at our flat yesterday."

"What package?"

"Some cakes . . . a note congratulating me on my latest novel, *The Mysterous Affair of Manchester.*"

"Was something wrong with the cakes?"

"They smelled quite bitter," Estelle said.

"Poison?"

"I think so. My husband's firm is looking into it."

"Why not call Simon and turn them over to him for testing?"

"I have no confidence in him."

"I see."

Hector took a deep breath, sat back in his seat, then let it out slowly, puffing out his cheeks. "And you came to find me to tell me this . . . why?"

"So you'd know the truth—that mourning for Brinke might not be worth your while on several levels. I'm sorry if that sounds harsh, but you're too good a man to allow to wallow in sorrow over a woman like that. Not after all she's done."

"It's good of you to say."

"I also remembered what you said the other day in your room."

"I was pretty doped up, Estelle. Prick my memory."

"You said if we identified a culprit in these crimes, and if we judged the evidence wasn't sufficient for officials to prosecute upon, that we might have to take matters into our own hands."

Hector looked taken aback. "I said that?"

"You did."

"So what are you saying?"

"I think we've come to that point now, Hector."

"What? You suggesting that we hunt down Brinke, wherever she's hiding? That we . . . render some *punishment* ourselves?"

"I'm asking you to think about it. I'm not sure I can do it alone. She's formidable."

They were on the Boulevard du Montparnasse again. They were approaching the Rue Vavin. Hector told the driver to pull over. He said to Estelle, "I'll think about what you've said."

"I've certainly given you plenty to think about," Estelle said.

"You have. And I had feelings for Brinke. I have to resolve some of this before I can think about trying to bring her to book."

"Of course. But you don't have much time. God only knows what she's plotting next."

"Interesting choice of words ... us all being writers and such."

Estelle smiled. She seemed to hestitate, then leaned across the seat and kissed Hector, a bit awkwardly, on the mouth.

He said, "What was that for?"

"I've been thinking quite a bit since I met you. Thinking about how wasted you were with that terrible woman ... that black widow. I feared for you."

Hector nodded. He kissed her back, hard. As a kisser, Estelle didn't live up—or down—to his dark, inexplicable earlier fantasies about taking her. But he acted as though she did. He rubbed her breast through her coat. He said, "You're a married woman."

She gave him a knowing look. "You're not really that old-world, are you? Think about what I've said. Think on it."

"I will. If you need to reach me, you can leave word at the Closerie des Lilas. I'll be checking in there occasionally over the next day or so."

Estelle frowned. "What about your apartment?"

"Figure it's being watched ... police ... maybe nihilists."

"Probably so. Well, *à bientôt.*"

*"Au revoir."* He paused. "Oh! How do you know about that dead man's hands? About how they were posed, I mean?"

"That policeman, while asking advice of me. He asked what I thought the hands might be trying to convey."

"Ah."


Snow flurries twirled in the brisk wind and it was getting colder. Hector figured by sunset there would likely be another sheet of ice forming across the Seine. It would be cold on the bridge at night. Thinking about that, Hector risked walking by the offices of *Intimations* again. The hair he'd pressed to the door was still in place.

He couldn't risk going home, although he thought if he did there was a fair chance that Molly might try to find him there.

After some searching, Hector finally found a pay phone. Simon picked up on the third ring. The policeman said, "You should be in hospital, Hector. I've expended resources looking for you. Come in, and let's talk."

"No time for that," Hector said. "But a question that will interest you. Did you ever show photos of Jeremy Hunt's body to Estelle Quartermain? Ever talk about his hands?"

"Are you daft, Hector?"

"No. And I didn't think that you did."

Simon said, "She has made a claim to the contrary?"

"Yes. She knows about the hands. I'm wondering how. One more question: Did you ever have reason to mention the name 'Molly Wilder' to Estelle … you know, during one of her visits to give you tasks?"

"Again, *non*."

"Have you found Molly yet?"

"*Non*, Hector. But we have found her brother. He was found murdered in an alley not so terribly far from your apartment. Shot once between the eyes … left dangling from a fire escape. He was not a small man—this Jackson Starr. Or, as we now know him under his other alias, Philippe Martin. It would have taken a strong man to hoist him up like that."

"Perhaps several men," Hector suggested.

"Perhaps. Your friend Hemingway is missing, too."

"I haven't seen Hem in several hours."

"Not since the hospital," Simon said. "Very adroit, that."

"I told you, I mean to find my other friend."

"Again with this matter of Brinke Devlin. I'm sure you're wasting your time, my friend."

"You have found her body?"

"Not yet."

"Then I soldier on, *solo lobo* . . . all alone in my hope."

"Come in—let's talk. At least let my men acquire you again for discreet surveillance. Peace of mind for us both, *n'est-ce pas*?"

"I'll think on it." Hector broke the connection.

He checked his watch: a little before five. Hector slipped into a store and purchased a notepad. Then he flagged down a taxi and asked to be taken across the river . . . someplace on the Right Bank where he could eat and write among strangers.

# Thirty-nine

*Snow falling on the* Seine.

It was half-past-nine: Hector had waited an extra fifteen minutes. He stared down at the river. Another icy fog crawled across the Seine. The lights of the bridge glowed in the cold mist. Hector wondered what to do with himself next. He couldn't risk returning to his apartment. By now the Hemingways would be on that night train . . . riding off in Hector and Brinke's stead to Italy. That thought filled Hector with immense sadness . . . some anger.

But at least Hem and his family were out of harm's way.

Hector was toying with finding a hotel.

Then he remembered a promise. He walked under one of the gaslights and pulled out his wallet. He searched its contents and found the small slip of paper with her address. Hector flagged down a taxi, slid in and said, "Rue Suger."

*    *    *

Hector knocked several times. Finally, a tentative voice:

"Who is it?"

"Victoria? It's Hector. The man who saved your life."

She opened the door a crack . . . looked him over.

"I thought you'd forgotten."

"Much has happened. May I come in for a moment?"

She stepped back from the door, said, "Come in."

He edged in . . . a small darkish room . . . fairly anonymous.

She had a derringer pointed at his chest.

"You won't need that," he said. "I'm on the side of the angels, remember?"

"You're no angel," she said. "Not after leaving all those other women to that maniac's hands."

"I couldn't foresee that. Something else precipitated that."

Victoria shook her head. "The man who did that? They say he got away."

"Not for long. He's dead. Someone shot him. It'll be in the papers tomorrow."

"Did you—?"

"No."

She was wearing a simple tweed skirt and black sweater. It unsettled Hector a little . . . it was a little like a thrift store version of the clothes Brinke had been wearing the night Hector had met her.

Victoria had her long, blue-black hair pulled up in a French twist. Hector said, "You must be stir-crazy by now."

"I'm trying to decide what to do next," she said. "My landlord's talking about setting me out."

"I'll see to him on the way out."

"You can't do that forever."

"I don't mean to," Hector said. "I'll just pay through Monday for now. Then we'll see about getting you work—something more in keeping with your dreams."

"You're a romantic . . . a sentimentalist . . . a fool."

"Certainly the last." Hector smiled, said, "I haven't had dinner. You haven't been able to go out in a few days. Let me buy you something to eat. Some good red wine. Someplace warm with quiet music."

"And then we return here and I reward you how? With my body?"

"We return here and you sleep in your bed. Alone. Though I frankly wouldn't say no to an invitation to spend the night on your couch. I can't go home."

"Why not?"

"Police, for one thing. They've been watching me ... thinking that in doing that, they might catch that other. This murdered man, the 'maniac,' was hunting me, you see."

"But you just said he's dead."

"But he has a few dangerous friends left. Really more like followers."

"So it's not over."

"For you? Yes. For me? Well, it may be another day or two."

Her cobalt eyes considered him. "All right, you can take that couch tonight. And this restaurant better have a *wonderful* chef. I haven't eaten in two days."

"Then for God's sake, let's go right now."

"What's your name again? Your last name?"

"Lassiter."

"All right, Hector Lassiter."


That night, Hector sat on Victoria's couch. Victoria was across the room, asleep in her own bed, her black hair spread out on the pillow. She was shivering a little from time to time; the windows were crooked in their casings and and there was a draft through two or three windows—the curtains rising and falling with the gusts of cold wind.

They had stopped for a couple of bottles of red wine on their way back from dinner. Hector sat by the window, next to a flickering candle, a glass of red wine in one hand and his notepad propped up on his knee.

But he wasn't writing.

Instead, Hector kept running scenarios in his head. Trying to reconcile recent events againt Estelle Quartermain's string of bizzare revelations, assertions, and theories.

Gradually, Hector evolved a theory of his own—one suitably bizarre to rival any of those of Estelle Quartermain's.

Hector decided there really was some kind of history between Estelle and Brinke—or, rather—between Estelle and Connor Templeton. Hector believed Estelle was being honest with him when she said that she'd only learned of Connor's true identity when Gertrude introduced Estelle to Brinke.

Hector also believed that Estelle had never heard of Molly Wilder. If that was so, then Estelle would only associate MW with Margaret Walker—not with Margaret "Molly" Wilder.

He sipped some of his wine, held it in his mouth before swallowing it. Estelle had claimed to have been shown photos of Jeremy Hunt's corpse. But Simon denied that was the case. Presuming that Estelle's husband, the alleged private investigator, did not have access to those photos of Hunt's body through back channels, then Estelle would have had to have actually seen Hunt's body to describe the dead man's hands. She would have had to have been present at the murder scene to describe the arrangement of Hunt's fingers to form the telltale M and W.

Philippe had denied that Jeremy Hunt was one of the magazine editors targeted by the nihilists for murder. The nihilisits had been courting Hunt, according to Hem. Presumably, the Nadaists were still pursuing that angle with Hunt when someone else killed him.

Then there was the woman in white—Lloyd Blake's alleged mistress—the one who had confided to Hector about Blake's planned meeting with a prospective magazine buyer named "Margaret W." Estelle knew that Gertrude had more or less assigned Hector and Brinke the task of snooping around Blake's murder.

Hector had told Gertrude Stein about Brinke's plan to attend Blake's funeral to look for clues. Estelle had been with Gertrude when Hector had informed Stein of their plans. If Gertrude shared Hector's plans with Estelle, then Estelle would have had the foreknowledge to place that woman in white on the hill . . . to tip Hector to this "Margaret W." Again, Estelle would have done that thinking the trail would lead him back to Margaret Walker, never knowing it would instead cast suspicion on Margaret "Molly" Wilder, of whom Estelle Quartermain knew nothing.

There was more: Estelle said her husband was some kind of detective agency operative. What if he had had Hector followed during the past few days—presumably followed by men more skilled than the nihilists in the art of shadowing . . . maybe better even than Simon's men?

If that was so, then Hector could have been followed by Estelle's agents to that brothel on the Rue Quincampoix. Through them, Estelle could have come upon the murder scene there, and planted the false note from Victor Leek implicating "the queen." And in a gambit to divide and conquer, Estelle might also have left that similar, threatening note on Hem's apartment's door.

Then, at the hotel where Brinke was "abducted," in a desperate moment of ill-conceived action, Estelle might have made a last bid to incriminate Brinke by scrawling that M and W on the bathroom door in lipstick before the police reached the scene. Those initials written in lipstick struck Hector as an act of regrettable innovation. As something a mystery writer would bin or strike in the process of revision. But Estelle couldn't take back that hastily scrawled M and W from that door. She couldn't edit away that impulsive false clue.

But *why*?

If Hector was right, why had Estelle done all this? What had happened between Estelle and "Connor" to prompt three murders?

Hector wondered if it didn't all come down to Charles Turner. That horrible, vicious poisoning—that was something straight out of one of Estelle's own books. It was an early murder, committed in public view. A killing whose execution—no pun intended—was set in motion, perhaps by Estelle, before she knew her nemesis, Connor Templeton/Brinke Devlin would be present to witness it. Later, conveniently, Estelle had gotten herself assigned by Gertrude to nose around that very murder.

The more Hector thought on it, the more he believed Turner's murder was the key to everything between Estelle and Brinke.

But where did that leave Brinke Devlin?

Philippe denied having taken her, though he left open the possibility Molly might have.

Estelle was echoing Hector's own belief that Brinke might still be alive. For Hector that was a hopeful thought; for Estelle, he began to think, it was a fearful one. And so Estelle had tried to vamp Hector—acting like a femme fatale from one of his *Black Mask* stories. Estelle had asked Hector to help her punish Brinke—to play judge, jury, and executioner.

"Why don't you come to bed?"

Startled, Hector looked up. Victoria, clad in a flannel nightgown, was sitting up in her bed. "I'm not offering more than to let you share the bed, Hector. It's cold and you're much too tall for that couch. If you'd like you can have the other side. But that's all."

Hector smiled and set down his wine and notebook. He took off his shoes and belt and sweater and blew out the candle. He said, "Thank you . . . that's so kind of you."

In his pants, socks, and shirt, Hector slid under the covers, rolling over onto his right side to leave plenty of room for her. After a time, Victoria nestled closer against him. Half-asleep, Hector wrapped an arm around her waist. She took his hand in hers, squeezed it once, then they both drifted into sleep.

# PART VII

vendredi
*(The Last Day)*

# Forty

*A goodbye at the* door: Victoria said, "You should let the police finish this."

"I'm not sure they can."

"Then you'll be needing the couch again tonight, Hector? Or rather, the other side of the bed?"

"Are you offering?"

"If you think you're still in danger when this day is over? Of course."

"I have no idea what this day may bring."

"I'll be up late . . . so if you need a safe place, come."

He risked leaning in to kiss her forehead. "Thank you so much."

Victoria hugged him back. He winced as her hands gripped his back. She said, "Thank you for saving my life. I think."

He smiled sadly. "Life is always worth living, Vicky."

She shook her head with a half-smile. "So you're an optimist as well as a fool."

"Not really. But dead is merely dead."


Hector went to a café on the Boulevard Saint Michel, ordered coffee and some eggs. While he waited for his order, he slipped next door to a pay phone and called Simon. He said, "What new horror has the day wrought?"

"*Deux* nihilists have been found hanged," Aristide Simon said. "I suppose they just couldn't face the void without their guide and guru . . . is that it?"

"Good a theory as any," Hector said. "Have you found Molly?"

"Lenore Starr remains missing, or well hidden."

"Not by me, if that's what you mean to imply."

"I imply nothing, Hector. I think you're desperate to find Molly, or Lenore, too. Before me."

"Could be. Any sign of Brinke?"

"*Non.* And the river is frozen over again. I doubt we'll be finding anything in the Seine for the next few days . . . not until we get above freezing again."

"Any clues as to who shot Philippe?"

"It was a cheap revolver . . . something small in caliber," Simon said. "As one might find in an antique store, perhaps. As a woman might carry in her purse. What they used to call 'a holdout.'"

A sleeve gun or derringer. Something small and unintimidating . . . comfortable and comforting in a small hand.

"You should come in or meet me, Hector. And Dr. Williams is worried about your wounds."

"I'm fine. I just want one more day to myself. One more day to try and put it all together."

"What about today is different from any other day?"

"Today is Friday."

"I don't understand."

"It doesn't matter. I think you should bring Estelle Quartermain in for questioning," Hector said. "I think she poisoned Charles Turner. I think she's been the one leaving the false clues, those initials 'M' and 'W' everywhere. I think she was trying to frame not Margaret Wilder, but Margaret Walker."

"Brinke Devlin, in other words. I concur. Mrs. Quartermain

has fled Paris, however. Quite abruptly. I believe she may be outside my reach. But I am trying."

Hector took a cab to the Rue Delambre. He walked briskly by the door of the *Intimations* offices, his head down and hat pulled low to hide his face. The hair he had left pasted across the door was still in place.

Hector stood in the archway of the church across from his apartment building. After ten minutes, he'd convinced himself that nobody was watching his place. He crossed the street and let himself in. It was strange to find the front desk unattended: at least Germaine had taken seriously his request to go away for a short time.

A stack of mail was mounded on the counter. Hector sorted through the pile for anything addressed to him. He stopped when he found a particular letter. The small hairs on the back of his neck rose.

In the left-hand corner of the envelope, where the return address should be, there was simply a name:

Bud Grant.

# Forty-one

*Hector sat at the* foot of his bed, reading Brinke's letter:

Darling Hector,
I am so so sorry my one true love.

What I've done is monstrous, but I really saw no other way in the short time left me by circumstances Wednesday. And, if I know you and your sharp brain, you never *really* believed me dead. You probably also doubt that I was kidnapped. I'm counting on the police thinking differently. The newspapers seem to indicate that is the case.

As I write this, newspapers are also reporting that Philippe Martin, or Victor Leek, has been executed by parties unknown.

I'm supposing that was your doing.

It might have been mine, if you hadn't gotten there first.

How deeply Molly is or isn't mired in all of this—in the killings—I don't pretend to know, and I wouldn't hazard a guess. I can't bring myself to punish her. I selfishly leave that burden to you. Pass judgment on her, or don't. You have to decide that.

But there is someone else you should be looking to—or perhaps pointing your policeman friend after:

Estelle Quartermain is also a killer, and responsible for at least two of these recent deaths in Paris, by my reckoning.

More on that in due course.

I promised you all my truths, my love, and in this letter, I intend to divulge them to you, my darling Hector . . . every last one.

My real name is Brinke Sinclair, as I finally told you the other night. My parents' real names are also as I told you then. And I really don't know if they are still living. My father was a Baptist minister. He also had a small farm holding mostly run by my mother with the assistance of a couple of hired hands.

Theirs—based on my young memories—was a largely loveless marriage. My mother was solitary . . . remote. My father was pious. Neither one of them was particularly affectionate toward me. And because they were relatively mature when I was conceived, I'm convinced I was an accident.

As an only child, I was lonely.

Ohio gets all the seasons, in full fury. Springs and summers—early falls—I used to go exploring the countryside with my dog, a Border collie I named Cricket. It's no exaggeration when I say that Cricket was my one true and best friend—there were no children within two miles of our house. At school, the other children tended to shy away because I was the minister's daughter; my father loomed over his parishioners as a kind of foreboding figure, I see now.

So I was lonely.

There was a neighboring farm.

One day in early May, Cricket, probably drawn by the scent, led me to the back of the neighbor's farmhouse. A plate had been left out on the back step . . . candies . . . a few cookies . . . some small sweet cakes. Nobody seemed to be around, so I snuck a bite of one or two of the candies. I fed one cookie to Cricket, and pocketed two more.

Then we ran home.

This happened five more times on consecutive days . . . the offerings on the plate getting just a little larger each time . . . little me risking taking just a few more pieces of candy each day . . . filling my pockets with candy.

On the seventh day, a man suddenly stepped out onto the porch with a rifle. He shot Cricket in the head, and then dragged me inside his house.

You can guess the rest. That dark imagination of yours will supply all the details I can't bear to put to paper, even after all these years.

I managed to escape after a few hours.

I was running home, half-naked and bleeding, when the county sheriff happened down the dirt road between that man's house and our family farm.

If I had reached my parents' house, I expect there might have been some kind of cover-up. I suspect my assault would have gone unpunished . . . certainly unreported.

But that sheriff was dealt a hand.

The man who attacked me, a fearsome old hermit named Leonard Sloane, was put to death. In the course of his brisk trial, they determined Sloane was probably responsible for at least three missing children in and around our town over a period of four years. Sloane claimed to have kept one of the other children a captive in his home for at least eight months.

I was told I was very lucky to have been in that house for less than a day.

But my parents were ashamed of what had happened. I think they were also quite ashamed of me. Shortly after Sloane's sentence was handed down by the judge, my parents sent me away to a Catholic boarding school.

Bad things happened there, too. But there was no end in sight, and no big-bellied county sheriff to run to that time.

At the age of fifteen, tall and athletic, I finally overpowered the particular nun who had abused me for so many years. I escaped and struck out on my own.

The good nuns did instill in me a love of writing and reading, and I guess I more or less found my writing voice through the composition of my own journal. I scribbled long entries nights at the boarding school and after, filling whole notebooks with my thoughts, fears, hopes, and, sometimes, little stories I told myself. But they were dark stories . . . revenge tales. Stories about clever and pitiless young girls turning the tables on their persecutors and vile parents.

Mystery stories.

Crime stories.

Left to my own devices, my reading tastes also ran to the

dark side . . . to crime and mystery novels. I supported myself as a reporter . . . a freelance writer . . . eventually as a writer of short stories in various regional magazines. After the war, I read about the exchange rates in Europe, particularly in Paris, and about how well one could live on so little there.

So I made my way to the City of Lights. I lived in Paris about a year, and then began to branch out to other countries . . . to see other places. Grist for my fiction.

The origins of Connor Templeton were exactly as I described them to you our first night together.

The first couple of Templeton novels were made up out of whole cloth, and, I think now, they read that way. Around the middle of the third novel, while living in Cairo, I found myself caught up in the coverage of an ongoing murder investigation. I decided to incorporate some of the facts related to that murder into my novel. I was looking to stir in some verisimilitude, I suppose . . . to give my novel some gravitas. Pursuit of truth.

Soon, newspaper accounts weren't enough. I began to ask some questions of my own around the edges of the actual crime. Through a kind of luck, or perhaps just some crazy knack, I overtook the official investigation . . . reached a solution of my own. I finished my draft of Connor's novel, then anonymously tipped police to my solution and set them on the correct investigative path.

A template was set. For the next several Templeton novels, I sought out real-life crimes—ongoing dramas—and appropriated them for my fiction. So, you see, this little escapade of playing sleuth for Gertrude, at least for me, wasn't a new proposition . . . it was more akin to my secret métier.

*My secret.*

As my rather peculiar work habits evolved, I realized

soon enough that if someone ever connected some of these real-life crimes to Connor Templeton's novels I might be at some potential for peril. I was already writing under a pseudonym. It seemed no great reach to adopt an alias in each new city I sought out as the backdrop for Connor's next mystery novel. Each new book brought a new city or country, a new crime to investigate and write about . . . and a new identity.

At least twice, I "solved" crimes in a manner that I knew precluded local authorities from ever replicating my results, despite all my tips. Eventually, in both cases—convinced other innocent lives were at risk—I acted on my own to mete out something I regarded as justice. I became a kind of chronicler cum vigilante.

Imagining the recipients of my private justice to be incarnations of Leonard Sloane made it easy.

I was in Egypt for a second time, in 1922. I was there researching my novel *Cleopatra's Curse.* I became aware of the presence of a second mystery writer, another woman, who was also living in Egypt to gather background for her next mystery novel, *The Ghoul of Giza.* You'll have guessed by now that the other mystery writer was Estelle Quartermain. The name I was using at the time was Margaret Walker. You'll take note of those initials . . . extrapolate out from there, I know.

I so know you, my darling Hector.

There was a murder. For a time, official suspicion fell on Estelle. The victim was poisoned—strychnine, again. There were dark whispers of some sort of affair between Estelle and the victim . . . a man named Robert Turner, who allegedly ended his affair with the mystery writer. (Estelle, I'm coming to learn, cuckolds her husband quite shamelessly . . . and takes rejection quite poorly.)

I put aside the plot for my in-progress novel, and instead

began writing a novel about Estelle's predicament. A novel about a female mystery writer who is herself suspected of committing a murder.

Estelle evaded prosecution; I completed and published my novel.

Through channels, I heard that Estelle was livid . . . that she wanted to sue Connor Templeton for his "brazen, lying roman à clef."

Of course, she couldn't do that and risk drawing the attention of those vast majority of readers who hadn't made a connection between the mystery writer in my book and Estelle Quartermain.

About three months after my book appeared, something very bad happened. A box of pastries was delivered to my publishing house, addressed to me. Since "Connor" was "abroad," one of the secretaries in the office set the box out for the office staff to enjoy. My publisher's secretary nearly died from the rat poison in the cakes . . . bleeding internally from the anticoagulants infusing such poisons.

Then, in March 1923, an anonymous fan letter was sent to my publisher. A mail room attendant was killed from inhaling the dust in the envelope—crystallized strychnine.

I had become, it seems, Estelle's bête noire . . . and the object of her murderous revenge. Fortunately for me, my identity remained a closely guarded secret. At least that was so until a few nights ago, when Gertrude shared my secret with Quartermain.

From that moment on, I knew I was living under a sword. I knew Estelle would come at me directly.

But there was a new wrinkle, unfolding almost simultaneously with Gertrude's revelation to Estelle regarding my identity. Estelle was about to murder Charles Turner . . . the brother of Robert, the man whom she was suspected of murdering in Egypt.

Only in the past few hours, through research, have I learned of Charles's relation to Robert. It seems that Charles was sparing no expense to employ private investigators and researchers in an effort to prove Estelle's complicity in his brother's death.

I think it was just a freak coincidence that Charles happened to attend the same party that Estelle and I had been invited to at Gertrude's salon. The poisoned snuff might have killed Charles anywhere, at any time.

Call it fate, call it serendipity . . . perhaps dumb luck. But the poison took Charles down in front of Estelle and I and the rest of you.

Reeling from the revelation about my identity, I think Estelle tried to get in front of events by immediately declaring Charles's death to have been the result of poisoning . . . to beat me to the punch, if you will. Then she got herself assigned by Gertrude to investigate a murder of her own devising . . . one Estelle had meant to be confused with the cycle of murders of little magazine publishers being committed by the Nadaists.

When those "Ms" and "Ws" started appearing, I knew that Estelle was setting about her revenge . . . framing me for at least some of those little magazine murders. I figured that Estelle was murdering others in order to make her frame a tight one. I think—and admittedly, this is a hunch—that Estelle had never heard of Margaret "Molly" Wilder, and so she couldn't know how those false clues she laid would be seen by you and by Simon. Estelle couldn't know that for some they would point suspicion at Molly Wilder rather than at me.

But I saw their true intent clearly enough.

In a perfect world, I would have insisted we go to Italy a day earlier, before time and circumstance overtook us . . . forced me to a brash decision—faking my own kidnapping and death.

When I heard from you that Simon was beginning to poke around Connor Templeton and those crimes from other countries informing Connor's books, I knew I was in terrible jeopardy. Simon strikes me as the committed kind, and I don't think the rationale for my just actions would ever be accepted by such a man.

I hope that you and your policeman friend will bring Estelle to book for her crimes. I know that if you do that, if you bring her in alive, Estelle will do everything she can to implicate me—either to lessen her own consequences, or, in spite, to see me destroyed along with her.

The world believes Brinke Devlin is dead.

With Brinke, dies Connor Templeton.

Connor will have a last couple of posthumous mystery novels, then his future royalties and such will be paid to Connor's "ward."

I'll be watching the newspapers. If I don't see Estelle arrested soon, I'll assume she dodged another bullet. I suppose then I'll try and settle matters with her directly. If she doesn't find me first.

My darling, darling Hector. I so much wanted to marry you and have our life together on that island. To laugh and drink and play with you naked in that Gulf Coast wind and water.

To perhaps buy a boat so we could explore Cuba and Bimini.

I'll be eagerly watching for *Rhapsody in Black* to see what becomes of wicked Alison Wilder.

I hope you'll be watching for Bud Grant's debut novel, *Triangle*, to see what becomes of Horace Lester. I suppose I'm falling in love with Horace, so I suspect he might see further installments.

And now the last:

I'm holding out hope we might yet still have that sweet life together on that island.

On February 14, 1925, it is my intention to be waiting in Key West in a back pew of Saint Mary Star of the Sea on Windsor Lane. I'm going to be there at seven P.M. on Valentine's night. I'll light a candle, and wait for an hour. I hope you'll walk through that door, Hector. I hope that you will come in and smile and sit down next to me and take my hand and tell me that we may start again.

It's a long time, I know, from this bitter, icy February to February of next year . . . particularly for a man like you, living in the City of Lights with so many vivacious, adventurous, and attractive women.

But if one has not stolen your heart by then, then you can know a woman just as good as any of those will be waiting for you on Bone Key.

If you don't come, I'll understand. But I will be devastated.

I want our beautiful life together.

I suppose you tire of me writing it, and that you perhaps doubt it, given all I've done, but I love you, Hector. I love you, I love you, I love you . . . with all my heart.

Always yours,<br>Brinke

Hector read Brinke's letter three more times. Then he folded it and inserted it into a compartment of his wallet.

Brinke was right.

It was such a long long time until next February.

# Forty-two

*Hector again passed by* the offices of *Intimations*. He looked at the door. The single hair he had pasted across the door now lay on the ground.

Looking around again for sentries, he risked knocking on the door. No answer.

Hector took a last look around the street, then knocked out the piece of cardboard taped over the broken window pane. He reached in and let himself in again.

One more dead mouse lay in a trap on the floor by the desk.

Molly's personal belongings, including her canister of lipstick, were gone.


Hector spent the long day writing in the Closerie des Lilas. It was warm in the café and Hector took a table at the back—Hem's customary table. Hector looked up from his notebook occasionally to rest his eyes and to flex his writing hand.

He was nearly three-quarters through the draft of his first novel.

Blaise Cendrars was again at the other table at the back of the café, writing poetry with his one good arm and slamming back drinks.

Old men were playing dominoes and arguing politics... still fighting the last war over drinks.

Hector looked out the front window. There was a terrible wind and the heavy snow flurries were falling nearly sideways and beginning to stick—covering the sidewalks and streets.

Hector took lunch and dinner at the café and drank a bottle of wine and several glasses of whisky, but he never really felt drunk.

At eight P.M., Hector closed his notebook, just one chapter away, he reckoned, from a full, first draft of *Rhapsody in Black*.

He stepped out into the cold night and hailed a taxi.

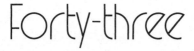

# Forty-three

*Snow was again falling* on the Seine.

It was a couple of minutes past nine and it was unusually quiet on the bridge ... very little street traffic because of the ice and heavy snow, and even less foot traffic.

Hector stood looking down off the Pont Neuf. The river was covered with a fresh layer of ice and the lights from the bridge shone on the hardened surface far below.

Another bank of fog crawled across the river. Hector stood in one of the hazy, solitary cones of light made weak by the snow ... stood there like a flickering beacon, or a target.

A lone figure was walking across the Pont Neuf ... crossing from the Right Bank to the left. Hector turned to watch her approach— the occasional glimpses of her silhouette as she passed from cone of light to cone of light left no doubt about her sex.

Finally, one light from the one he was standing under, Molly said, "I didn't want it to end this way ... couldn't imagine it ending this way, Hector." She reached the place where he was standing.

She looked like hell ... dark hollows under eyes ... gaunt. Her violet eyes were hazy ... unfocused.

He reached out with a gloved hand and tipped her chin up to

better see her features in the light. "Oh, Molly, honey. What have you taken? Cocaine? Opium?"

"It doesn't matter, Hector. It doesn't matter anymore. It didn't help, and it doesn't matter."

*"Molly."*

Her hand rose to his lips. "There's really nothing left to say, Hector. It's over. The police are looking for me. They'll never let me be. Never believe me innocent. And in many ways, I'm not."

Hector said, "That's not true. Philippe said you knew nothing about your parents' murders. Or about what he was doing here in Paris. He said you didn't know until I told you—until Brinke did—that Nada had become a kind of murder and suicide cult."

"I suspected even before then," Molly said. "But I didn't ask the hard questions, Hector. I just went along, a kind of silent accomplice." Molly shivered and said, "Can I have a cigarette?"

Hector pulled out his pack of cigarettes, shook loose two, and put them between his lips. He lit them both, cupping his hand to protect the match from the wind, then passed one to Molly. He turned and propped his forearms on the bridge rail, staring off down the Seine, Molly mimicking his posture. She said, "It's depressing, isn't it? The view, I mean."

"That's a matter of perspective," Hector said softly. "We need to change yours."

Molly blew a thin stream of smoke off into the darkness. "No, I'm seeing things as they are, Hector. I killed Lloyd Blake, you know. I was sleeping with Lloyd for more than a month... spending nights in his bed when his wife was away. He kept talking about a special publication of several of my poems in the spring issue of his magazine. He was going to publish several pages of my writing, he said. He reneged and I went berserk. He was so horrible... a horrible man to make love to. He made me wear wigs... red and black... calling me by different names. Sometimes he hurt me. We were in bed that last night together, when he told me my writing is horrible...unfocused. He said my poems are 'ponderous,' that they are like 'unleavened dough.'"

Hector sighed, said, "Oh, Molly...that's just wrong."

She pressed on: "Lloyd kept a silver dagger by his bed. He used it as a letter opener. Sometimes he would hold it to my throat while he made love to me. I picked it up, raging, and drove it into his chest...slashed his throat."

Molly shrugged, looking off down the river toward the Conciergerie Palais de Justice. "Philippe never knew about that."

Hector heard the rawness in his own voice. "That might almost have been justifiable, in its way." He didn't really believe that, but Hector knew too well his own ego. He had a sense of how he might have reacted if he was placed in Molly's position. He said, "Were there others? Other murders?"

"Just one." Her jaw was tight. "I saw you leaving La Rotonde yesterday. Like you, I was looking for Philippe. I followed you, following him. I saw you attack Philippe. While you were hauling him up the side of that fire escape, I made my way around the block, into the building behind you, where I could watch and hear. I listened to all that Philippe said to you. I realized what he had cost me in terms of you, and my writing...ruining my chance with *Intimations*..." She hung her head. "I was horrified about all the people he had killed in my name. Even our parents, who weren't, as you wrote in your letter, 'abusive' or 'evil,' but not loving either. But they didn't deserve that. When we came to Europe, Philippe, or Jackson, as you know now, convinced me that some crazy people back home were spreading rumors about the fire, and so it was better we lived under other identities. Again, I didn't press hard enough for more from him. Just went along. We were in London. He became Oswald Rook. I took a different name there. He fell in with Crowley. After the...accident...I mean well, Jackson has no—"

"I know about his self-mutilation," Hector said.

She nodded. "We decided then, or I decided, to pose as lovers, so he would be spared pressure from women coming after him...

expecting things from him. I never thought about the effect it might have on my own life . . . until I met you, and you saw me as Philippe's lover. So stupid of me."

Hector steered her back to the events in the alley. He said: "You shot Philippe?"

"I fired a shot down the alley to lure you away. Then I shot Philippe. He saw me pointing the gun at him . . . started to call out. I killed him." Molly smiled, a terrible and tragic smile. "I didn't feel anything. Isn't that *funny*?"

Hector wrapped an arm around Molly's shoulder. "Where'd you get the gun?"

"I bought it for myself earlier that day. I was working up to turning it on myself."

"*No.*"

"I tried before. Last Christmas . . . I took some pills."

"I've heard."

Molly searched his face. "And you've heard why?"

Hector nodded slowly.

"I can't stand the guilt on your face. That's why I came here a last time to talk with you, Hector. Just to say you have nothing to feel guilty for. Not from before, and not now. Don't ever feel guilty, Hector. Please, don't *ever* feel guilty."

It happened quickly then.

Molly said, "I love you Hector. I choose to think you love me, just a little."

Then she threw herself over the rail.

Molly underestimated Hector's reflexes: he caught hold of one of her arms. Hector tried to hook his foot under the bridge's rail to secure himself. His back was in agony—the whip wounds reopening from the strain of carrying Molly's dangling weight.

She stared up at him desperately. "You're ruining this, Hector. Please—*let go*. I've made my decision. Let me go, I beg you."

"You can't do this," he snarled, feeling blood spread across his back.

"It's all hopeless now, darling," she said, digging at his hand with her nails, trying to free herself. "There's no future for me."

"There *is* a future. We'll get you away from this city ... get you another identity! You'll start over, darling ... without the weight of that psychotic brother of yours. Without this twisted infatuation with the void he's tried to instill in you. This love of meaninglessness."

Her eyes were imploring. "Start over? *Where? Alone?* Do you love me enough to come with me, Hector? To help me?"

Hector stared down into her wild, crazed violet eyes. What choice did he have? His back was in agony ... his arms felt as if they were being ripped from their sockets. Hector couldn't sustain her weight more than another minute or two. The muscles in his arms and hands were already trembling.

"We'll go away together, Molly. Tonight. I swear to you. We'll go to Italy ... wait for things to get quiet, and then we'll find a place where you can be the poet you've dreamed of being."

Molly was watching him closely. "Guilt, my darling Hector. That's guilt talking, not love. I see it in your face, and I hate it. I can't live any more lies. Goodbye, Hector."

Molly struggled harder against him. She got one foot against the bridge and then the other, then kicked off away from the rail, tearing loose from Hector's failing grasp.

In horror, Hector watched Molly fall backward off the Pont Neuf, her arms spread wide ... her eyes watching him. She fell without screaming.

There was a terrible crack as she hit the ice spread across the river far below.

The ice was evidently thicker than it had been the night just a week before when Natalie Champlin had gone off the bridge and through the ice.

Molly lay on her back on the frozen river, her arms outstretched. Hector thought he might still be able to get down to her ... perhaps crawl out across the ice and pull her to the shore. But there was something spreading out behind her head . . . something dark like blood. Then there was a cracking noise and the upper portion of Molly's body slid into a hole in the ice. As the current caught hold of her coat and her arms, the river dragged Molly the rest of the way under the ice.

Hector stared at the steaming hole for a long time.

When he looked up, the snow was falling heavier . . . blocking out the lights at either end of the bridge. It was like the entire city had gone dark.

Shaking, bleeding, Hector tried to get a cigarette going, but his hands were trembling too hard. He felt nauseated and afraid . . . empty.

Freezing, he looked for a cab, but saw no traffic. It was like he was alone in Paris . . . horribly solitary . . . the last man in the City of Lights.

*Solo lobo.*

Hector could barely stand by the time he reached the Rue Suger.

Victoria opened the door, then frowned at his appearance.

Silent, she helped him off with his coat. She dipped her head better to see his face, then felt compelled to hug him. Victoria bit her lip and held up her own hands, bloody from touching his back.

"Here," she said, undressing him. "We need to get these clothes off you . . . wash these wounds."

Hector helped her unbutton his shirt. He kept seeing that hole in the ice . . . that black maw into which Molly had disappeared.

A line from Nietzsche ambushed him: ". . . the abyss also gazes."

Wincing as she got a look at his bleeding back, Victoria said, "Please tell me this nightmare is over."

"It's finished," Hector said.

He reached out then . . . took down Victoria's long, blue-black hair. He spread it out across her shoulders . . . her long dark hair falling down over her breasts.

She said, "What are you doing, Hector?"

He smoothed her black hair. He was unsteady on his feet. His hand was trembling. "Trying to annihilate a memory." He said, "You've never thought about writing, have you?"

Victoria looked confused . . . and a bit alarmed. Hector could hear a thrumming in his ears. He felt light-headed . . . maybe from blood loss. He began to see spots. Scowling, he heard Victoria say, "Lord no, I'm no writer."

From far away, he heard his own voice: "So much the better." There should be more. He struggled to shape one true sentence; came up short.

The last of the light receded.

In the blackness, Hector felt himself falling.